FINDING DAISY

From the Deep South to the Promised Land

ISBN-13: 978-0-9992014-2-8
ASIN: 0999201425

Library of Congress Control Number: 2019916934

FIRST EDITION

Cover design and quilt artwork
by Kathy Lynne Marshall

Kanika Marshall Art and Books Publishing
PO Box 1202, Elk Grove, CA 95759-1202
www.KanikaMarshall.com/books.html

FINDING DAISY

From the Deep South to the Promised Land

KATHY LYNNE MARSHALL

DEDICATION

Our Grandma Daisy was
a complicated woman who
led an admirable life of service
and excellence. This book
is dedicated to her tenacity,
strength, and tutelage.

Daisy Dooley Marshall, Trustee of St. James AME Church,
Cleveland, OH, circa 1953.

TABLE OF CONTENTS

INTRODUCTION

"Write our stories, write our stories now!" My spirited ancestors began hounding me day and night in 2016. Our accomplished eighty-three-year-old family historian, M. Lavata Williams, had stepped down from the position she held for thirty years. I was the sole person in my mother's *and* father's family lines who accepted the challenge to assume responsibility for leaving a published legacy of our African American presence in America.

With each tick-tock of the clock during my sixtieth year of life, I developed a visceral need—a hunger—to complete this task, one book at a time. The ultimate goal would be to publish family history books that would be referenced and available in the Library of Congress, as well as research libraries and historical societies in the cities and states where my ancestors lived. I want to make a significant contribution, imprinting our Afrocentric stories on the American historical record. As an old African proverb maintains, "Speak my name and I live on..."

The genealogy bug initially bit me hard in 1976. A white-skinned elder coworker at the California Highway Patrol—who I could tell was African American—asked about my European lineage. "What are you talking about?" I responded as politely as possible, knowing both of us could see the truth in the mirror. I had long disavowed any genetic connection with Caucasians because it suggested our enslaved female ancestors were forced into "relations" with their white masters to produce children who looked like me.

But lo and behold, after taking the first of three DNA tests in 2012, I learned that almost half my ancestral blood did not come from Mother Africa. Who were those people whose pale fingers left an imprint on my heritage? For forty years, I searched for our roots ineffectively, because I didn't know how, or was unable to follow, recommended genealogy protocols, such as: listening to stories from the elders (there were few), researching the slave master's family (I didn't know their names), and visiting the land of our ancestors (I didn't know who they were pre-1900), etc. Roadblocks abounded, but the ancestors wouldn't let me sleep, so I had to figure it out.

It wasn't until October 1, 2016, that my ancestral itch could be scratched, after listening to a webinar from writing coach, Anita Henderson. She told me two things that got me on the fast track to writing a book of family stories. First, she urged, "Start today by writing what you already know." I've been collecting boxes and binders full of genealogy "data" for four decades, and I had already written biographies of my mother's and father's lives. I knew enough about myself and a little about Grandma Daisy to get a book started that day. Second, Anita cautioned to focus on one ancestor and accept that it was okay if I didn't find all of my answers for a First Edition book.

I taught 600 analysts at the California Highway Patrol how to approach every writing assignment, by creating a template outline of the finished product at the beginning of the research and analysis process. It finally occurred to me that I could employ the same approach to write family history books. I immediately created a word processing document in the format of a book and began filling it with stories I already knew well. I started taking genealogy research seriously, examining all available historical documents, attempting to interview our few living relatives, utilizing more online tools besides Ancestry.com, and attending writing and genealogy workshops to learn how to craft credible stories based on facts.

My first writing effort focused on the descendants of my enslaved great-great-grandfather, Otho Williams. The intense, multiple-hours-per-day researching, interviewing kinfolk, and typing the manuscript until my fingers were numb, resulted in my self-publishing *The Ancestors Are Smiling!* in July 2017. That was a book of emotional, funny, sad, uplifting, life-affirming stories that were told from the point of view of Otho Williams' descendants.

For my second book, *Finding Otho: The Search for Our Enslaved Williams Ancestors*, I combed through hundreds of land and probate records; purchased and read scores of genealogy and history books; joined writing critique groups; and composed, typed, edited, and revised, seemingly a million times, what would become a well-researched, genealogy guidebook of sorts, which I self-published in December 2018. Happily, it won an award from the Northern California Publishers and Authors group.

This third book, *Finding Daisy: From the Deep South to the Promised Land,* is a literary nonfiction storybook about my paternal grandmother, Daisy Dooley Marshall Schumake, and her ancestors. Some of the conversations in this book were imagined by me, using as many historical references, online searches, census, and other genealogy data as was available.

I struggled for forty years to find Grandma Daisy's parents. Part of the problem was that I was looking in the wrong place! You see, Grandma Daisy told me, and darn near everyone else, that she was born in the Midwest, but she was actually born where plantations and slavery society had been prevalent pre-Civil War in the Deep South. Although the bread crumb trail to Grandma's true history was obscured, at long last I picked up the tasty clues that led me to the truth.

Stories from known relatives and those met through DNA testing, as well as an eye-opening trip to the Deep South in April 2019, added contextual accuracy, a ton of research documents, and a stimulating sense of place. There is *nothing* like walking in the footsteps of your ancestors, feeling the glow and warmth of the sunrise, seeing and touching the soil in the cotton fields where they toiled, and smelling the air they breathed.

The anecdotes and memoirs presented in this book are from our enslaved and free ancestors who were farmers, Pullman porters, hotel waiters, cooks, postal carriers, funeral home directors, embalmers, doctors, and nurses. Some tales included the white slave owners who hailed from Ireland and Germany.

In 2006, after joining the online Ancestry.com website, I began researching my lineage in earnest. Professional genealogist Darlene Nowels, a tangential Dooley relative, righted my course and set me straight on *where* my grandmother was actually born. My family tree changed back and forth over the years because of those uncertainties. It wasn't until 2018 that dozens of people who matched my DNA helped me figure out the true story of Grandma Daisy's roots. I had to find out why Grandma Daisy was so driven to be involved in civic, political, and church events, yet so dictatorial at home? And most of all, why did she lie about her birthplace?

Finding Daisy was based on several information sources, including:

- Telephone and personal visit interviews with kin;
- Letters from ancestors who are now in the beyond;
- Binders of ancestral documents;
- My mother's personal journal discussing her in-laws;
- My father's cigar boxes full of sentimental papers and letters;
- Property records and cemetery deeds;
- DNA testing results, which uncovered many other relatives;
- Articles and photographs from the Cleveland *Call and Post* and *Macon Beacon* newspapers.

To enhance the authenticity of this book, I traveled to Georgia, Alabama, Mississippi, and Ohio, to experience firsthand where my paternal progenitors lived in the 1800s and further back in time.

I had been in Grandma Daisy's presence a handful of times before she died in 1986. All I knew was that she was attractive, petite, smart, no-nonsense, tough, serious, demanding, mentoring, caring, and had accomplished remarkable feats during her lifetime.

I had three specific goals in mind for this book. First, was to learn about Grandma Daisy's upbringing. What caused her to lie about her origins and did those experiences influence her inner beast? My second goal was to extract memories from Daisy's descendants and to validate their stories with documentary evidence. Third, was to weave DNA testing with traditional genealogy research into interesting, literally non-fiction stories told from my ancestors' points of view.

The opening chapter gives us a glimpse into the morning routine at Grandma Daisy's house, circa 1944. One soon begs to question which demons and motivations drove this woman who excelled at everything she did outside the home, but ruled everyone inside with an iron fist.

DAISY DOOLEY MARSHALL TREE

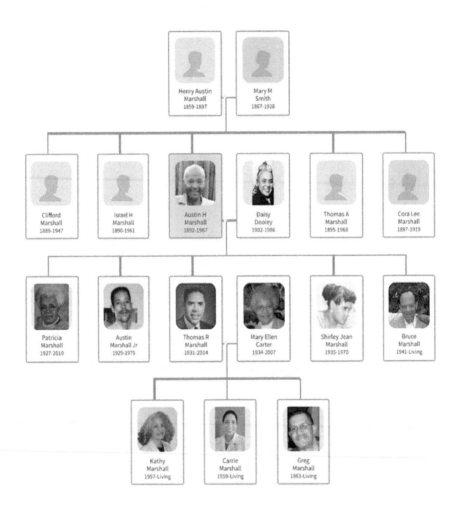

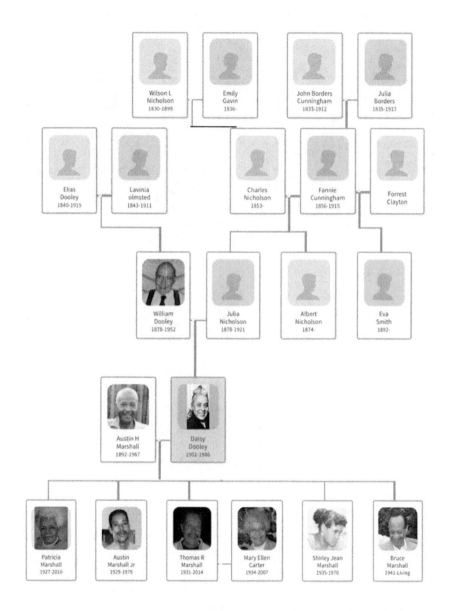

Quilt made by Kathy Lynne Marshall for this book, representing the fields
in the Deep South and skyscrapers and Lake Erie in Cleveland, OH.

PART I - DAISY'S STORY

Daisy Dooley Marshall, Cleveland, OH, circa 1944.
Photograph: Thomas Marshall.

2182 81ˢᵗ Street, Cleveland, OH.
Photograph: Kathy Marshall,

CHAPTER 1 - GOOD MORNING!

(2182 East 81st Street, Cleveland, Ohio, 1944)

"Children, come on over here," demanded the formidable, five-feet two-inch dynamo, her lustrous brunette hair styled in a neat French chignon. Daisy Dooley Marshall Schumake, the author's paternal grandmother, wore a flowered cotton day dress in the pale colors of spring, which could not hide her shapely bosom, waist, and hips. Beige support hose wrapped legs that stood so many hours each day. Her dainty feet were fitted into medium-heeled black shoes to make her exactly one inch taller.

THE DRILL

"You children know what time it is. It's time to get your medicine," Daisy commanded her five children that chilly spring morning before they left the house for school. "One must pay the piper before enjoying life's treats," she continued, with her signature, barely there Mona Lisa smile.

Everybody knew the drill. The kids lined up in the cramped kitchen at one end of the long, two-story house, by age, starting with Patricia Rae who was seventeen years old. Next to her was fifteen-year-old Austin Henry, then thirteen-year-old Thomas Richard (the author's future father), followed by Shirley Jean, eleven, and the youngest, Bruce Cyril, four years old.

As a mouth-watering meaty pork aroma wafted through the moist air, Daisy inspected their hands, fingernails, and faces for cleanliness. She ensured the boys' short wooly hair was combed and the girls' ebony hair was plaited, or hot comb-pressed and curled. Thankfully, their school clothes passed their mother's "properly ironed" scrutiny.

Remaining as still and quiet as possible, the children awaited the most dreaded activity of the day. Daisy had a teaspoon in one hand and in the other, a dark bottle containing the most odious substance in the universe: castor oil.

"Now, you all know that the only way to salvation is castor oil in the morning to move your bowels, prayers to the Good Lord at night, and weekly enemas to keep the body clean and pure."

Daisy moved down the line of children, their mouths open wide for a teaspoon of that viscous delight drizzling into their orifice. Once the hated dose was administered, each child ran to his or her assigned seat at the kitchen table, grabbed a tall glass of orange juice, and drank it down quickly, before the fishy castor oil ruined their taste buds for the rest of the day.

After the children guzzled the pulpy salvation, they remembered to unfold the napkin and place it on their lap. You better believe everybody's mouth watered at the addictive smell of fried bacon strips sitting next to the sunny-side up eggs that Patricia had cooked, from the eggs Shirley Jean had gathered from the chicken coop in the backyard.

Without a sound, they all dipped their spoons into the hot Cream of Wheat cereal, flavored with brown sugar. Then each child cut a pat of yellow butter from a white ceramic dish to spread onto their fragrant toast. Some children also added a thick layer of marmalade on top of the buttered bread. Others preferred the blackberry jam their mother had canned last summer, harvested from the prickly berry bushes growing along the chain-link fence in their backyard.

ETIQUETTE

"Stop blowing on your cereal, Shirley Jean. It's not that hot," Daisy warned. The youngest daughter stopped immediately, but had the temerity to pout at her mother when her back was turned.

"Thomas, get your elbows off the table. How many times do I have to tell you to keep one hand in your lap while you eat?" Daisy continued. Her middle son obeyed quickly, but said some choice words under his breath.

The Table Manners Nazi added, "Austin, must I remind you yet again not to talk when your mouth is full of food? You are not a cow." Austin shook his head and looked down at his plate, glancing at Thomas making funny faces when their mother wasn't looking.

Young Bruce was using his fingers to put some egg on his toast when he also received an etiquette reminder his offending hand would remember.

Later in life, the children would appreciate those lessons in manners and would teach them to their own offspring. This morning, though, they hoped to get through breakfast without any more helpful instruction.

The only one who didn't hear from her mother was Patricia. Being the eldest, she knew all the rules by heart. But Patricia had an embarrassing secret, and she worried the all-too-apparent truth would catch her mother's watchful eye.

THE RITUAL

You see, every night Daisy inculcated upon her children a ritual that was impacting Patricia this morning. At seven p.m. last night, after the dinner dishes had been washed and the homework completed, Daisy called out from the front room, "Time to take your baths, children." Each night, the children took a hot bath, without playing around. They were expected to scrub their bodies clean with a harsh washcloth before they donned flannel pajamas, said their prayers, then slid into their beds. The eldest child got into the tub first, getting to enjoy the freshest and hottest water. Then it was the second-oldest child's turn, and so on. By the time poor little Bruce got into the tub, the water was cold and dirty brown.

Following the bath, each child brushed his or her teeth for two minutes, using an egg timer to ensure that each tooth was cleansed just so. Their mother came in to inspect their work.

"Bruce, I still see collard greens from dinner stuck between your front teeth," Daisy admonished. She grabbed his toothbrush and applied a paste of baking soda and water to the bristles. With unabashed relish and an uncharitable gleam in her beautiful brown eyes, she scrubbed not only his front teeth but the rest of his mouth too. "There, that's how you should brush your teeth every night," Daisy concluded, giving Bruce's toothbrush back to him, her smile more a satisfied smirk than a loving grin.

"Ya-yes, ma'am," Bruce whimpered. Crocodile tears leaked from his red-rimmed almond-shaped eyes, his pummeled mouth smarting from his mother's rough treatment, which was veiled as "care and concern" about his dental hygiene.

In addition to the nighttime bathing and toothbrushing ritual, Patricia and Shirley Jean were required to wash their pretty faces using Pond's Cold Cream—never with soap. The creamy Pond's left an oily film on the surface of their skin, which made it feel as soft as a baby's bottom. Unfortunately, the Ponds also allowed bacteria to be trapped underneath the surface of a teenager's already oily skin, resulting in unsightly white-topped pink mountains on her face.

THE ESCAPE

The next morning before breakfast, Patricia found three "whitehead" pimples looking like they would burst on her forehead. She tried to hide them under her sponge-rolled bangs. You see, Grandma Daisy had a special cure for acne. If she saw a pustule of imperfection anywhere on her child's face, Daisy would use a dry, rough washcloth to scrub the pimples off with all her might, leaving the recipient's face bloodied and raw. She said she was purifying the area.

Patricia wasn't looking forward to that remedy, especially not in the morning, right before high school classes began. Just imagine how embarrassing it would be if Paul, the boy she ogled in secret, saw her with the red, crusted remains of her mother's severe remedy? Thankfully, Daisy somehow missed the facial eruptions, so Patricia's secret was safe for now.

While the kids finished their breakfasts, Daisy—an active member of the St. James African Methodist Episcopal (AME) Church—continued to preach. "Now I expect you all to listen and learn in school today. That is your job. Your marks better all be A's, or we will have a serious discussion later on. DO YOU HEAR ME?"

"Yes, ma'am," the four older children shouted in unison, vigorously nodding their heads up and down. They grabbed their heavy coats, hats, gloves, books, and lunch sacks and plodded down the four wide porch steps. They strode from their house on East 81st Street in Cleveland, Ohio, toward their school several blocks away. Young Bruce didn't look forward to spending the entire day alone with his mother.

Deep down, Daisy was a caring woman, but they knew better than to ever question their mother's motives for how she ran their lives. She could get angry quickly, and nobody needed that so early in the day.

Peace

Daisy:

Whew! Now that those noisy children are gone, I can hear myself think. After I remove these dishes from the table I can get started on my busy morning. I volunteered to work at the Democratic Party Committee office today, then I will drop by the American Legion Post this afternoon, with Bruce, before the older children get home from school.

I fitted the round rubber stopper into the white porcelain sink basin and prepared to wash the breakfast dishes. As I turned on the hot water spigot and watched the aerated frothy liquid pour into the sink, I harkened back to my childhood, after the turn of the twentieth century, when I had to bring buckets of water from the well into our tiny kitchen, to be warmed on the wood-fired stove before the dishes could be washed. I remember getting up after dawn to milk our gentle cow Maisy, so we would have milk for breakfast.

Life was so much more difficult back then. These children nowadays don't appreciate how easy everything is for us Negroes here in Cleveland, compared to where my folks grew up. One day I'll tell them all about the ups and downs of my extraordinary life.

East Boulevard, Cleveland, OH

CHAPTER 2 - SHE ARRIVED LIKE A QUEEN

(1543 East Blvd., Cleveland, Ohio, 1976, Daisy)

The day of our country's Bicentennial celebration, July 4, 1976, I was living the seventy-fourth year of my life. On that humid summer afternoon, I walked down the front steps of my upscale, apartment building in Cleveland, Ohio.

1543 EAST BOULEVARD

The apartment building on this site from 1907-2007 was home to a prominent industrialist early in its history. Phillip Dressler was founder and president of American Dressler Tunnel Kilns Inc., providers of specialty kilns, providing heat-resistant ceramics for molding specialty steel and aluminum products. Founded in 1915, it merged in 1930 with William Swindell and Brothers to become Swindell-Dressler Corporation, whose headquarters today are in suburban Pittsburgh. As the surviving entry arch demonstrates, these were luxury apartments, long spacious units spanning from front to rear, two on each floor for a total of six. In 1910 its tenants were William H. Kefauver, a driller in an automobile factory; Abram E. Brown, Manager of the Philip Carey Company; Sigmund S. Lederer, President and Manager of the Lederer Flour & Grain Company; Walter C. Runyon, Jr., President of the Lake Erie Builders Supply Company; and Arthur M. Smith, Treasurer of the Gas Machinery Company. Among its other early occupants were Samuel and Edward Dettlebach, real estate agents who built this building and lived here from 1907 through at least 1929; Mrs. Edith Phillius, widow; John R. Staniler; Monroe A. Loeser; and Malcolm B. Duncan. Albert A. French designed this building.

Plaque where Daisy's 1543 East Blvd., apartment complex stood.
Now part of the University Circle area of Cleveland, OH.
Photograph: Kathy Marshall, 2018.

I had moved into the apartment in 1958, after marrying my second husband, Lawrence Schumake, a retired postal employee, upgrading my name to Daisy Dooley Marshall Schumake.

We lived in an upscale apartment building located at 1543 East Boulevard, belonging to what would now be considered a condominium association. All tenants had an equal say in any property improvements, hiring of custodians and other things that would typically fall under the perks available to an owner rather than a renter.

Two dozen or so cultural gardens dotted nearby Rockefeller Park, which is eye-catching in the spring when the flowers are in full bloom. Our home presided amongst stately brick houses where rows of groomed hedges guard leaded bay windows in one of the grandest residential districts in the city. Comprised of mostly Negro residents, our houses in the East Boulevard Historic District would fetch ten times the price than those in the nearby suburb of Cleveland Heights.

Our spacious home looks onto Wade Park, and is within easy walking distance of the Cleveland Museum of Art and other cultural and "University Circle" institutions.

On the way to visit my next-door neighbor, Theodora Handy, I was surprised to find a letter in my mailbox from my granddaughter, Kathy Marshall.

"Look at this, Theo," I exclaimed, flapping my postal present in the face of my on-and-off-again neighbor-friend as she opened her door. "I just received a letter from my granddaughter Kathy! Remember? She's my middle son Thomas's eldest child who lives in Sacramento, California, with his sweet first wife Mary."

"Oh my! You are indeed a lucky woman, Daisy. I never hear from my grandchildren. Well, come on in and tell me what it says."

As we walked through Theo's immaculate home full of French Provincial furnishings, I skimmed the letter, becoming more and more perplexed. However, I said, "Oh, my granddaughter just wants to know about our family lineage." *Odd, why would Kathy want to pull our skeletons out of the closet for everyone to see?*

Hoping to change the subject, I crooned, "Aww, Mary, it's too bad Thomas let her go and married that flashy, red-lipsticked white woman from Michigan. Pam—I think her name was—had been Thomas and Mary's ballroom dance instructor. Can you believe that she enticed my tall, good-looking son to start attending dance lessons by himself, so she could 'show him how a man is supposed to lead his partner?' I bet she did show him a thing or two!" I glowered, as my head snapped from side to side as I spoke.

My friend's eyes opened wide, hand covering her gaping mouth in an exaggerated fashion. "No! You can't be serious,

Daisy. Come sit down in the kitchen, girl, while I brew us some tea, and you can tell me all the details." She put on the flowery apron that matched her kitchen curtains and tablecloth.

I sat my seventy-four-year-old arthritic bones into an ornately carved wooden chair at her mahogany kitchen table. An expansive view of stately maple trees in Wade Park across the street spread before my eyes, allowing a brief glimpse at the lagoon in the distance. "Thomas, you better watch out for that woman!" I warned. "But adult children don't pay us elders any mind," I shook my head woefully.

As Theo filled the white enamel teapot from the sink at the far end of the kitchen, she uttered, "Uh-huh, we try and try to help our kids avoid pain, but they just seem to run right toward it, like a deer in the headlights. They act like we don't know what we're talking about just because we have a few gray hairs."

"A few?" I chuckled. "Anyway, I never said, 'I told you so,' when Pam divorced him in 1972 after a few years of marriage. Can you believe she had the nerve to claim my precious Thomas had anger issues because he demanded perfection from her at all times? Sure, he sometimes laid his hands on her, but that was because she didn't perform as expected."

Theo replied, "What's wrong with demanding people do their best? That's how I was raised, have always lived my life, and how I taught my children."

"I agree wholeheartedly. If the wife or child isn't doing what they're supposed to do then, as my blessed mother used to say, 'you git what you git and don't throw a fit.' Anyway, Pam sure took my Thomas to the cleaners! They lived in California which is a community property state, and you know what that means. Husband and wife split their assets and debts from the marriage, half and half. So she got half of his twenty-acre parcel in a tiny town named Loomis, but he was allowed to keep their rustic, three-level executive home on the property. You better believe he had to pay her a hefty sum for half its value! Well, that's enough of those unpleasant memories."

"Yes, tell me more about your daughter-in-law."

Hmm, haven't I told Theo about Mary before? I can't remember who I've told what story to, especially lately.

"Just thinking about Thomas' first wife—my little country girl, Mary Carter—brings back wonderful memories. I so enjoyed having her live with me those couple of years starting in the Spring of 1957. Back then, I was living in the house my first husband, Austin Marshall, and I had purchased in 1923. We lived in a once-lovely tree-lined neighborhood at 2182 81st Street, which sat right around the corner from our family business, the Marshall Funeral Home, which we bought in 1939, at 8115 Cedar Avenue."

"I remember your mentioning that once or twice in the past," Theo replied. *Hmm, was that a smirk on her face?*

Mary was in her third trimester of pregnancy with their first child. Thomas was completing his last year at The Ohio State School of Medicine, in Columbus, Ohio. The funny thing was that my brilliant son was studying to become an obstetrician. His unpredictable school schedule could have interfered with him attending the birth of his own child. What an irony that would have been, right?" Theo laughed just as the tea kettle started whistling its signal the water was hot.

"That's why Mary stayed with me, so when she went into labor I could be with her," I added.

Theo got up and selected a teaspoon and two delicate tea cups she had purchased from her visit to Stoke-on-Trent, England, ten years earlier. As she prepared the orange pekoe tea, I continued my story.

"Mary arrived at the Cleveland Union Terminal train station, stomach out to here." I gesticulated with my hands a foot in front of my belly. "The Terminal Tower Building was a fifty-two-story, landmark skyscraper located on Public Square in downtown Cleveland, built during the skyscraper boom of the 1920s and 1930s. It was the second-tallest building in the world, with the train station on the lower levels and various buildings on top of it."

Theo asked, "Remember the Fred Harvey concessions located in that building? I heard it was the world's largest railroad service operation. It's too bad Negroes were not often allowed to eat there before the 1960s."

I nodded absent-mindedly, a serene look coming over my face, replaying an invisible movie in my head.

"Mary stood in front of the terminal by the curb as I drove up. After getting out of my 1956 blue and white Maverick, I patted my daughter-in-law's back as we embraced. You may have noticed I'm not much of a hugger…" A stifled laugh came from my catty neighbor-friend and she tried to cough to cover it up. I ignored her rudeness.

"I asked a porter to carry her bags into the trunk. Once we got into the car, the normally quiet Mary could not stop talking about the heavenly experience my ex-husband, Austin, had given her in his Pullman Sleeping Car, on the short trip from Columbus to Cleveland."

Mary exclaimed, "Oh Daisy, I couldn't believe it! Austin treated me like royalty from the moment he took my suitcase up the steps into that luxurious train. He escorted me into a plush deep burgundy seat in the middle of the car. Hunter green curtains were draped over the windows. Art-deco style lampshades covered the overhead lights. Murphy-type beds were closed into the wall above the seats. Such an efficient use of space. I had never seen anything like it!

"In his official role as a Pullman Porter, Austin brought me the same fine food the rich patrons ate, instead of me having to waddle to the dining car. He served me Waldorf Salad as my first course: walnuts and diced apples on a bed of mixed lettuce, green grapes cut in half, celery bits, and a tangy mayonnaise dressing. I'd never tasted a more delicious salad in my life! Have you had that before, Daisy?" she asked.

I nodded yes and she beamed at me when I said I would teach her how to make it.

"Sounds like she was looking forward to you being her second mom," Theo interrupted.

"Indeed, and I was the perfect person to teach her all she needed to know to be a proper wife and mother." I noticed that Theo didn't jump up and agree with that statement. Oh well, she's probably just jealous that she doesn't have my skill set.

"Anyway, Mary continued expounding on her trip to Cleveland and slathering more praise onto my ex."

"And then Austin brought me a pork chop smothered in gravy, with well-seasoned, buttery mashed potatoes on the side.

For dessert, I received a healthy piece of pound cake covered with fresh strawberries and a dollop of whipped cream. Everything was delicious and fresh and delivered with a gracious smile. I now understand why he wanted me to hop on the train at lunchtime."

"My dear father-in-law served me my meal on gold-rimmed porcelain plates with what looked like real silverware. That is a world away from the plastic or chipped ceramic plates my poor relations had growing up. He even shined my shoes! And Austin smiled at me the whole trip, making me feel he was only administering to *my* needs. He introduced me to the other porters as his *beloved* daughter-in-law. Daisy, my first experience on the most luxurious of all passenger trains was incredible! I never felt so loved by a father in all my life. Basically, Austin treated me like a queen, just like he would any white person who had bought an expensive ticket in that car. The entire journey was more memorable than I can adequately describe," Mary sighed as she finished her reverie.

"I must admit to being a little jealous about how she blushed and gushed all over what Austin did for her. It was evident she loved her father-in-law, cherishing him more than her own absentee father whom she remembers meeting only once on her fifth birthday when he gave her a nickel. Isn't that the saddest thing you've ever heard?"

Theo nodded with a dispassionate, "Uh-huh." Oh, that's right. Theo had a similar experience with her father leaving his household in Georgia while he made his way Up North for better job opportunities during the Great Migration.

"Mary strained to recount that her father was only around long enough to make another baby. He would soon leave again, going who knew where, doing who knew what. Her grandfather, Otho Sherman Williams—with whom Mary and her mother and siblings lived—forbade Mary's shiftless father from ever visiting the house again. It was the sole way to ensure no more fatherless babies were created.

"Thomas' pretty first wife grew up in the small town of Mt. Vernon, Ohio, with her six living siblings and mother, Pearl Williams Carter. Pearl did 'day's work', as Mary called it, in other people's homes, cooking and cleaning houses during the day and a dental office at night. Even though her mother had lots of experience cooking and cleaning, I was shocked to learn Mary knew almost nothing about cooking or taking care of a household. That poor child—bless her heart—couldn't even boil water!"

"Normally, as you can imagine, Theo, I would not have approved of a union with a such girl of low social standing. But my precious Thomas was so head over heels in love with her, even after dating long distance for three years before they married. During that long courtship, I had a chance to meet Mary and her no-nonsense mother, Pearl Williams Carter. Did I ever tell you that Mary's maternal grandmother, Myrtle Booker Williams, came from an esteemed family in Mt. Vernon, Ohio?" Theo nodded her head.

"And did I ever mention that Mary's paternal grandmother, Ella Roy Carter, worked for Christopher Columbus Delano, a former United States Representative for the State of Ohio, *and* that he was Secretary of the Interior under President Lincoln?" Another nod.

Holding up my index finger to make a point, I continued, "In fact, Representative Delano was not only related to President Franklin Delano Roosevelt, but more importantly, he was one of President Lincoln's closest allies who convinced him to sign the Emancipation Proclamation in 1863, freeing all the slaves in rebel states! Mary's lineage is as close to royalty as a Negro could be in this country. Yes, Mary comes from great stock, so they got my blessing.

"Well, Theo, it's time for me to pick up Lori from school. Thanks for the tea," I said leaving quickly.

I'm glad my neighbor didn't ask again about that letter and how I was going to answer Kathy. I will have to figure out how much of the truth I want to reveal to my granddaughter.

Mary Carter and Thomas Marshall, Columbus, Ohio, 1953.

CHAPTER 3 – TEACHING THE YOUNG OLD TRICKS

(2182 East 81st Street, Cleveland, Ohio, April 1957, Daisy)

"Ok now, Mary, while you are living with me, I shall teach you everything about cooking, cleaning, organizing a household, and taking care of a husband and baby. You will get the benefit of my many years of experience, just like you were my natural-born child."

"I certainly appreciate your guidance and *anything* you wish to teach me," responded twenty-three-year-old Mary.

That first day with me at my home on East 81st Street in Cleveland, my pregnant daughter-in-law hardly said a word after exclaiming about the train trip from Columbus with my husband. She was such a quiet little mouse and watched me intently, doing her best to learn all I had to teach her.

"So Mary, what is your favorite dish to cook?" I expected her to say something like roast beef with scalloped potatoes, or pork chops simmered in gravy, or Sunday baked chicken with salad greens. After an unexpected silence of several seconds, she hung her head and mumbled something unintelligible. "What did you say?" I questioned. Another utterance issued from her lips. "Mary, speak up! I can't hear you."

She raised her head a bit defiantly, with fire in her eyes. "I hate to say it, Daisy, but I can't do much in the kitchen. My mother insisted on doing almost all the cooking at home, even though she was dead tired from being a domestic employee all day long. My oldest sister, Norma, would sometimes cut up vegetables, but Mom preferred to do all the cooking herself. Truthfully, I can only make a jello mold," Mary revealed, embarrassed about her naïveté.

My eyebrows arched in surprise, but I took charge and said, "Now, Mary, after I come home from my nursing duties at the hospital, I am going to teach you how to cook. My son is going to be a doctor and his nutritional needs must be met every day to keep his brain and body functioning at top speed. And your baby is going to need a mother who can take care of all its needs. I shall teach you how to cook, manage a household, and take care of a baby and a husband. You are in good hands, my dear."

Mary nodded her head in acknowledgment, her lips pursed tight. I imagine she was embarrassed to be so helpless. As long as she has a teachable spirit, we will get along just fine.

THE FIRST COOKING LESSON

I escorted my big-bellied daughter-in-law into our bright yellow kitchen and showed her around. The deep white enameled sink was at the far wall, with wood-topped counter space on both sides and milk chocolate painted drawers and cabinets underneath. Next to the sink was a narrow pantry flanked by lots of overhead storage for dishes, glasses, mixing bowls and the like. The fridge was on an adjacent short wall next to the door leading to the backyard. Smoke from fried chicken and bacon exited an open window next to the combination stove/oven, signaling to the neighbors what we were having for dinner every night.

"Mary, we are going to cook roast beef with mixed vegetables and a smooth, flavorful gravy for tonight's dinner." *Look at her beautiful smile. I knew she would enjoy that menu.* "Another day I'll teach you how to make the fluffiest chicken and dumplings and my famous potato salad. I'll also show you how to make a flaky crust for my delectable sweet potato pie. And I'm sure Austin Sr. will share his secret Down Home Georgia family recipes for rum cake and bread pudding."

"You know, Daisy, I appreciate your patience. It's amazing to me too that my siblings and I didn't learn the basics of cooking or sewing. I need you to know, though, that I have never been a lazy girl. I was the Art Editor for our High School Yearbook and I helped my mother clean the dentist's office when I wasn't dressing windows at Ringwalt's Department Store after school. Mom didn't raise any slouches. However, I do feel bad that she was on her feet all day long cooking and cleaning white folks' homes, then had to come home and fix dinner for us too. Now is the time to correct that situation. I am ready to learn! Mold me into the woman, wife, and mother I need to be."

"That's the can-do spirit I like to hear," I responded. "Let's start by learning how to cut meats and vegetables. Pointing to the lower cabinet door next to the sink I said, "Get the cutting board out of that cabinet over there." Mary squatted, her belly supported by her bent knees. She retrieved the well-worn wooden cutting board and placed it on top of the counter. I grabbed a large yellow onion from the pantry and set it on the board, then removed a large chef's knife from the drawer.

After washing our hands, I said, "First, we remove the outer layer of skin, like this," demonstrating by cutting the root end of the onion and pulling off the outer layer of brittle skin. "Now cut the onion in half lengthwise, top to bottom. Place one half cut side down on the board, then make vertical cuts every one quarter-inch. Then cut crosswise, perpendicularly, making neat and even bits, like this."

I sliced and diced one-half of the onion, then scooped the pieces into a bowl. Passing the knife to Mary, handle first, I encouraged her to give it a try.

She took the knife with her outstretched dominant left hand and handled it as though she were going to cut off a finger. "Child! You don't even know how to hold a knife properly, let alone cut with it? Here, let me show you again."

Mary began to sniffle, either at her helplessness or the fumes from the onion, but she continued trying her best to accomplish this new task anyway. The next hour passed slowly as I had to demonstrate over and over again how to hold the knife, cut the onion into one-quarter inch cubes, then how to peel and dice russet potatoes and carrots. I made sure Mary practiced those skills under my watchful eye.

Next, I showed her how to preheat the gas oven to 375 degrees.

"What is the purpose of that?" she asked.

"The food will cook properly if the oven is already hot before placing the food into it," I replied, trying hard to be patient.

I reached under the oven and pulled out a drawer which contained my dark blue enameled roasting pan freckled with white spots. "Go ahead and grease the pan first."

Mary hesitated, not understanding my direction.

"On top of the stove is a can of bacon grease," I said, somewhat irritably. "Grab a spoon from the top drawer over there."

I pointed to the dish rag so she could wipe her greasy hands.

When Mary stood with the spoon in her dominant left hand waiting for further instructions, I said, "Now take a heaping tablespoonful and plop it into the baking pan. Use your fingers to coat the bottom and sides with grease." She made a face as her oily fingers rubbed grease into the bottom and sides of the roasting pan. "Greasing the pan now will make it easier to clean later and will add a fragrant aroma."

I placed a cylindrical slab of marbled red meat into the roasting pan. "Watch me tie this roast with white cotton twine. See, I'm tying knots every two inches or so."

"What does the twine do?" she asked.

"It keeps the roast's shape as it cooks. OK, now it's your turn to tie the last two segments." Mary fumbled a bit with the knots, but she finished her task satisfactorily.

"Good. Now pour the cut vegetables into the pan." There was a colorful mound of yellow onions, orange carrots, and white potatoes surrounding the trussed red meat. "One can of beef consommé will help steam the vegetables and keep the roast moist while cooking. Go to the pantry and look on the third shelf for one can of consommé."

I pointed to the can opener and was surprised she knew how to use it. "Carefully pour the brown broth around the edges of the pan. OK, that's good. We're almost done."

"Now we need to season everything with salt, pepper, garlic powder, and maybe some sage." I pointed to the spice rack on the pantry door and let her find the sage and garlic powder. "Here's the salt and pepper shaker. I leave them on top of the stove because I use them so often. You just turn them upside down like this and shake evenly over the beautiful marbled roast and vegetables."

"How do you know how much to shake on?" Mary asked innocently.

"You'll get to know with practice, but for now, that's enough. Do the same thing with the pepper, garlic powder, and sage." She did as I instructed.

I retrieved a meat thermometer from one of the drawers and inserted it into the center of the roast. "We need to ensure the internal temperature of the meat reaches 145 degrees before we remove it from the oven." Mary nodded in understanding.

"Good, now put the roast on the middle oven shelf but be careful not to tip the pan for the roast might slide off into the oven, or worse, onto the floor."

One of the things my son loved most about his wife, besides her good looks, was that Mary was a competitive tomboy. She was a "take no prisoners" tennis player and golfer, and the Queen of marbles in her hometown. Thomas said she could skate backward and forward and she dominated on the basketball court. But even though she had a strong two-handed backhand in tennis, she admitted to having little grip strength.

So as Mary struggled to distribute her unaccustomed girth in order to set the heavy pan onto the oven shelf, I could see it starting to tilt. The roast was sliding forward as her grip began to fail. The scene rushing before my eyes was the roast and all our hard work splashing onto the oven bottom in a messy heap. I rushed over, grabbed a pot holder hanging on the wall next to the stove, and supported the bottom of the roasting dish with my right hand, guiding it onto the oven shelf just in the nick of time. Whew! Disaster avoided.

"I'm so sorry, Daisy. My grip is the weakest part of me, well…and my love of chocolate!" We both had a good laugh as I closed the oven door and stood up, rubbing my back after my heroic effort to save our dinner. Mary would have to learn how to do these things herself, though, with or without a child in her belly.

I continued our lesson. "The instructions from my Betty Crocker Cook Book indicate we should let the roast cook twenty minutes per pound of meat. Our roast is a little heavier than three pounds, so that's about sixty minutes." Assuming she didn't know how to do this either, I showed Mary how to turn the manual timer on by twisting the knob clockwise around to the sixty-minute mark on the dial. Done.

Mary looked tired after our first two-hour cooking lesson, so I suggested she lie down on the sofa while the roast was baking. Teaching someone how to cook is hard work and I too dozed off in my rocking chair, with an unopened novel on my lap.

The hour flew by in a heartbeat. The steady *ding ding ding* of the timer woke us up at the same time.

I helped Mary off our long, cushiony olive and gold brocade couch.

The savory smell of roasted meat pulled us back into the warm kitchen. I lifted the pan out of the oven and set it on a cast iron trivet on the counter. The thermometer read 144 degrees, which was close enough. I explained the internal temperature might inch up another degree or so while sitting in its hot juices. I showed Mary how to use a fork to test the potatoes for doneness. Yes, they were soft.

"Ok, Mary, the last step is to cover the roast with tin foil and let it rest for at least twenty minutes. Yes, that's right, grab those pot holders, place the foil loosely over the top of the meat, then mold the wrap around the sides of the pan. Don't burn yourself. Now turn on the timer for twenty minutes." Mary did as I asked, a satisfied look on her face.

"What is the purpose of that?" Mary asked, pointing to the foil.

"Allowing the meat to rest allows the juices to redistribute throughout the meat. As a result, it will lose less liquid when you cut it and be far more tender and juicy to eat," I explained.

"Hmm, that's good to know. I can hardly wait to taste it!" Mary smiled mischievously.

Things were looking up. We were almost ready for dinner.

A PROPER TABLE

"Now it's time to set the table in the dining room. The plates are in the cabinet over there, above the sink. Four is all we need, one for you, me, Larry, and Bruce." Mary got the plates and put them around the table. "Larry always sits on the far end by the window and I sit here on the end closest to the stove. Bruce sits there (pointing to the left) so you can sit on the right side." Mary did as she was instructed, with a curt nod of her head.

"Napkins are in that second drawer down under the plates." After she brought four napkins over, I showed her how to fold them in half then halved again into a neat three-by-six-inch rectangle placed near the left rim of the plate.

"Silverware is in the drawer above the napkins. We'll need four forks, serrated knives, and spoons."

I taught Mary how to set a simple table for daily dining, by placing the fork on the napkin, the knife with its cutting edge toward the right side of the plate, and the spoon next to the knife. Growing up, Mary revealed her household had only a few serrated knives to share amongst eight people. Imagine that!

I filled the water glasses and set them on the upper right of the plate next to the wine glass, then placed a bottle of red wine on the table. Pregnant Mary was not a drinker or smoker, so she just needed the water glass.

"Mary, my ancestors had been 'House Negroes' who worked inside the slave owner's plantation house. They were not only responsible for cooking the meals and cleaning the house, but also learning the ways of white people. They learned how to sew fine clothes and quilts, how to dress like a lady—because they had to dress the mistress of the house. They knew how to wear their hair stylishly—because they did the mistresses' hair. They were expected to set a fine table with silverware and china plates and serving ware for the family and for large parties that well-to-do planters often had for their friends and business associates. I had learned the proper way to set a table when I was a youngster from my mother, and she from her mother, back generations of house slaves. So, even though we may not have had the same type of fine clothes, or houses, or china, or fancy wine glasses growing up, we learned the proper way to dress and set a fine table. You better believe that I expected my children, grandchildren, and daughters-in-law to follow the rules of decorum that our ancestors practiced every day for their owners."

"I appreciate your sharing your knowledge with me, Daisy, I really do," Mary responded.

The timer signaled the end of the twenty minute rest period for the meat. The last step for tonight's dinner was to cut the roast and arrange the slices onto a silver serving tray. First, I had to cut off and remove the strings around the roast. Using a pair of tongs in my non-dominant left hand, I showed Mary how to hold the roast so it wouldn't move around the platter. I used a long, sharp chef's knife in my right hand to slice through the roast, cutting off half-inch slices of meat. I left three slices at the butt end for Mary to cut. We piled the moist roast beef slices on one side of the serving tray, overlapping them to fan out the slices. I had Mary spoon the vegetables onto the other side of the tray and add a sprig of parsley between the meat and vegetables. Voila!

"Oh, I forgot the gravy!" Quickly, I placed a small saucepan on the burner and poured in one-quarter cup of cooled beef drippings from the roasting pan. Adding two tablespoons of flour, I quickly whisked them together to form a smooth paste. I poured in more of the beef drippings and some milk, stirring until the mixture was incorporated. Then I turned the fire on high, stirring all the while until the flour magically thickened the mixture in a few minutes. I poured the viscous brown mixture into its designated gravy bowl and placed it on the table.

"Larry! Bruce! Dinner is served." I had invited my husband-to-be, Lawrence Schumake, to come over for dinner. A few minutes later, we all sat down and enjoyed Mary's first cooked meal. It was a tiring experience for me, but much more so for her, being pregnant. I was glad to find out that she does indeed have a teachable spirit, and wouldn't give up until the task was done. She went to bed early that night, bone-tired, but proud of her efforts!

HOUSEHOLD ORGANIZATION

The key to a successful life is having an organized and clean house, a healthy body, and sharp mind, as well as helping your fellow man. My parents taught me to present a good example of those characteristics to my children and community, and to always be a beacon of light to others.

The next morning was my day off from the hospital so I showed Mary how to make pancakes and scrambled eggs. She got the same dose of castor oil and orange juice that I gave my children every morning at breakfast, and she made the same sour face they did.

After washing and putting away the dishes, we examined how I had arranged food in the refrigerator. "Now, Mary, notice that I put fresh vegetables in the left bottom drawer and fruit in the one on the right. That shields the fresh foods from strong smells. Milk, containers of fruit juice, and other taller items must be on the top shelf. Proteins are on the second level: eggs on the right side and meats taking up the rest of that shelf. Cheese, butter, and condiments are placed in cubbies in the door. Other short items are on the third shelf. Casserole dishes sit on top of the fruit and vegetable drawers. The freezer is rather small but it's easy to forget items in the back until it is defrosted every month. I'll show you that task later. Breads rest in the pantry, but they must be eaten quickly or they will mold when the humidity is high."

I taught Mary how to organize plates, bowls, and glasses into the upper cabinets within easy reach of the sink. That way, after washing and drying, it's easier to put away the implements that are used daily. Pots and pans are stored in the cabinet next to the stove.

"Silverware and other utensils are placed in partitioned plastic trays, just so, inside the drawer next to the sink. This reduces the steps needed to put them away after washing. A place for everything and everything in its place makes for an efficient, orderly kitchen, as the basis for an efficient, orderly life. That's my motto and I expect you to abide by my rules while you are living with me," I proclaimed.

With a smile and nod of her head, Mary responded, "You can count on me!"

MORE COOKING BASICS

"Ok, now let me show you how to use the oven to avoid burning the meal."

"Daisy, I don't understand. If you are following a recipe, why would you ever burn the food?" Mary asked in a serious voice.

"That's a good question. Not all ovens are alike. Electric ovens take longer to heat up than gas-heated ones. If you have not preheated the oven to the correct temperature before inserting the food, and cook the food according to the recipe, the end result may be underdone. You may have to cook it for a longer time, which may be too long," I replied.

"Well, that certainly makes sense. So, how can you be sure the food has finished cooking?" Mary asked.

"There are lots of different ways," I started. "Take the potatoes from your first dinner here, for example. When the timer indicated the roast and vegetables should be done cooking, we took a fork and pierced a few pieces of potato to see if they felt soft, right?" Mary nodded yes.

"For some cookies, you can look through, or open the oven door a tad to see if they have risen a bit in height and whether they are just starting to turn golden brown around the edges."

A dreamy, faraway look clouded Mary's vision and she admitted, "The sweet smell of my mother's tasty oatmeal cookies wafted out the open windows and always brought us kids inside asking, 'Do you need help with those Mom?' Of course that was just a ruse to savor the scrumptious morsels!"

I laughed, imagining seven children bursting through the kitchen door clamoring for a taste.

"Daisy, do you have a good recipe for oatmeal and chocolate chip cookies?" Mary asked innocently, her eyes still bright, just thinking about her mother's delicious baked goods.

I nodded, responding, "On the back of the Quaker Oatmeal box is the recipe I use."

"And what about lemon cake and buttery pound cake and gingerbread? How do you know when cakes have finished cooking?" Mary asked, looking like she was salivating at the mere thought of sampling a forkful of buttery pound cake right now.

"Most cakes are a little trickier than cookies," I replied. "Some rise maybe an inch or more from the poured batter level, but others rise well above the top of the pan.

The toothpick test is perhaps the most widely used method for determining doneness. Did you ever see your mother do that?" Mary shook her head no. "Well, take a toothpick or dinner knife and insert it into the center of the cake and quickly pull it straight up and out. If the toothpick or knife comes out clean, without any trace of raw batter on it, then the cake is completely baked.

Another method is to open the oven door and lightly press your index finger on the center of the cake; if it bounces back, the cake is done. If not, close the oven door quickly, so no more heat is lost, and let the cake cook another couple of minutes before checking again for doneness."

"I will teach you how to make a proper peach cobbler, as my mother taught me, and her mother did before her. Whenever I smell the peaches and nutmeg wafting through the kitchen, it always takes me back to the enjoyable times I had baking with my mother." I had to catch my breath for a moment, as memories crowded my brain. *I still can't believe Mama died so soon after we moved here to the Promised Land. I miss her.*

"Cobbler sounds good, but what about fudge?" Mary asked, breaking me out of my reverie. "Daisy, that's one of my favorite desserts. Really, just about anything that's chocolate is my favorite."

I tried not to smile. We had to stay on track because Mary had a lot to learn. Speaking seriously, I indicated that, "Making candy on the stove—like caramel topping for apples or popcorn—or taffy, toffee, or fudge, requires a candy thermometer be affixed to the inside of the cooking pot. The recipe will advise the correct temperature which must be achieved for the end product to be successful. The hotter the temperature, the more the sugars in the recipe will cook and the harder, or more brittle, the finished candy will be. That's called the 'hard ball' stage."

"Why would they call it that?" Mary asked.

"Most candies have a good amount of sugar in them. When white granular sugar is heated it becomes a liquid. With more heat the chemical compounds in the sugar meld with other ingredients and become a thicker substance which, when cooled, becomes a firm solid.

"If you take a bit of the boiling sugar mixture and drop it in a glass of ice water, then grasp the cooled drop between your fingers, it will feel like a hard lump or ball, which is what you want for peanut brittle, for example. Hard ball stage means the mixture is cooked to between 250 and 266 degrees.

"For softer candies like fudge or toffee, you want to cook the mixture to the 'soft ball' stage, which is 235 degrees. That means the cooked sugary mixture forms a 'soft ball' when

35

dropped into a glass of ice water. I'll show you the next time we make fudge."

"How about this evening?" Mary asked with a wink and playful grin. Even *my* mouth started watering at that thought.

"Stop trying to divert my attention, Mary! Let's get back to the lesson." Mary jumped a bit with my unexpected outburst so I calmed down.

"Various meats require a specialized meat thermometer. In general, poultry should have an internal temperature of 165 degrees to be considered cooked properly. Steaks, roasts, veal, lamb, and fish should be cooked to 145 degrees, but ground pork and beef to 160.

Checking the oven for the proper temperature is the key for cooking meat. People could get sick if the food isn't cooked properly. Also, harmful bacteria may grow if certain foods like meat and dairy products are too long left out of a refrigerated environment."

"I didn't realize that could be a problem. Food was so scarce in my home that we never had leftovers for bacteria to grow on!" Mary said good-naturedly. "What about BBQ'd hot dogs and hamburgers?"

"There are other means for checking doneness for grilled meat if you don't want to use a thermometer. Personally, I like the palm method." I held up the palm of my left hand.

"Really? Using the palm of your hand can tell you how done grilled meat is?" Mary queried, eyes squinting, acting like I was pulling her leg.

"Exactly," I responded, using my fist to show her what I meant. "Let's take grilled steak, for example. You could do a touch test by making a fist. First, make a relaxed fist. The fleshy area of your palm between your thumb and forefinger is soft, which is how a rare steak feels if you were to press it with your finger. If you slightly clench your fist, it's a little firmer, like medium doneness. Clench your fist a bit more tightly and the area will feel like a well-done steak."

"Daisy, you are a marvel. I'm learning so much from you. The next time I visit my mother, I'll feel proud to cook a sumptuous meal for her! And wait until Tom gets to taste my new cooking skills. He's probably told you that he is often the one who cooks our meals, because I never learned how."

I kept my composure, but I was *not* overjoyed to hear my son had to cook, along with studying for his medical exams. "Well, Mary, Tom did mention that once or twice. That's why I'm helping you become the wife and mother you *need* to be."

Mary was an organized person in general, so she caught on quickly. While she lived with me, I expected her to help cook and clean to reinforce my training, which she did without complaint.

THE SEAMSTRESS

After graduating from medical school, my son Thomas would not be making a lot of money during the four or five additional years required for obstetrics internship and residency.

Mary needed to do her part by learning how to sew clothes for herself and the baby, to save money.

My pregnant daughter-in-law and I went to the gargantuan, eight-story May Company department store in downtown Cleveland. They sold everything there.

I bought her a Necchi brand sewing machine, with the intent of teaching her the basics of sewing garments and quilts. We bought some sewing patterns for baby clothes—one-piece outfits, pants, shirts, and rompers. We also bought a couple of patterns for simple house dresses and blouses for Mary.

We explored different types of fabrics and which ones were most appropriate for children and adults, depending on the garment. We looked at 45-inch wide bolts of fabric, how to read the pattern, and to buy the correct amount of material.

Back home, I taught her how to pin each pattern piece to the fabric and cut them out. Threading the needle and bobbin took a few tries but she mastered that task. Then I showed her how to sew a straight stitch, suggesting she frequently clip the dangling threads to keep her work neat. Under my tutelage, she sewed her first baby quilt, a simple infant gown, and a loose floral house dress for herself that she could wear after the birth. The seams weren't totally straight but the items were usable.

As each day passed, we had the sensation that something momentous was about to happen. My grandchild was due to enter the world in just three short weeks! We had to get the baby's room ready.

The latest Montgomery Ward catalog came in the mail last week, so we pored over various baby items that we would buy in the next day or so.

Time was collapsing around us, moving faster and faster, warning us to complete our preparations soon.

Chapter 4 - The New Mommy

(Cleveland, Ohio, May 1957, Daisy)

Baby Kathy and her mother Mary Marshall, Cleveland, OH.
Photograph: Thomas Marshall, 1957.

Almost There

At breakfast one morning in early May, I presented Mary with an important gift. The peach-colored *Better Homes and Gardens Baby Book* was the most well-regarded publication for mothers-to-be at that time. That "baby-bible" of sorts contained information and instructions for all stages of babyhood, from prenatal care through the sixth grade. I began that morning by giving Mary daily reading assignments and quizzed her when I returned home from work. She needed to understand how to maintain herself during the remaining weeks of pregnancy, prepare for the baby's arrival, and know what to expect during labor, delivery, and beyond.

The book was right on time. The next day at work I received a frantic telephone call from Mary right before lunch. She was experiencing sharp pains in her belly.

"No, Daisy, these (gasping) are definitely not the same sensations as when the baby is kicking. These are much stronger. I think I'm having my baby *now*. Please come home!" Mary panicked through the phone.

Mary had been reading her baby book and felt sure she was in labor. I imagined beads of sweat appearing on her upper lip as she contemplated the impending birth. She didn't know what to do, being all alone in the house while Bruce was at school and I was at work. My husband, Austin, and I had divorced by then so Mary was all alone in the East 81st Street house while I performed my nursing duties.

"Now, Mary," I tried to sound comforting, but I was starting to become impatient. "As a first-time mother-to-be, I am pretty sure you are having pre-labor pains, called Braxton Hicks contractions. You are most likely *not* having your baby right now," I said slowly. "Listen to me. I want you to sit down on the couch and put your feet up, then rub your belly in a slow circular motion. Breathe deeply and TRY TO RELAX!" I said a bit too forcefully.

"I don't think that's going to stop these pains!" she continued, working herself into a frenzy.

In my sternest voice, trying to get her attention, I said, "Mary, listen to me. Breathe in five seconds, hold your breath five seconds, then breathe out s-l-o-w-l-y for eight seconds. Do that several times to relax yourself. I'll have my next door neighbor, Edith Bradfield, come over right now and sit with you until I get home. Calm down. I'm sure you'll be fine. The baby isn't due for another couple of weeks."

"Are-are you sh-sure I am not in labor?" Mary whimpered, sounding a bit more composed.

"I had those same pains when I was pregnant with all my children. Wait for my neighbor to come over, then prop your feet up like I told you, and do the breathing exercise I just gave you."

I hung up the phone, then called my neighbor to look in on Mary to assuage my daughter-in-law's fears.

That evening, Mary and I prepared a corner of the guest room where she was sleeping, for the baby. I had Bruce retrieve the woven bassinet from the attic that I had used for my children decades prior. We cleaned it thoroughly with Pine Sol and wrapped a clean sheet around the tiny deodorized mattress. I put Mary's rather shabby first-effort quilt on the sheet. The sunny yellow quilt covered with blue birds and pink flowers that *I* made would wrap the baby for the trip home.

I was off work the next day, so we went shopping on the fourth floor of Higbee's Department Store to purchase everything the baby would need: cloth diapers, knitted caps, tiny white socks, two cotton infant gowns, bath towels, baby washcloths, baby shampoo, baby powder, baby oil, Vaseline, burping cloths, and more blankets for the bassinet. We got a few more items at Montgomery Ward. By mid-May, we were ready, and none too soon.

At Last!

My third granddaughter, Kathy Lynne Marshall, was born on May 22, 1957, at Lakeside Hospital in Cleveland. Thankfully, Thomas was able to "attend" (assist) in the operating room for the birth of his first child. After all, he was studying to be an obstetrician and needed some "on-the-job" training. Most fathers-to-be back then were only allowed to pace back and forth in the hospital's "father's" waiting room. As a nurse at University Hospital's Hanna Pavilion, I was also allowed to be present for the birth of my granddaughter.

"Mary, you may not remember, but I came in a few times to ensure they were treating you well."

"Seriously, Daisy, mostly what I remember about the birth was the small, dark room," Mary told me afterward. There was a nurse who sat there with me and even though she didn't do or say much, I was comforted knowing a professional was nearby. My contractions were coming frequently for about an hour and I thought, I've just had about *enough* of this. Thankfully, the nurse offered me something for the pain. Tom arrived about then from Columbus.

"After the anesthesiologist gave me a shot in my spine, I felt the next contraction but then nothing at all. My buttocks, inner thighs, hips, and the area between my legs were dead to the world. There must have been something else in that shot because the next thing I knew the nurse was saying, 'Wake up and see your darling little daughter.' I opened my eyes, but all I remember seeing was Tom holding a little round face surrounded by lots of silky black hair looking at me. Then I went right back to sleep."

When Mary and the baby finally came home days later, I was in charge because Thomas had to return to school right after the delivery. During the next couple of weeks, I stayed home and showed Mary how to swaddle her precious baby tight. Kathy was wrapped in layers of thin blankets, even though it was nearly summertime. Everyone knew a tight wrap was the best thing for a newborn.

[Author's note: This common swaddling practice may have contributed to my lifelong claustrophobia in tight spaces, and the overwhelming feeling that I had once been buried alive in a tight box.]

The living room was bathed in light from the window that overlooked the shady trees across the street. Mary and I sat on the brocade couch after a lunch of egg-salad sandwiches and iced tea which she had proudly prepared for us.

After a few seconds gazing at her week-old daughter, who was asleep in her lap, Mary said to me, "Can you believe the doctor had the nerve to proclaim, 'You were made for having babies. Your daughter slid right out of those wide hips while you were in La-La-Land.' Well, as much as I love this precious little baby, I am *not* going to be like my mother with seven mouths to feed! At this time, Daisy, I have *no* plans to go through that experience ever again!" Mary smiled, gently moving a lock of black hair from Kathy's warm forehead. Then she took a sip of cool orange pekoe tea from the glass sitting on a lacy, white doily on the walnut coffee table.

"I understand perfectly, my dear. Five children was enough for me!"

I tasted a bit of her white bread sandwich filled with egg-salad and iceberg lettuce. "Maybe a little more salt and yellow mustard next time. It needs a bit more spice to enhance the blandness of the eggs," I advised Mary.

"OK, thanks for the feedback. I never learned how to use spices." Mary took a bite and washed it down with sweet tea. "Daisy, it was so strange having to stay in that noisy hospital for four days. They brought Kathy in and showed me how to bottle-feed her. I loved watching that miraculous little being that Tom and I made—clenching her hands and squinting her eyes open at the light.

"After the second day, I felt fine, walking a few steps by myself to and from the bathroom, but they wouldn't let me go home. They said it was hospital policy, so they could ensure all was well with me and the baby."

"Staying so many days in a hospital may be inconvenient, and it certainly is noisy, and the food isn't as good as mine"—smile—"but it's a precaution they take with everyone. I'll take good care of you both now. I've arranged to stay home with you for two weeks until you get your 'new mommy' feet wet. Then you should be able to watch her by yourself."

MAMMA MIA!

After lunch, infant Kathy woke up and began whimpering for some unknown reason. Mary walked with her from one end of the house to the other, cradling the newborn in her arms. When that didn't work, she put the baby on her shoulder, speaking in soothing tones, but Kathy would not be consoled.

Back then, bottle-feeding was thought to be better and more convenient than the mother's breast. Mary and I had purchased a dozen bottles and nipples, along with Similac formula—the same commercial milk-based baby formula I fed my babies decades ago. Kathy thankfully quieted.

"Ah, there's my baby girl, all happy now," Mary crooned.

Retreating to the makeshift baby room, Mary put her daughter on the tatty yellow and green baby quilt she had made, atop a small chest of drawers which doubled as a changing table. "Mary! Watch that she doesn't squirm off the edge," I screamed.

43

"You must keep one hand on her body at all times as you change her diaper." I showed my receptive daughter-in-law how to fold the fluffy, twelve-inch by twelve-inch white cotton diapers into thirds, placing the baby's tiny bottom in the center of the cloth, covering her belly button on the front and her buttocks on the back. Then one flared out the top edges and overlapped them around the baby's waist, carefully securing the edges with large diaper pins.

Cleaning and washing the cloth diapers was a dreary but unavoidable task. We had a special diaper pail for the soiled ones. If the child had a bowel movement, we dunked the diaper into the commode until the particulate fell into the water. Quickly affixing the close fitting lid to the diaper pail kept undesirable odors from overtaking the house. We generally washed diapers every other day, using white vinegar and baking soda, along with regular clothing soap. The wet diapers were pulled through the wringer on my modern Maytag washing machine. Then we used clothes pins to hang them on the clothes line outside to let them dry in the sun.

After the umbilical cord had fallen off about a week after the birth, we gave Kathy her first bath. I had purchased a small plastic infant bathtub that could fit inside my kitchen sink. I warned Mary to check the water temperature by dipping the outside of her elbow in the bath to ensure it was room temperature.

Mary gushed, "Oh, Daisy, don't all baby products smell delicious? Johnson's baby bath, shampoo, baby oil, and baby powder make me want to cuddle my freshly washed baby." Her arms akimbo, Mary continued, "I'm feeling so much more confident now, knowing I'll be able to care for her properly. Thank you so much for all you've given me. I am lucky to have you as my mother-in-law."

A Mona Lisa smile crossed my lips with her gratitude, but I knew that mothering isn't always a bed of roses. Even so, it was marvelous being with the new mother during her baby's first year of life. I had been used to a full house of children in the 1930s and 1940s. The only child still living here was Bruce, fourteen going on forty, if you know what I mean.

I found myself surprised at how much I enjoyed watching every new accomplishment and milestone baby Kathy reached each day. Opening her eyes, focusing on our faces, holding onto our fingers, smiling when she passed gas. It was one risible day after another in the company of a baby, seeing the world for the first time, and her mother who delighted at every new discovery.

Walking in the park next to our house, Kathy tried to focus on the green leaves of the trees, then at our beaming faces. Eleven years later, when Kathy was in fifth grade, a routine eye-test revealed she was nearly legally blind and needed thick glasses. That's why she squinted so much, sat so close to the television, and held books so close to her face! It's incredible nobody knew she was visually impaired, especially considering her father was a medical professional and her mother an elementary school teacher.

It was all somewhat magical looking at it from a grandmother's point of view, instead of the day-to-day drudgery of a parent. I had mostly raised our children alone, since my first husband's Pullman porter job kept him so often away from home. Parenting was hard. Grand-parenting was so much easier and more enjoyable. It was kind of nice to have my ex-husband, Austin, stop by to visit me, Thomas, and six-month-old Kathy. It almost felt like old times when we were married.

Once Thomas graduated in 1958, he moved his young family across the country to Seattle, Washington, where he completed his medical internship, and fulfilled his military obligation as a Navy Lieutenant in the Medical Corps.

Many may think I am a cold, mean biddy, but after Thomas, Mary, and Kathy left my house, I felt a deep void in my heart. Thankfully, I still had other grandchildren living nearby whom I could guide on a regular basis. All my children and grandchildren needed to learn the proper way to do things and believe you me, I was just the person to teach them!

Yes, I had big plans for each of my children and grandchildren. I led by example, showing them how they, too, could be a successful entrepreneur, community leader, and solid citizen. I may not have constantly said, "I love you" or hugged and petted them like other mothers, but I made sure they had whatever they "needed"—not necessarily what they "wanted." I groomed each of them to live up to their potential.

Kathy, Thomas, Daisy, and Austin Marshall.
Photograph: Mary Marshall, 1958.

For example, it was me who encouraged Patricia to attend Oberlin College, and perform at local social events, aggressively encouraging her to become a concert pianist and music instructor at a performance high school. While my first husband financed Patricia's and Thomas' educations, it was me who saw our middle sons' phenomenal mathematical and scientific potential. I strongly suggested that Austin Jr. take the U.S. Postal Service examination to become a postman, which was considered a respectable job for Negroes. Youngest son Bruce had the bug to be his own man and I helped him become a savvy—some would say ruthless—entrepreneur. I vowed to plant the seeds for my grandchildren to excel, whether they felt my diktat was punitive or nurturing.

I shall carry on the traditions my parents taught us and their parents taught them. The ancestors are smiling!

46

THE LETTER

Back to that muggy July day in 1976 when I received a letter from my then-teenaged granddaughter, Kathy. It had been a long time since any of my California grandchildren had written to me.

In fact, the last time I saw Mary and her three children was in 1967, the year after she and Thomas had divorced. That was when the four of them rode the California Zephyr train across country and visited me for a couple of weeks, after spending time with Mary's mother in tiny Mount Vernon, Ohio. By then, I was raising my daughter Shirley Jean's three children—Michal, Carolyn and Lori—who were roughly the same ages as Mary's kids. My second husband, Larry, and I had a full house of children once again.

Or, maybe the last time I saw Mary was actually in about 1970 when I took Michal, Carolyn, and Lori with me to visit Thomas in his modern, tri-level house in Loomis, California. No matter, those details are unimportant now. I had a letter to read.

What an interesting surprise! Kathy wanted to know about my family's background. She asked where and when I was born, what my parents did for a living, who my siblings were, when and where I got married, who my mother was, and whether we descended from Caucasians.

Huh, that last question was strange. Why would she ask that? Well, one look in the mirror tells the tale that some of us Dooleys do appear to have a lot of cream in our African coffee!

Kathy explained that an elder coworker from her brand-new job at the California Highway Patrol had asked why her skin coloring was so light. Kathy could not answer the question, hence, this letter.

Should I tell her the truth, or take my secrets to the grave?

The Deep South.

CHAPTER 5 – SUGAR AND SPICE?
NOT SO NICE

(1543 East Blvd., Cleveland, Ohio, 1963, Daisy)

"For as long as I can remember, Aunt Eva, I have purposely given people the impression I was born in St. Louis, Missouri. Technically, that was not true, as you know all too well."

"I don't blame you at all, girl. Had I been smarter, I would have done the same thing," my seventy-four-year-old Aunt Eva Clayton Smith Craggett replied, picking up a flaky biscuit and spreading it with butter and blackberry jam. Between sips of freshly brewed coffee and bites of the fluffy biscuit, my mother's younger sister seemed to be looking forward to reminiscing about our years in the Deep South.

"Many die-hard Southerners affectionately call their homeland 'Dixie' for the Mason-Dixon Line, which divided the slave south from the rest of the country. I chose to exorcise Dixie altogether from my life," I bragged indignantly, sliding my head saucily from side to side, as some Negro women do.

Appearing self-conscious, Aunt Eva carefully ran a hand over her silvery, pressed curls as though she wanted to ensure they were still in place. She had mentioned a strong wind greeted her when she exited the streetcar on East Boulevard, just a few doors from my house.

I could tell Eva was always conscientious about looking her best. Her mother was my grandmother, Fannie Cunningham Nicholson Clayton. GramFannie—that's what we kids called our grandmother—taught all of her children: "You get one chance to make a great impression on someone, and that could influence how they view and treat you, so always look your best." I found that to be sage advice that I practiced, choosing to dress myself memorably every day.

From the balcony in Larry and my spacious East Boulevard home, one could glimpse several frothy water fountains spouting in nearby Rockefeller Lagoon. This elegant setting was the perfect place to help us appreciate how fortunate our lives had turned out, in spite of our humble beginnings Down South.

"Aunt Eva, didn't you come out and visit when we were living at Windsor Place in St. Louis in 1920, when I celebrated my eighteenth birthday?" Eva nodded.

"Yes, Daisy, I came out once while y'all were there. I remember how difficult it was for folks to maneuver a car down that long narrow lane, with all those houses alongside the road. Y'all weren't there more than a year before you moved up to Cleveland with Hampton and me, right?" I nodded. "I was so impressed by how nice the places were in St. Louis and wondered how so many Negroes were able to afford them," Eva said, before taking another bite.

Getting a browned biscuit for myself, slathering it with butter and marmalade, I continued to rewind my memory clock. "Yes, when I look at this gorgeous scene here, I just pinch myself! I so wish Mama could see how well we've all done in the forty years since she passed."

"Indeed. My sister, Julia, would be proud of all her children, but especially you, Daisy. I still can't believe she died in 1921, just after y'all moved here. It's hard to imagine that you were perhaps the first Negro woman to be a certified mortician, and for a while you were running the Marshall Funeral Home here. You are a Trustee at St. James A.M.E. Church and team leader at the colored YMCA, as well as being President of the PTA. You're also an activist in the Democratic Party, and you take care of three grandchildren. How do you do it all? You are amazing!" Eva smiled and continued, "And to think all of us were born near that dusty small town of Macon, in Noxubee County, Mississippi, a million miles away physically, mentally, emotionally, and religiously from this urban city with so many opportunities for advancement."

Happy about the compliments, but wanting to appear humble, I got up and walked over to my shiny new General Electric percolator on the kitchen counter, filled my coffee cup, and offered to refill Aunt Eva's.

"Yes, I spent most of the first two decades of my life in that despicable place Down South, and I survived to tell the tale! Is it any wonder why so many Negroes like me preferred to claim a St. Louis birthplace, instead of Mississippi, Alabama, or Georgia? Aunt Eva, did you know that Noxubee County was named for the Choctaw word 'nakshobi' which means 'to stink?' Need I say more?"

Both of us laughed heartily at that, slapping the table for emphasis. Tears started streaming down our eyes, both because the stink was hilarious and because it went *far* beyond the smelliness of the Noxubee River.

"Sugar and Spice, Mississippi was *not* nice, at least for most people of a darker hue. Can I get an Amen?" Eva, asked.

"A-men!" I replied on cue.

Even though Eva was slightly duskier than my lighter, cafe-au-lait skin tone, we all knew that if you weren't white, you weren't treated right.

I said, "The Civil Rights Era of the 1950s, up to now, has boldly brought the issues of blatant racism onto television screens all around the world. I still can hardly believe the vile hatred spewing from the lips of those screaming white Mississippians. It is abhorrent to many people on the world stage. Police brutality was, and is, an everyday occurrence. Many men and women have been carted away to jail for the flimsiest of reasons, beaten in the paddy wagons, as well as in jail."

"Negroes still—even now in 1963—have to pay a poll tax in order to vote. Oh yes, Jim Crow segregation is alive and well in Ol' Miss. Their grandfather clause allowed any adult male whose father or grandfather had voted prior to the abolition of slavery to vote, without paying the tax. But because most of our Negro ancestors"—pumping my fist for emphasis—"had been slaves, many of us still have to pay a poll tax to vote! It's not fair!" I nearly screamed in frustration.

"Well, I don't know if it's true, but I heard some states make all their citizens pay poll taxes, no matter the race." Eva countered.

"Maybe so. Anyway, I shudder to think that I was born a third of a century after the official end of slavery!" I mused, shaking my head.

"Well," chimed in Eva, "I was born twenty-five years after it was abolished, only *one* generation away from being a slave myself. I tremble at that thought. Right after slavery was abolished in 1865, Mississippi became the first state to enact the 'Black Codes' that restricted the rights and status of us Negroes.

Even now, our children rarely have access to an equal education Down South and even here in the Promised Land.

"To be fair, though, Daisy, not every white person spews hatred and not every black person has been treated with ill will. There are good and bad people everywhere, but the overwhelming persona of the Deep South was odious for us."

I interrupted, "That's precisely why I didn't want my reputation to be besmirched by that birthplace. It used to be if you said you were from Mississippi or Alabama, people made certain assumptions about you. They acted like you were uneducated, sheltered in ignorance, and poorer than dirt. It's like saying you're from the ghetto state of America. I made sure my children and grandchildren, as well as all official records, believed I was born in the more prosperous and forward-thinking St. Louis, Missouri. And I see no reason to change that perception this late in my life!

"Girl!" is all Aunt Eva responded, and that one word said it all.

HOPE SPRINGS ETERNAL

"Hallelujah!" Eva shouted, raising her arms up excitedly in the chair. "We certainly thought our situation was looking up when the 14th Amendment was ratified in 1868. I can just see our ancestors lifting their voices in song when everyone…except folks in jail…were finally granted national citizenship. States were finally prohibited from restricting the basic rights of citizens, black and white.

I can only imagine how jubilant Negroes were when one hundred delegates, including seventeen colored men, gathered for the 'Black and Tan Constitutional Convention'? It was the first time Negroes were able to participate in the political process in Mississippi. And the new State Constitution included a strong clause requiring the state to provide an equal education for *all* children regardless of race."

Nodding my head, I said, "Yes, Reconstruction was certainly a period of great hope for a better future for our people. Colored men registered to vote using their new political status, in hopes of voting in people who would craft more favorable public policy for us, as well as for whites."

Eva smiled, "Yes, and this helped the race achieve equity in terms of community services, the courts, even police protection, and freedom of expression and movement."

"Auntie, I remember learning in school that by 1875, I think it was, one-third of the Mississippi Senate and fifty-nine members of the House of Representatives were Negroes. Incredible! Colored men served as Superintendent of Education, Lieutenant Governor, Secretary of State, and Speaker of the House. They played a leading role in pushing for equal public schools. GramFannie told me that people back then were proud, joyful, and hopeful the future would be better for us and our children."

"Hope sprang eternal," Eva said, "at least until our hopes were dashed to the ground a few years later."

How Bad is Bad?

Flipping the bright light of Reconstruction off, Eva continued in a heavy tone. "That Redemption movement which swept across the South eventually led to the adoption of Jim Crow laws. Racial segregation became the norm across the region. Remember how all those young white men formed armed militias to intimidate colored voters?"

I nodded my head, getting madder and madder at what I knew was coming out of her mouth next.

"Those white democrats easily regained control of both houses of the Mississippi Legislature. By 1890, only four Negroes still served there. Those white folks were like a pack of wild dogs fighting to rip apart some bones...our black bones." Eva took in a big breath and blew it out slowly, trying to calm her nerves.

"You know that's right, Aunt Eva. The new Constitution that Mississippi adopted greatly diminished the political power of colored men by restricting their voting rights. A prime example was many states implementing poll taxes that many Negroes and poor whites could not afford to pay. Or, if they could afford the tax, many coloreds were coerced with bodily harm *not* to pay it. And if the two-dollar tax wasn't paid, one couldn't vote. And don't get me started on those literacy tests that were generally only given to Negroes, Indians, and poor whites."

I felt my eyes well up, but from frustrated anger, as I continued fuming. "While I was growing up in Ol' Miss, I heard Mama complaining that the local *Macon Beacon* newspaper annually listed—and probably still does—those who didn't pay their poll tax. My daddy, and most other Negroes we knew were on that list, year after year. Even though the two dollar cost was not out of reach, we couldn't answer the literacy questions. We still didn't have adequate schools to teach us what we needed to pass the test. That meant our folks could not vote for people or issues which might have bettered our living conditions. Year after year, this unequal treatment has kept us behind the eight ball," I finished, in a bit of a huff.

It was Aunt Eva's turn to fuss. "And that new restrictive Constitution created racially segregated schools. The wealthy school districts for you-know-who levied taxes for education revenue far in excess of the taxes generated in our poorer school districts. The die was cast. There were few opportunities for our children to receive a decent education by the turn of the twentieth century."

"That's right," I agreed. "Sure, we did go to school a few months out of the year when we didn't have to help farm Daddy's crops, but our threadbare school had few textbooks, pencils, paper, chairs, slates, or bathroom facilities, when we could attend. We had already moved to St. Louis before I could get my diploma, and we didn't stay there long enough before moving here to Cleveland for me to graduate. I was devastated not to be able to finish high school. It wasn't until I went to John Hay Adult School at night, in my thirties, when I earned that precious piece of paper confirming I had achieved a twelfth grade education. You know, I had to graduate high school before I could go to mortuary school to become the professional I had always dreamed of being."

"Um-hmm," Eva muttered.

"Daddy always drummed into us kids that running our own business was a sure sign of success. He didn't want us to work for crumbs off other people's tables. 'Entrepreneurship, not farming cotton, is the way to the American Dream,' Daddy maintained."

Eva nodded her head in agreement.

AFTER THE CIVIL WAR

"You know, Auntie, Mississippians have come a long way, even though they still have miles to go. I think all people deserve to have an equal say in this Land of the Free."

"Um-hmm," Eva slowly intoned.

"I remember Mama telling me about those census takers who would come around every ten years in our 'Township 16' neighborhood in Noxubee County. They wanted to know all about our families. Can you believe there was one white person for every five Negroes in our neighborhood in 1870, after the war? Of course, the well-regarded 'farmers' were white and colored folks were nearly always the farm laborers."

"You know that's right, niece!" Eva broke in.

I continued, "Mama said Moses Cotton was the only Negro in our neighborhood who owned his small plot of land, compared to thousands of acres owned by just a few Caucasians."

"That's how it was, for sure," Eva mumbled, shaking her head.

"Daddy told me before I was born, my grandfather, Elias Dooley Sr., and many other Negroes, were farmers on their *own* land in 1880, just fifteen years after slavery was kicked to the curb. Fewer coloreds were farm laborers as time went on, with more being farmers on their own, or rented land. Many of our children were in school, even though it might have been a few months a year. By 1880, the economy had improved and there were even a few house servants, as well as one black cook, one nurse, one washerwoman, and a nineteen-year-old teacher named Effy Marant. Do you remember her being your teacher when you and my mother were in school?"

Eva replied, "Well, I wasn't born until 1889, eleven years after your mother. So, no, I wasn't in school with a Miss Marant, even though Julia might have been. Julia's blood daddy, Charles Nicholson, was out of the picture by the time she was two. My blood daddy was Forrest Clayton who had married your GramFannie—Fannie Cunningham—sometime in the mid-1880s," Eva finished her recitation of their family ties.

I mused, "Well, I probably wouldn't have my favorite aunt—you—in my life, if Grandpa Charles was still in the picture."

Eva smiled with acknowledgment. "I love you too, niece. Anyway, I can't for the life of me remember the names of my teachers that long ago. But I sure do cringe when I think back on that horrible system of 'tenant farming' that evolved after slavery. 'Renters' paid the land owner directly for the use of his acreage, but were able to keep the revenue from their entire harvest. 'Share tenants' on the other hand, had to turn over a percentage of their harvest to the landowner. 'Sharecroppers' were the poorest in this system, turning over at least one-half of their harvest to the landowner. That left the 'cropper' with little to live on, or to invest in toward the next year's crop. Most of our families and poor whites were croppers, never being able to get ahead in life."

Shaking my head, "I still think it's incredible that colored workers never seemed to fight that system. They went on and on for years like that, living hardly better than when they had been slaves. That's why I am so involved with the new Democratic Party and Labor Unions. I want to help ensure that *all* workers receive the same pay if they do the same job, and that workers can't be fired capriciously. Unions are the future for *us*."

Eva nodded and said, "Well, I think some coloreds did try to change the system, but they often ended up swingin' from a tree. I think it was after the turn of the century when folks started trading the awful working conditions Down South for better opportunities in the 'Promised Land' up north in St. Louis, Chicago, Detroit, and Cleveland."

The usually so prim and proper Eva took a huge bite out of the biscuit, I imagined as though she were biting the head off the hated tenant farming machine. I had to laugh, even though it wasn't a laughing matter.

"Excuse my language," Eva cut in, "but Mississippi was a hellhole for Negroes and was the most racist state in the Union."

"You know *I* agree with that shi-et, by refusing to tell anyone I was born there!" Both of us giggled like school children getting caught cursing.

Eva continued, "Many 'majority' Americans wanted to reinstitute slavery-era laws that would keep colored people in the most lowly of jobs, forever in debt as sharecroppers, or jailed in chain gangs which made the captives forever working for free."

"Yes, ma'am," I said. "Those chain gangs were the worst. Negroes were always being jailed for the tiniest of contrived offenses, like not stepping aside for a white person on the sidewalk. You remember Uncle Henry got put in jail for looking at a white man in the eye, and Uncle Bobby Joe for not saying 'Yessuh' quickly enough when spoken to. The powers that be could do whatever they wanted with our folks on the chain gang. Lots of city improvements, then and now, have been made with free chain gang labor. It's just a new form of slavery, I think."

Eva said, "You are preaching to the choir, girl. That's precisely why Louisiana, Mississippi, Alabama and Georgia—the deepest of the so-called Deep South states—were places where enslaved men and women in more northerly slave states dreaded to be sold. To be 'Sold South' was to be banished to serve the cruelest of masters, to be subjected to the most difficult and backbreaking work of picking cotton or tobacco, or farming sugar cane. And most dreadfully, there was the greatest chance your relatives would be sold away.

I can't even fathom what it would be like to lose you or my sister's other children, never seeing you guys again." Eva had a faraway look on her face. Tears formed in our eyes, imagining we might have family members we knew nothing about—folks who had been sold away during slavery.

I gently took my seventy-four-year-old aunt's warm hand in mine and patted it reassuringly. While she composed herself, I said, "We know all too well the Deep South is where lynchings occurred with such regularity that it was gleefully anticipated, like the gladiator spectacles from old Rome. Gladiators were pitted against each other, or against vicious lions and tigers, until one was ripped apart and the other was the victor.

White people have always the victors over Negroes, Asians, Mexicans, and Indians, no matter what the scenario. It's still hard for me to believe that many white families brought children of all ages, with blankets and picnic lunches, to cheer on a good ol' lynching."

"At a young age, many southern white children were taught to hate anyone with darker skin color than theirs. They were taught *they* were superior in all things. They believed that then—and many still do! *Their* opinions, needs, and wants are the only ones that matter in this world.

Caucasians are the only good guys portrayed in American History books that all children must study. There are few positive mentions of contributions from anyone else. Where are the kudos to the Chinese who built the railroads, or understanding that Indians were only protecting their land from the European invaders? Where are the nonwhite family traditions and accomplishments? Where are the Mexican-Americans, Negroes, and Asians who have toiled for decades—no, centuries—growing our nation's food and doing the various jobs Caucasians felt were beneath them? There are, of course, plenty of pictures of ragged shacks, poor, half-clothed waifs, and Negroes in jail. Those degradations and slights are shown on everywhere in this country, but particularly in Mississippi."

Regaining her voice, Eva said, "And that's why Mississippi tops the list with the most total lynchings in the United States. Remember that lynching of fourteen-year-old Emmett Till who was accused of whistling at a white woman? The brutality of his murder and the fact that his killers were acquitted drew attention to the long history of violent persecution of Negroes in America. His brave mother took an unusual stand to protest the barbarism her son experienced. She decided to have an open-casket funeral service so everyone—especially the news media—could see how her son had been battered and broken. This created a big to do around the world, bringing clarity to the inhumanity against Negroes, particularly in the southern part of America."

"And therefore," I concluded, "our conversation has convincingly explained why many of us don't claim our Mississippi birthplace. I chose to alter my own life story, to help me become the successful businesswoman I am today. I'm choosing to rewrite the historical narrative about Negroes and show America that our lives *do* matter and that we do make valid contributions to this country!"

"Bravo!" Eva clapped at the end of my soliloquy. "Well, Daisy, it's been fun—well, maybe let's say cathartic—traipsing down memory lane with you this afternoon, but I've got to get on the road, get home, and start dinner." Eva retrieved her purse, hat, and gloves. I walked down the steps with her, holding her arm, and we moseyed toward the nearby streetcar stop. I waved goodbye, then walked back home, thoughts of the past lingering in my mind.

Cliftonville, Noxubee, MS. Photograph: Kathy Marshall.

Cunningham Cattle in Noxubee County, AL

CHAPTER 6 - GOOD TIMES

(Life in Noxubee County, Mississippi, About 1910, Daisy)

The pastel sky of sunrise greeted me at the door, pail in hand, as I trudged sleepy-eyed toward the ramshackle barn in back of our house. When I was six or seven years old, Mama started sending me outside during the early tendrils of dawn to milk our dun-colored cow. "Maisy" slept on a straw pallet in the six-foot-square barn in the back of our house.

"Mornin', Maisy," I chimed, in my bright little girl voice. She was already awake, grazing on a delectable yellow flower in the uneven sod. She raised her lumbering head and mooed in response. She was more than happy to stand patiently while I deposited the pail under her swollen udders. Sister Wilda Lee, who used to have this job but now got to go to school in the morning, had shown me how to grab the cow's left teat with my left hand and the right teat with the other, squeezing them rhythmically, one after the other, while pulling downward. Release. Squeeze and pull. Soon, two warm streams of milk sprayed into the awaiting vessel. It took about five minutes to fill it three-quarters full, just enough so it wouldn't slosh out during the short trek back to the kitchen. A parting "moo" was Maisy's thanks for relieving her discomfort.

I GUESS WE DO COUNT

My life wasn't totally abysmal in Noxubee when I think back on it some seventy-five or so years after the fact. Parts of it were pretty nice: the emerald green pastures after a brief rain, the leafy pine forests containing song birds, shimmering catfish ponds during the golden hour of evening, the morning breeze generated from the Coosa River before the sun turned it humid, and memories of the rich, red clay soil. Even the predictable daily routine could be comforting.

But my favorite memory was having lots of family and friends living all around me. Our grandparents and cousins lived in nearby Prairie Point and Zion Hill, in what was called on geological maps, "Township 14, Range 17." When I was born, we lived near the county seat of Macon, and the tiny one-mile-square towns of Brooksville and Cliftonville, where families of former slaves and slave owners farmed rows upon rows of cotton. I imagine those communities are still dotted with cleared land ready to plant seed in April after the spring showers.

The rich black pasture land in Prairie Point was used for grazing cattle, and sparkling ponds harvested catfish.

My closest cousins were surnamed Dooley, Nicholson, Cunningham, Clayton and Moore. They lived within a two-mile radius of us. There were plenty of Walkers, Williams, Mays and Thomas's who were my friends living nearby. There was always someone to play stick ball or tag, or giggle with, after the chores were complete.

Adults supported each other by babysitting each other's kids, helping to farm each other's properties during harvest season, having quilting bees to make blankets for beds or wind screens for inside house walls, and lending emotional support to each other.

I don't remember much of my life when I was a baby or a young child. But I do remember seeing women who had to work in the fields, swaddling their young babies in a cloth pouch, similar to an Indian papoose. *Was that also the African way?* Babies were on their mother's backs all the time while they worked in the sweltering heat, and in rainy weather. I imagine my mother had to do the same with me, stopping work several times a day to feed me and change my cloth diapers—if I wore any—but generally carrying me on her back while she toiled.

When I was about eight years old, I remember a pale white man coming by our house holding a clipboard in his left hand, knocking on our door. It was hot outside and I was sitting under the shade of our peach tree laden with ripening fruit, so I imagine it was during the summer time.

"Ma'am, are you the lady of the house?" asked the tall, lanky man.

"Yes, I am Julia Dooley. May I help you?" She replied, wiping the bread flour from her hands.

"I'm here from the United States Census Bureau and I'd like to ask you some questions about your household. Do you have a few minutes?" he queried amiably, pushing his glasses up higher on the bridge of his nose.

"Well sure, come on in. Didn't you come by my house some time ago asking about us?" Mama asked, her eyebrows raised in question.

"No, that wasn't me during the previous 1900 census. This is my first time." Mama smiled politely, but later made me laugh when she told me, "They all look alike to me!"

"Ma'am, may we sit down somewhere? That will make it easier for me to write down your responses neatly and correctly." Mama nodded and escorted him into the house, pulling out a kitchen chair for him. I followed them inside the house to hear what he had to say.

"Would you like a glass of water before we start?" she invited.

Shaking his head, "Oh no, thank you. This will just take a few minutes." Mama sat down across the table from him and I crouched in a corner, watching and listening, invisible, hoping to learn some juicy secrets.

The strange man lit up a smelly cigarette and then started asking a bunch of questions, like: "Who lives in the house, in order of the oldest to the youngest? What is their relationship to the head of household? What is everyone's age and sex? How many years have Mama and Daddy been married? How many children does Mama have? Where was everyone born and where were their parents born? Is anyone an immigrant (*whatever that was*)? Did we all speak English? What does everybody do for a living and what type of work was that? Were they an employee or an employer? Do they have a job now? If not, how many weeks have they been out of work?"

Whew! Would he ever stop asking questions?

"Can you all read and write? Do you own your own home, or have something called a mortgage? Do you live in a house or farm? Is anyone a survivor of the Union or Confederate Army or Navy?" And finally, "Is anyone blind, deaf or dumb?"

I don't know why he asked if we were stupid. That's a dumb question!

After the man left, Mama and I sat on the porch and listened to the birds chirping for a while, wondering what that man was going to do with all of Mama's answers. Then we resumed our household chores.

OUR TOWN

The largest city in our area was Macon, the Noxubee County seat, founded in 1833. Sure, there was only one main road going down the center of Macon, but there were several streets with businesses bordering it and residential streets beyond that. To support the cotton industry, Macon had a cotton compress which squeezed bales of cotton down to ten inches thick for more efficient shipping. They also housed a cotton seed oil mill, four cotton gins, a large plant for making bricks, and water bottling works. My family extended members were sometimes able to get menial jobs in the cotton gin and brick plant. Brooksville, Cliftonville, and Shuqualak were other towns of any size in Noxubee.

Between 1840 and 1860, Noxubee County's population doubled, with the number of free persons growing to 5,171 and the number of slaves growing to 15,496 (75 percent of the total population). One of Mississippi's most productive agricultural areas, Noxubee County ranked first in the production of corn, fifth in cotton, fourth in livestock, and sixth in sweet potatoes. Its farmland had the third-highest value in the state. Seventy-two people labored in industry, with most making bricks or working in lumber mills. In 1860, Noxubee County was home to thirty churches: fifteen Methodist, ten Baptist, four Presbyterian, and one Catholic.

In the postbellum period, Noxubee became a popular destination for African Americans looking to improve their lives. While the number of whites remained stable, the African American population increased by almost 10,000 between 1860 and 1880, making the county one of the state's largest, with 29,572 people. Noxubee had by far the largest number of Alabama natives who relocated to Mississippi; we were one of those families. As in many black-majority counties, Noxubee had a large number of tenant farmers. Only 38 percent of the county's farms were run by their owners—like many of us Dooleys—a figure well below the state average.

Noxubee remained an important center for agricultural production, ranking first in the state in corn and oats, tenth in cotton, and sixth in the total value of farms. The county's 4,373 mules constituted the fourth-highest total in the state.

In 1880, Noxubee's manufacturing firms employed 113 men, 6 women, and 18 children. In addition, the county was home to 89 foreign-born residents, most of them from Ireland (e.g., our Cunninghams) and Germany.

Farming was not all Macon was about, though. During the Civil War, it served as the capital of Mississippi, because the fighting did not reach its borders. All the principal religious denominations were represented in a variety of churches. Several lumbering plants had their offices there, as well as two lumberyards with a large planing mill. Macon also had two hotels and three livery stables. In 1900, the population had grown to over 2,000 people, with Negroes always outnumbering the white population by at least two to one (four to one during slavery).

When the Gulf & Mobile (G & M) Railroad came to Macon in 1856, the railyard came too, lasting until sometime in the 1890s. Many jobs were available to Noxubee workers in the 1870s, such as: conductors, engineers, firemen, laborers, helpers, yardmaster, brakemen, blacksmiths, machinists, carpenters, and telegraph operators.

Even though the pay was low, the most menial job was sought after by the few Negro men who were able to get them. If one was industrious, he could be trained to be a machinist or blacksmith or carpenter helper. Sometimes our women were cooks or washerwomen. This meant many people in Macon didn't have to be cotton farmers. Though badly damaged in the terrible tornado of 1880, the railyard shops continued to provide jobs for the locals, until Macon took the depot area within its city limits, prompting G & M to leave, with its payroll and jobs.

The Merchants and Farmers Bank was established in 1888 and the Bank of Macon in 1899. They handled large sums of money generated by the agricultural pursuits stemming from the Deep South to the northern states and England. Negroes weren't allowed to bank there, so our meager savings were often kept in a clay crock in the back of the cabinet that held our dishes.

Near the end of the 1800s, Macon embarked on a series of improvements. The building of the Electric Light Works was a step out of the dark ages. The lighting illuminated the streets, public buildings, stores, hotels and some houses. We couldn't remember what life was like before the streetlights…and never wanted to go back!

Everyone knows how hot and sticky it gets in the Deep South during the summer months. Another great improvement—some say a necessity—was the Ice Factory and Creamery. Established in June 1896 (in the nick of time for summer), the acre-sized building on the banks of the Noxubee River, was equipped with an ice machine that could manufacture over three tons of ice. This created many jobs for strong men who could use hooks, tongs, and ice picks to wrestle the large cakes of ice from the factory into a wagon. They would deliver the ice to houses and hotels, chipping them down to size to fit into ice boxes, which were the precursors to refrigerators.

The Creamery was the beginning of the dairy business in Noxubee, made more prosperous when Borden Creamery was established in the late 1920s. Some of my Dooley family members benefitted from good jobs in the dairy and cattle industry.

In August 1908, a dense volume of smoke approached several of us sightseers on the streets of Macon. The fact that it was moving and wasn't stationary puzzled us for a while. Some thought it was a prairie fire. But in a few minutes, a handsome automobile emerged from the smoke with Mr. The Irish at the wheel (yes, that's what everyone called him) and Mr. K. T. McLeod on his right. "Ooh how beautiful!" A slew of questions came from the crowd: "How fast does it go? Will it get stuck in the mud when it rains? How does it work? What do you feed it to make it run? How much does it cost? When can I buy one?"

It was Noxubee's first automobile. It was attractive in shape, seemed strong and substantial in construction and size, and looked comfortable with its cushioned seat back. How helpful such a vehicle would be, carrying people and products. In hot days when horses cannot be driven fast, the car would be a great improvement. Unfortunately, most of our roads were still hard-packed dirt in the summer and thick, impassable mud in the winter; few roads were graveled. The *Macon Beacon* newspaper placed an announcement on the front page stating Black Motor vehicles would soon be sold for $375. McLeod claimed the car's high wheels were suited to rough or muddy roads, up to twenty-five miles per hour. Helpful or not, it would be years before my family could dream to afford such a vehicle. Such a purchase wouldn't likely be allowed by Negroes in Ol' Miss anyway.

Finally, many of us Dooleys were involved in the meat industry, as Noxubee land was prime for cattle grazing. Borden Dairy became a large presence in Noxubee starting in the 1920s and some of our Dooleys became foremen. This meant some Dooley families, black and white, had more comfortable lives than other Negroes. Uncle Anderson Dooley became a well-respected butcher in Macon, always giving mama the "family discount" when she came in for a pot roast or steak.

RULES OF BEHAVIOR

"Do it now," was a common refrain amongst our elders. It was drummed into our heads that we should do what we could *today*, instead of procrastinating, for tomorrow might present a whole new set of problems and difficulties. In the Deep South, Negroes had to be creative to reach their goals, because so many unnecessary impediments were put into our paths, making it hard to live an equitable life in America. Planning, being organized, thinking ahead, doing what you could do proactively, as well as having a whole lot of luck, were ingredients for having a successful life.

But oh the many rules about what you could, and could not, say or do. Breaking the rules would result in some kind of unpleasant disciplinary response, ranging from a harsh word or quick slap to more painful treatments like a punch, or a tree switch on bare skin (called a whuppin'), to a full-fledged beating, to being locked in a cellar or other dark place for a while. Punishment could include extra chores, withholding of food or water, restriction from playing, extra homework, etc. Sometimes girls received other unwanted, invasive punishments…to their bodies.

Good times also included restraints that were meant to make us better people. Here's a sample of rules we were expected to follow. We were not allowed to use the "N-word" (nigger). We couldn't call anyone a liar—we had to say "storyteller" instead. We were expected to say "be quiet" instead of "shut up." A Dooley should never say typical low-class Southern expressions such as: ain't, y'all, or fixin' to.

A child could never answer "what?" when their name was called by an adult, or overheard by an adult if you were answering a peer or older sibling. The term "half" siblings was never spoken about, even if you were one. People did what they had to do back then and skeletons in the baby-making closet were to stay in the closet.

On the flip side, many Dooleys would use the word "commode" instead of "toilet." And when one was using the bathroom, one was "indisposed." "Aunt" was pronounced "Uhnt" instead of "Ant" or "Awnt." "Nox'bee" is how people pronounced "Noxubee." "Brefix" was often uttered instead of "breakfast." "Bitty bodies" was a term used when describing nosy and gossiping older women. "Heffa" was a term for fast girls...never used for a woman who had children. To be "ceitful" was to be untrustworthy or two-faced. And "she has torn stockings" was a euphemism for being pregnant.

There was no talking back or rolling your eyes or arguing with adults, for any reason. To do so was to feel the peach tree switch on our bare legs or buttocks, or experience more invasive types of discipline. There was no warning with these violent outbursts. No reminding us about the rules, just an immediate and painful reaction if we transgressed them in any way.

Sometimes I felt Daddy took his anger out on us kids and my mother when he was particularly peeved, perhaps with the ill treatment he sometimes endured from the powers that be. But Mama explained that was just his way to teach us right from wrong. I must admit that I brought those same expectations and punishments to my children and grandchildren. If it was good enough for my daddy, it was good enough for me in my adult household. The lessons we learned at home served us well in the wider world when we got older. During our old age, we would be able to laugh at these sometimes hard, sometimes funny, life lessons.

DADDY DEAREST

My father, William Dooley Sr., was a complicated man. He was born in Noxubee County in about 1876. Being a "general farmer" meant he did whatever needed to be done on his own farm, such as plowing the soil, sowing the seeds, weeding, watering, harvesting the cotton crop, baling hay and wheat, etc.

All I knew or cared about was that he was my daddy and I thought he was the strongest and most handsome man in the world, albeit a little scary and unpredictable sometimes.

Daddy stood about five-feet nine-inches, was of medium weight, with large brown eyes, long eyelashes, and soft black hair that he sometimes pomaded to make it look straight (before he went bald, that is). He was a light-skinned mulatto—we all were—with "lots of cream in our African coffee," as Mama used to say. I got my bad eyesight from him. He was definitely the man of our house and made all the important decisions.

William Dooley Sr.
1876-1952.

Daddy could be kind sometimes, especially to us girls, but more often than not he was quite strict concerning our chores. We rarely heard "good job," or "thank you," or "you're so smart" from him. If we did our tasks correctly and quickly, there was no punishment, and that in and of itself was our reward.

We didn't hear a heartfelt "I love you," or receive affectionate hugs. But we could count on admonishments like "Get your work done before you play," and "Don't talk back to adults." We could expect a swat if we didn't do what we were told. On a regular basis, we did hear from him hurtful phrases, like "Stupe!" (for stupid), and sometimes even, "You're so worthless you don't deserve the air

69

you breathe." I don't remember a lot of laughter when Daddy was around.

Oddly enough, I adopted the same general parenting style, and my kids passed those dysfunctional traditions onto their children.

Daddy could often be unpredictable. He might be smiling when he came in from working all day, but blow up unexpectedly for no reason. He could lash out at us in a split second. Those violent outbursts could occur more frequently if he had been drinking alcohol. Mama called that "being in his cups."

We kids never knew which Daddy would walk through the door. If we sensed he was in a bad mood Mama would hold up a finger to signal we needed to be quiet and on our best behavior. She would try to protect us when Daddy was in one of his tempers, by singing a soothing hymn to cut through any discord that intruded into our well-run household.

On the other hand, Daddy could be so gentle, sometimes combing our frizzy hair with such care and tenderness. Or he might tell us how pretty we looked in our church clothes. Rarely, he might praise a cake we made for dessert, or a good grade we got on a test. My sisters liked it when he said, "You're going to make someone a good wife someday." But I preferred hearing from him, "I bet you'll be a great businesswoman when you grow up."

Being a good provider was never an issue, even though Daddy wasn't always living with us during my teenage years. He was like so many Negro men, leaving the South for better prospects in the industrialized North, but I'll tell you about that story soon. We never wanted for anything major, because our Grandpa Elias and Grandma Lavinia made sure we were taken care of in our Daddy's absence.

MAMA JULIA AND THE COOKING GENE

I inherited the cooking gene from my mother, Julia Nicholson, who got it from her mother, Fannie Cunningham, who got it from her mother, Julia Borders. Anyone coming into our home would be greeted by the smell of something delicious in the air: buttery pound cake, braised pork ribs, sweet potato pie, fried chicken, greens and ham hocks, cornbread, and peach cobbler. I could go on and on. Cooking and baking weren't necessarily our passions, but we were born with the knack. Of course, helping our mothers prepare meals for our brood or, in GramFannie and Great-grandma Julia's case, the slave master's family gave us plenty of practice. All cooks in Mama's kitchen had to wear a blue-and-white striped apron—her favorite colors—to keep our clothes clean as we cooked.

Those of us blessed with the cooking gene didn't need a recipe book, for we knew what spice went with what dish, how to double a recipe in our heads when company was expected, how much to beat a cake batter so it was as light and fluffy as angel wings, and how long to fry chicken so the skin was crunchy but the meat was succulent inside.

I remember Mama making pastry crust for a pie or cobbler, flour dusting her already pale skin. Her shoulder-length ebony hair often piled on top of her head, sometimes in a bun or chignon, was a stark contrast to her barely tanned face. Her scrunched eyebrows indicated she was thinking about something, maybe the next ingredient in a recipe, or the next step in a plan, or staying one step ahead of Daddy and us kids.

Mama always looked young to me, but she was too thin. I thought of her as being rather delicate and willowy, not like Ruby Lee and me, who were sturdy, buxom girls who seemed taller than our five-feet two-inch height, simply by our confident bearing. Maybe that's why Mama was always a bit sickly, her cough heard throughout the day during wintertime. Wilda Lee and I used to joke that Mama needed to eat more of her own good cooking.

When she told us bedtime stories, though, Mama's normally weak voice would assume an inner power, transporting us to whatever setting she was describing. Yes, storytelling does run through our veins.

My Siblings

I loved my siblings, even though sometimes we had our problems and disagreements, like everyone else.

My older sister, Wilda Lee—who was sometimes called Willie Lee—was born in 1898. She was as tall as Mama with long, thick, dark brown hair, light olive skin, and full lips. She liked the finer things in life, always preferring to be dressed in the latest fashions. Mama taught us both how to sew and make our garments special by adding buttons and trim to customize them.

Wilda was perhaps the most cultivated, yet headstrong, of us children. Being the eldest, she endured privations that often accompanied the first child of new parents. Rules were first tried out on her, but she was not afraid to challenge some of those controls. She and Daddy didn't always get along well for she had a habit of asking "Why?" and Daddy would respond, "Because I said so," which did not satisfy her spirited nature.

Wilda could be bossy. She was often our second mother when Mama had to be out working. What soothed her (and my) inner beast was growing beautiful flowers amongst the vegetables in our garden. She also loved to make peach ice cream, but it was difficult to keep it frozen in the early decades of the twentieth century, before iceboxes were in every home.

My elder sister always had to be the center of attention. She liked people and they liked her. Her social life, and dressing as fashionably as a girl could in rural Noxubee, were often more important to her than reading, writing and 'rithmetic in school. Those behaviors caused problems with Daddy and strained their relationship.

Fast forward: Wilda married David Shackleford in Cleveland in 1921. In her adult life, she was often mentioned in the *Call and Post* newspaper, hosting the Wisteria Bridge Club and other luncheons at her beautifully appointed home on Hampden Avenue. She was also well-known for her "swanky" fashion sense, as observed at the numerous dances and social functions she regularly attended with her prosperous husband.

Brother William was one year older than me. He wasn't much of a talker, but like most boys, he was always jumping up and down or running here or there. However, William did excel at math. He liked numbers, figuring out how much something would cost, and how long it would take a worker to earn enough to pay for it. A bit taller than Daddy, brother William had a broader face and wide-set black eyes with the typical Dooley nose. Like most of us, he did not smile often, but occasionally could tell a wicked joke or two. William grew to enjoy accounting work as an adult. He was often seen with a clipboard in his hands, even at family gatherings. He stretched his entrepreneurial wings to establish "Dooley's Place" which was a combined bar, night club, and rooming house in Twinsburg Heights, Ohio, near Cleveland. He was married twice, first to Sarah Davis in 1920, then Deotha Hill in 1971.

Ruby Lee was my three-years-younger baby doll, born in 1905. When our parents and the older children were out working in the garden or fields, or were at school, I was often left in charge of her. My goodness, that adorable child was busy! Even as a toddler, she was always chattering, walking, or climbing. She loved to smile and laugh. Her giggle caused the rest of us more stoic folks to laugh too. Everybody looked out for little Ruby Lee, which helped humanize the rest of us. As usual, the youngest child enjoyed the most freedom. Rules were relaxed a bit, the household ran like clockwork, and everyone was settled into their roles during the 1910s in Noxubee.

Ruby Lee was certainly the most nurturing of us kids. She cared about animals, taking care of our mutt dog, Ralphie's, feeding and grooming needs. She could gently capture a beige spotted garden moth in her small hands, exclaiming at its beauty before she released it. She watched birds in flight and attempted to emulate their calls and whistles. She even had a soft spot for red-legged grasshoppers, who sang so beautifully at twilight.

Ruby Lee married Essie Spencer in 1922 in Cleveland, then divorced him a few years later. In 1930, she was living with brother William and his wife Sarah Dooley and their sons— Marion, Elbert, and Austin Erwin. By 1934, Ruby Lee and a second husband, James Daniels, were taking care of William's three teenage boys. My nephews thought of Ruby Lee like their own mother, and since she had no children of her own, that suited her just fine. Unfortunately, Ruby Lee died in 1941 and the boys had to return to their parents in Twinsburg Heights.

EDUCATION IS ALL IMPORTANT

Our parents constantly reminded us how important it was to learn to read, write, and "do our numbers" so our lives could be better than theirs. I was proud my daddy owned his own farm; that was unusual for a Negro in Mississippi at the turn of the twentieth century. My parents could read and write, and they made darn sure we children got as much education as possible. Even so, the normal colored child in Mississippi only received about five months of schooling each year. I found out that was inadequate to be competitive in America. This is embarrassing to admit, but I didn't earn my high school diploma until 1936, when I was thirty-four years old.

Ours was probably no different than the experience of most sub-standard colored schools in the Deep South. We had a one-room structure with no interior walls or ceilings. There were crude, hard wooden benches with no backs, and plank blackboards. There was a pot-bellied, wood-burning stove near the center of the room which provided some heat during the colder months. The front door was the entrance and exit. Small side windows produced little light, so candles were sometimes necessary to see our school work.

Children in each age grouping, from kindergarten to eighth grade, had one teacher to educate them all. Busy farming parents could rarely assist the teacher, although occasionally one of the grandparents spent the day helping in the classroom. Many of them never learned to read and write, because it had been illegal to teach them, so some elder helpers came to learn for themselves.

Boys wore faded overalls patched at the knees and bottoms. Girls had homemade gingham dresses or denim jumpers under ill-fitting, hand-me-down coats from their older siblings. The girls' hair was often plaited in neat squares of braids from their scalps.

The children's rubber boots trudged through muddy gravel roads to get to school. But they did the best they could. Every day they marched into school with faces glistening with Vaseline, to oil their ashy, dry skin. We were proud to be in school. Discipline was generally not a problem because most of the students understood their parents expected them to learn as much as possible.

We played outside until the school bell rang in the morning, then filed into the dim room, quietly taking our seats, awaiting the teacher's instructions.

My sister Wilda (10) and brother Willie (7) were enrolled in school in 1908, as were our Dooley cousins Doll (17), Viola (12), Amanda (12), Fannie (11), Robert (8), Charlie (6), and Anderson (5). I was almost six years old, but had to stay home with Mama and Ruby Lee.

The first teacher I remember was Miss Ida Goodwin. In 1910, she started teaching at the age of nineteen. She knew so much compared to the rest of us, having been raised by educated parents. She tolerated no nonsense in her classroom, though, and expected us to perform our best. If we failed to meet her high expectations, she would stare at us and drill us on our addition and multiplication tables even harder. While some students felt she was too intimidating and mean, others of us understood she had a deep concern for our well-being. I modeled myself after her no-nonsense approach.

Our teacher was determined to teach us how to apply her mathematics instruction to daily living. She used common sense examples that a farmer might encounter, since most of us would likely work in the agricultural field. For example, "Who knows how much seed would be needed to cover a one-acre plot of land if one bag of seed would cover one-quarter of an acre?"

Brother William raised his hand, went up to the blackboard, and grabbed a piece of white chalk. He drew a square and wrote "one acre" at the top of the drawing. Then he drew a vertical line down the center of the square and a horizontal line across the middle of it, making four equal quadrants inside the square. He wrote "1/4" in each of the four quadrants. Then he turned toward the other students and said, "There are four quarters in one acre, and one bag of seed is needed for each quarter, so we would need four bags of seed to cover one whole acre."

"That is not only correct, but also presented in a clear way that everyone can understand. You would make a great teacher, Mr. Dooley. You get an 'A' for the day," Miss Goodwin replied, smiling. She had noticed many of the students nodded their heads, obviously understanding how William figured out the problem. A more difficult question at the end of the school year might be, "How much money would a farmer earn in a week if each of his four workers harvested 200 pounds of cotton every day, and cotton was selling at $14 per pound?"

Teaching these useful skills helped us become savvy about finances and accounting. The wool would not be pulled over *our* eyes, as it had been for our parents and grandparents who could not read or write for most of their lives.

Most of our teachers over the years concentrated on reading assignments, though, for they felt the ability to read could propel us to success faster than any other school subject. Like most colored schools, there were few textbooks, so teachers relied on the generosity of a few white people to donate books for the various age groups. Even so, there were not enough reading materials for each child to take home to practice their studies. However, if there were two or more children in a household, they could check out one book amongst themselves and share the knowledge.

To stimulate younger pupils' thirst for learning, some teachers made up rhyming songs and had the children read limericks like:

There was an Old Man with a beard,
Who said, 'It is just as I feared!
Two Owls and a Hen,
Four Larks and a Wren,
Have all built their nests in my beard!

Teachers in rural colored schools had a difficult row to hoe. Their paltry pay was inadequate for their effort. Their housing was meager, like that of most students. Transportation to and from school was difficult.

They had few teaching resources: books, paper, pencils, maps. And their charges came irregularly to class due to farming and other responsibilities at home. On top of that, teachers and students endured weather issues inside the school house itself, which was often dilapidated, dim, drafty, and musty.

Thankfully, most of our teachers had a goal to mold each of us into intelligent and productive citizens. Our brave teachers wanted to fortify us against life's disappointments and prepare us for the reality of Negro life in post-slavery America. With their help, the unfairness, abuse of power, and neglect from the rest of America would *not* deter us from our path.

Education would liberate us to foster our own personal goals and dreams, thus ensuring our generation, and each generation of Negroes to come, would be better off than the last.

Extended Family Ties

was born on January 16, 1902, in Macon, Mississippi, Noxubee County, to William Dooley and Julia Nicholson. Before I was born, my parents' families lived next door, in Beat 3, District 66, which was west of the Mobile and Ohio railroad tracks. Here is a list of our closest neighbors in 1900. My great-grandfather, Elias Dooley, and his wife, Lavinia, were raising my cousins James Wingate and Viola Moore.

The Walkers lived on the other side of them, with parents William and Lucy, and their children Tom, Frank, Willie, Jonnie, Inez, and Lucius.

Fannie Clayton—who was called GramFannie by us kids—produced my mother, Julia, and my uncle, Albert, with Charles Nicholson in the 1870s. I'm not exactly sure what happened to Grandpa Charles, but I was told he was gone from the picture by about 1885.

GramFannie later married Forrest Clayton in Noxubee and had several children with him. But it was hard to find decent work in Noxubee, so Grandpa Forrest left us in Mississippi in 1896, to drive a delivery truck for the Galloway Coal Company in Memphis, Tennessee. He continued working there until 1900, when he got a job as a servant in the Harbest household. GramFannie continued to live with her younger daughters Stella, Eva, and son Buddie, next to Great-Grandpa Elias in Noxubee. Having family nearby was critical to our quality of life.

Daddy's sister, Annie, and her husband James Moore, were living next to GramFannie. Their daughter, Viola, was living with Grandpa Elias for some reason.

Daddy's older brother, Elias Jr., his wife, Annie, and their kids Anderson, Amanda, Alfred, Harry, Minnie, and Ollie lived next door to the Moores. All of us felt safe being so close to relatives.

Things had changed considerably for our families by 1910. My favorite aunt, Eva Clayton, had married Hampton Smith in 1908, and was living in Birmingham, Alabama, with her thirty-five-year-old husband, and his nephew, seventeen-year-old Clifford Marshall. I missed her dearly, but as luck would have it, we would reunite in the future.

How Daddy Got His Land

Vegetable gardens that fed the sharecropper's family were usually discouraged or prohibited by landowners, because they wanted the tenant farmers to concentrate on growing the cotton, the cash crop for their boss. During 1907, though, the boll weevil destroyed most of the cotton crops in the state. So some farmers started growing other plants, like tomatoes. Because my daddy *owned* his land, he could parcel out a garden plot for fruits and vegetables for our

1900 & 1910 U.S. Census, Noxubee, MS		
196 Walker, William		Head
	Lucy A	Wife
	Tom	Son
	Sarah	Son
	Willie	Son
	Jonnie	Son
	Lucius	Son
197 Dooley, Wm		Head
	Julia	Wife
	Wilda	Dau
198 Dooley, Elias Sr.		Head
	Lavinia	Wife
	Wingate, James	GSon
	Moore, Viola	GDau
199 Clayton, Fannie		Head
	Stella	Dau
	Eva	Dau
	Buddie	Son
200 Moore, Jas		Head
	Annie	Wife
201 Dooley, Elias Jr.		Head
	Annie	Wife
	Ollie	Son
	Minnie	Dau
	Henry	Son
	Alfred	Son
	Amanda	Dau
	Anderson	Son
223 Dooley, William Sr.		Head
1910 Census	Julia	Wife
	Willie Lee	Dau
	William Jr.	Son
	Daisy	Dau
	Rubie Lee	Dau

personal use. That way, we would be sure to have a good stock of food, canned or fresh, all year round.

When I was about six years old, I wondered how Daddy got his land in the first place, since most Negroes seemed to be sharecroppers on someone else's property. I wondered how much land there was among his Dooley relatives. I asked Mama one day while William and Wilda were in school, but I never expected the story she told me...

"Oh, Daisy, we are indeed fortunate people. Have I not told you about your Grandpa Elias' daddy and where he came from?"

"No, Mama, at least I don't remember that story."

"I have a few minutes. Let's sit on the porch and rest for a bit while I tell you his interesting story." Mama sat in the rocking chair and I sat cross-legged on the porch slats, feeling the cooler air coming from beneath the slats underneath my outstretched legs. Three-year-old Ruby Lee played with the dog in the front yard.

"Where to begin?" Mama sighed as she stroked her narrow chin with her fingers. "So you know your dad's father—your grandfather—is named Elias Dooley, and his wife is Grandma Lavinia, right?" I nodded. "Elias' father was named Billy Dooley. I know you don't know about the history of the United States yet, but Billy was born about 1820 in a place called Elbert, Georgia, which is two states away from here. It could take us a whole month to walk from Elbert, Georgia, to this place."

"Oh, that sounds far. I wouldn't want to do that," was all I could think to say.

"Billy's daddy was his slave owner, a white man named William Dooley. You know 'Billy' is a nickname for 'William,' right?" Mama finished.

"Is my daddy named for the white man too, then?" I asked.

"Well, yes, it's common for parents to name their children after other family members. There is a long line of William Dooleys among your daddy's kin. Grandpa Elias' brother was named William, after their father. You are smart, Daisy, to make the connection about men named William Dooley!" I could feel my cheeks getting warm with pride at her kind words. Praise did not come often in our house.

"So," Mama continued, "That's how your daddy, and his daddy and uncle, bought several plots of land over the years.

79

When slave owner, William Washington Dooley—they called him WW—died in 1852, he owned about 440 acres of land in Township 15, and about 300 acres of cattle-grazing land in Prairie Point where GramFannie lived before she moved far away to Tennessee. WW was a cattleman, like some other relatives I'll tell you about later.

"Your great-grandfather, Billy, owned two lots in Macon Town worth $300 by 1870, and about sixty acres in Township 15 by the time he died in 1879. That, combined with being more educated because his white daddy taught him to read, and having a supervisory job at a cattle ranch, helped your daddy's folk be better off financially than most Negroes, right?" I smiled uncertainly. She just said I was a smart girl, so I needed to live up to her high opinion of me.

VICTUALS

When the first rays peeked out from the pastel-colored horizon, we heard through our dreams, "Mornin' everybody! Time to get up!" Mama was shouting before sunrise. We knew to get up right away and, on non-farming days, dress appropriately for school. Those who tarried felt the switch on the back of their legs.

We began eating the breakfast Mama had prepared: hot porridge, blackberry jam on a slice of bread baked the night before, bacon, and milk from our cow in the backyard.

When I was very young, the men left to tend the cotton or corn crop in the main acreage. The women and girls cultivated the kitchen garden, with simple tools like a hoe, trowel, or shovel in one hand and seeds or fertilizer in the other. We grew corn, tomatoes, cucumbers, collard greens, and sweet potatoes—which was a vestige of our African ancestors. In August, along the fence, we couldn't help but sample the stickery blackberries bush whose thorns discouraged animals (and humans) from snacking in our garden space.

Our main victuals were centered around flour, cornmeal, sorghum, salt pork, lard, dry peas, molasses, chitterlings, rabbit, butter, milk, and sweet potato pie. We were able to grow enough of our own vegetables to eat reasonably well throughout the year, if we canned the excess produce for winter meals.

Nowadays we know that such high levels of carbohydrates and fats tend to cause or exacerbate problems with diabetes, but we did the best we could with what we had, paying the health consequences later in life.

My father and brother were proficient hunters and fishermen. We have eaten everything from turtles and birds to possums. In the wintertime, we ate wild greens and rabbits and squirrels, and catfish from the lakes.

OUR HOUSE

Our house was an unpainted double-winged, shingle-roofed building with five small drafty rooms. The house was built about a foot off the ground to stave off the mud that accumulated from winter rains and provide a bit of ventilation in the summer months. The strong March wind whistled through the side boards, nudging the structure ever so slightly so that over the years, most of our houses sagged and leaned.

The deep, slatted front porch, was a haven under which dogs and other animals might escape the sun and rain. A basket-weave swing hung from the rafters of the front porch, which was conveniently screened from the scorching rays of summer by a scented lattice of yellow honeysuckle vines.

The wide, covered porch held a couple of low chairs which accommodated my parents' tired bones after a hard day of work. We kids sat at the edge of the porch, swinging our short legs over the side, playing with our hands:

"Miss Mary Mack Mack Mack,
All dressed in black, black, black,
With silver buttons, buttons, buttons,
All down her back, back, back."

The back porch, off the kitchen, was a smaller landing which had two rickety chairs on either side of the door.

There was a window next to the front door and a couple of windows along the sides of our twenty-foot-long house. Mama made white lace curtains to drape inside the single-paned windows. We kept those sash windows open during the summer months, hoping to catch a breeze wafting through the house. It was hard to sleep when a lost firefly made its way into the house. There was one chimney in the center of the wood shingled roof which led down to a coal stove.

Example of a home in rural Mississippi, circa 1910.

Most Negroes didn't have running water in the home. Before I was born, people had to drag heavy buckets of water from the nearby Noxubee River for drinking, washing, and cleaning. Can you imagine how hard that must have been during the rainy months when water-soaked dirt roads sucked at the water bearer's shoes? Mama said they had a cart they could load with water jugs when the ground wasn't too soft that the wheels got stuck in the mud. Thankfully, there was a well and pump in the side yard by the time I came along in 1902.

Home is where the heart is and Mama made our two-room house as nice a place as she could. Daddy had built a multi-tasking eight-foot table. This served as a meal preparation countertop where we could shuck peas and corn, stir cornbread batter or Mama's special pound cake recipe, and cut tomatoes and cucumbers and carrots from the garden for meals. Covered with a blue-and-white checked cloth, it was also our dining table around which the six of us squeezed, sitting in narrow high-backed wooden chairs, also made by Papa. We also used it as a homework desk during the weeks when we could get out of farming duties to attend school. During the day, the table served as a sewing surface for Mama and Wilda Lee to construct shirts, dresses, sheets, and diapers from feed and flour sacks. Bed quilts were sewn from tattered garments and were often stuffed with newspaper or feathers.

A painted oil cloth covered part of the floor, a coal stove cooked our meals and heated the house, a butter churn provided fresh butter and cheese, a basin held dishes to be washed, and cleaning rags hung from the walls. Assorted metal pots and pans hung on the wall near the stove. Plates, cups, bowls, forks, spoons and knives were placed in a cabinet near the sink. We girls had to wipe down the kitchen surfaces and sweep the floor every day. Dust was a major problem in our neighborhood.

There was no insulation in the walls so during the winter months it was cold, cold, cold inside if a fire was not kept lit in the coal stove. Mama hung quilts on the walls to stop wind incursion. Conversely, the house was sweltering hot in the summertime. There was no electricity, no telephone, and no cars back then. We did the best we could with what we had.

Beds of flowers and scattered rose bushes softened the scruffiness of a large front yard overgrown with patchy crabgrass. A small cluster of scrub peach trees blossomed cheerfully every spring in a corner of the yard, but withered during the sweltering summer heat after harvesting their fruitful bounty.

After dinner, our favorite part of the day, we sat outside enjoying the balmy weather, listening to the cicadas, smelling the men's cigars, and catching phosphorescent fireflies as twilight turned to dusk. While the children played tag and jumped rope, the elders watched the sun saunter through the sky toward the far horizon, treating us all to a magnificent display of colors, from light blue, to pink, to orange, to red, to a combination of colors, and to purple as night fell. We had candlelight inside the house, but generally we hit the sack once night firmly took the sky.

Ruby Lee and I slept on one end of a double bed and Wilda slept on the other. Our mattress was stuffed with sweet-smelling straw. Lucky William had a narrow bed to himself. Mama and

Daddy had a double bed. Cheery, hand-sewn quilts covered our beds for warmth, as well as to pretty up the space.

What is *your* most awful memory of childhood? Mine was the outhouse on the farm. Only about six feet tall by three feet deep and four feet wide, it was made out of leftover slats of wood. The steeply pitched roof ensured rain would easily flow off the top and not drip onto the head of the user. The wooden bench had a round hole in the center that led to a deep storage pit. "What goes in must come out," and when the pit filled with the "out" a new one had to be dug and the rickety outhouse moved accordingly. Nobody wanted that job! There was a clothes hanger on the wall draped with sheets of newspaper for wiping the "out."

In the summertime, the odors were so unbearable the door had to be propped open, resulting in hordes of flies landing on our faces, arms, and even our nether regions from the pit, making the call of nature deposit more unsanitary than optimal. In the wintertime the door often froze shut, or it was raining so hard we had to use chamber pots inside the house.

Admittedly, my family fared better than many Negroes and whites in Noxubee. Daddy's family was among the minority who owned land in Macon and rural areas of the county. Uncle Anderson Dooley had a butcher's shop. Other Dooley relatives had supervisory positions in the budding dairy industry. My family had some nice pieces of furniture, a few china pieces, and our clothes were a little more fashionable than many of our neighbors.

So many memories of my childhood, but they weren't what I wanted to dwell upon in my adult life. There are some experiences that I never wish to share with anyone…

CHAPTER 7 - TRUE CONFESSIONS

(1543 East Blvd., Cleveland, Ohio, 1976, Daisy)

SHOULD I TELL MY SECRETS?

Fast forward to 1976 when I received Kathy's letter asking about our lineage. No. I don't want to remember those Jim Crow years in Mississippi. However, I am getting older and Kathy is the first of my children, or grandchildren, to express a deep interest in our lineage. Maybe I should reveal what Eva and I, and other family members experienced, so Kathy will understand what our lives were like in Noxubee County and why I told that innocent little lie about my birthplace.

Honestly, the whole subject of slavery, Night Rider Ku Klux Klansmen, and how masters forced themselves on their female slaves to create us mixed-race "yellow pickaninnies," was just too painful for my relatives to talk about. There were lots of things we had to do against our will. Nobody could blame adults for not wanting to speak about those times, right? Especially when they felt so powerless to run their own lives. Few secrets were revealed from one generation to the next, and those few were in whispers amongst adults only.

And that's why, as formidable as I am, I was horrified when my son, Thomas, the doctor, began dating a white woman named Virginia, a few years after his divorce to the other white woman, Pam. The new gal was born and bred in Alabama, of all states…and she was blonde, to boot.

Pictures of "Miss Anne," the stereotypical pampered, blonde southern belle mistress from Alabama were emblazoned on my mind. My friend, Sally, revealed that in some salacious romance novels, Miss Anne, the slave owner's wife, loved her some muscular Mandingo warrior slave, in secret. The darker his skin, the better. The unobtainable golden princess would lust after a particularly strong, glossy slave, and order him into her bed. When the mistress came up pregnant with a pigmented child, she would swear she had been raped. The ebony "perpetrator" would be treated to the most unimaginable torture and eventual death in front of the entire enslaved and white population on the plantation. That was to teach all black men a lesson: to never ever think about even touching a white woman, especially a blonde one.

Unfortunately, it had the reverse outcome. Many black men and some white women developed a thirst for one another after slavery—a seemingly unstoppable magnetic attraction—which generally left us black women in the dust with regard to black male companionship. And yes, many mixed babies were produced and those "mulattos" have upended.

Thankfully, contrary to this dismal picture, Thomas' third wife was as sweet as pecan pie and always showed him the utmost respect, loyalty, and all-encompassing love throughout their lives together. I guess you can't judge every book by its cover. Love is love.

Hmm, maybe I *should* tell Kathy the truth about our lives in the Deep South, maybe in a true confessions-type journal. I could write:

Dear Kathy,

I was surprised to receive your letter last week, but happy you wrote to me. I am getting old and it makes me feel good to know you were thinking of me.

So you want to know about our lineage and about how I grew up? Let me start with your first question. My mother always said her mother was one-quarter Blackfoot Indian, which accounts for our silky hair and bright skin color. Every summer we would go to the ranch and ride horses, pick apples from the orchard, and run and play all day long. To answer your second question, I was born in St. Louis, Missouri, in 1902. I lived there with my parents, sisters and brother. I had a normal childhood there. I hope that answers your questions about our forebears. Thank you for writing.

Love, Grandma Daisy

I feel like a coward, but I just couldn't do it! I couldn't tell my own granddaughter where I was actually born. Then everyone would know the truth. I have to maintain the lie my father demanded us to tell. He lived through the ostracism of people knowing he was a mere Mississippi "boy." He didn't want me to experience the condescending stares and jokes about our accent, with northern people thinking we were country bumpkins who didn't know anything about the world.

Yes, there were many good times in Noxubee, as I described earlier, but the overarching experience in the Deep South was not a positive one.

What would my society friends think if they knew the unspeakable truth of where I spent the first seventeen or so years of my life? I doubt they would continue inviting me to the Vagabond and Vaguettes Ball, or allowing me to be the President of the PTA, or being on the YMCA Board, or being a Democratic Precinct Woman. Maybe I would even be kicked out of the Order of the Eastern Star. No, I can't tell the truth of my humble beginnings. Not yet. Maybe not ever!

But…what if I ever *were* to unburden myself at some point in the future? What would I say to my granddaughter? Hmm, maybe I should make the attempt to write a journal. Yes, I could leave the information to her in my will so she would know the truth…after my demise. Yes, I could do that.

REVELATIONS FROM THE DEEP SOUTH

A Memoir, by Daisy Dooley Marshall Schumake

This journal was inspired by a 1976 letter from my granddaughter, Kathy Marshall, who was curious about our ancestors and where I grew up. What follows may shock my family and friends, and that's why I have left instructions this journal shall be released after I have passed on to my Maker.

From the time I was 17, I told everybody I was born and raised in St. Louis, Missouri. Not East St. Louis, Illinois, mind you, which was mainly a Negro town, but the whiter side of St. Louis, on the west bank of the Mississippi River.

But the truth is that I was born on January 16, 1902, in Noxubee County, Mississippi.

The United States had entered into the Treaty of Dancing Rabbit Creek with the Choctaw Indian Nation in 1830, in the southwestern portion of what came to be Noxubee County, a few years later. My grandmother, Fannie Cunningham Nicholson Clayton, often told me she was one-quarter Indian. Unfortunately, I don't remember ever hearing her name any specific Indian relatives. Even so, I wrote to my Granddaughter Kathy Marshall in 1976 telling her I thought we had Blackfoot Indian blood, which accounted for our less-than-kinky hair and barely tanned skin.

Knowing what I know about the uninhibited Caucasian-Negro goings on in the "Piney Woods" near my home, and the "yellow" children that were produced there, I wonder if our coloring came from Caucasians with slaves.

Noxubee was one of twenty-six counties in the State of Mississippi, carved from the last Indian cession east of the Mississippi River. This was after the Indians were forced to give up their rights, property, and territory to the American settlers, who wanted to move west where the soil was ripe for farming and raising cattle.

Most of the early Caucasian settlers to Noxubee came from the Carolinas, Georgia, and Alabama, farmers looking for land on which to rear their families. Few of them were wealthy, and slightly less than half were slave owners. Those migrants lived in log cabins with few furnishings. I learned in school that by 1840, in the county seat of Macon, there were churches and schools, and one hotel.

Like most of the Deep South, Noxubee County is part of the Bible belt, being home to over one hundred churches. Negroes were generally not invited to participate in those white churches, so we had to build our own houses and places of worship. In 1916, Missionary Baptists made up more than half of all churchgoers; Methodist Episcopal, Southern Baptist, and the Colored Methodist Episcopal churches accounted for most of the remainder.

Everybody knows that most Negroes in America are Christians, even to this day. I myself have been a proud member of the St. James AME Church for fifty years here in Cleveland. But in Noxubee, we attended the New Zion Church in the Prairie Point area, or the Friendship Community Church in the Piney Woods area. Every Sunday, rain or shine, we made sure we worshipped in church, praying for better times, then celebrating a big Sunday dinner with our large families.

More than 3,000 Negroes were tenant farmers who had their own mules. A tiny proportion were farm owners like my father. Most Negroes were sharecroppers, working for the same white farmers who were their former slave owners. No "cropper" could ever get ahead with that system, and they were poorer and of lower status than tenant farmers, and those who owned their own farms.

Noxubee has always been an agricultural area. Cotton was "King," as it was in most parts of the Deep South, but corn was also an important crop, because it fed people and livestock.

For many Caucasians in the southern states, slavery was seen as a necessary way of life in America. I don't know for sure how many of my dad's Dooley ancestors were slaves, but I expect Grandpa Elias and his kin were. I knew my grandmother, Fannie, and great-grandmother, Julia, were slaves. But that was not a subject often discussed in front of us children. All I knew was that my daddy owned the land and the house we lived in by the turn of the twentieth century.

Mississippi had been the second Southern State to secede from the Union in 1861, when President Abraham Lincoln was elected. Seven companies of men came from our neck of the woods to serve in the Confederate army and cavalry. I remember hearing that Macon, Brooksville, and Shuqualak opened their churches, schools, and homes to the soldiers wounded in Civil War battles. When Mississippi's capital city, Jackson, was destroyed, the state government was set up in the town of Macon, near where we lived after slavery ended.

We heard the adults whispering that early on, slave masters wanted to "break" slaves who were brought directly from Africa. That means the whites wanted to eliminate the tribal names, languages, and religious traditions of their enslaved "property."

I don't know if any of our ancestors came directly from Africa though; based on our skin tone, probably not.

Now I don't believe it, but some people said slave owners used the Christian Bible to keep our people enslaved. They said Abraham, the Father of Faith, and all the patriarchs, held slaves without God's disapproval (Gen. 21:9–10). They said Canaan, Ham's darker son, was made a slave to his brothers (Gen. 9:24–27). They said the Ten Commandments mentioned slavery twice, showing God's implicit acceptance of it (Ex. 20:10, 17). They even said the Apostle Paul specifically commanded slaves to obey their masters (Eph. 6:5–8). They interpreted the Bible saying darker-skinned people should always be slaves.

One night when I was a child, I overheard Grandpa Elias tell Daddy a crazy story. Grandpa's parents had been slaves in Georgia, where I think he was born, so I believe he knew what he was talking about. He whispered to Daddy that the owners had conspired to convince their slaves that if they worked hard enough, and didn't run away from their masters, they might get into heaven. They were promised that with golden wings, it would be easier to serve their masters on the other side of the Pearly Gates. It was supposed to be something slaves could look forward to, but I imagine it put the fear of God in them against running away or shirking their work efforts.

It was illegal for anyone to teach slaves to read or write, and their masters drummed "obey your master" scriptures into slaves' heads to keep them from running away to freedom. The plan didn't always work, though, as some decided to take their chances on heaven and run anyway. I don't recollect if we had any runaways.

Our unsubstantiated history is that my great-grandmother was a concubine of sorts who willingly had children with the grandson of her former slave master. In 1976, I told Kathy we had Blackfoot Indian blood. If this story about my grandmother is true, it may have been Caucasian blood mixed with our enslaved female ancestors that accounted for our skin tone.

Additionally, I believe several of my female ancestors were offered as "night comfort" for their slave owners, or the overseer, or visiting friends of their slave owner. It was a common thing, I've heard my mother whisper to other women.

I have no names or any proof of this, except the visage I see in the mirror.

I do know that after the Civil War, during what was called "Reconstruction" between 1865 and 1876, the American Union tried to heal its devastation from the war. That was a short period of enlightenment when my grandfathers could vote and a few Negroes were elected to the Senate and House of Representatives. That peaceful time didn't last long.

The Ku Klux Klan (KKK) organization, initially formed in the 1860s, rose up again in the South and flourished nationwide at the turn of the century and into the early to mid-1920s. The KKK advocated tirelessly for white supremacy, white nationalism, and anti-Jewish sentiments. Dressed in their ridiculous white robes and hoods, they became a familiar sight, marching through our towns and sometimes burning crosses near our houses. They wanted to instill in us Negroes the fear of death, and they usually succeeded. But nearly three-quarters of the population in our neck of the woods was Negro, so we may have felt less fearful than some other counties.

There were almost 600 lynchings in Mississippi alone. In Macon, around where we lived, James Jones and Henry Williams were lynched in 1898. Fred Isham and Henry Isham were lynched in 1901. G.W. Edd and George Somerville were taken from the sheriff and hanged by a mob for an alleged shooting in 1912. On June 27, 1919, in an incident described as part of the Red Summer, a mob of white citizens including a banker and a deputy sheriff, among many others, attacked prominent black citizens. I don't remember exactly, but that's about when we left Macon for St. Louis, Missouri. There was no way my daddy was going to keep exposing his children to that dangerous behavior.

From 1916 to 1970, an estimated six million Negroes willingly left the rural southern states in droves, migrating to urbanized city centers where the jobs were plentiful, such as St. Louis, Detroit, Chicago, and Cleveland. We were no different. We all wanted a chance to live the American Dream in a free land—the Promised Land—with honest work that paid a fair wage. We wanted to start our own businesses and become the captains of our own ships instead of low-paid swabbies constantly working for others.

Even though I only stayed in St. Louis for about a year, I chose to represent myself as coming from a place of industry and progress. That Missouri city was more acceptable, more progressive, more modern, and more diverse than anywhere in Mississippi.

My daddy cautioned us to steadfastly maintain we were born in St. Louis so we would be thought of as being more intelligent, more cultured, and more credible. I feel it helped me become the powerful woman I was known to be in Cleveland.

I do apologize for misleading my descendants, but if I had the chance to relieve my life, I would do exactly the same thing again. May you all find peace and prosperity in this world.

Daisy Dooley Marshall Schumake, 1976

PART II - THE STORYTELLER

Alex Haley's masterpiece novel, *Roots: The Saga of An American Family*, was released to grand acclaim in 1976. In 1977, it became the first, and still most-watched, TV miniseries in the world. It was an emotional tale about a young African boy called Kunta Kinte, born in around 1750 in the Mandinka village of Juffure, in the African country of the Gambia.

One day, while teenage Kunta was searching for wood to make a drum for his younger brother, four men chased him, surrounded him, and took him captive. They sold him to white slavers. The story chronicled his horrific journey in a cramped slave ship across the Atlantic Ocean to life on a plantation in Virginia.

Throughout his adult life, Kunta taught various African words and traditions to his children and they, in turn, passed them down through each successive generation to Alex Haley. He decided to bring those remarkable stories to life in *Roots*. His family's story lived on because each generation had at least one storyteller who passed along their history, memories, and stories to their children.

Daisy's mother, Julia, and her grandmother, Fannie, were natural-born storytellers. Their gift was like that of Kunta Kinte's. Daisy and her dearest elder, Aunt Eva, often recalled stories they heard from our talented mothers. Their narratives were birthed from fact, spiced with wonder, and sprinkled with a touch of wisdom.

It's time to honor our mothers by revealing those stories to you now. So sit back, relax, and listen to how it was back in the 1800s and 1900s in the deepest part of the Deep South.

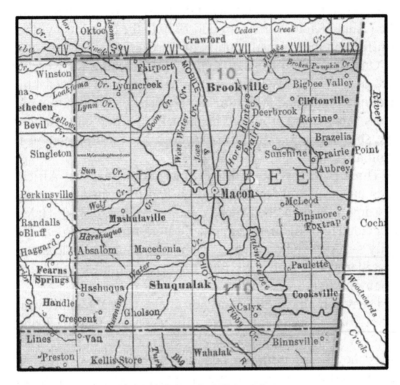

Noxubee County, Mkississippi.

CHAPTER 8 - GRAMFANNIE

(Noxubee County, Mississippi, March 1910, Daisy)

Anticipation. Silence. Marvel. Those three words preceded any description of our most cherished treasure. Affectionately called GramFannie by us, her grandchildren, Fannie Cunningham Nicholson Clayton, was the most intriguing storyteller in the world...perhaps only rivaled by Scheherazade from the Persian tale called *One Thousand and One Nights.*

High-spirited and still attractive, her graying hair was often piled on top of her head, pompadour style, or sometimes it was hidden by a colorful bandanna. GramFannie could manipulate her face to take on any character. At the blink of an eye she could become a young child scared by the dark, a wizened old man telling his life story, our cow Maisy enjoying the release after being milked, the mistress overseeing her household slaves, an old Indian woman describing her disappearing way of life, a teenage boy learning about love, a fish swimming in the Noxubee River, or sometimes she was just herself.

As a little girl, GramFannie had dreamed of becoming a teacher, but like so many of her caste born into slavery, she was relegated to farming and housekeeping activities during her lifetime.

My mother Julia was a good bard too, having learned the narratives from her master storyteller mother, but she couldn't touch GramFannie's skills. Sometimes the mother-daughter team would regale us with a dazzling interplay of characters from the past, the setting most often played out right here on our front porch near Macon, Mississippi.

My lifelong appreciation of learning started with GramFannie. Every time she visited us, we children clamored for her to tell us histories from the old days, especially from Indian and slavery times. She was bodacious and dramatic, and loved to tell tall tales about her interesting childhood. One of our favorite stories included how she learned firsthand—literally—about the end of bondage, but I'll tell you about that one later.

On cool spring mornings or better still, warm summer nights, GramFannie introduced us to her mother and father, brothers and sisters, famous aunts and uncles, and other ancestors within the scope of her recollections and imagination. As warm and friendly wraiths, our progenitors would come and sit with us in the night, under the twinkling stars, filling our heads with the truth that we came from a vigorous, enduring lineage. Those stories taught us lessons and made us feel strong and confident enough to go out into the harsh world, without wavering from our intention. We would make a good life for ourselves and our posterity.

The front yard had transformed into a portal to the world, the launchpad for our dreams and aspirations. How we loved sitting next to GramFannie on the porch, listening to her wondrous, alluring stories about the "old days" in Alabama, or her experiences in Mississippi and Tennessee. Our bodies, tired from working in the fields or trudging to and from school, became refreshed anew in her scintillating bath of faraway ideas, family history, jokes, riddles, limericks, poems, and seemingly magical tales.

Sometimes she spoke in an old tongue before formal education was legal, and other times she used perfect diction. We never knew what to expect and that made the experience even more delicious.

Now get yourselves ready…it's story time!

THE METAMORPHOSIS

"Ok, chil'ren, come on over here and sit down. Wait a minute. Wilda Lee, get the broom and sweep the porch so y'all chil'ren can sit and not get yo clothes dirty." Everybody yearned for The Storyteller to begin tonight's recitation, so twelve-year-old Wilda Lee quickly did as she was told.

"Daisy, while yo sista's sweepin', bring me a glass of that sweet'n lemon water, in case my lips get parched as I'm a talkin'."

I jumped up, ran into the house, grabbed a tall glass in one hand and the pitcher of honeyed lemon water in the other. I poured the aromatic, barely yellow liquid into the glass, careful not to spill a drop on the blue-checkered tablecloth. I didn't want to spoil my grandmother's good mood.

When I exited the house with the refreshment, GramFannie was already sitting in the well-worn rocking chair on the porch, between the door and front window. My brothers and sisters, and cousins Eva and Stella Clayton, were flailing their tanned legs off the edge of the porch slats. Everybody became as quiet as church mice until the show began.

GramFannie took a long drink and licked her lips as she placed the glass on the overturned bucket-table next to the chair. She rocked slowly back and forth, back and forth, as her eyes assumed a glazed, faraway look. As she appeared to go into a trance-like state somewhere inside her fertile mind, all of the worry lines from her forehead began to relax and disappear. Her leathery skin became satiny smooth and taut. Her lips became full and cherry red. Her gray, wispy hair seemed to turn back to its original luscious walnut color. Her ample girth melted away to the lithe young woman she had been thirty years prior. Even the skin on her hands became smooth and blemish-free.

As The Storyteller prepared to regale us with her favorite tales from the olden days, she metamorphosed into the former beautiful girl of legend. Watching her magical transformation from elder to vivacious younger lady was part of her mystique. We all wondered where tonight's story would take us. GramFannie's raspy voice became strong and animated in the mouth of The Storyteller.

The Choccolocco Creek Archaeological Complex

CHAPTER 9 - INDIAN COUNTRY

(Calhoun County, Alabama, 1830s and 1840s, Daisy)

THE CHOCCOLOCCO VALLEY

"Long ago, in the Choccolocco Valley in what used to be called Benton, but is now Calhoun County…" The Storyteller always began her tales in the same way, talking about our ancestors from central-east Calhoun County, Alabama, located near the Georgia border.

"My Mama, Julia Borders, who was sometimes called 'July,' was raised in what used to be Indian Country. Julia was born in 1834 in Jackson, Georgia. It was a year or so before 1840 when she and twenty-seven other slaves traveled about 150 miles on foot, which took them around twenty days. Their master, John Borders, and his brood rode to Alabama in covered wagons. They were all moving to Massa Borders' newly built house on Old Choccolocco Road in eastern Alabama."

"What does Choccolocco mean?" we kids asked on cue.

"Well," The Storyteller began, "in the Creek Indian language 'chahko' means 'shoals'. What do you think a shoal is, children?"

"It's a large number of fish swimming together," we cried in unison, having heard this question many times.

"That's right. Now what kind of fish were found in those parts of 'Bama?" The Storyteller asked, deliberately stringing out the story for as long as she could before getting to the good parts. This also served as a teaching lesson, for she felt it important the children understood the history and geography of where their ancestors had lived.

"Darter, pygmy sculpin, and blue shiner," we responded together.

I added, "And there were also lots of slimy snails and clams and black mussels in the water." The Storyteller smiled at my addition, and I flushed inside with her approval. Being eight years old at the time, I was the second youngest of the grandchildren and, therefore, was usually treated as though I didn't know a thing. But I listened to what was going on around me, so I learned a lot about my world and was rarely afraid to speak up when I had something to say, even though the expectation was that children be seen and not heard.

The Storyteller closed her eyes and resumed speaking, as she continued to rock back and forth in the creaky, wooden rocking chair. "The Indian word 'Iago' means 'big.' The Choccolocco Creek is a wide shallow stream with big shoals of fish. The Choccolocco Valley went from the Coosa River all the way to the Georgia boundary. Long ago, this was Indian Country." She paused for effect. Shivers went up and down our arms, just imagining that GramFannie's mother had lived among Indians!

We children had heard terrible scary things from white people about Indians scalping settlers, stealing their cattle and horses, and causing all sorts of mischief. But white people often lied, so we children didn't know what to think of the people who had brown skin like ours. The Indians wore pretty feathers around their heads and animal hides around their bodies. They had their own language and culture, as was explained to us in intricate detail by our wise grandmother. We wanted to learn more about them.

INDIAN COUNTRY

Another day, we kids walked to GramFannie's house, fighting the March winds all the way. It was too cold outside, so we gathered inside the house, settling ourselves on the painted floor rug near the warm hearth. GramFannie sat in her rocking chair. After her mesmerizing transformation to a youthful Storyteller, she started in her usual manner, "Long ago in Calhoun County, Alabama...

"Brown-skinned Indians with straight black hair called the Choccolocco Valley home for a long, long time. Nobody knows how long they had lived there. In the process of farming, present day people have found tools and bowls. Indians didn't speak English, of course, but spoke their own Indian language, and drew strange pictures on rocks. Nobody knows what those pictures meant, but they might have been their way of writing, like our ABCs. Answer me this, children. The residents of Choccolocco were the ancestors of which modern-day Indians?" The Storyteller cupped her hand behind her ear, waiting for the children to answer.

"The Muscogee Creek Indians," Eva and Stella cried out first.

A nod of the head told them they were right.

My younger sister Ruby Lee asked, "Where did all the Indians go, GramFannie?" as she pulled her knees up to her chest, not sure if she had asked a smart question or not.

Our elder replied, "When 'Bama became a state in the year 1819, almost one hundred years ago, all except the southern territory of this country belonged to the Creek Indians. It was usually not open to white settlers or us colored people. Indians lived there for maybe thousands of years. Who knows?

"William Mallory was the first of the white settlers to come. Mallory set up a trading post near White Plains, which is a town near the northern end of Choccolocco Road. He acquired several hundred acres of land on the creek directly from the Indians. What does 'acquired' mean?"

"I think acquired means to buy or to get something," William—the numbers man—spoke up.

"That's true. Very good, William." He beamed, crossed his arms, and smiled at the other children, seeming satisfied with himself.

The Storyteller continued, in spite of his drama. "I swan, Mallory must have treated the Indians with respect for they freely traded the pretty glass beads, animal skins, and strong drink he brought with him, in exchange for some of their land. Then a few of Mallory's other friends started coming in too, all wanting Indian land because of its rich soil and forests, which could be cut down to make houses and other buildings."

"By the terms of the 1832 Cusseta Treaty, the Creek Indians were forced out of Alabama and 'removed' in 1836, about seventy years ago. What's a 'Treaty,' children?"

We younger kids looked at William and Wilda Lee, the ones with the most education, for their answer. Wilda Lee spoke first, "Well, white men came into the Choccolocco area in the 1830s wanting the land for themselves. The Indians were forced to sign

101

a piece of paper that said they agreed to give up their land; that agreement on paper was called a treaty."

William piped in with, "The treaty said the Indians agreed to move their families west of the Mississippi River."

"That's exactly right," The Storyteller replied. "The unfortunate natives were removed from the land they had lived on for generations upon generations. Then the government 'surveyed' the Indian lands. What does that mean?"

Most of the children looked at each other and shrugged their shoulders in an "I dunno" gesture. Wilda Lee had heard this part of the story before and said, "To 'survey land' means to describe and draw the boundaries of a section of land onto paper. Like when Daddy had that man come out and divide up our land so that part of it would be planted with wheat, and some with cotton. So maybe it means the government divided the Indian land up." She had a satisfied look on her face when The Storyteller shined a beatific smile at her. I glared at my smartypants sister.

The Storyteller continued, "Gold was discovered in Georgia in 1828, Cherokee territory. The immediate consequences were a bunch of white squatters and settlers coming in, doing illegal gold mining, and Cherokees being forced off their own land. After the relocation of Indian tribes along what was called the 'Trail of Tears' was complete, the Choccolocco Valley was opened in 1834 to white settlers. The Trail of Tears was a series of forced Indian removals from the Southeastern United States to west of the Mississippi River. The Indians suffered from too much sun, wind, disease, and starvation. Sadly, thousands of Indians died before reaching their destination, some having to walk 900 miles from their original homeland."

"Did all of the Indians agree to move away?" Stella asked.

"Oh no," GramFannie shook her head. "My mother said the Creeks were most reluctant to leave their homelands. After the treaty was signed, the American government tried to get two groups of Creek Indians to fight each other, instead of the whites who were taking their land. This was called the Creek War of 1836. But the unsuccessful Creeks were removed even farther west, to Arkansas. Afterward, the Choccolocco Valley was rapidly occupied by settlers who were mainly from North and South Carolina.

"In the late 1830s, William Johnston came from South Carolina with his wife, children, and slaves. Also amongst the early settlers was a man named John Borders, who investigated the territory, swore loyalty to the U.S. Government, bought land, and had a plantation house built for his family.

"This part of the story may or may not be true, but some of us believe my mother, Julia Borders, was born in the new Alabama territory. Whispers suggest that she might have been the daughter of one of the Indian women in the area where John Borders explored. If that is true, it means each of us (pointing to all us children) are part Indian by blood…"

We looked at each other, not knowing whether to be excited or disappointed that we might be part Indian. The Storyteller broke into our thoughts by saying, "My mother believes she was born in Jackson, Georgia, before John Borders' family moved to Alabama. I don't know what the truth is."

I said I liked the "We come from Indians story." Throughout my life, I would keep that as the true story of our heritage. But somehow over the years, I forgot the "Creek Nation" name and started saying our ancestors were "Blackfoot Indians" instead— because some Negroes have black feet.

In an instant, The Storyteller was gone, replaced by our old grandmother. "I think that's enough for today, m'dears, I'm mighty tired now," GramFannie concluded, taking a gulp of cooled tea.

WHO CAME TO CHOCCOLOCCO?

On another day, we were treated to an impromptu visit by The Storyteller when she dropped by for a cup of tea after church.

After the metamorphosis, GramFannie said, "Long ago in Calhoun County, Alabama…" and the story began as usual.

"Do you know the names of the people who were marched on the Trail of Tears that we talked about the other day?"

I said, Cherokee, Eva said Muscogee Creek, William said Seminole, Stella said Chickasaw, and Willie Lee said Choctaw.

"You're all correct, but who else lived here and was marched away?" The Storyteller asked. We all looked at each other, not knowing about any other Indian tribes who were affected.

"What about the African slaves?" she added. "Yes, some Indians owned slaves and if you dig far enough, I believe you may find that some of your grandfather's Nicholson ancestors had been the slaves of Indians here."

Our eyes grew wide hearing that titillating detail. I would ask my Nicholson cousins about that the next time I saw them.

"As I've mentioned before, white settlers came to the Choccolocco Valley in droves. To make it easier to travel from Georgia, a crude road was dug through the Valley, through a gap in the Appalachian Mountains, to the town of Oxford. The mail came by horseback and stagecoach to White Plains, where there was a post office as early as 1842. That's where our Cunninghams lived, a couple of miles away from the John Borders plantation.

"When the Georgia Pacific Railroad laid tracks through the Valley, a train depot was placed at a spot convenient for the loading of iron ore. At about the same time, three brickyards were built in the area. The towns in the Choccolocco Valley began to grow, as people could become specialized in more than just farming. Bricklayers, iron workers, sawyers, and all sorts of other jobs from those industries, caused more people to come to the land. And some of our Negro ancestors became skilled in those fields too, as I shall describe in future stories."

"Aw, GramFannie, can't you just tell us another story now?" But the vibrancy of The Storyteller had already left, leaving a smiling, pleasant, older woman in her place.

105

Borders-Blackmon House, Calhoun County, AL. Registry of
Landmarks and Heritage, Alabama Historical Commission, 1935.

CHAPTER 10 - THE BORDERS PLANTATION

(Calhoun County, Alabama, 1830s and 1840s, GramFannie)

On this balmy spring evening, I was dressed in a periwinkle blue-and-white checkered dress, my hair in a puffy Gibson Girl style, which made me look more girlish than my fifty-some-odd years. As the children watched, transfixed, while sitting cross-legged on the porch, I transformed into The Storyteller in less than a minute this time.

I took a deep breath and began today's story.

Long ago in Calhoun County, Alabama, in the early days of the Choccolocco Valley, a wealthy community was made up of large plantations. The beautiful rolling hills were dotted with large homes and never-ending brown fields of fluffy-headed cotton bushes, worked by many strong slaves.

Massa John Borders was one of the first to receive several land grants from the United States Government in the mid-1830s, amounting to about 1,200 acres in total.

"Wow!" The children exclaimed, not understanding how much land that was, but it sounded like a big number to them.

That's about two miles wide and two miles deep, like a square with one side about the distance from our house to your school.

All around the space where he wanted his plantation house built were rolling hills, surrounded by longleaf and yellow pine forests. There were also pasturelands where cows and other animals grazed on the grasses that grew there. It was a gorgeous piece of land. As time went on, the Choccolocco Road curved through large properties of men who, like Massa Borders, became the biggest planters in the area. One end of the road went to the town of White Plains and the other toward Jacksonville and Oxford.

After the Indians were removed in 1836, Massa Borders brought two trained carpenters, Griffin and Levic Borders, to his new land. He wanted them to build him a grand home, on a prime spot next to Choccolocco Road where it met with DeArmanville Road. It would look similar to the house they had already built for the Borders in Jackson, Georgia. And guess what?

"What?" The children responded on queue.

Those two brilliant builders, Griffin and Levic, were slaves. That's right. Not all slaves were cooks, maids, or field hands. Some were trained carpenters who built houses and furniture, others were blacksmiths who used heat to bend metal into tools and machines. Some were expert brick layers.

One of the first things Massa Borders did was to have Griffin and Levic build him a sawmill near the Coosa River that I've talked about in other stories. Men used heavy broad axes to chop down trees in the thick forests. Massa Borders needed a river nearby with a strong current so logs from the forests could be cut and floated downstream to his sawmill. Branches and tree trunks could then be cut with special saws for further shaping into pieces of lumber so thick—

"How thick were they?" Daisy asked.

They were so thick they could be used for houses and other buildings. The sash saw could cut tall trees down to twelve or sixteen feet long, some about as deep and wide as your daddy's foot. Notches would be carved into the ends of the wood so the cut logs could be crisscrossed at the corners to make log cabins, like their neighbor, Mr. Barnabee's, house. Workers stuffed the space between logs with smaller pieces of wood, covered with a mortar made of lime and sand, called "chinking."

When settlers first came to Indian Country, many lived in one-room log cabins like I described, maybe sixteen by eighteen feet in length and width.

I gestured what I meant by length and width using my hands.

They sometimes constructed a second building for the kitchen. Often the two buildings were connected by a 'dog trot' which was an open-ended passageway between the two buildings. Each little house had a well and a garden. A spinning wheel could be heard in every home from wool shorn from sheep, and women used a loom to weave the thread into cloth for 'homespun' clothes, curtains, and blankets.

As time went on, the richer planters had grander plantation homes built for their families. Their old log cabins became slave quarters.

Massa Borders was a smart man. He wanted his new house to have a good supply of water, in addition to having a well dug in the backyard. Do you know what he did?

The children shook their heads and shrugged their shoulders.

He had his slaves build a reservoir, which is like a pond. This reservoir was at a waterfall about a mile from his home. He had it cemented so it could hold water. The slaves cut logs and hollowed them out so water would run through them. They cemented those hollowed-out logs together and the water ran from the waterfall into the reservoir and then through the long log pipes to the Borders home.

By 1840, Massa Borders had brought his kin from Jackson, Georgia, about 150 miles away, and enjoyed showing them their new home. His wife was named Cynthia Knox. Their children were Mary Adaline, Narcissus Virginia, Malinda, Serena Ann, Eliza, Samuel, Evelyn, Abner, Cynthia, and Georgianna. Narcissus was the most important to our story.

"GramFannie, why did the slaves have the last name 'Borders'?" I asked.

I'll tell you that fascinating story another time, I winked.

Our Family Arrives

Long ago, in Calhoun County, Alabama… The Storyteller (me) began the day's tale.

Last time, I told you about how John Borders and his two carpenter slaves, Griff and Levic Borders, came to the Choccolocco Valley to build the Border's sawmill and house. I also mentioned the names of the Borders who came to live there. Guess who else Massa Borders brought with him?

Ruby Lee offered, "Dogs?" Everybody laughed, knowing Ruby Lee loved her animals.

Still chuckling, I replied, maybe, but what I had in mind was the twenty-six slaves he brought in from Jackson, Georgia, to live on his property and work his land. Other slave names that I can remember now, were Charlotte, Dicey, Wash, Willie, Dennis, Orange, Dave, and Eva, in addition to Griff and Levic. That group included my Mama, Julia Borders, when she was about four years old. All twenty-eight of them would live in five log cabins near the newly built plantation house.

Daisy piped in bravely, "Or was Great-grandma Julia born in Choccolocco from an Indian mother and John Borders when he first went there in the 1830s?"

I stared at Daisy for a moment, as I didn't remember telling her about our possible Indian connection. Without answering her, I continued the story.

During what was called the Antebellum Period from 1840 until 1861 when the War Between the States started, white settlers cut the forests, built big plantation homes, and farmed the land. And who do you think *actually* did most of that work?

After a brief silence, "Their slaves did all the work!" some of the children shouted.

"What's a slave?" little Ruby Lee asked innocently. She was too young to have already heard my prior stories about our lineage. It was a good thing to repeat our history more than once.

When I was born in 1856, my mother was the property of John Borders. She was forced to obey him. If he wanted her to cook his food at midnight, or clean his clothes outside in the rain, or kiss his nasty feet at the end of a hard day—

"Yuck!" the kids shouted.

She had to do whatever he wanted immediately, or get into trouble. Slaves that disobeyed their masters could be slapped, whipped, tied to a post all day, go without food, or be put into jail. Slaves had to till, plant, care for, and harvest all kinds of crops. They had to milk the cows, feed the pigs, spin the sheep's wool into thread and cloth, and sew clothes and quilts for their fellow slaves and sometimes for their owner's family. Slaves had to clean the house, cook the food, and do whatever the slave master and his descendants wanted, whenever they wanted it.

Slaves trained in carpentry skills, like Griffin and Levic, built the master's houses and furniture. They had to know how to work with wood, make bricks, and build brick and stone walls. This country was built on the backs of slave labor, to be sure.

"GramFannie," smart-aleck William spoke up, "it sounds just like today's children having to obey their parents!" We all laughed at his truth.

In a somber voice, I added that sometimes enslaved relatives—even children—were sold to other slave masters, never to be seen again.

The kids were silent, perhaps thinking about what it would be like to never see each other again. After a few moments, I continued.

After the Civil War ended in 1865, the Choccolocco Valley began to take on its modern-day appearance. They had sturdy bridges across the creek, trains transporting people and products to and from valley towns which produced most of what a diverse community needed to survive. Next time, we'll learn more about what life was like for our ancestors on the Borders plantation, OK? *The children always want to hear more, but I am tired.*

As I said those last words, my face began to sag like a too-ripe pumpkin, the blotchy age spots from too much sun reappeared on my face and hands, my hair faded to gray, my shoulders and breasts drooped from gravity, and my lips thinned considerably. I was the beloved GramFannie again.

Ruby Lee walked over and gave me a big hug, thanking me for yet another memorable story. She was the only hugger in our family, besides cousin Eva. The rest of the children thanked me for telling them more about our history, but kept their distance physically. They weren't shown much physical affection from their parents or grandparents, so most of them didn't feel comfortable showing that type of emotion to me.

But little Ruby Lee was a hands-on little girl who loved to cuddle and hold hands and even rub noses. She gave each of us a kiss good night on the cheek. They all believed she would make a caring parent one day. Frankly, it was hard for me to imagine cynical William, self-absorbed Wilda, or clinical Daisy becoming caring parents. *Hmm, we'll see.*

Borders-Blackmon (now Gibbins) House, Calhoun County, AL.
Photograph: Kathy Marshall.

THE BORDERS PLANTATION HOUSE

Metamorphosis complete, The Storyteller began in the usual manner. Once upon a time in Calhoun County, Alabama, the view from Choccolocco Road, between Oxford and White Plains, led to the expansive lawn of the Border's plantation house, set way back like a castle.

"What's a castle, GramFannie?" Daisy asked.

Oh my, haven't I told you about castles? The younger children shook their heads.

A castle is the grandest type of house for kings and queens, and other important people in some other countries of the world. Castles are often made out of stone or brick and they have many rooms. In fact, one castle in France has 365 fireplaces in separate rooms—one for each day of the year. Some castles have tall towers at the corners, called spires, like what you see on some churches in town." The children all nodded their heads in understanding, thinking about the single pointy white spire that extends above the roof of most churches in Noxubee.

There were two buildings that made up the Border's house, joined together by a "Whistling Walk," which was kind of an open-air hallway. A four-foot-wide brick pathway led up to the house. In slavery days, slaves carrying food to the master would have to whistle as they walked through the hallway to signal to the master that they weren't eating any of the food. You see, slaves were not allowed to eat the same fine food they prepared for the master's family, but they might sometimes get to eat their leavings.

"What! You mean they ate the food scraps from the master's plate?" Wilda Lee asked, her eyebrows raised.

Yes, that's exactly what I mean. Otherwise, the slaves just got the fatty parts of the pig and other food stuffs that weren't as desirable. Eating the master's leftovers at least gave some variety to the house slaves' diet. I'll talk more about the slaves' lives in another story.

At the top of six steps leading to the front door was an eight-foot-wide porch. One side had a built-in bench where a person could sit and relax and enjoy the view of green lawn, trees, and slave houses in the distance. Farther away, they saw fields cultivated with wheat or corn crops, surrounded by forests.

To avoid flooding, the home was built a few feet higher than the ground, with the lower two or three feet of the house's foundation sided with brick.

Tall, white, double doors welcomed visitors to the stately Borders plantation house. Inside the doorway, a wide foyer had beautiful yellow-pine floors that extended thirty feet to tall, double doors leading to the backyard. The back doors were large enough to ride their horses into the house during bad weather.

"Really? Horses inside the house?" William exclaimed.

That's right, I nodded. There were no stairs outside the back door. Since the house was built on a sloping hill, horses could walk right through the white double doors at the back of the house.

Turning left from the front door led through the Whistling Walk hallway, to a dining room and kitchen at the far end. Turning right from the front door led to one of two downstairs bedrooms for the Borders' children. In fact, Ansel John Hopkins

Borders engraved his initials on the wall in his bottom floor room.

A stairway in the middle of the foyer, with extra-steep steps, led to the second floor containing three more bedrooms, each with two windows in one side of the room. Two of the rooms overlooked the backyard garden and pasture. One could view the front yard from the third upstairs bedroom.

The two-story portion of the structure was flanked by two chimneys, one for two of the upstairs bedrooms. A one-story 'bump out' was flanked by two smaller chimneys to heat the main living spaces just inside the back-door entrance.

The Kitchen

The kitchen was the castle where my mother was Queen. Nothing happened there without the say-so of Mama Julia or the Missus of the house. The kitchen and dining room were *so big*—

"How big were they?" the children screamed.

I continued, laughing, They were so big they were in a building by themselves, almost bigger than this whole house. My head turned around the entire room with my arms extended, palms up, encompassing the entire space in which we sat.

The hearth was so wide...

"How wide was it?" the children asked.

That all you children, and your Mama and Papa, could stand next to each other inside it. Imagine a huge piece of wood, nine feet wide and about one foot tall, crossing sideways above my head. I gestured with my hands above my head, as wide as I could stretch them apart. That's what the fireplace was like standing inside it.

The red brick chimney was *so tall*...

"How tall was it?" the children screamed.

You could see the smoke coming out of it from across the road in the slave quarters, and also when working in the field beyond that.

The hearth was so *huge*...

"How huge was it?" the children screeched.

The black cast iron pot in the left corner of the hearth, stayed on top of the always lit fire. Whenever hot water was needed, like for cooking, washing dishes, or bathing, it would be heated in that pot.

The hearth was red brick from top to bottom, side to side. The smokestack was so massive…

"How massive was it?" the children yelled.

That it vented up through a square hole in the back of the red brick wall, up through the roof. An assortment of black cast-iron pots and pans, and long-handled cooking tools, hung from hooks on both sides of the hearth.

Years later, before I was born in 1856, Massa John installed a cast-iron stove and oven in front of the open fireplace. The toasty warm kitchen was the place to be during the freezing winter months, but it was almost unbearable during a hot and humid summer day.

Borders-Blackmon (now Gibbins) House, Kitchen Hearth, Calhoun County, AL. Photograph: Kathy Marshall, 2019.

The kitchen also had *so many* shelves…

"How many were there?" the children shrieked.

On two of the walls, all the pots and pans and plates and serving trays and utensils were in easy reach for the slaves to cook the most sumptuous meals, as needed for large parties.

Borders-Blackmon House, Kitchen building, Calhoun County, AL. Alabama Registry of Landmarks and Heritage, Alabama Historical Commission,

The four windows were *so spacious…*

"How spacious were they?" the children inquired.

That the cooks could open them and let the fresh air in. They could see whoever was walking or riding by the front yard, and they could watch the slaves entering and exiting their quarters across the road. And…from the kitchen windows, the cooks could see cattle across the gated fence in the pasture area, and people coming up to the house.

CHAPTER 11 - THE ENSLAVED

(Calhoun County, Alabama, 1840s - 1860s, GramFannie)

I put on the blue-and-white apron I often wore when it was time for The Storyteller to make her grand appearance, then trudged toward the well-worn rocking chair near the window. My long, graying hair was plaited in the back and rolled around in a bun on my head today. But as my metamorphosis completed, I felt the bun unraveling and my wavy hair flowing down from the top of my head over my shoulders.

My loving gaze rested on each child sitting on the floor around me: William, Wilda Lee, Daisy and Ruby Lee were joined this time by their Clayton cousins Stella, Eva, Mary, and Buddie. I sat in the old rocking chair as usual, took some deep breaths and relaxed into my yesteryears as I always did. But this time, I held up an old newspaper and showed my grandchildren a picture of a house that looked similar to their cow barn.

Grayed wooden slats were nailed to vertical posts at the four corners, with little slits where the boards should have butted up to one another to keep out the cold winter wind. The small structure leaned a little to one side. The roof was shingled. There was a door—maybe five feet tall—in the center of one wall, and a small window on the side wall covered with a white cloth.

Children, I began. This is what a one-room slave cabin looked like on the outside. It may have housed six people. There was room for a bed in the corner that four people might sleep in and two more might sleep on the floor. They stuffed grass, bird feathers, moss or straw inside a bag that served as a blanket on the bed and a pallet on the floor.

A blackened fireplace, lined with red brick made by the slaves was on the opposite wall with a hole in the ceiling that acted like a chimney to let most of the smoke outside. There was a chair or two and a small table on the other wall and maybe a small closet for one pair of work clothes per member. Pots and pans would hang on the wall or from the top of the hearth. Dishes were stacked on the table. Does this look like a house you would like to live in?

Most of the children wrinkled their noses and shook their heads no. Daisy spoke up and admitted, "Well, GramFannie, it does not look all that much different from what we have here, except we have three rooms for the seven of us."

I smiled in approval that Daisy made my point even before I said anything.

Yes, that's right, you smart girl. We, as a people, have not progressed much since slavery days as far as where and how we live. The big difference is that now we are able to send you children to school so you can be smarter than we were with book learning, numbers, and such. During slavery it was against the law to teach a slave to read.

What else do you think is different now than during slavery times? I searched their faces for an answer.

William stood and said, "My daddy owns his own land and he can grow whatever he wants and earn the money from his harvests, instead of being a slave who has to work for someone else, growing what that person thinks is right, and not getting any money for his hard work. Slaves had to work for free and could never do what they wanted." He was scowling by then at the injustice of that unfair system, his hands clenched in anger.

Yes, slaves had to work from sunup to sundown in the fields for the master. Morning meals were prepared and eaten at daybreak in the slaves' cabins. The day's other meals were usually prepared in a central cookhouse by an elderly man or woman no longer capable of working in the field. Sometimes they used peas, beans, turnips, and potatoes, all seasoned up with meats and sometimes a ham bone. All that was cooked in a big iron kettle and when mealtime came the field slaves all gathered around the pot for a-plenty of helpings. This took place at noon, or whenever the field slaves were given a break from work. A water boy or girl gave them water during the day.

A boss called an overseer cracked a whip to get the slaves to work faster. At the day's end, some kind of dinner would be prepared by a wife or mother in individual cabins. Then they went to bed, getting up before sunrise the next day to do the same thing all over again. Slaves generally had to work for Massa Monday through Friday and half a day on Saturday, rain or shine.

"What's an overseer?" Wilda Lee asked, even though she already knew the answer. She wanted me to explain it for the younger kids.

I began, "An overseer is a man who is supposed to make sure slaves follow the master's orders, ensuring they work as hard as they can. They need to harvest as much rice or corn or cotton as possible so the master can make as much money as possible. An overseer sometimes rides on a horse up and down the fields, shouting at people to work harder, using a whip or a stick to beat those who are not working every second of the day. He writes in a little book how much work each slave did every day and reports back to the master who, in turn, can have disobedient or slothful workers disciplined.

"What kind of discipline, GramFannie?" Daisy's eyes were wide open.

Well, for a small mistake, they could get hit with the whip or a stick or the overseer's hand. Or they could be forced to work on a Sunday instead of being able to go to church and be with their family. Or they could be forced to go without food. Or their head and hands could be chained into the stocks if they did something wrong, like stealing food.

But if they did something *really* bad, like try to run away, they could get their foot cut off, so they couldn't run anymore. Or they could be sold to another master—maybe so far away that he would never see his kin again. Or they could be hung from a tree.

I remember hearing about a hard-working, handsome black-skinned man named Clyde who the overseer said had whistled at the master's wife. Now the overseer was just jealous because all the slave women were always talking about how attractive, big and strong Clyde was. He could lift a cut tree trunk by himself, his arm and back muscles rippling like they were alive with the effort. But the overseer was short, pink-faced, and ugly. He wanted to cause trouble, so he lied to the master. Clyde denied ever doing such a thing to any woman, but the master didn't believe him. Guess what happened?

All the kids had a different guess: "He got spanked," said one child. Another, "He had his dinner taken away." A third, "He got tied to a tree and left there overnight." A fourth, "His little finger was cut off."

That last answer was the closest to the truth. He did get something cut off, something very important to a man. William understood instantly, and covered his private parts with his hands. I nodded my head yes, and William shuddered.

William, a few minutes ago, you captured perhaps the most important difference between how our people were treated then and now. Nowadays, your mother and father get to make more of their own decisions instead of having a slave master who makes all the decisions for them and their family.

Sadly, even though a few of us do own our own land, most are sharecroppers, renting land from an employer, often their former slave master, living in the same slave shacks, growing whatever the planter commands, hoping the planter is truthful about the value of the crop harvested, having to buy whatever the family needs from the planter's store, and almost always owing the planter money by the end of the growing season. Most former slaves are essentially living just like the slaves, never getting ahead in life.

Everybody looked at their fingers, not knowing what to say after that sad pronouncement.

"Were you ever a slave, GramFannie?" Ruby Lee, the littlest one, asked, looking at the floor.

Absolutely! When I was about the age you are now. Six, right?

Ruby said, "Seven on my next birthday."

Ok then, you will like the soldier story. I'll tell you that story soon. I finished, stifling a yawn. That's all for now, my dears, I have to take a nap. I closed my eyes, pretending to be in a deep sleep. They all left, whispering.

"Ah, nuts. She always stops right before the good stories," Daisy pouted.

MAMA JULIA

Today, my hair was covered with a bandanna like most slave women wore. After my entrancing metamorphosis and my "Once Upon a Time in Calhoun County, Alabama," opening line was complete, I began an important story about my Mama, Julia, the revered cook of the John Borders plantation. This time, though, I chose to use a heavy southern accent to talk like our folks spoke back in the 1840s to 1860s, before the Civil War began.

Taday, chil'ren, Ima gonna tell ya 'bout ma mutha, July Bordas. She tol' me many stories o' her life workin' in da Bordas' kitchin'. Ya see, she be brought ta da Choccalocca Valley wit da rest o' da Bordas when she's on'y a few years ol', in 'bout 1840. Dis was afta da slaves, Levic an' Griff'n Bordas, built da main plantashun house. I cain't 'member if'n those two carpenters was her brothas or her uncles, but they was close kin ta her. I know dat. Why for I know? Cuz Griff name one o' his daughters after Mama July and I be named after Levic's first wife, Francis. Fannie be a nickname for Francis, doncha know? That's wha' families do…use da same names from gen'ration ta gen'ration.

"Like my name, GramFannie?" William inquired.

'xactly. You not on'y named for yo daddy, Willem Dooley, but also for his daddy brotha, Willem 'Billy' Dooley. And Wilda Lee, she named for…oh, I be forgettin' who right now. Anyway, I named your mother, Julia Nicholson, ta honor my muther, Julia Borders. Maybe y'all chil'ren will carry on that impo'tant naming tradition and bless one o' your daughters wit da name Fannie, after me.

As y'all know, my Mama was da cook for da Bordas family. She live in a lil shack next ta da Big House where da Massa live. Her place was unda some big trees just 'cross da driveway. Beside me, two udder house slaves live der wit us. There was four udder slave quarters 'cross da roadway, wit Levic and Griff and der wives, Ellen'n Florence, sharing a nice two-story house.

Mama, she hab ta wake up real early, before da sun come up. She plaited her'n my hair, an' wrap a head scarf 'round each o' our heads, like dis one." I pointed to my head. "If it rain oba night, we put on boots ta cross da muddy driveway ta da Big House. We be's quiet when enterin' while da Bordas was still 'sleep.

Mama hab ta wake up da hot coals in da nine-foot-wide fireplace in da kitchin'. She hab ta make a roarin' fire that would boil water in da big pot. The Bordas 'spected coffee first thing in da morning, so Mama brewed dat first, while she got ready ta fix da brefix. Den she put da grits on ta cook sof', and got bacon out da larder, and made biscuits, and hab me set da table. We hab ta have everthang ready for they brefix.

Brother William asked, "What else did she cook, GramFannie?"

Well, with da hep o' her sisters'n me, Mama tend da veg'table garden out back o' da kitchin', when she wuddn't cookin' meals for da family. Let's see if'n I kin 'member. She grew white'n sweet taters, beans, black-eye peas, cayenne peppa, winta squash, and, o' course, collard'n mustard greens. Yes, four long rows o' crops, surrounded by a fence ta keep da pigs and udder animals out o' it. They slaughter pigs fo' pork chops'n, ham'n bacon, doncha know.

Dey hab a chickin coop down da hill a little ways near da barn wit a dozen hens layin' everday. Eggs was used for brefix and for making Mama's famous pound cakes. It seem ta me dat I hab ta beat twelve eggs in a big bowl 'til they was light'n fluffy. Den, I beat in da sugar, den flour'n other things 'til I thought my arm would fall off, mixin' dat much batter!

We all laughed, then I continued, but da sweet smell scenting da house as the cakes bakt, and da taste o' da small "test" loaf Mama made fo' us house slaves, was well wurt da trouble.

'Nuther day, I'll tell y'all 'bout our mos' famous relatives." And with that last sentence, I shuddered out of my trance and returned to the present, noticing for the first time the children's stunned faces.

What did you think of that story, I asked in my normal voice.

"It was *fascinating!*" Wilda replied, and the other children began talking all at once.

"How did you wake up before the crack of dawn?" "Did you have a clock?" "What was your favorite thing to cook?" "How many pigs did you have?" "Will you make us some of that pound cake?"

I answered so many questions that day. It made me feel good to know the children were interested in our family's history. *Maybe they'll even pass our stories down to their children, so our legacy will live on forever.*

THE FAMOUS SLAVE BUILDER/ARCHITECTS

Twinkling stars began to pop into focus from the ever-darkening sky. The cicadas made their thrumming, sawing sound, and frogs croaked in the damp areas of the yard. Black as midnight crows were having a spat, and fireflies floated hither and yon before our excited faces. We had just finished Sunday dinner: me, my husband Forrest Clayton, my daughter, Julia, my grandchildren and their other grandparents, Elias and Lavinia Dooley, and the Dooleys' other grandchildren, James Wingate, and Viola Moore.

Chairs were brought outside for the elders with the kids sitting on the grass or the edge of the porch. It was going to be a big audience for tonight's story time and my performance had to be extra special.

Everyone was quiet as I walked toward the rocking chair, mustering as much excitement as I could by moving deliberately. I adjusted myself on the seat cushion, closed my eyes, then inhaled deeply, producing a low "ahhh," as the old air left my lungs through my open mouth. Again I breathed in and out, then slower still out. My hands lay limp in my lap as I relaxed so the metamorphosis could begin.

My forehead was the first to loosen from the stress of the day as I breathed out the stale air. The wrinkles around my eyes disappeared, my hollow cheeks plumped up, pulling the sagging corners of my mouth upward. My lips became full and kissable. My blood-shot eyes cleared and the sienna irises glowed. My face felt young and supple. The thick cords in my neck retreated and the skin smoothed itself down my neck and collarbone.

When I breathed in again, my shoulders and breasts raised as my chest expanded with the inhale. My shoulders relaxed with the exhale but my chest stayed lifted. With each breath, my Gibson Girl hairstyle unraveled a bit, falling over my shoulders and down my now-straight back. My hands and feet lost their spots and calluses.

Good evening, everyone. Tonight's story will be about our most famous relatives, Griffin and Levic Borders, who were related to my mother Julia Borders. I don't rightly remember if they were her uncles, or brothers, or if one of them was her father, but I do know they were beacons of light to our family and to the residents of Calhoun County, Alabama.

Levic and Griffin Borders were brothers, both born in Jackson, Georgia, Griffin in 1815 and Levic in about 1820. I don't know for sure who their parents were, but even though Griffin was a brown-skinned man, some believed Massa Borders was their daddy. I don't have any proof of that, but people wondered why Massa John Borders sent them to be schooled with master craftsmen. The brothers built the Borders house in Jackson, Georgia, and learned lots of dos and don'ts about wood, tools, and construction. They even learned how to make their own nails.

Trained in carpentry, the brothers made a respectable name for themselves, creating furniture and building homes in Calhoun County, while still bound in slavery. The first task Massa John gave them was to build the Borders Plantation house about 1836, using the same basic floor plan as their Jackson house from Georgia, with a few improvements.

Levic, especially, was a master carpenter, constructing sideboards, tables, cabinets and other furnishings which showed his cabinetmaking skills.

Each of their nine fireplace mantels throughout the home has a different design, which illustrates their skills and craftsmanship.

Two of nine existing fireplace mantels at the Borders-Blackmon house, built by Griffin and Levic Borders in the late 1830s. All mantels are different. Photograph: Kathy Marshall, 2019.

The brothers also built five small homes for all the Borders slaves, four structures were across the street from the front yard of the plantation house, and the other was next to the big house for Mama Julia, me, and two house slaves. The brothers built themselves a two-story house and lived in it with their twin wives, Ellen and Frances. Both of them were excellent quilters and seamstresses. Griffin and Milly lived upstairs and Levic and Francis downstairs.

By the way, did you know 'Fannie' is a nickname for 'Francis'? And that my mama named her first-born, Ellen, after somebody else's wife—sorry, I can't remember who right now.

Griffin and Levic were tasked to build the Harmony Baptist Church on Old Choccolocco Road. The buildings were faced in red brick and the tall white spire could be seen from the Borders plantation. The church was dedicated in 1855.

Harmony Baptist Church and Cemetery, Calhoun County, AL.
Photograph: Kathy Marshall, 2019.

Griffin and Levic had saved up enough money from their carpentry work to buy their own, and their wives' freedom. They were well known in Calhoun County for their expert building and carpentry skills. They had built John Borders family home

126

in Jackson, Georgia, and in Calhoun County, Alabama, along with homes for John and Cynthia's children, the Harmony Baptist Church, brick smokehouses for the Borders and Allens, and various and sundry other building projects.

Unlike most slaves, Griffin and Levic received some payments for their brilliant efforts. Unfortunately, on January 25, 1860, the Alabama legislature repealed all laws and portions of laws authorizing the emancipation of slaves before any court in the state. Thus, Griffin and Levic's plans were thwarted and they had to remain slaves.

Just looking inside Griffin's fifty-some-odd tools listed on a bill of sale after the Civil War—planers, smoothers, files, an oil stone—shed light on the tools and techniques, and the methods used by him and other fine craftsmen. Can you believe when he was freed after the Civil War, he was forced to buy back his own tools from the Borders for $62.75? Here this man made all sorts of money for the Borders who farmed him out to build furniture and houses for their cronies, but he had to buy back his own tools? Well, that's just how life is for colored people." All the adults nodded. A truer statement was never told.

Griffin and his wife Milly were living in the town of Oxford, in Calhoun County in 1870. He owned land worth $500 and tools and other property worth $300. A few years later, he got a bank account with the Freedmen's Bureau when he and his wife were visiting friends in Memphis, Tennessee. In 1874, they moved to Cotton Plant, Arkansas, where he farmed his own land, until he died in 1885.

Levic was a carpenter in 1880, living with his wife Emily in Oxford, Alabama. Several people lived with them, including daughters Rene and Anna, son-in-law Jake Anderson, step kids Gus and Jane Freeman, grandsons Borders Freeman and Travis Anderson, and niece Amazonia. Levi made a good life for himself after slavery, continuing to ply his trade, sharing his excellence far and wide.

I wanted to share with you some positive news about our ancestors. We some from capable, hardworking stock. Don't ever forget that." And with those uplifting last words, I became myself again, to the dismay of my family, who expressed their desire for more stories.

John Borders Cunningham (1833-1912), from
My Forebears by Linda Cunningham Ewing.

CHAPTER 12 - JBC

(Noxubee, Mississippi, 1911, GramFannie)

Good mornin', children. On this bright, beautiful day, I am going to reach back into my memory bank so you can learn about several important people in my life. But first, I'm going to need some of that lemonade your mother makes so well. This is going to be a long story, so go on to the bathroom now, or you might miss part of it later on.

Ruby Lee ran to get the juice this time, Wilda Lee swept the porch steps, as was her usual job, Daisy puffed up the pillow on my chair seat, and William helped me into the rocker.

A bunch of Clayton cousins came today to hear this story: Eva, Stella, Mary, and Buddie who visited the outhouse as suggested. Everyone quieted themselves and found a comfortable position, watching for the first sign of my transformation to begin.

I tapped my foot a few times, then began rocking back and forth. In an instant, I blinked my eyes and became the youthful Storyteller. A feathered hat came from out of nowhere and a red cape whisked around my shoulders. My black shoes had delicate pearlescent buttons up the sides, which matched the buttons on my white silk blouse.

OK, children, I am ready to tell one of the most important stories I know, so listen up. The slave master, John Borders, had many children, but perhaps his favorite was daughter, Narcissus Virginia, who was born in 1813 in Jackson, Georgia.

Also living in Jackson in the 1830s, was the Ansel Cunningham family. I heard tell their family originally came from Ireland centuries ago, whereas, the Borders came from what is now called Germany. Do you older children know where those places are?"

"They are somewhere in Europe, but I wouldn't be able to find them on a map," Wilda Lee admitted.

"I know, I know," William shouted, "Ireland is on the same island as England."

Who says you can't get a decent education in our colored school? I responded appreciatively.

Ansel was about sixteen years older than John Borders, and had fought in the Revolutionary War. Do you know what that war was about?

Wilda spoke first. "People who lived in this country were fighting to break away from England's rule so we could become the United States of America. Wasn't that war fought around 1776, GramFannie?"

Indeed, granddaughter. Very good. It was the war which created our country, and Ansel Cunningham fought in it. Anyway, Ansel and John Borders knew about each other because they were both farmers who traveled in the same social circles. One of Ansel's sons was named Ansel Griffin Cunningham, and he was born in Wilkes County, Georgia, which is next to Elbert County, Georgia, where your Dooleys came from. Are you starting to get the picture?

I stared into the eyes of each child to see if they were putting two and two together.

No? You don't see that as being strange, that your Dooley white folks and Cunningham white folks came from darn near the same place in Georgia?" No lightbulbs came on. Ok, let me continue, then.

Ansel Griffin Cunningham met Narcissus Virginia Borders. Maybe they were at the same dance in Jackson or Wilkes. Maybe they met at a picnic. Or *maybe* their fathers thought they would be a good match and suggested they get married." Daisy's face brightened first. *That's my girl!* Guess what, children?

"What?" Most of the children replied automatically, without actually guessing.

My smart girl, Daisy, asked, "Did Ansel Griffin Cunningham and Narcissus Borders get married?"

Good girl! Now it was Daisy's turn to strut a bit, curtsying toward her siblings in triumph.

Ansel Cunningham and Narcissus Borders married in 1830 in Jackson, Georgia, when he was twenty and she was seventeen. A year later, their first child—a daughter named Mary Ann Elizabeth—was born.

Two years after that, a privileged baby named John Borders Cunningham was born, when the fall leaves of October were particularly brilliant in 1833. 'JB'—as he was often called—was a healthy baby who grew into a friendly, broad-faced boy with brown hair, wide, dark brown eyebrows, and smiling eyes. Sometime between 1833 and 1835, the Cunninghams moved from Georgia to…

Children, where do you think the Cunninghams moved? I looked around to see who would win the brass ring this time.

My eyes closed for a second when I heard a little voice ask, "To here?"

Correct! Who said that?

"Me, little Ruby Lee," the tiny girl almost whispered.

Oh my goodness. All of you are *so* clever! Before I could say another word, Ruby flung herself into my lap, then turned her face to mine, and gave me a big kiss on the cheek. Now it was my turn to blush. She stayed in my lap, so I continued the story.

Cotton fields ready to seed, Cliftonville, Noxubee, MS.
Photograph: Kathy Marshall, 2019.

Ansel Griffin's young family—Narcissus Virginia, Mary Ann, and JB—moved to Cliftonville, Mississippi, just on the other side of Macon from us. They had several parcels of land they owned in Noxubee and Lauderdale, Mississippi, mostly planted in cotton. And do you know what that means? I waited for an answer.

"They had more children?" William mumbled, as if unsure of his response.

Well, yes, they eventually had more children, starting with Serena Adaline in 1835, then Victoria, Cynthia, Henry Clay, Samuel Knox, and finally Ansel Griffin Jr. who was born in 1848. But that wasn't the answer I was looking for. I said they had a few cotton plantations and asked what that might mean.

Wilda Lee let out a disgusted sigh. "People, that means they owned slaves to work those cotton fields." She already knew she was right and didn't wait for my congratulations as she pirouetted across the floor.

Excellent, Wilda Lee! Yes, that *should* mean they had lots of slaves to work their plots of cotton. But in 1840, Ansel only had five slaves and twelve white people, all living in Cliftonville. I wondered if maybe they weren't farmers at all, at least not cotton farmers. You see, some of the land in Noxubee was prime pastureland for raising cattle. Maybe that's why the Cunninghams had so few slaves, because they were ranchers, instead of cotton farmers who would have needed lots of slaves. Maybe you children will be able to find out the truth when you grow up. *Only Daisy smiled a bit at that, and that gave me hope that she was interested in our history.*

Anyway, a terrible thing happened in 1848, right after their youngest child was born. Ansel Griffin Cunningham died when he was only thirty-eight years old. He was buried in Deerbrook Cemetery to be with his ancestors. Young JBC was left the responsibility for caring for his widowed mother and his siblings.

"How old was JBC when that happened?" Daisy asked.

Barely sixteen. Imagine having that much responsibility at your age now, Wilda. She looked down and shook her head.

After Massa Ansel died in Noxubee, JBC and his family moved back to Alabama, occupying a plantation built by Griffin and Levic around the bend from Narcissus' parents. By 1850, Narcissus had eleven slaves, from two newborns to a thirty-eight year old female. One of them was a 13-year old "black" girl.

Narcissus' father, John Borders, who lived a hop, skip and a jump down Choccolocco Road, had a 15-year old "mulatto" slave girl living with him. Do you think either of those girls have been my mother Julia? I peered at each child listening to my story, but none answered my question, so I continued talking.

In 1860, Narcissus had sixteen slaves working for her in Calhoun County, Alabama. Her son, JBC, was still living with her.

The kids looked bored. Too many names and dates, I guess. I'd better get to the good stuff to keep their interest.

Listen up now, children. All eyes looked at me. Massa Borders, had thirty-two enslaved human beings working for him in 1850, and thirty-six in 1860, according to the U. S. Census. One of them was listed as a twenty-five-year-old 'black' female—that could have been my Mama Julia. Some of the others on the list of his slaves could have been our relatives. There were no names on those lists, though, just the age and sex of each person owned by the slave master, so we can't be sure. What do you think about that, children?

As might be expected, there was silence. I hoped the children were thinking about what it meant, that our family had been *property*, without having proper first or last names on a document. I needed them to appreciate they were better off nowadays over their enslaved ancestors. I wanted them to continue the struggle for equality in all things. Maybe they'll understand the next time I tell this story.

JBC also had slaves to work his land. In Cliftonville and Brooksville, there were wide, flat fields planted in cotton. Rows and rows, as far as the eye could see, with nary a tree to shade the workers during the hot, summer sun.

My Mama said slaves on the Borders plantation were treated better than most. Massa Borders and JBC allowed their slaves to meet at, and after, church services at the Harmony Baptist Church. That church was built by our famous ancestors, Griffin and Levic Borders, just down the windy Choccolocco Road, not even a mile from the Borders plantation. JBC also had a Harmony Baptist Church built in Noxubee. The Christian religion principles were very important to them, even though they owned slaves.

Most slave owners never allowed their slaves to congregate, for fear they would plot running away to freedom. But our people *were* allowed to meet and talk and sing and trade goods before and after church. That's why I said they were luckier than most.

Now I'm going to tell you a little secret, children. Listen carefully. All the kids sat with rapt attention—finally.

Narcissus Virginia Borders had lots of children. Some of her boys took a *liking* to the enslaved women on their farms. Lo and behold, plenty of bright-skinned children like you"—I pointed to Daisy, then William—"were born in Calhoun County. In fact," pausing for emphasis, "JBC Cunningham was *my* daddy.

The children looked at each other. How would they react? Would they be happy about my revelation? Shocked? Sad? Embarrassed? Angry? Some were too young to know how babies were made so they might be clueless about the import. The older ones looked at their fingernails and yawned.

I continued, not addressing the children's mixed expressions. "The law at the time said whatever the mother was, so were the children. So all of us children born of slave women were slaves, even though our daddies were the white grandsons of the free slave master, John Borders.

Oh…now the children understood what I was talking about. My Daddy was a white man, so that means I am the half-sister of his white children, and you are related to them too. They looked at each other with widened eyes, whispering amongst themselves.

When their chatter died down, I began again. In 1860, right before the Civil War started…Wait a minute. Do you know what the Civil War was about?

William spoke up this time. "The Civil War was between the states that wanted slavery and the states that didn't."

In the simplest sense, yes, that is correct. There were other reasons, though. The southern states came up with some cockamamy story that it wasn't about slavery. They insisted it was all about the rights of states to do what they thought was good for their state. Basically, they wanted to have the right to keep slavery if they felt it was necessary for their plantation lifestyle. Of course, that meant they wanted to keep their *property*—our ancestors—who did most of the work.

In 1861, eleven Southern states—like Mississippi and Alabama and Georgia—broke away from the United States to form their own country called the Confederate States of America. But the bottom line is exactly what William said: Confederates wanted to keep slavery, but the Yankees in the North wanted to free the slaves so they could help win the Civil war and make America whole again." I beamed at my grandson for his to-the-point response. He returned my gaze with a confident smile.

JBC spent four years in the War Between the States, enlisting in June 1861 in Company H, 10th Alabama Regiment. His first battle was at Bull Run under General Kirby-Smith. Then they went to Yorktown and on to Richmond, Virginia, which was the capital of the Confederacy. That's where JBC was wounded in the hip and was released from the army.

In 1862, he went home to Choccolocco to heal his wounds. One Sunday at church, he was introduced to Margaret Malinda "Linda" Gibson who was visiting from Tennessee. Sparks flew, and they were married within three weeks. She remained his beloved companion for thirty years, and she aided him in building up a splendid estate. She wrote a book of biographies about the Cunningham and Borders families which you might want to read someday.

No response. No interest?

I started again. Linda's mother was a Clayton. Wouldn't it be something if she was related to your Claytons?" Once again, no response from my Clayton listeners, or anyone. *I'd better try another story.*

When JBC visited us kids, he enjoyed talking about his adventures during the war, along with the amusing and horrible things that happened to him. One time he was famished, not having any food for two days, when he rode up to the window of a small cottage asking for something the eat. The lady apologized, saying that she only had buttermilk and bread. He ate while sitting on his horse and said it was the best meal he ever had.

My mama told us she was married to JB Cunningham and had five babies with him: Ellen in 1855, me in 1856, Lee in 1868, James in 1870, and Minnie in 1872.

"What did your daddy look like?" Ruby Lee asked.

I remember Daddy JBC having kind, dark brown eyes and silky brown hair. He had a big, soft, white and gray beard that

135

he sometimes let me comb when he visited our house. You see, JBC didn't live with Mama and us kids, because he had an official white wife. Things were complicated back then. A white man could not marry a Negro woman then any more than they can today in 1911. But love is love, and babies are often created when there is love between a man and a woman. Plain and simple.

My brother, James Cunningham, was born in 1870. At that time, Daddy JBC was managing 900 acres of black prairie land in the Prairie Point area of Noxubee. He became the largest cattle rancher and beekeeper in the county. We sometimes got to see him when he traveled back and forth to visit his mother, Narcissus, in Alabama. When JB's first wife died in 1895, he married Mattie Dantzler. There are lots of Dantzlers around these parts. Daddy's still living here in Noxubee, but he's been ailing a bit lately. In fact, I think he went to New Orleans to find a cure for his ailment. Would you like to meet him someday?

"Yes! That would be interesting, now that we know about our connection." Daisy cried.

[Author's Note: John Borders Cunningham died in 1912 in New Orleans, Louisiana, from complications—some say he had a gall bladder infection, others say it was a more "personal" problem. He is buried in Deerbrook Cemetery, Brooksville, Noxubee, Mississippi. See Appendix B for a Timeline of historical and family events and Appendix C for Dooley, Borders, and Cunningham family trees.]

Cemetery in Noxubee, MS

CHAPTER 13 - WAR BETWEEN THE STATES

(Noxubee, Mississippi, 1911, GramFannie)

As The Storyteller, I had laid the groundwork in previous visits, explaining to my grandchildren about the history of the Choccolocco Valley, which was once Indian Country before 1836.

I described how white settler John Borders had his plantation built in the late 1830s by his architect/builder slaves, Griffin and Levic Borders, then brought his family and twenty-six additional slaves to live there. The children learned what it was like to be a slave in Calhoun County, Alabama.

Now, it was showtime. I sat in the rocking chair, cleared my throat signaling for Daisy to bring a glass of sweetened lemon water, then relaxed into the comfy chair. Breathing deeply, the wrinkles and double chin melted from my face as I exhaled. My eyes closed, lips plumped, and hair cascaded down my shoulders as I eased into the trance. The metamorphosis to youthful storyteller was complete, and I began the best tale of all.

In 1861, Alabama was the fourth state to secede from the Union to join the Confederate States of America. At the outbreak of war, the state's economy was weak; during the war it declined further. The full crops planted in 1861 were harvested by those left behind, but the 1862 planting was smaller, partly due to a drought in 1862, which further reduced harvest production.

Alabama was fortunate that it did not suffer through as many battles during the war as other states did. In fact no battle was fought in Alabama until 1863, almost exactly two years after the beginning of the conflict. The war did not come close to Calhoun County, perhaps due to the hilly terrain and lack of major industries, but newspapers chronicled the devastating effects of the fighting throughout the country.

One day in mid-1863, it was all quiet on the home front and the skies were a limpid blue. The quack of ducks in the pond, noisy honk of geese flying overhead, and the ever present buzz of cicadas were heard while slave workers carried out their normal planting duties in the fields. Occasionally, the workers would burst out into an African-style 'call and response' type of work song, like:

I'm gonna jump down, turn around, pick a bale o' cotton
Gonna jump down turn around, pick a bale a day.
Oh Lordy, pick a bale of cotton,
Oh Lordy, pick a bale a day.

These songs helped us endure the drudgery of the work performed day in and day out in the planting fields.

Wilda, William, Daisy, and Ruby Lee, your great-grandmother, Julia Borders, was cooking lunch in the over-heated kitchen in the Borders plantation house, getting a meal ready for Mistress Cynthia's lunch.

"What was she fixing for lunch, GramFannie?" Daisy asked. I assumed she was trying to prolong the end of my story.

I don't rightly remember, Daisy, but I 'spect it was maybe egg or potato salad, ham sandwiches, and sassafras or mint tea.

Mama Julia told me later that she glanced out the window at the landscape all around the plantation. She said she was surprised to see several men in blue uniforms, some marching and some riding horses. They were coming toward the fence which bordered the property.

I stopped talking, reached over to the bucket table next to my chair, and sipped a bit of lemon water. After several minutes enjoying my drink, I started rocking again.

"What happened next, GramFannie?" the children cried, impatiently. I had left them panting for more, as does any good storyteller.

Well, Mama Julia told me later that she figured they must be Yankees from the Union Army, because they didn't wear the same gray colors as the Confederate boys from the South. Mama could not believe her eyes when the lead soldier got off his horse and picked up her pretty young daughter—me.

I had been playing in the yard with our dog, Mellie. I was almost seven years old, too young to work all the time in the fields, or be much help in the kitchen either. Sometimes I play with the dog, or run after butterflies, or pick vegetables from the garden, or play with my doll…

"GramFannie! What happened next?" William whined like a baby.

The children all knew the game. I would build up their excitement, then throttle back to talk about something nobody cared about, until they clamored for me to continue with the meat of the story. Okay, okay, I chuckled.

The soldier lifted me up and placed me on the fence rail. In a kind voice, he said, "Hold the gate open, gal, so me and my men can enter your master's property."

I was taught to do what elders commanded, without question—unlike some people I know. *I looked at Wilda Lee.* So I held the gate open, as instructed. I could see my mother through the window, and I waved at her with my free hand. Later, Mama told me she dropped the bowl of potato salad she was mixing when she saw that strange man touching me. Mama rushed outside to save me from the Yankees. She plucked me off the fence and held me tight to her side.

"Who are ya and whatcha doing with my chile?" Mama asked.

Any fear she might have had about a strange white man vanished when my safety was at stake. As I recall, the lead man in charge, dusty and dirty from his ride, asked Mama to prepare him and his men some food, as they were mighty hungry.

Looking the strange white man in the face, Mama said, "My Massa isn't here right now, suh, and he would be mighty upset if I fed Yankees from his larder."

Slaves were not supposed to look white people in the eyes. But my revered Mama, who was called "Miss Julia" by the other slaves, was not a subservient woman. She wanted this man to know she was not afraid of him, and would not permit him to proceed farther onto the property.

"The Missus would not want you here," Mama continued. "You bes' leave now, suh,"

The soldier didn't move. He said, "Ma'am, we come to bring all you slaves good news. President Lincoln signed the Emancipation Proclamation, so you are now free to leave this place, free to work your own land, free to do whatever you please. Now, are you going to fix us bearers of freedom some food?" he smiled.

After a few seconds, Mama began to wail. It was just like those ladies in church when the Spirit gets 'em, and just like people keenin' during a burial ceremony: long and loud.

"Holy Sweet Jesus!" Mama screamed. "We is free? WE is FREE? WE IS FREE!" she screamed, louder and louder, with each iteration of the magic words.

As you can imagine, slaves from the fields and the house came a-running to see what was happening. Was their Miss Julia being hurt? When they finally assembled around Mama and me, the soldier told them *all* the good news.

Out of the corner of my vision, I could see the Missus standing in the front doorway, listening to the commotion. She must have seen her slaves with the strange white men in blue uniforms. Yankees! Wide-eyed, Missus raised her hand to her open mouth. Did she realize what was going on? I suspected she was worrying about what we *now-free people* might do *to* her, the *former* property owner.

I took another long sip of my lemon water and sat back in my comfortable chair for several moments.

"What did the slaves, uh, *former* slaves do next?" Daisy ached to know. "Did they run into the kitchen and start making food, like the man wanted?"

Wilda asked, "Did the rest of the slaves dance and shout with joy like Great-grandma Julia did?"

William asked, "Did they try to beat up the Missus?"

I turned toward William and said, "Oh no, child, they wouldn't hurt the Missus." I was a bit shocked at my grandson's leap to violence. It must be a boy thing.

We were all in a tizzy and didn't know what to do. Mama got her wits back quick as lightning, though, and told us all to be quiet. The white man walked up the red brick pathway toward the Missus. He spoke with enough volume for everybody to hear.

"Ma'am," he removed his hat and dangled it at his left hip, as he extended his right hand for her to shake.

The Missus didn't make an effort to return his friendly gesture. Hmm, what happened to her Southern hospitality?

"That's wasn't very polite, was it?" asked Ruby Lee.

I shook my head.

"What is the meaning of all this commotion?" Missus asked in her usual sharp voice.

"What are you and your men doing here on *my* property?"

Missus tried to look angry and menacing, but I bet she was scared. I would have been in her shoes.

"Ma'am," the soldier started again, "I bring important news. President Lincoln signed the Emancipation Proclamation, freeing all slaves in states which seceded from the Union. Your slaves are now free..."

Missus' face changed so many times in ten seconds, I didn't know whether she was shocked, scared, or just plain angry.

"Ma'am," the soldier continued, "We was hopin' to get a bite ta eat. We been riding all day with nary a morsel of food, nor drop to drink. We'd 'preciate anything you could give us."

Missus didn't seem to know what to do. Her mouth opened like she was going to say something, then closed just as quickly. She looked at the soldiers, then at all us slaves watching her. She made a quick about face, walked back inside the house, and slammed the door behind her. Maybe she decided to stay inside her room in case trouble began—trouble against her. Her husband was gone, and the pink-faced overseer was nowhere to be seen.

Well, children, my brave Mama took it upon herself to nod to the soldier. Then she turned to me and sister Ellen and said, "Let's go into the kitchen and fix these men some food."

I skipped behind her to help. I wanted to ask what the men were here for, I but knew better than to say anything right then because...

"I know, I know," Daisy inserted, "Children are to be seen and not heard." The kids rolled their eyes at that tired old sentiment, heard *so often* from us adults.

Smiling, I resumed the story.

Thankfully, the huge bowl of potato salad was still sitting where she had dropped it on the table before she ran out to grab me off that fence gate. Mama started humming:

Wade in the water,
Wade in the water children,
Wade in the water,
God's gonna trouble the water.

141

Mama instructed me to get some bread and butter from the larder. She asked Ellen to grab "this many"—holding up both hands with her five fingers spread wide—"long sausages from the storeroom."

Mama said we could serve them sausage sandwiches and tater salad, and the pound cake she made that morning. She told me to fill the large pitcher, take it out to the summer kitchen, then come back and help her make the sandwiches.

"Yes, ma'am," Ellen and I replied. We both scurried to do as Mama asked. We didn't understand what was going on with those men, but felt in our guts that it was a good thing. When the food was prepared, we took it outside and served the bedraggled soldiers first, then all the *former* slaves.

Just Imagine that celebratory meal with the Yankee soldiers and newly freed men, women, and children. Glory be! I can tell you there was a joyful noise inside *my* head once I understood what "emancipation" meant! You never heard such jubilation!

Next story time, I'll tell you what happened right our family became free people of color.

Now That We're Free

Once upon a time in 1863 in Calhoun County, Alabama, our once-enslaved family was now free. The day after the Yankee soldier delivered that momentous information, we free people didn't know what to do with ourselves. The Missus had barricaded herself inside her bedroom and wouldn't, or couldn't, decide what to do with us. In the absence of Massa's leadership, Levic and Griffin Borders took over. They proposed to the field and house slaves that everyone performing their normal duties for now. Things could be sorted out when Massa Borders returned later that day.

Some refused and chose instead to pack their belongings, determined to strike out on their own as free men and women.

"Where were they going to go, GramFannie?" Daisy asked, riveted to every word of this story.

Well, some wanted to reunite with family who had been sold to other masters in the area. Hugging, crying, laughing, joyously slapping hands, a few slaves left the Borders plantation that morning. However, the majority stayed, including Mama

Julia, me, Griffin and Levic and their wives, Orrang, Dave, Dicey, Dennis, Willis, and Wash, among others.

Massa John Borders rode up on his horses the afternoon after freedom was announced. He was surprised to see his former slaves working the fields as usual. He respected the leadership that Levic and Griffin had shown in his absence, and included them in discussions about what would happen next to his former *property*.

Children, you have to understand that the Emancipation Proclamation freed slaves in the *rebel* states in 1863, but not everywhere in the United States. Wintertime was only a few months away when we found that out. Where would we go? What would we eat? How would we take care of our families?" The Civil War fighting was still intense in many areas, and would be for the next two years.

Some freed slaves joined the Union Army to defeat of the Confederacy who demanded to keep slavery the law of the land. Others fled to the northern states, like Ohio or Pennsylvania.

In general, Calhoun County was not affected as much as other places in the Deep South, if at all. But people still had to eat, right? And they still needed a place to live, right?" The children hesitated, looked at one another, then nodded slowly.

The nation was still unprepared to deal with the question of full citizenship for its newly freed population. What would *you* have done if someone suddenly announced that you were free?"

William shouted, "No question. I would have left as soon as the soldier told me I was free. I'd take one of Massa's horses, a bridle and saddle, pack my clothes, grab some food to eat, say goodbye to y'all, and be on my way to join the Union Army. I'd be gone!"

Sassy Wilda said, "I'd walk down the road where my boyfriend was working—because you know I'd have a *fine* man—and I'd convince him to marry me and leave town. I don't know where we'd go, but I'd want to celebrate freedom with him.

Daisy chimed in, "I would learn what Massa would offer me to continue working for him, then I would make my decision."

Little Ruby Lee hugged her mother, "Mommy and GramFannie, I would stay and take care of you both." My daughter, Julia, and I smiled at her sweet sentiment.

After the Civil War, in 1865, the Thirteenth Amendment to the U.S. Constitution freed all U.S. slaves wherever they were. But we Negroes did not know how to be free, and the white folks didn't know how to act with free colored people around them.

So the United States Congress—a group of decision makers from every state—implemented something called 'Reconstruction' from 1866 to 1877. Reconstruction was aimed at reorganizing the Southern states after the Civil War, providing the means for readmitting them into the Union, and defining how whites and blacks could live together in a new, non-slave society. They created an organization called the "Freedmen's Bureau" which created schools for colored children—that was the first time our people could legally be taught to read and write.

The Freedmen's Bureau also created work contracts which required new employers to pay former slaves for work they continued to do. In 1865, ten of Massa Borders former slaves—including Mama Julia, Dave, Dennis, Eva, Dice, Griffin, Levic, Orrang, and Willis, agreed to continue working five-and-a-half days a week, for six months, doing exactly what they did as slaves, and continue living in their slave shacks. John Borders would pay them a whopping $25 in December 1865, after six months of hard labor. Such an improvement, right? I couldn't help but frown.

A "Freedman's Bank" was created to help the newly freed people safely store their money safely. Griffin later opened a bank account and bought a farm in Arkansas.

Glory be! Freed men could now vote. In 1867, twenty-six former slaves surnamed Borders—some our relatives—proudly registered to vote in Calhoun, Barbour, Cleburne, Macon, and Russell Counties in Alabama. Six were from the John Borders plantation: Dennis, Griff, Levic, Wash, Willis, and Wiley.

"By 1880, the Agricultural Schedule indicated that several of the Borders' former slaves were still living in Calhoun County, farming their own land, raising their own animals, and selling their own products. Some stayed near the Borders, but some, like Mama Julia, moved a few miles away to Oxford or Davisville, Alabama.

CHAPTER 14 - THE LAST STORY

(Noxubee, Mississippi, 1912, Daisy)

I was nine or ten years old when GramFannie last visited us. There was something different about her that time. Yes, it was a hot day. Maybe that's why she acted like she was a bit confused. Maybe she needed more water, or sleep. Maybe she wasn't feeling well. Her eyes were milky in appearance. She just didn't seem *right*.

Everyone—Dooleys, Nicholsons, and Claytons—was invited over for dinner to celebrate GramFannie's and Grandpa Forrest's visit. Our esteemed grandparents had come on the train from their home in Memphis, Tennessee. It had been many months since their last visit and we would soon find out a lot had happened in the meantime.

We ate dinner outside on that balmy summer night. GramFannie was sitting in the porch rocker, as usual. The other adults sat in chairs taken from the kitchen, with beverages in their hands and plates of food on their laps. We kids sat at the edge of the porch, swinging our legs, or sitting on large blankets spread over the uneven sod in our front yard.

The blue-black night was ripe with stars and the butterscotch-colored moon was full, winking at us from *way* over there. We pointed at the Big Dipper in the distance.

Our beloved grandmother seemed to have forgotten us and the usual storytelling ritual. We waited for her to ask for something sweet to drink, as she often did, but she was silent as a corpse. I ran to get her a glass of sweet tea anyway. Maybe that would help. No, she continued to sit still, seemingly oblivious to what was going on around her. A zombie.

GramFannie, rock the chair to generate the magic, I suggested.

"What? Oh…yes. I'm sorry. I, uh, forgot," she said in a weak voice.

"I'll help." Ruby Lee started rocking the chair for her, slowly, back and forth. Back and forth.

GramFannie's cloudy eyes glazed over more. We wondered if she was going into the trance. We could feel a lackluster charge of electricity extend from around her body. But her hair didn't change from gray to brown, her sallow skin didn't smooth or become vibrant, and her voice remained wispy and quiet. She was still an old woman, sitting in the magic chair. We watched, concerned. Could she remember even one story?

"Julia, honey, help me, would you?" GramFannie mumbled.

"Mother, you were going to tell the children about how our family came from Alabama to live here in Nox'bee," my mama prompted, as she sat in a straight-back chair next to her fifty-five-year-old Storyteller mother."

Something strange—alarming—must have happened to our grandmother since we last saw her, but we didn't know what it was. I had heard mother and Aunt Eva whispering the other day…"Yes, she's slipping…" "Forrest not sure what to do…" "Doctors suggest moving her to a home…" "Maybe her last visit…" "It's incurable…"

Were they talking about our beloved GramFannie? I didn't tell anyone what I heard, for fear voicing it would make it come true. I held my breath, hoping for a miracle.

Back and forth, again and again, Ruby Lee rocked the still silent Storyteller in the well-worn chair. We were all quiet, praying she would find her way back to the Land of Story Time.

Finally, GramFannie began, the words coming slowly at first. "Once upon a time in the Choccolocco Valley, in what used to be Indian Country…" her aging voice murmured, becoming louder and stronger with every word.

We kids sighed with satisfaction, our tense bodies relaxing into the familiar words of the narrative. At that moment, though, we had no idea it would be her last.

GramFannie was now The Storyteller again, finally. She said, "A young slave girl named Julia Borders was born in Jackson, Georgia, in 1835, or thereabouts. A couple of years earlier, a young white boy named John Borders Cunningham—called JBC for short—was born in the same place. He was the slave master's grandson. Julia and JBC were playmates, both being too young to do anything useful around the plantation. Not that the slave owner's grandson would ever have to do anything on the farm.

"In 1840, five-year-old Julia and her parents, joined twenty-five-some odd slaves, owned by John Borders, and started a twenty-day walk about 150 miles west, to the Choccolocco Valley in east Alabama. Massa John Borders and his family rode to their new home in a week, in a horse-drawn carriage. JBC and his parents, Narcissus and Ansel Cunningham, went with their slaves, traveling an additional 200 miles or so farther west to Cliftonville, in Noxubee County, Mississippi.

"After JBC's father died in 1848, JBC and his mother, and some of their slaves, moved back to the Choccolocco Valley, near Massa Borders' house. Julia and JBC, now teenagers, renewed their friendship. But time had changed their bodies. Julia's titties had popped out, as did other things on JBC. They took a liking to each other, much more than friends this time. It was illegal for them to marry, but love is love, so eventually they had five children together: Ellen in 1855, me in 1856, sister Lee in 1868, James in 1870, and Minnie in 1872. There were five of us mixed-race children with the last name of Cunningham. I was about 14, sometimes living with my Uncle Wash Borders in Oxford in 1870.

"After fighting in the Civil War on the Confederate side, JBC spent a few years in Nox'bee, but moved back to Calhoun County for a spell to help care for his ailing grandfather. Once Massa Borders died in 1873, JBC moved back to Nox'bee to take care of his cattle ranch and beekeeping farm in Prairie Point. I went with him as a servant.

"Oh GramFannie, that's how you came to be here in Noxubee? I wondered how that happened," Wilda confided.

GramFannie resumed. "My first Sunday in Prairie Point, I attended Mt. Zion Church, and that changed my life forever."

"What happened at Mt. Zion?" I asked.

"Well Daisy, that's when I met Charles Nicholson at the church. He was tall, slim, and attractive in my eyes. When he looked at me with his pools of brown, I got the shivers, thinking he could see right through to my soul. We were seventeen years old and at the peak of our teenage bodies," GramFannie smiled.

The women and teenage girls listening to the story sighed deeply. I was only nine or ten and didn't understand why they were acting that way.

GramFannie crooned, "Ah, Charles and I fell head over heels in love. One thing led to another and in 1874, our first child, Albert Nicholson, was born. Four years later, my darling

147

daughter, Julia here, came along." GramFannie smiled at my mother, Julia, who was sitting next to her.

Looking at me, Wilda, William, and Ruby Lee, GramFannie said, "I named *your* mother, Julia Nicholson, after *my* beloved mother, Julia Borders." A tear rolled down both GramFannie's and Mama's faces.

Hmm, I wondered what they were crying about.

GramFannie continued, "Even before my second baby was born, Charles and I began having disagreements. I thought he should be working harder for us, but he preferred to play poker instead. Soon, like many men, he got into the devil liquor and started staying out all night. He claimed my 'rich' family had spoiled me and that's why I was always fussing at him. Without getting into the heartbreaking details right now, I'll just say that Charles found someone else to love, then left us high and dry." She sighed and remained quiet for a moment.

Even though I wanted to know whether GramFannie and Grandpa Charles had officially married, we children knew better than to ask adults personal questions like that. She would tell us if she wanted us to know. So I stayed quiet and listened.

GramFannie cleared her throat, "If I may humbly say," using her hands to gracefully encircle her face, "I was in my mid-twenties and still looking pretty good for a woman with two kids..."

Then, she just stopped talking. All eyes turned toward our beloved Storyteller. Nothing. She was immobile, not blinking or acknowledging any of us, like a timepiece that needed rewinding. It scared us to death watching her blank look. What did it mean? What was wrong with our GramFannie?

My mother, Julia Nicholson, stepped up and in a bright voice, said, "In 1880, your GramFannie, my brother Albert, and I lived a few houses away from the Claytons, in Prairie Point. That's where the land was almost black, it was so fertile. Green grasses with tiny yellow flowers grew in profusion making the prairie the perfect place for grazing cattle. My granddaddy, JBC, was the largest cattleman in the area and he also had the largest beekeeping business in Noxubee County.

My mother continued, "The Hannah Clayton family lived a few doors down from us, and your father's mother, Emily Gavin, and his father, Wilson Nicholson, lived a few houses away, on the other side of us. So even though my natural daddy, Charles Nicholson, left us, my brother Albert and I were close to our paternal Nicholson and Gavin relatives." Sitting quietly in chairs on the lawn, Grandma and Grandpa Nicholson smiled.

My mother continued, "By 1880, Caroline Clayton lived close by with her five sons and her daughter Eliza. I saw them at church and school. A few years later, in about 1883, I guess, the oldest Clayton son, Forrest"—I pointed at him, sitting at GramFannie's left—"started walking us home after church. He was younger than her, but she was attractive, and he took a liking to her, more than just a friend."

Mama glanced at her step-dad, Forrest Clayton, who was sitting beside his wife, our GramFannie. He held her stiff hand in his, tears glinting on his face in the moonlight.

Mama turned toward us kids, and continued talking. "Your GramFannie started inviting Forrest to stay for Sunday supper. He came around more often during the week, sometimes bringing her flowers, and sometimes a piece of cloth for her to use in a quilt. They got along like two peas in a pod, and he was kind to all of us. Albert and I started calling him Daddy when he married your GramFannie in about 1885, when I was seven. We had the bigger house, so Daddy Forrest moved in with us.

"Kids, my brother, Albert, and I were thrilled when your Aunt Stella was born in 1887, followed by Eva, Mary, then Elbert, who we all called Buddie. We were a close-knit family and got along well, then and now.

"That's true," Aunt Eva affirmed, smiling at my mother.

"But it was hard to find decent work in Nox'bee, so Forrest left us in Mississippi in 1896, and started driving a delivery truck for the Galloway Coal Company in Memphis, Tennessee. He worked there, coming home on holidays, until 1900, when he got a job as a live-in servant in the Harbest household. GramFannie moved to a boarding house in Memphis last year, so she could be closer to her husband."

Stella Clayton (lower right) and other Claytons, circa 1970.

Mama tried her best to keep us entertained. But the more she spoke, the more we could see our Storyteller GramFannie receding from the chair, from the porch, from us, from life. When Mama finished talking, GramFannie seemed to be an empty shell of herself. Our eyes sore from crying, we all got up to hug our treasured grandmother like there was no tomorrow, because there wasn't...

The next morning after they left for the train station, Mama confirmed that our grandmother was very sick. She would be moved to the Home of the Incurables in Memphis, and probably would not be able to return. She passed away in January 1915 from cancer in her leg, and she suffered from blindness too.

Crushed beyond words, we were crestfallen. No more stories from our precious treasure? We would always remember GramFannie as the best storyteller in the world and vowed to pass her family histories down to our future children. We would begin each story with, "Once upon a time, in the Choccolocco Valley, in Calhoun County, Alabama, in what used to be Indian Country..."

[Author's note: There is quite a bit of speculation as to whether Fannie Cunningham—GramFannie--lived in Noxubee, MS, in 1870, or in Calhoun or Talladega County, Alabama. There is also uncertainty about whether Fannie died in Memphis, Tennessee, in 1915, in the Home of the Incurables. A Death Certificate for "Fannie Clayton" said she was born in 1845, instead of 1856 as other records indicated. It also described her as a white woman (it "is" possible she looked like a white woman; just look at her white-haired sister, Stella, on the previous page).

A man named Forrest Clayton (Fannie's second husband) was a driver by 1896, in Memphis, then a servant in the Harbest household by 1900. His presence in Memphis can be tracked there until his death in 1931. Forrest Clayton was sometimes living at the same address as a woman named Fannie Clayton, as indicated in Memphis City Directory entries from 1909 to 1915. There was also a 1904 deed involving a Mrs. Julia Borders (Fannie Cunningham's mother?) and Mr. and Mrs. Rose, in Shelby County, TN, who may have been connected to the Harbest family where Forrest worked.

Further investigation is warranted to determine whether Forrest and Julia are definitely Fannie Cunningham Nicholson Clayton's kin. These speculations will be revisited in a Second Edition book.]

African Americans migrating to St. Louis, Missouri, in the 1920s.

PART III - THE PROMISED LAND

Chouteau Street, near where William Dooley lived in 1917, St. Louis, MO

Typical street corner in St. Louis, MO, 1917.

CHAPTER 15 - MIDWEST BOUND

(Noxubee, Mississippi, 1916, Daisy)

It's time to experience the American Dream," my father pronounced after breakfast one March morning in 1916. "This is the last time they're going to charge me for a poll tax just to vote, and the last time the cropper merchant will hoodwink me when I buy supplies, and the last time I have to step aside when a white person walks toward me on the sidewalk, and the last time I have to say 'Yessum' or 'Yessuh' when I could perfectly well say 'Yes, sir.' I need to get out of this Godforsaken area and make some real money for this family. Some train workers I know say there's plenty of work for us colored men in St. Louis, Missouri, and that's where I aim to go."

"But Daddy, why do we have to move? And where is St. Louis anyway? I don't want to leave my cousins," I whined, forgetting for a moment that children are to be seen and not heard. A quick slap upside my head reminded me quick enough.

"Daisy, didn't nobody ask your opinion on grown folks' business. You might be fourteen, but don't be acting like you think you have a say in this household," Daddy replied, with not an ounce of pity.

"*I* am moving to St. Louis in a few days. You all will stay here. Your grandparents will watch out for you. I'll rent out my land to Mr. Walker and he'll give some of his earnings to your mother. I'll be sending money back here to take care of you, so don't worry."

"Daddy, we're gonna miss you *so* much! What will we do without you here leading us?" Willie Lee pouted. She later told me she was secretly glad he would be gone, so she could see her seventeen-year-old boyfriend without Daddy's constant reproach.

"Don't worry, children, I'll be able to come home every so often. And you might be able to visit me during the summers using the train service to St. Louis. You kids will continue to go to school here and learn how to read, write, and do your numbers, along with helping your mother."

Wagging his finger at me and my brother and sisters, he added, "That is the most important thing you children can do to give yourself a better chance at a good life. Nobody's going to get rich being a farmer or dairyman here in Noxubee. After all, we never got our forty acres and a mule, right?"

Everybody shook their heads in agreement, looking at each other quizzically not knowing what he meant. Daddy was excited and we didn't want to change his mood before he left by asking questions.

My daddy, William Dooley, pushed himself away from the table, stood his five-feet nine-inch frame, and stretched his muscular arms to the sky, having said his peace. I wondered whether Daddy had been thinking about escaping Noxubee for a long time. He said St. Louis was where Negroes could find work that paid double what he earned here. He said they could own a profitable business. In St. Louis, he would be treated like a human being with all the rights Americans are supposed to be accorded. Daddy often talked like that, especially after he'd been drinking some of that moonshine Mr. Walker made behind his barn.

I also knew there was some kind of trouble between Grandpa Elias, his son Henry, and some other folks regarding land. I overheard them saying Grandpa had posted a warning in the *Macon Beacon* indicating, "Trespassers would be shot." What was going on? Were white folks trying to get Grandpa's land or was someone taking his cattle? Was daddy involved in the trouble? Is that *really* why he's leaving us?

"Stop day dreaming Daisy! You had better get this table cleaned up so you can get started on your chores. Do you hear me?" Daddy commanded, but with a hint of a smile. Perhaps he was going to miss his bugaboos...at least a little bit, I hoped.

We answered in our sweetest voices, "Yes, Daddy," in unison, knowing not to press him for any details about this new development, or to question what the "forty acres" meant. We could ask Mama while washing the breakfast dishes.

"Children, there was no forty acres and a mule," Mama explained in a tired voice. "Not when the Civil War was won, not when the Thirteenth Amendment abolished slavery in 1865, and not when Reconstruction attempted to piece together our broken country after the Civil War."

"But what does that mean, though, 'forty acres and a mule'?" Willie Lee asked, as she scrubbed out the bowls which held the remnants of grits, now sticking for dear life to the insides of the bowl.

"My understanding, which may not be wholly correct, was that some believed newly freed Negroes had a *right* to have their own land—particularly land from those confederate plantations taken by U. S. troops during the Civil War, like here in Mississippi. The forty acres and a mule was supposed to be a reward of sorts for hundreds of years of our unpaid labor during slavery times.

"After slavery was over, twelve years of a period called 'Reconstruction' started. An organization called the Freedmen's Bureau helped former slaves get on their feet, money wise. The Bureau helped them find their loved ones who had been sold during slavery. They also started schools to teach former slaves to read and write, to help us coloreds become true, equal Americans.

"That's why we colored parents want so badly for your generation to get a good education. Most of us still can't read or write well, because it was illegal to teach that to slaves. Did you know that?" We kids nodded, having been told that story a million times already.

Mama continued, "So the white man could lie to us about how much money our crops were worth. He could keep working us like dogs, as he did during slavery times, saying we owed him more and more money. We could never get ahead from sharecropping, but many of us felt there was no other choice. Most of us had to stay here and do the farm labor that generations of our families have always known."

"But Mama, you and Daddy can read and write good," said Ruby Lee.

"Well," Mama corrected, "We can read and write 'well,' Ruby Lee. But your point is true. Some, like us, are fortunate enough to be able to read and write a bit, own our land, and be farmers working for ourselves. Most aren't as lucky as us. Although, the droughts of 1902 and 1914 dried up the crops and we couldn't pay for the feed for our animals, or the seed for next year's crop. Most of us can't even pay the annual poll taxes that

Negroes have to pay in order to vote, or to feed, and clothe our families.

"Some of us, like your Daddy, are tired of the disrespect here, and the backbreaking work just to survive in Mississippi. Many of our neighbors and church members have been talking about pulling up stakes and moving to the big cities. We hear there's well-paying jobs for whites *and* Negroes in St. Louis, Chicago, Detroit, and Cleveland. I'm sure your teacher must have mentioned 'the Great Migration' being a mass movement of former slaves and freed men and women to the northern and western United States. This is precisely the movement your father has decided to join. He wants us to move up the ladder of success. So we have to do our jobs here to help that plan work, to better all of our lives," Mama finished explaining.

When it was time for Daddy to leave, we all gathered around him and listened as he told us to mind Mama and learn all that we could in school. He didn't give us the usual lecture, as he needed to hurry and catch the next train. He hugged us all, grabbed his bag of clothes, and trudged out to start a new life, far away from his family.

WORKING IN EAST ST. LOUIS

In Daddy's first letter home, he wrote that he had found work within a few days after arriving in St. Louis. Several of our neighbors, who had already left for the big city, helped him find a temporary place to live and showed him the ropes of how to get around the city. Here's what he wrote:

Dear family,

How are you? I am happy to tell you I already found a job here. I am working for a man named William Cooper in a freight house in East St. Louis.

A freight house is a long building owned and operated by the railroad. Our freight house has a long door that slides open next to the train tracks and more sliding doors on the opposite side of the building. That makes it easy for us to unload items from the trains into trucks and wagons, which take the items to businesses in East St. Louis, in Illinois, and across the river to St. Louis, Missouri. We move farm equipment, tools, boxes of food, bales of hay, you name it, we move it from the train to wagons outside. It is always busy here.

It is hard labor lifting boxes and large barrels all day long, but I make $2 here for every $1 I made back home. I should be able to save up a lot of money so I can send for you all to move out here in the near future.

Oh, and I found a place to live. You can write to me at 3707 Chouteau Road, in St. Louis, Missouri. That's a French word that is pronounced 'Shoo-toe'. I'll tell you more about this place in the next letter.

Be good children. Write to me.

Love, Daddy

Well, children, it sounds like your father is doing well. I'm glad he found work so quickly," Mama said, looking away so we wouldn't see the tears forming in her eyes. After a moment, she turned back around, cheeks wet, and said, "I want each of you to write him something on this letter that I started. I don't want your dad to think we forgot about him already."

Each of us took turns writing a few sentences to Daddy, starting with the oldest and finishing with the youngest. Willie Lee told him about the "A" she got on her last history test. William talked about being the high scorer at his last stick ball game. I mentioned how Maisy squirted me in the face the last time I milked her. Ruby Lee said she found a dead bug in her bed that scared her. Mama wrote something private that she didn't let us read. We all told Daddy we missed him.

Life went on for us as usual, getting our chores done, going to school, and playing with the neighbor kids when we had free time. We often visited Grandpa Elias and Grandma Lavinia and our cousins, Viola and Fannie, who lived with them. A few days later we got another letter from Daddy with a picture of the Eads Bridge that connects St. Louis, Missouri, and East St. Louis, Illinois.

EADS Bridge, circa 1917, St. Louis, MO.

Dear family,

How are you? I am doing fine. Sinn Williams and me are sharing a room in a boarding house with other fellows who came from Mississippi, Alabama and Georgia. All of us think we can do better for our families because there is so much work here.

We live next to a train hub where lots of trains pass day and night. It was built on top of what used to be Chouteau Lake many years ago. The water in the lake used to be filled with clear, cold water with lots of fish and a flour mill. That's before people started dumping all sorts of junk in it, including dead animals, garbage, and other things that made it an open sewer. Then the water turned bad and smelly, and was full of flies and mosquitoes. Many people got sick with cholera and died here. White people moved away to better parts of the city, leaving us Negroes to live on the south side of the train tracks. It is smoky and noisy all around us, but we are happy to be working and getting paid.

Chouteau is a major road here that flows about six miles to the wide, brown Mississippi River. People and cars and buses and street cars cross the Eads Bridge that goes over the river into East St. Louis. That's where I work. It takes me about an hour and a half to walk to work in the morning, but I'm so tired at the end of the day that it might take me two hours, or more, to get home. Sometimes I use the streetcars to get from my house to work. Negroes can sit wherever they want in the cars, not like in the South where they are forced to sit in the back of the car, where the smoky fumes are greatest.

I am finding out that East St. Louis is an important industrial area. Railroads slice through neighborhoods, like the Mobile & Ohio, Illinois Central, Louisville & Nashville, Chicago, Burlington & Quincy, and Great Northern. There are large train yards and acres of repair shops and freight houses. Some say this makes the city a national railroad hub, only second to Chicago.

There are meatpacking and food processing plants, iron and steel foundries, and glass factories all around here. That's why so many Negroes are coming here for lots of jobs.

Well that is all for now family. I hope you are all doing your chores and not giving your Mama any problems. Remember, I am not so far away that I can't come home and take a switch to your backsides, if you don't behave.

Love, Daddy

We got a letter from Daddy a few days later, telling us more about his work, how sore his muscles were, and how the first few nights he went to sleep early. Two weeks passed before we received another letter. He wanted to know what we were doing to make Mama's life easier, so we each wrote back a few sentences assuring him we were working hard and being good. I'm sure Mama might have added a few more descriptive words on the status of his family. All in all, life went on. We could always run to Grandpa Elias and our Nicholson grandparents if something was needed. Mama and bossy Wilda Lee pretty much kept the household running smoothly.

A few more weeks passed before we heard from Daddy.

Hello all,

I am sorry it's been a while since I have written, but I have been so busy here. This place is promising a better way of life, especially

161

for those of us who escaped the violence of the Deep South. We are changing from people who only knew how to work the land, to becoming an industrial working class.

Colored people here are opening all kinds of businesses like barbershops, clothing stores, shoe stores, and grocery stores. And can you believe that there are Negro doctors and dentists and lawyers and people who sell houses? There are Negro bankers and insurance salesmen and newspaper reporters. Just about anything the white folks do back at home in Noxubee, Negroes do here. It's wonderful.

And there are trade unions and political parties made up of colored people. Folks here are trying to gain political support to eliminate those horrible Jim Crow laws in the South.

I'm putting my money together so you all can come out this way. Are you helping your Grandpa around the farm?

William Jr. I am mighty proud of your marks in math. You should see how much money accountants make here!

I'll write soon. Write me too, you hear?

Love, Daddy

Dear family,
All had been going pretty well for me until the other day when a piece of metal flew off a pallet I was loading. It got stuck in my left eye. I was rushed to the railroad doctor, and he was able to remove it. Unfortunately, he wasn't able to save my eye. Maybe in the future I'll be able to get a fake eye to fit into my eye socket, so I don't scare people away. Until then, I'll wear a patch over my eye. I do feel OK, but I look like a pirate. Don't worry about me. I will be fine. Most importantly, I can still work, and my employer will keep me on if I don't complain.

Love, Daddy

Dear family,
I hope this letter finds you well. I am excited! The world isn't standing still, you know. We Negroes are ready to become power brokers in city politics. I've joined a labor union that is fighting to get Negroes the same pay as whites. And there are political clubs that oppose segregation and violence against our people.

Thousands of black Southerners are migrating to northern cities. We are taking advantage of manufacturers' need to supply Great Britain and France in the war against Germany. We have been filling job openings that have been created because the war has sent many immigrant laborers back to their homelands.

Some of us have applied to job advertisements placed in Mississippi newspapers. We tell our friends and family about the available jobs at the Suburban Railroad Company. Others were able to secure jobs at American Steel Foundries.

Many of us, like me, are sending money home to our wives and families, who will later follow us here. Glass factories, railroads, meatpackers, packinghouses, and many other businesses are encouraging black laborers to migrate north. It is an exciting time to be here. Looking forward to seeing you all soon.

That's all for now.

Love, Daddy

Dear family,
You might have heard about the East St. Louis riots in late May and July 1917. They were caused by labor- and race-related violence by whites. They thought Negroes were taking over their jobs. White people caused the death of hundreds of black people, as well as property damage. Thousands of Negroes have been left homeless in East St. Louis and other northern cities. Some people in the Chamber of Commerce even called for the police chief to resign because the police force did nothing to stop the brutality and destruction against Negroes. At the end of July, some 10,000 people marched in silent protest in New York City to condemn the riots. Some colored folks left the city because of the violence. But that didn't stop me from signing up with the military in September 1917, after the race riots.

I felt I should join the forces that wanted to fight for freedom. Maybe if Europe becomes free, we Negroes who fight in the war will be treated fairly and equally too. So far, I haven't been called to war and am still working in the railyards and freight yards. Don't worry about me. I am fine. I've almost saved enough money to have you all come here to live. Until I see you, be good to your mother, and do what she says.

Love, Daddy

William Dooley's Registration Card, 1917.

It's Time To Go

Dear family,

You must have heard by now about the new riots in what is being called the "Red Summer of 1919." When Negroes came back from World War I, they expected to be treated with thanks for their service. They expected to come back to their old jobs on the railroad and in the factories. Unfortunately, the returning white soldiers wanted those jobs.

This time, Negroes would not back down. They had learned how to use guns overseas and had no fear about fighting for their rights here in America. But the whites revolted due to competition for jobs and housing among white and colored people.

I was not involved in the riots and I am OK. Do not worry. Things are getting back to normal. I am still working.

It pained me not to be able to get off work for Daddy's funeral before Thanksgiving. He had been such a comfort to you all, and to me, while I've been gone.

Now it's time for you all to come to the Promised Land in St. Louis. I'm sending money for your train tickets. Take the 2/4 train at 2:30 and I'll meet you at Union Station in St. Louis, on December 1, 1919. I look forward to spending the holidays with you in our new home at Windsor Place. You will love this place.

Love, Daddy

165

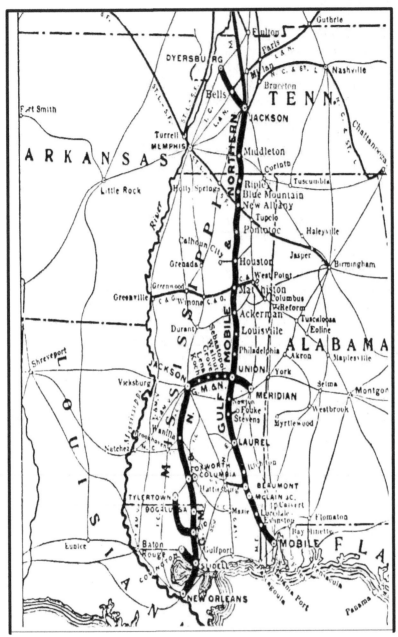

Train routes from the Gulf Coast of Louisiana, Mississippi, and Alabama, north to Tennessee.

CHAPTER 16 - REUNION AMID TURMOIL

(Noxubee, Mississippi, about December 1919, Daisy)

MOVING TO ST. LOUIS

I have good news, children. I received a note from your father. He sent money for us to come to St. Louis...today. The train leaves the Macon station at 2:30 sharp. You need to pack up your things this morning. Don't dawdle, or your few prized possessions may be left behind. I'll give you each one flour sack, so make sure you fold your clothes to fit in as much as possible. Now get moving!"

The noise in the household was intense. All kinds of questions went into the air but dropped to the floor, unanswered: "What?" "We're moving when?" "Can't we say goodbye to our cousins and friends?" "What about cousin Doll's birthday party tomorrow?" "What about school graduation?" "How will we get there?" "Where will we live?" "Is it colder in St. Louis than here?" "Can't I take a few moments to say goodbye to my boyfriend?" "When do we leave?" So many questions, but no answers from Mama who would simply point to the clock on the wall, signaling we needed to hurry and pack.

Just like that, a few hours later our bags in hand, on a bitter cold afternoon on December 1, 1919, we jumped into the fifth from the last car on the northbound Streamline train on the Mobile and Ohio Railroad. After stowing our bags under the seats and in the racks above, we fought over who would sit next to the windows. The eldest kids, William and Wilda, won. I sat next to William. Ruby Lee sat next to Wilda, with Mama in the aisle seat. I was seventeen years old, taking my first train trip out of Noxubee.

"All aboard!" The ticket master called out, slamming the heavy door shut. Then a *chug, chugga chug* could be heard as the steam engine huffed and puffed, getting up enough energy to propel the train forward. Our necks craned to see out the windows, as our familiar homeland passed before our wide eyes:

Macon, Crawford, Artesia, West Point, Corinth, Jackson, Cairo, then Rives.

After a while, our lips were silent as we began to understand the gravity of our undertaking. This would not be a quick visit. We might never see Mississippi again. What started out as excitement turned to reflection and maybe a little fear. We crossed the border from Mississippi into Missouri at Union City, heading out of the former land of bondage for the Promised Land. We were sad to be leaving Noxubee without having the time to say a proper goodbye to our friends and family, but we were unimaginably excited to see the town Daddy had been writing to us about for a few years.

We passed Columbus, north of Macon, crossing over the majestic Mississippi River under our train tracks, then on to Cairo, Sparta, and Millstadt, in Illinois. The train ride was often bumpy, to be sure, making it difficult to use the bathroom on board. But even that couldn't lessen our excitement. Seeing so many towns, different types of land formations, cattle, and houses, was eye-opening. Each train station we stopped at along the way was unique. People exited and entered the train at what must have been fifty station stops along the way north to St. Louis, Missouri.

Being kids, we had to run up and down the train cars to the caboose at the end of the train, at least until someone complained, then we had to stay put in our seats with Mama. We had sack lunches of fried chicken, biscuits, and peaches that Mama had put together while we were packing our suitcases that morning. Drinking water was available near the bathroom car.

Our eyes could not be peeled away from the windows. Our first view of St. Louis was not to be believed. The tallest buildings we had ever seen looked like they touched the sky. The train stopped at Union Station, a massive building that looked like the castles GramFannie had described to us.

The Grand Hall in the station was breathtaking: a huge arched ceiling with incredible arched, stained-glass windows. And thousands of people with suitcases and hat boxes milling about, buying tickets, looking at the huge "arrivals and departures" board, getting a bite to eat or drink at the bar. Not wanting to get lost, we kids stayed by Mama's side. So many people. It was a little scary.

Behind us came a familiar voice. "Welcome to your new home, children." It was Daddy come to pick us up. What a joyful reunion! Hugs, kisses, and tears aplenty. We took the streetcar from Union Station to our new home at 3868 Windsor Place.

We couldn't believe we would be living in such a large house on such a gorgeous street. This was *nothing* like where most Negroes could live in Noxubee, even those who were supervisors for the dairy industry, living in Macon. Daddy must have been doing *really* well in St. Louis. Our new home had indoor bathrooms, three bedrooms, a sitting room, and a kitchen with indoor plumbing, and a stove, and an icebox. Wondrous!

Our second day in St. Louis, was memorable. Daddy showed us how to use the streetcars and buses. He took us to the shopping areas in the extensive colored neighborhoods of St. Louis and East St. Louis amongst so many tall apartment buildings. The National Negro Business League supported numerous black-owned insurance companies which served bankers, publishers, lawyers, funeral directors, retailers, and insurance agents. So many movie theaters, clubs, and churches. The culture shock was hard to describe. It was marvelous. We were living in the Promised Land. Our futures were bright in

The Windsor Place neighborhood where the Dooley family lived in 1920, St. Louis, MO. Photograph: Google Earth, 2019.

169

ALL WAS NOT A BED OF ROSES

We loved this new place, but Daddy had not adequately described the extent of the racial tensions in St. Louis. We soon learned the truth from our new neighbors.

You see, in 1917, the United States had an active economy boosted by World War I. Many white workers were drafted or enlisted in active military service, creating a shortage of labor for industrial employers in major cities like Detroit, Gary, Pittsburgh, Cleveland, Akron, East St. Louis, and Buffalo. Those places became popular destination points for Negroes who wanted to fill local labor shortages in 1916 and 1917, since European immigration had almost stopped during that time due to the war.

Daddy said the major industries in East St. Louis included Aluminum Ore Co., American Steel Foundry, Republic Iron & Steel, Obear Nester Glass and Elliot Frog & Switch. Nearby National City had stockyards and meat packing plants, attracting more workers. East St. Louis was a rough industrial city, where saloons outnumbered schools and churches. Negroes like us began the "Great Migration" from the rural South to seek better work and education, as well as to escape from lynchings and Jim Crow conditions.

As World War I was winding down, Daddy explained that Negroes were arriving in St. Louis and East St. Louis at such a tremendous rate their population had increased to 10,000, or one-sixth of East St. Louis' population of 60,000. There weren't enough jobs for immigrants, whites coming back from the war, and Negroes. Tensions flared to the point of riots.

When it all came down to it, St. Louis wasn't much better than the Deep South when it came to equal treatment. Those of us who migrated from the horrors of the Deep South to St. Louis and Detroit became disillusioned about the poor treatment of Negroes especially after the 1917 riots. Unlike what we were led to believe, we got the lowest, most menial jobs. Non-white people were corralled into the low-rent district—well, that's what the houses looked like—but landlords charged us more than they were worth.

170

WHERE CAN WE GO NOW?

St. Louis was better than Mississippi, certainly, but Daddy was still looking for the true Promised Land. Some of his friends said the feeling toward Negroes in Cleveland was kind. They reported there were Negroes who were master carpenters, painters, shopkeepers, growing richer every year. The Negro community there boasted a sizable number of success stories.

Daddy was told the average income and occupational level of Negro Clevelanders was higher than most in the north. He made up his mind to move us northeast to Cleveland, after our presence was recorded in the 1920 Census in St. Louis. I made up my mind to use that official documentation to alter my life story, proclaiming from that point on that I was actually born in St. Louis, Missouri.

We packed our bags and took the train to Cleveland—this time with Daddy. When we arrived, we found the claims of milk and honey in northern Ohio, at the edge of lake Erie, were an exaggeration.

Blacks weren't residentially segregated in Cleveland, although they were generally clustered in certain parts of the city, like around Cedar Avenue. Most of the colored newcomers to the city moved into the central Scoville Avenue area between East 17th and East 55th Streets, the oldest and most prominent sections of the town between 1915 and 1920.

Jane Edna Hunter, the nurse who would found the Phillis Wheatley Society, described her search for a place to stay when she arrived in the city in 1905. This area was well on the way to becoming a black ghetto because there was a growing discrimination in real estate sales to colored people, no matter how much money they had.

Many of the city's former integrationist policies began to fail after 1915. Restaurants, hotels, and even the Young Men's Christian Association (YMCA) and YWCA began keeping colored folk out. White hospitals were united in keeping Negro doctors and nurses off their staffs. Colored patients were only admitted to "Women's Hospital" on Saturdays. Most hospitals adopted segregated wards.

171

Most good positions in the foundries and mills were being filled by foreign-born whites. Carpenter and brick-layer unions remained integrated, but most other unions excluded us entirely.

These are the reasons the Negro middle class could grow through membership in Masonic organizations like Prince Hall and Order of the Eastern Star. Some independent crafts, like electricians, could not join the union, but they could sometimes get work if they took on the most undesirable jobs, like working during the sweltering summers when union workers didn't.

Most Negroes could not aspire to white collar jobs, but instead were often funneled to janitorial jobs in those offices. It was in federally controlled post offices that our people could make any inroads in clerical employment prior to 1930.

City employment for Negroes was relegated to street cleaning, garbage hauling, spittoon cleaning, truck driving, etc. Black women often had to get jobs outside the home, like immigrant women.

Migration from Southern states made the black population quadruple between 1910 and 1920, and double again in the next decade. The exodus was uncontrolled, with some Negroes leaving their southern homes in the middle of the night and never returning.

The central woodland area of the city contained neighborhoods of Italians, Russian Jews, and the majority of the colored folks. By the end of the 1920s, the Italians and Russians began moving out into other areas. This left coloreds able to fill into those deserted areas around Central and Scoville. By the 1930s the Woodland area and Euclid to the north were often segregated. East Cedar and East 55th to East 105th was mostly Negro by the 1930s.

With all of that less-than-stellar news, we were still excited to move to Cleveland in 1920. We moved in with my Aunt Eva and her first husband, Hampton Smith, at 2194 East 69th Street in the heart of the Negro Community.

I was eighteen years old. I had left the only home I knew in the Deep South, spent a short time in the progressive City of St. Louis, and became exposed to a whole new way of life. I loved the excitement, the activity, the opportunities now opened to me and my family. I looked forward to starting my adult life in this exciting urban center in the Promised Land.

172

CHAPTER 17 – LOVE IN THE PROMISED LAND

(Cleveland, Ohio, 1920, Daisy)

I am eighteen years old, but I know I have a lot to learn. Romance? Well, I had a few dates in Noxubee and St. Louis, but achieving my life plan for success before the age of thirty far outweighed doing something stupid with a boy. No, I would not be saddled with children before I had made my mark on this world. I might tease 'em but I wasn't going to please 'em, at least not before *I* was ready.

It all happened so long ago, when I first met Austin Henry Marshall, the Pullman Porter who altered my self-imposed straight path to glory. Little did I know at our first meeting that he would become my husband and the father of our children.

Austin Henry Marshall, coming home from his Pullman porter job, 1930, Cleveland, OH.

Austin's train route took him from Columbus, Georgia, where he was born in 1892, northwest through Alabama and Mississippi to St. Louis, Missouri, then continuing northeast through Columbus, Ohio, ending in Cleveland.

How did we meet? It could have been possible he had a layover in Mississippi or St. Louis and saw me there, our eyes met, and we knew we belonged together. But no, that's not how it happened.

Or it could have been that Austin ran into my father while daddy was working in the freight house in St. Louis. My father could have taken a liking to him and wanted to introduce him to his eldest marriageable daughter, Willie Lee. But that's not how we met either.

No, it was much simpler than that. You see, in November 1908, my favorite aunt, Eva Clayton, then nineteen, married thirty-five-year-old Hampton Smith from Tuskegee, Alabama. He had three children from his first wife. His uncle, Clifford Marshall, lived with them. In her letters to me, Eva spoke about Clifford and his brothers Israel, Thomas, and Austin Marshall, who visited them from time to time in Tuskegee, and later at their home in Birmingham, Alabama.

Even though Austin was ten years older than me, Aunt Eva thought I might want to meet him once we moved to Cleveland in 1920. She felt we had similar goals in life, so she arranged us to meet at her house one afternoon.

I dressed in a crisp, white A-line dress, with cinched waist, the skirt of which flared out around my hips. I wore matching white shoes, the heels making me one inch taller. I wore a pearl necklace with matching earrings. Not-too-boring red lipstick, a bit of eyeliner, and touch of blush would give me a fresh, natural look.

I had no idea what to expect when I took the trolley to meet with Aunt Eva and Austin at her house. She planned to make lunch for all of us.

Aunt Eva would not tell me exactly what Austin looked like. I hoped he would be a tall, slim man with black, wavy pomaded hair as she described the looks of Austin's his youngest brother, Thomas. Whoever I became involved with needed to know how to dress and have clean fingernails. I would be attracted to a man who could talk on various subjects. A plus would be someone who had an entrepreneurial spirit like me.

I rang the doorbell, with a bit of trepidation. I would finally meet this man Eva felt so strongly about. I took a deep breath with my hand on the doorknob, my head tilted upward to meet the gaze of my tall man. The handle turned and the door opened.

Where was he? Oh. My eyes had to train themselves lower than expected. Austin was diminutive, about five-feet seven-inches tall, a few inches taller than me with heels. I tried not to look disappointed, but instead smiled, then shook his hand. "Hello, I am Daisy Dooley. Eva has told me quite a few nice things about you."

"The pleasure is all mine, I assure you, Miss Daisy," he crooned in a deep voice, pressing my right hand to his lips. "You are even lovelier than your Aunt Eva described." Some might think that was a corny approach, but he was smooth and self-confident. Nothing like *any* man I had been exposed to. *Hmm, this will be an interesting date.*

Let's not pretend. Austin was not my ideal man. He was short and slight of build—that's not what I considered physically attractive. Medium-brown skin, squinty eyes, small mouth, distinctive nose, and already nearly balding at thirty years of age.

But Austin was so suave and debonair. He was dressed in a white suit over a white shirt, white pants, with white and black spats, and a black fedora. Everything about him was clean, pressed, sharp, and smart.

He was a charmer and about as good a storyteller as GramFannie. He'd traveled to so many places and met many important and interesting people on the train as a Pullman porter: politicians, powerful businessmen, famous musicians. It was an attractive quality. We did not want for conversation during lunch. Every time I looked toward Aunt Eva, she was beaming at her effort as a matchmaker. She was successful. I was more than willing to go out on a second date with Austin Marshall.

My new friend was savvy about the best places to eat in Cleveland, and he personally knew many of the up-and-coming musicians in the juke joints, and he knew which side of town had apartments and houses that were welcoming to Negroes. In fact, there wasn't a question he couldn't answer. He was a confident man—not cocky—but sure of himself. I liked him.

I soon learned it was Austin who *had* persuaded my dad to move from St. Louis to Cleveland, where there were more opportunities for jobs and investments. You see, his train route had passed through St. Louis, and he and Daddy had met there on a few occasions at the freight house, and other places where Negroes working on trains congregated.

Austin explained that Cleveland was the fifth-largest city in America by 1920. One could find whatever was needed from its urban, industrial, and neighborhood streets. There were a huge variety of eateries and businesses that catered to Negroes. There were many jobs available, especially during wartime. The political climate was active and exciting. We had arrived in time to celebrate our first Thanksgiving and Christmas in Cleveland.

Austin recounted that he and his brothers, Israel and Thomas, had moved from their hometown in Columbus, Georgia, to Cleveland between 1915 and 1917. His brother Clifford and sister Cora stayed in Georgia. However, Thomas, Austin, and Israel Marshall did their civic duty by fighting for democracy in World War I and brought back an understanding of other parts of the world where Negroes were treated with respect. This fascinating guy had big plans to purchase property in Cleveland. He said he was in the middle of brokering a deal to establish a Realty and Life Insurance Company, and he and his brothers wanted to go into the lucrative funeral home business one day.

Love was in the air for me, brother William, and Sister Wilda Lee. I think we all wanted to be free of our parents and start our own lives, on our own terms here in the Promised Land. Brother William started his new life in Cleveland, with a new wife, marrying Sarah Davis on December 11, 1920.

Austin and I continued to date when he was in town. He had captivated me by Christmas 1920, and we spent New Year's Eve together. You know what they say—whoever you spend New Year's Eve with is who you'll be with for the entire upcoming year. Austin ensured that would happen by proposing marriage that pivotal night and I said yes.

It was cold, cold, cold in Cleveland that winter of 1920. The winds surfed across Lake Erie, adding to the chill factor. Then the unthinkable happened. Mama died the first week in January 1921. She was always borderline sickly, but the damp cold and wind did her in. I felt sad that Mama did not get to witness my wedding on October 3, 1921, nor Wilda Lee's marriage to David Shackleford two days later. Mama missed sister Ruby Lee's wedding to Essie Spencer on April 15, 1922.

I believed that if we only we had a doctor in the family, maybe Mama could have been saved. That idea to have a medical professional in the family stayed with me for three decades, until I did something about it.

APPLICATION No. 163163   FILED AND MARRIAGE LICENSE ISSUED   October 3

Name   Austin H. Marshall   Name   Daisy Dooley
Age 29   Residence 2269 E. 43 St.   Age 19   Residence 7209 Cedar Av.
Place of Birth   Columbus Ga.   Place of Birth   Macon Miss
Occupation   Porter   Occupation
Father's Name   Austin Marshall   Father's Name   Wm. Dooley
Mother's Maiden Name Mary Smith   Mother's Maiden Name   Julia Nicholson
Number of times previously married none   Number of times previously married none
                                             Married Name

Marriage to be solemnized by Rev. H. Bailey,E. 43 St.   License issued by H.W.Beckman
Consent of   Filed   19   Consent of   Filed

THE STATE OF OHIO, } ss.
CUYAHOGA COUNTY,   RETURN

I CERTIFY, That on the 3rd   day of October   1921, Mr. Austin H. Marshall
and Miss   Daisy Dooley   were by me legally joined in marriage.

                                   Rev. J.B.Redmond

Marriage application between Daisy Dooley and Austin Marshall,
Cleveland, OH. 1921.

Winter blizzard in Cleveland, OH.

CHAPTER 18 - HOME SWEET HOME

(East 81st Street, Cleveland, Ohio, 1923, Daisy)

The waning golden rays of the late May sun dipped below the horizon, heralding my favorite part of the day. Restful twilight is the magical time between daylight and darkness when light from the sky often appears pinkish. The sun is below the horizon, but its rays are scattered by Earth's atmosphere to create a stunning rainbow of colors.

After dinner, my husband, Austin, and I enjoyed sitting in the cushiony porch swing next to the front door of our new house. A bowl of creamy vanilla ice cream was a cushioned platform for a piece of Austin's homemade rum cake. The flavorful yellow-crumb-with-walnuts recipe had been passed down from father to son for generations. We would settle in for an enjoyable hour or so, swinging ever so slightly as we savored our boozy dessert. It was one of the few days each month that my husband was home from his job working on his Pullman train. We wanted to enjoy each other's company on our swinging perch.

"Good evening, Mrs. Thompson," I cried out to my eighty-year-old neighbor across the street, who was sipping her favorite sweet mint tea from a tall glass, relaxing on her porch swing.

"Evenin', Miss Daisy. Lookin' sharp as usual, Austin," she replied, smiling at my handsome, brown-skinned husband, who wore a white fedora and partially unbuttoned white shirt, exposing a bit of his taut chest. He nodded and flashed his most brilliant smile back at her.

"Howdy, folks," Harlell Jones from next door uttered in our direction, a fat stogie clenched between his pearly white teeth. He and his wife, Josie, had welcomed us to the neighborhood with freshly baked sugar cookies and pleasant banter about the people living on our street. Austin and Harlell shared the love of sweet-smelling cigars, and they were both puffing away on their favorite blend, with not a care in the world.

One by one the street lights began to illuminate the darkening neighborhood as twilight turned to dusk. The butterscotch glow of the lamps reached into the balmy night.

Thousands of crickets were tuning up their orchestral strings, with frogs adding to the bass chorus, and the hoot of an owl keeping the beat. The sky had turned from light to dark blues to purples that could be glimpsed over the leafy tree canopy.

Low conversations about the events of the day could be heard from both sides of our porch, interspersed with occasional laughter, as we adults watched the young children play tag in the tree-lined street. By eight p.m., our dessert a delicious memory and the day's gossip discussed, we entered our new home.

Purchasing our first home in 1923 from Mr. and Mrs. Bubetz was so exciting. That it was near shopping in Shaker Heights was icing on an already sweet cake. I could now write "2182 East 81st Street" as my return address, when sending letters to relatives in Macon and St. Louis.

The smell of pink and red roses wafted up from the bushes bordering the front steps. And the tasteful vegetable garden in the backyard, surrounded by daisies and roses, was about the only remnant of my years in the Deep South. Tending my garden of fragrant flowers soothed my inner beast when it was riled up...and the older I got, the more it made its disturbing appearance.

CHAPTER 19 - THE IN-LAWS

(Cleveland, Ohio, 1921-1952, Daisy)

One does not get married in a vacuum. There are always family issues that come with a new spouse—sometimes good, sometimes bad. I counted myself lucky to become part of the driven and successful Marshall family.

All of Austin's siblings were born in the City of Columbus, in Muscogee County, GA, between 1889 and 1897. Their parents were Henry Austin Marshall, born in Talbot, GA, and Mary Smith, born near Tuskegee, Alabama. Clifford was the oldest, followed by Israel, then my husband Austin Henry, Thomas Alfonso, and their baby sister, Cora Lee. Cora Lee died in 1919 in GA, so I never got to meet her.

Austin was the shortest at five-feet seven-inches tall and the darkest of the brothers; Thomas Alphonso was the tallest with a smooth milk chocolate coloring.

Tall, brown-skinned, slender, with brown eyes and black hair, brother Israel was the most famous of all of us. The National Urban League bestowed him posthumously with the Opportunity Award for contributions to citizenship, interracial good will and high American ideals. For twenty years, Israel was the extraordinary, polished headwaiter at the Hollenden Hotel, known as the most prestigious hotel in Cleveland.

> CONGRATULATIONS! Now in order for congratulations are seven Clevelanders who were presented with awards for outstanding achievements by the Urban League. They are CLARENCE GENERETTE, engineer of the Cleveland Transit System; RALPH FINDLEY, manager of the Fireside Mutual Insurance Co., for achievements in the field of business; REV. CHARLES SPIVEY of St. John's AME Church for service in the realm of religion; ISRAEL MARSHALL, head waiter of the Hollenden Hotel's banquet service; MRS. ERMA

Call and Post newspaper heralds Israel Marshall's National Urban League honor. Cleveland, OH.

When the Hollenden opened in 1885, it was considered a technological marvel because every room was equipped with electric lights and the building was fireproofed. Adding to the hotel's glamour, it contained 1,000 rooms, 100 private baths, a theater, barbershop, several bars and clubs. The hotel's interiors consisted of paneled walls, redwood and mahogany fittings, and crystal chandeliers. During the hotel's history, it had a reputation for hosting celebrities, industrial giants and various politicians.

Israel began working there as a waiter in about 1915. After twenty years of exemplary service, he was promoted to headwaiter, a job intended to ensure the entire wait staff performed at the highest level at all times. He contracted tuberculosis, though, and in about 1956, he was committed to Sunny Acres—a sanitarium—for the last six years of his life. Israel died peacefully in 1961.

My brother-in-law, Israel, had more to his life than his important job. He married Blanche Margaret Mitchell in Columbus, GA, in 1912. They had one daughter, Elizabeth Ann Marshall, and she produced three daughters: Sally, Blanche, and Jamie. Israel's 1917 WWI registration indicated he was a Pullman porter before his exemplary forty years at the Hollenden. Israel lived one street over from Austin and me, at 2181 East 80th Street, in Cleveland. Like me, Israel was active in civic affairs, the Cedar Avenue YMCA, the Phillis Wheatley Association, and the Congregational Church.

Austin's father had left his family by 1900. I never could find out exactly why, but maybe he died. Austin's siblings and mother, Mary Smith Marshall, were living on Fifth Avenue in Columbus, GA, with his grandparents, Israel Smith and Laura Ligon Smith. Israel Smith was a righteous preacher who was born in South Carolina, I think. He could read and write, had been a shoemaker during much of his lifetime, and owned his home. Grandmother Laura did laundry. Austin's mother, Mary, was a cook who taught him several indispensable recipes like rum cake and bread pudding.

Also living in the Columbus, GA, house were Austin's Aunts Annie and Laura Smith—both doing laundry. Uncles Hampton (a store porter who married my Aunt Eva Clayton in 1908) and Milous (a day labor) lived there too.

By 1920, Israel and Blanche Marshall invited Austin to live with them at East 43rd Street near Central Cleveland Avenue. After we got married in 1921, we newlyweds lived with Israel and Blanche until we got on our feet financially.

My brother-in-law, Clifford, was living in Birmingham, Alabama, with his Uncle Hampton and my Aunt Eva in 1910. Like other family members, he was working on the railroad. He registered for WWI in June 1917, claiming exemption from the draft due to a lung issue, and was honorably discharged in December 1918. He married Myrtle Comer soon thereafter and they had one son, Clifford Jr., in 1919.

Clifford Sr. drove an ice wagon in 1920 and moved his wife and young son to Fourth Avenue, in his Columbus, GA, hometown. They divorced and Clifford moved to Cleveland and was living with Israel's family by 1930. He was a quiet fellow who kept to himself, and died in 1947.

I had the closest relationship with my tall brother-in-law, Thomas Alfonso Marshall. Initially, we hit it off famously. Both of us were ambitious and wanted to have a successful business. Thomas had attended Tuskegee Institute. He and I both received degrees in embalming from the Cleveland School of Embalming.

Thomas, Austin, and I decided to establish the Marshall Funeral Home late in 1939. Austin made the most money and had the best credit, so he would be the official owner on the mortgage at 8115 Cedar Avenue. Thomas and I both interned at Rogers Funeral Home and for a time were co-directors of our Marshall Funeral Home. I'll talk more about the details of our Funeral Home adventure later, but suffice it to say that Thomas and I had a good relationship for many years. Austin even named our third son after Thomas.

Thomas was a 32nd degree Mason, Prince Hall, and treasurer for St. James AME Church. He married Hazel Harpoole in 1949. I think his new wife, Hazel, resented my working so closely with her husband, sometimes attending out-of-town conferences together, etc. She succeeded in souring our relationship and that, in turn, caused many of the reasons the relationship with my husband deteriorated. Blood comes before anything else. Although estranged, I was saddened when Thomas died in 1968.

Thomas Marshall
Mortician Dies

Well known among the city's morticians, Thomas A. Marshall, 72, a retired funeral director was buried last Thursday in Lakeview Cemetery. Marshall collasped last Saturday night in his home at 1575 East Boulevard. He was later pronounced dead at Mt. Sinai Hospital.

Marshall came to Cleveland from Columbus, Georgia before World War I. He attended Tuskegee Institute in Tuskegee Alabama. In Cleveland he received his degree in embalming from the Cleveland School of Embalming.

A 32d degree Mason, Prince Hall, Marshall worked for the well known Rogers Funeral regarded with regret at St. James AME Church, 8401 Cedar Avenue, where he was named Trustee emeritus.

Funeral services for Mr. Marshall were conducted last Thursday at St. James AME Church. Slaughter Funeral Home, 2116 East 90th Street, was in charge of the services.

Mr. Marshall left his wife Hazel to mourn. The Marshalls were married November 10, 1949. Other survivors include three nephews and two nieces: Dr. Thomas A., Austin, Bruce Marshall. Mrs. Patricia Conners, and Mrs. Jean Chick.

Call and Post newspaper announced Thomas Marshall's obituary, Cleveland, OH. 1968.

CHAPTER 20 – BEING RIGHT WITH THE LORD

(Cleveland, Ohio, 1921-1976, Daisy)

For over fifty years, I was an active member and trustee of the St. James African Methodist Episcopal (AME) Church, located at 8401 Cedar Blvd., just a few blocks away from our Marshall Funeral Home location and our residence on East 81st Street.

St. James AME Church, 8401 Cedar Avenue, Cleveland, OH.
Photograph: Kathy Marshall, 2018.

St. James AME evolved from a small prayer meeting in 1894 to become one of the city's leading Negro churches. In 1925, the church acquired the former Trinity Congregational Church at 8401 Cedar Avenue. The membership grew from 94 at the turn of the century to 516 in 1925.

My husband, Austin, and I were married at St. James AME Church in 1921. We met so many fine, industrious, welcoming people there who helped us navigate the business and social milieu of Cleveland. From learning about the neighborhoods, places to shop for food and clothing and furnishings, to making contacts with city employees and politicians who could help us establish our businesses, St. James congregants were our rock. I remained an active member there until my health deteriorated to the point I could no longer attend. I regarded St. James as my home and its members my family.

Reverend D. Ormonde B. Walker led the congregation from 1926 to 1937. He was quite prominent in civic and political affairs, founding the nationally acclaimed St. James Literary Forum where many of the city's best-known religious, civic, and political figures appeared, garnering it regional and national fame.

In February 1935, the church gave me a surprise baby shower for the birth of my daughter, Shirley Jean Marshall, as well as for Mrs. Frankie Williams' impending baby.

The church suffered $100,000 in damage from a devastating fire in January 1938. Reverend Joseph Gomez stepped into that dire situation. With the help of many fundraising efforts—several of which I spearheaded—he oversaw the church rededication ceremony in May 1941.

During March 1940, I was the Treasurer for St. James' "Daughters of Allen" (being named for Richard Allen, the illustrious founder of African Methodism). We had vowed to eclipse all former records for raising money for the church. One way was via selling ticket sales for an upcoming Religious Drama that many of us acted out.

Two years later, in March 1942, amidst the cheers of several hundred people, the Women of St. James surpassed all previous records by bringing in $2,288 during their six-week-long Annual Daughters of Allen Drive. That drive concentrated on clearing up the outstanding building debts. That same year, I was "General of the Blue Army." We raised $3,775, which was more than the Youth, Red, or White Armies. For the second year in a row, I was crowned Queen. I love to raise money for a good cause and I go at the task with as much gusto as I can muster.

As part of the St. James A.M.E. Booster Club in June 1947, I was one of fifty beautifully dressed hostesses who arranged a wonderful program honoring Dr. Joseph Gomez, who had presided over our church from 1937 to 1948. We prepared a delightful tea one Sunday afternoon, with Attorney Jean Capers as the guest speaker, whose interesting subject was, "Wanted. People Who Think." We also arranged vocal solos and a piano duet as part of the program.

Another fire destroyed the church in March 1950. This time, Reverend Hubert Nelson Robinson led the next rebuilding, rededicating it again in April 1953. Surviving the 1938 and 1950 fires, the current building's Gothic front (see the beginning of this chapter) is what remains of the original structure. Reverend Donald G. Jacobs led the church during the tumultuous civil rights movement. It became a center for civil rights activism. A $180,000 Education Annex was added to the church during Jacobs' tenure.

I was honored to serve on the Board of Trustees during this time of rebuilding in 1953 and gladly donated my time and efforts to fundraise for the good of the church.

Reverend Alvia A. Shaw led a congregation of about 1,300 members in the mid-1970s and oversaw the acquisition of additional church property.

"Pastor's Aids" at St. James AME Church, Cleveland, OH. Daisy in the center of the bottom row. 1953.

Inside of St. James AME Church, Cleveland, OH. Source:
Rededication Edition, April 12-17, 1953.

Sadly, the educational system for Negro children was
poor in Cleveland, as it was in most parts of America. In order
to get some of my grandchildren into the best school available,
I had to convert to Catholicism—on paper—so they could attend
Catholic school for a few years. Back then, you had to be a
member of the Catholic parish to send a child to their school.

Truthfully, I wasn't what one would call a devout Catholic.
My real church home was always St. James AME, but
sometimes we have to do what is best for the next generation. I
kept close tabs with my St. James congregation during those few
years that I jumped the AME ship.

Thomas Richard Marshall, May 2, 1931
(Author's future father)

CHAPTER 21 - ON BECOMING A PARENT

(Cleveland, Ohio, 1947, Daisy)

"What am I supposed to do now, Aunt Eva?" I panicked, getting more than a little worried. Sure, I had taken care of my younger sister Ruby Lee when she was little, but that was ages ago. Now here I am in Cleveland, pregnant, feeling alone, and about to have a baby at the age of twenty-seven. My mother is dead, both sisters are childless, and I am somewhat estranged from my father. My husband is usually gone, working most days and nights on the train. Who can I rely on to help me during this last stage of pregnancy? Who will help me during labor and the first weeks after the birth? I feel a lot of stress right now, and that is not good for the baby." A heavy sigh escaped my lips as I imagined the difficulties coming my way all too soon.

"Honey, you know I'll be here for you. Whatever you need, just ask. I'll even move in with you for as long as you need me. I'm sure Hamp won't mind," Aunt Eva soothed. Her calm voice relaxed me a bit.

"I can't take you away from your husband, but I do appreciate your offer. I might take you up on it after the baby is born. I'll speak with the Nursery Ministry at church to find out what services are available for pregnant women. I'm sure I can find other new mothers with whom I can talk. Even though I've been in Cleveland now for six years, I haven't surrounded myself with mothering types of activities. Instead, I've been running our Peoples' Realty Company and Crusaders Mutual Insurance Company, and connecting with the big shots in town. I had so many plans, Aunt Eva, to become the businesswoman Daddy always said I could be."

Eva crooned, "I know, honey, and I'm proud of the mark you've made in Cleveland, but this is the time to think about how your life is going to change. Now you remember what I'm saying. I'll be glad to accompany you wherever you want to go, and I'll help get the baby's room ready. We'll get through this with flying colors, don't you worry, Daisy."

Fast forward two months. The baby's nursery was ready: white woven bassinet, chest of drawers with hats, booties, shapeless one-piece garments, stacks of cloth diapers folded in thirds, diaper pins, lotions, burping cloths, bath towels, blankets and a pastel pink and blue quilt I made. I sewed several loose-fitting dresses with belts which could be cinched up as I lost the baby weight. They're easy to unbutton for nursing.

When the labor pains started at eight a.m. on August 10, 1927, I asked Aunt Eva to get word to Austin at the railroad, with the hope he could come home right away.

I had been talking with many women and nurses about what to expect on the *big day*. But anyone who has had a child knows there is no way to prepare for the *excruciating* pain of labor. I can attest to that now, having spent what seemed like a thousand hours in hard labor. Sweating, panting, praying for relief, accepting the saddle block anesthesia, getting through the birth, smiling when they put my baby girl, Patricia, into my arms.

The Good Lord gave women extra-special endurance, though, and a brain that immediately forgets about the pain of birth when a new baby is placed in our arms. Staring at the angelic, trusting face looking up at me gave me a sense of love I never knew I could have. I *am* a mother.

OH MY KIDS!

"What's all that noise goin' on in there?" I demanded from the upstairs hallway. "You're all supposed to be quiet and getting ready to sleep," I reminded my young children. I had marched them to their bedrooms right after they bathed their bodies and scrubbed their teeth.

"We're *almost* asleep mother," they sniggered.

Those darn kids! I heard them giggling, thinking I didn't know they were playing cards in their bedroom. Well, who *could* go to sleep at seven thirty on a warm summer night? I know they want to be outside under the golden glow of the street lamps, playing tag with their friends, but I need some peace and quiet after a hard day's work. My children had to stay in their bedrooms.

I heard rumors that my mischievous middle son, Thomas Richard, bragged that he often escaped through the two-story bedroom window, climbed across the roof, then scampered down the tall sycamore tree next to the house, to play with the neighbor kids. If I ever catch that boy, he will get the *what for* with my hand!

By 1940, Austin and I had four children between the ages of five and thirteen, with a fifth little bugger in my belly. Patricia Rae was born in 1927, Austin Henry Jr. in 1929, Thomas Richard in 1931, and Shirley Jean in 1933. I thought we were through, but Bruce Cyril made his appearance on April Fools' Day in 1941.

With Austin gone for long stretches of time working on the railroad, I was left to raise all these kids by myself, AND be Co-Director of the Marshall Funeral Home that officially opened in 1940, AND keep up with my many civic and social organizations. It was too much, even for me. For a while, I had shipped out Thomas and Shirley Jean, to live with a distant cousin, Della Green, in her group home on Quincy Avenue, until Austin could come back and help me with my responsibilities.

Though I was a petite five-feet two-inches without heels, I've always prided myself on being a formidable "can do" woman. Some said I was larger than life. I commanded respect and demanded excellence in whatever I did. My children and husband knew that. They were expected to perform in that same exemplary manner at all times. My motto was: be impeccable with your word, don't take anything personally, don't make assumptions, be skeptical but learn to listen, always do your best, and practice the Golden Rule to do unto others as you would have them do unto you. My parents taught me those rules for success and believe you me, my kids would learn them too, if it was the last thing I did.

Now that I have a moment to think, with those crazy kids in bed, I remember back when I was pregnant with Patricia, my first child. We had purchased this house on East 81st Street in 1923. Little by little we began furnishing it. First came the couch and matching chairs for the front room, so we could entertain friends in style. Then came a beautiful walnut kitchen table, with matching chairs. I sewed tasteful white lace curtains, and a matching lace tablecloth. We painted the walls a creamy white everywhere except the kitchen, which received a sunny yellow coat.

As money came in from various financial ventures at our Peoples' Realty Company and Crusaders Mutual Insurance Company, in addition to Austin's Pullman porter salary and tips, we were able to finish decorating the house. Everything had to be perfect for the many teas, bridge games, Order of the Eastern Star meetings, and my daughter Patricia's music recitals which I hosted.

All my children were expected to excel in school and in life, even though they were born during the Great Depression, an era of lowered opportunities for most Americans. Even though I couldn't get my high school diploma until 1936, education was key and we Negroes in the Promised Land of Cleveland drummed that critical life component into our children and grandchildren as often as possible. As a result, we raised them to be independent and successful, each in their own right. I am exceedingly proud of all my kids' accomplishments. And like any proud Mama, I'm going to tell you about them.

My first-born, Patricia, was considered to be a child prodigy on the piano. She began her musical career at St. James AME Church. She was one of the first Negro women to graduate from East High School in 1945, and attended the prestigious Oberlin Conservatory of Music in 1949. Several years later, she received her Master's in Music from Cleveland State University.

My talented daughter was dedicated to music and music education. She began her teaching career as a music instructor at Tennessee State University, then returned home six years later to teach voice and instrumental music at Empire Junior High and John F. Kennedy High School. She led several dynamic choirs to first place in state competitions, and for several years served as the piano accompanist for the renowned Cleveland All-City Chorus. Upon retiring, she led choirs part-time at Cleveland Community College and taught privately at Rainey Institute of Music.

She was the mother of five children: Jocelyn, Scott, Marsha, Francina (nicknamed "Cino"), and Kevin. Her grandchildren were Brittanie, Sterling, Jason, Sydney, Owen, Christian, Joshua, and Gabriel, and great-grandchildren were Jaelun, Treasure, and Braylon. I could not have asked for a more devoted daughter than Patricia. She helped me raise the other children—whom she affectionately called 'knuckleheads'—

while I was busy with my many entrepreneurial and social obligations.

Austin Henry Jr., my eldest son, was an amiable fellow. Tall and lanky, he loved all sports, but especially baseball and football. He was happy to be a postal carrier in Cleveland for most of his life. He married Bernadine Maddox in 1956 and they had two children, Pershell—a teacher—and Austin David—a draftsman with the Ohio Transportation Department. His children profess their father was a gift from God who always put family first over his own personal wants or needs. He believed education was the key to freedom and spent what little money he had to make sure his kids, got a college degree. But most of all he was the happiest when around his brothers, sisters, and family.

Even at nine years of age, my son Thomas seemed interested in how the body was put together. I taught him about bones and muscles and other structures of the body that I had learned about at the School of Mortuary Science. That's why I began calling him "doctor" at an early age, because I believed the good Lord felt he had what it took to become a medical professional.

I'm proud to say he made my dream come true when in 1958 he graduated from The Ohio State University College of Medicine. He saw the end of life every day growing up in our funeral home. His lifelong goal, as a future obstetrician and gynecologist, materialized in Sacramento, California, in 1965, as he opened his first medical office. Over a thirty-five-year period he brought thousands of babies into the world and kept their mothers healthy. Ever since my mother had died when we moved to Cleveland, I had wanted to have a doctor in our family. Now I am happy.

Shirley Jean was the most darling little girl. She and her beautiful smile were featured in the Cleveland *Call and Post* newspaper, Social Whirl section, when she was ten months old, and again at her fourth birthday party. Shirley Jean was as cute as she was hard-headed. Once she learned how to talk, she started talking back. That didn't fly well with me. We had as many battles as we did moments of joy and kinship. Having a mind of her own and being quite the party girl, Shirley Jean demanded we let her marry at a young age. She had three children—Michal, Carolyn and Lori. Unfortunate lifestyle choices resulted in Shirley Jean's early death at thirty-five years of age, leaving her three children in my care.

Bruce Cyril, the youngest, received the Dooley and Marshall entrepreneur gene, which had been passed down for generations. He became a sales promoter in Northern California, becoming involved in several businesses during his lifetime. He married the beautiful Rae Evelyn Gardner in Cleveland. They had four sons—Bruce Jr., Terrell, and twins Jason and Chris, then moved to Sacramento County, California, near his older brother Thomas Richard's family.

Bruce Jr. was a sharp dresser, like his father, and always wanted the finest things in life. For example, in 1968, he owned a Corvair convertible car and was one of two people in Sacramento who had a car phone (the other person was the Mayor). My youngest child sometimes employed *debatable,* creative means for achieving his grandiose goals. Bruce and Rae had my grandchildren Christina, Monica, Terrell Jr., Jordan, and Marissa, who were as beautiful and handsome as their parents and grandparents.

A FATHER'S LOVE

I was the one who raised our kids, day to day, but they all *oohed* and *aahed* as soon as Austin returned from his shifts on the train.

Frankly, I was jealous of my husband and his loving relationship with our kids and grandchildren. He was a Good Time Daddy, who was home only a few days each month. But with silver dollar coins jingling in his pocket that he earned from tips on the railroad, he was able to buy kids candy and sodas for days. He was their favorite, the life of the party. He was so warm and friendly and cuddly to our kids and grandkids that they swarmed around him.

Having traveled through many states, Austin told fascinating stories about his adventures on the train, and the relationships he enjoyed with important people whom he serviced, including politicians, movie stars, and musicians. Storytelling ran in his family as much as it did in mine.

Everyone felt loved around Austin. He smiled all the time, at work, and at home. Whether it was just a practiced smile or not, he seemed sincere and liked to chat with people about their lives.

I resented his popularity. I had to do all the work in his absence, being both father and mother, the disciplinarian, and the cook. It wasn't fair that he was so likable. That jealousy fueled some of my beastly anger toward him.

IT'S MY TURN NOW

It is embarrassing to admit that I had to enroll in night school at John Hay High School—a seven-minute drive from our house on East 81st Street. I finally earned my high school diploma in 1936. Educational attainment, speaking with proper diction, improving one's vocabulary has always been incredibly important to me and my family. Now that I had a basic education, I strove to get a college degree to prepare myself to become a magnate in business.

CHAPTER 22 – USHERING THE DEAD TO GLORY

(8115 Cedar Avenue, Cleveland, OH, 1939-1952, Daisy)

Can you believe I was an embalmer and Associate Director of the Marshall Funeral Home? Yes, it was unusual for a woman to have co-managed such an establishment. I not only co-directed our family's funeral home for about a decade with my brother-in-law Thomas Marshall, but I held leadership positions in the Cleveland Funeral Directors Association, being voted in as the Director in 1947 and Vice-President in 1950. I was serious about making this a career to be proud of.

WHY CHOOSE EMBALMING?

It may sound gruesome to be an embalmer, but in the Negro community, "ushering the dead to Glory" has always been a deeply honored occupation, which started in Egypt.

Most people have heard of King Tut and the mummies found in tombs in ancient pyramids. The Egyptians perfected the technique of mummification. They believed that when someone died, their soul left their physical body. The soul would then return and be reunited with the corps after it was buried. However, the soul needed to be able to find and *recognize* the body in order to live forever.

Embalming slows the natural decomposition process so family can see their deceased loved ones still looking like themselves in an open casket, before they are interred. Mummification goes one step further by wrapping the embalmed body in thin strips of linen to preserve it for hundreds of years, or more.

Some may be unaware that at one point in the Americas, it was against the law for slaves to give their loved ones a decent funeral and proper burial. This is largely because slaves were prohibited from gathering together in groups of four or more. Whites feared they would plot to revolt against their masters.

Most slaves were denied the opportunity to mourn their dead using the traditional rituals from West Africa. Those preparations included bathing the body, wrapping it in cloth, and laying it out on a perforated wooden cooling board placed over ice. This would slow down the decomposition process while people gathered for a "wake" at night before the burial. Prayers and worship were important activities before carrying the body to the grave, which had to be done before dawn. Afterward, everyone would gather for a post-burial feast called the repast.

Deceased slaves in America, on the other hand, were often buried without ceremony in unmarked graves. Those graves were sometimes dug by children who were too young to work the fields. When allowed, slave funerals took place late at night in secluded areas near the slave quarters.

However, when a member of the white master's family died, trusted house slaves were expected to wash, prepare, and dress the dead, as well as prepare the repast for mourners who gathered after the funeral.

Enslaved people with no hope of escape began to see death as a relief from the agony and humiliation of slavery. When Christianity was brought to the slaves, death offered the chance to be with Jesus and go home to their promised "mansion in the sky." Therefore, for Negroes, the funeral evolved into a "homegoing" or a "homecoming" celebration.

Some slave owners allowed their slaves to meet for religious services and funerals. Their joyful behavior celebrating the homegoing of their loved ones was not understood by white people, as whites could not fathom death as being preferred to a life of unpaid labor. After all, the master provided everything a slave would need here on Earth, right? Many whites viewed slaves as nothing but children who had to be cared for by their benevolent masters.

Before the 1860s, caring for the dead was viewed as a woman's role. Death care tended to take place in the home, because women were thought of as being more caring. Women were the ones who helped deliver infants. In 1850, almost one in five live Caucasian births and one in three Negro infants died, so dealing with death was seen as part of the birthing process, which fell into the realm of women. Women collected the corpse, washed it, and rubbed it with herbs to reduce the natural rotting smell which accompanied death. Women dressed the body, and posed it for its wake and burial. In most cases, men were relegated to constructing the coffin and digging the grave.

Well, all this changed during the Civil War. Male Negro soldiers were recruited to dig the holes to bury the war dead. Some were also responsible for keeping burial records of soldiers killed in combat. Male Negro assistants were trained by doctors to learn embalming techniques. Negroes conducted much of this type of work, which prepared them to become pioneers in the funeral service business.

With thousands of American men dying far away from home, families began requesting that their loved ones be embalmed and shipped from the battlefields. Up until then, most Americans viewed the practice of embalming as unnatural, something scary and unholy that took place in medical schools.

When the use of embalming became more widespread during the Civil War, both races considered it taboo for a white undertaker to handle a colored man's corpse. This segregation of the dead created a parallel funeral industry, complete with a self-contained network of Negro-owned casket companies, and embalming chemical suppliers.

Funeral parlors were among the first businesses to be opened by Negroes after slavery was abolished. Becoming an undertaker was a promising profession for any aspiring Negro entrepreneur. The funeral director was a well-respected, well-dressed, and well-spoken figure in the community.

In 1880, my daddy's family lived a few farms down from the neighborhood gravedigger. Before the turn of the twentieth century, when Daddy was old enough, he and his brothers sometimes helped the gravedigger, in order to earn some spare change. They learned about the funeral business by watching the bathing, dressing and burial process. Our father passed that information on to us children.

In 1900, the National Negro Business League included some 500 male and female funeral directors. That number swelled to thousands through the mid-century, including me. Yes, I am a proud alumnus of the Western Reserve School of Mortuary Science, having earned my embalming license in 1939. I interned for a time at the Rogers Funeral Home with my mentor, James Alsip Rogers, who was always in my corner and sang my praises.

THE MARSHALL FUNERAL HOME

On May 3, 1940, at a cost of $5,355 dollars, Austin bought a four-unit house at 8115 Cedar Avenue, from a nine-acre plot that used to be owned by Harris Jaynes. He and his brothers had been saving up for years to purchase this business. This would start their, and my dream of owning a valued and valuable business in Cleveland.

Austin was the official property owner on paper, as women were not allowed to sign financial contracts at that time. I am listed as a mortician on the 1951 City Directory and an embalmer on the 1953 City Directory. My husband is listed as a funeral director in the 1943 City Directory, even though he worked as a Pullman porter on the railroad and was gone most days of every month. Thus, I wore many hats: the mother and acting father of five children, Associate Director with my brother-in-law who often claimed it was the Thomas Marshall Funeral Home. You can imagine that created some friction between us...

We worked hard to ready the new building. There was a wide, covered carport on the right side of the house for the hearse. A door on the back side of the house led down to a "preparation" room where the bodies were washed, dried, makeup applied, hair styled, and the body dressed for the funeral.

We had a viewing room on the first floor where guests could say goodbye to their loved ones which we helped look their best. Some families elected to have the service in our funeral home, but most preferred a church for the ceremony. In either case, our staff handled the necessary paperwork and ensured the burial was handled in the most caring and careful manner possible.

One of the most important additions was having a two-foot tall and six-foot wide front façade sign which proclaimed this building was the "MARSHALL FUNERAL HOME." I have a charming photograph of our four children standing in front of it. Patricia was 13, Austin 11, Thomas 9, and Shirley Jean was 5 years old. We officially opened the doors of the Marshall Funeral Home in the fall of 1940.

Marshall Funeral Home, 8115 Cedar Avenue, Cleveland, OH. Thomas, Austin Jr., Shirley Jean, Patricia Marshall (Bruce not yet born), circa 1940

THE PLACE TO BE

Cedar and Central Avenues were the main streets that provided various and sundry services to the majority of Negroes who lived on the eastern side of Cleveland. Our Funeral Home was at the corner of Cedar Avenue between East 81st and East 82nd Street.

There were notable landmarks and buildings in this vicinity. The Majestic Hotel was located at 55th and Central.

The Vera Apartment building at 78th and Cedar was a type of apartment housing where African-American newcomers from the South could live. Typical of the multi-family buildings that existed along Cleveland's streetcar lines, newcomers to Cleveland could be tutored on how to find employment among the many industries available. With a lot of effort, some were able to move up and out to single-family residences.

The Phillis Wheatley Association—the former Young Women's Christian Association—was located at 4450 Cedar Avenue, a settlement house for black working women relocating from the South.

Built in the 1930s, the Outhwaite Homes Estates, along with the Cedar Apartments and Lakeview Terrace, were the first three public housing projects to be completed in Cleveland. Outhwaite's brick Art Deco buildings, grouped around grassy courtyards, originally contained 557 units.

Of course, churches were a mainstay in the Negro community and there were many in the Cedar-Central area, including St. James AME, Shiloh Baptist, Emmanuel Baptist, Olivet Institutional Baptist, and Antioch Baptist Church, to name a few.

Sometimes on Friday nights we would take the kids to the Pla-More Roller Skating Rink in the Cedar-Central Fairfax neighborhood.

There were also numerous music-oriented establishments, such as Gleason's Musical Bar and the Chatterbox Bar and Grill in the 1950s, along with many restaurants in this populated corridor of the city. Of course there were numerous barbershops and hairstyling businesses owned by Negroes. Hair care was an important part of grooming.

And one of the most stalwart Negro businesses was that of the undertaker. There were numerous funeral homes owned and operated by Negroes in Cleveland by the time we opened ours in 1940.

THE UNDERTAKERS

In a time when few professions were open to Negroes, mortician Elmer F. Boyd started a funeral parlor in 1905 on Cleveland's east side. In 1938, after a few venue changes, Boyd planted his business at the corner of E. 89th St. and Cedar Avenue. His son,

William F. Boyd, joined the business and the establishment was renamed E.F. Boyd & Son Funeral Home. They were our closest competitors, but since the funeral business—like most other businesses—was segregated, we and other local Negro funeral homes didn't want for business. We generally got along well and helped each other succeed.

In fact, as mentioned earlier, I interned with the venerable James A. Rogers who came to Cleveland in 1895. A successful barber for eighteen years, he had always wanted to be an embalmer. So he followed a white mortician around, who let him bathe and dress his dead bodies. Mr. Rogers kept an eye on how the white undertaker practiced his skills. Then, Rogers studied embalming in the evenings at the Myers School of Embalming. In 1901, Mr. Rogers became Cleveland's first licensed Negro mortician. Nine years later, he purchased his funeral home on Central Avenue, operating it with the help of his wife. When her health failed, I asked if I could learn from him, to which he welcomed me aboard.

"I believe Mrs. Daisy Marshall to be second to none in the embalming profession," my mentor told the Call and Post newspaper on more than one occasion. "It's plain poppycock that women aren't as smart as men," he continued.

Mr. Rogers has helped me become the powerhouse that I am in the funeral home business. To show my gratitude for his tutelage, I helped him manage his wife's illness by teaching him to be a housekeeper, cook, and handyman at the ripe old age of 83. He and his wife lived over his unpretentious funeral home. Even though his voice was harsh sounding, he wore a diamond stickpin and a 33rd degree masonic ring, and attended as many functions as his body would allow.

Being the Assistant Director and Mortician for the Marshall Funeral Home, I was a member of the Progressive Business Alliance. In May 1947, I was enjoying one of their many business events with Mrs. Lawrence Schumake...whose husband would become *my* husband twelve years later, but that's a story for another time.

My brother-in-law, Thomas Marshall, was also at many of the events I attended alone, since my husband was away on business. My being in such close proximity with my business partner was a worry for his new wife, Hazel, and caused debilitating problems for our business, as you will soon learn.

We local funeral directors were pictured in the *Call and Post* as we prepared for the Ninth Annual session of the National Negro Funeral Directors Association meeting, which would convene in Cleveland at the Central Senior High School. We would feature the latest funeral furnishings and automotive equipment, and even offer a cruise on Lake Erie later in June 1947. I was there, amongst the best of the best.

In September 1947, I was photographed by the esteemed Allen E. Cole at his studio at 9904 Cedar Avenue. He was the most famous and prolific photographer in Cleveland, with twenty-two years of experience in photographing prominent people. I was honored that he promoted my credentials on one of his newspaper advertisements: "Mrs. Daisy Marshall, a licensed embalmer & undertaker." That's precisely how we colored folk helped each other grow our businesses in the city, raising up our community as a whole.

Allen E. Cole. Introduces:

MRS. DAISY MARSHALL, a

licensed embalmer & Undertaker

On a recent date Mrs. Marshall was photographed at Cole's Studio 9904 Cedar Ave. She took advantage of their 22 years of experience in photographing prominent people.

Allen E. Cole, Photographer

9904 Cedar Ave.   CE. 1063

Mrs. Daisy
Marshall

"Somebody, somewhere wants your photo.
Let Allen E. ole make it."
Watch for our studio guest next week.

Allen Cole was the most lauded African American photographer in

In 1950, at the Mercury Lounge, I celebrated with other members of the Cleveland Funeral Directors Association, which had been organized by the late Elmer F. Boyd twenty-three years prior. We were celebrating the induction of his son, William F. Boyd, into the President's chair. I was the Vice-President at that time, and was honored to be pictured with Mr. Boyd, Secretary Alvin Gibbs, and Treasurer (and mentor) James A. Rogers. I always wanted to be on the forefront of organizations, preferably as the leader, so I could have a strong voice in their policies and procedures.

TROUBLE LEADS TO A NEW START

I don't want to bore you with the tawdry, sordid details. Let's just say my business partner and brother-in-law, Thomas Marshall, and the shrew he married in 1949, Hazel, and I did not get along. No, not one bit. I don't know if she was jealous of my spending so much time alone with her husband, or she envied my looks, or the respect I had *earned* for three decades in the Cleveland community, but there was friction in our Marshall Funeral Home.

Additionally, due to irreconcilable differences, my husband had moved out of our house in 1952. That's all I'll say about that difficult time right now. All you need know is that I had been virtually ex-communicated from the Marshall Funeral Home by 1952. I presume they didn't want me to partake in any financial benefits from the business. You know how it is. People take sides in a separation. Blood sticks with blood. So be it. They will soon find out just how much work *I* did as the primary mortician, representing them at Funeral Director meetings, marketing their business, and interfacing with customers.

Thankfully, I had a *great* reputation with members of the Cleveland Funeral Directors Association. My mentor, Mr. Rogers, invited me, with open arms, to join his business. I readily agreed and began working for him, and none too soon.

When my precious sister and best friend, Wilda Lee, died in 1952, I was proud to help usher her to Glory via the James Rogers Funeral Home. I selected the perfect outfit for the occasion, reflecting Wilda's snazzy clothing sense. And I made sure her hair was stylish for her open casket service. Her short obituary read:

Mrs. Wilda Shackleford, age 55, of 10922 Hampden Ave. Services were conducted Saturday, Sept. 6, at St. James Parish House. Interment followed in Lakeside Cemetery with the James Rogers Funeral Home in charge. She died on September 3 in the Women's Hospital. Born in Mississippi, she came to Cleveland from St. Louis, Missouri. She was a member of St. James Church. Survivors include her husband, David, two sisters, a brother, a father, three aunts, and an uncle.

Our father was not happy sister Wilda left her entire $7,000 estate to her husband, David Shackleford. Daddy felt she should have left him something to help him in his old age. They were never particularly close, even though he lived with Wilda and her husband for a few years.

Mr. Rogers was grateful for my help during his old age. He even decided to change the name of his venerable establishment to the "Rogers-Daisy Marshall Funeral Home" in 1953. I was humbled and honored.

Later that year, I attended the Annual Cleveland Funeral Home Director's dinner. A picture was taken of me with the other local Funeral Home Directors. Thomas Marshall chose not to attend. I was the sole woman Funeral Home Director in town, and the other women in the picture were spouses of the male Directors. Their wives certainly helped in their family businesses, but none were certified morticians like me.

Not to brag, but I like to stand out wherever I go. While the men and their spouses usually dressed in black suits, I sometimes wore a sleeveless, mid-length, white dress which accentuated my small waist and shapely figure. The outfit was accessorized with a stunning white hat, gold earrings, and medium-heeled white shoes. My sister Wilda and I had that in common: the love of unique clothing styles that helped us to stand out in a crowd.

The Rogers-Daisy Marshall Funeral Home was chosen to conduct interment services for James E. Beckwith in November 1953. He was known as Captain Beckwith, captain of drill teams for both the Spirit of Ohio Elks Lodge and the Odd Fellows Lodge, for about fifty years. Mr. Beckwith and his wife, Mary, were also the owners and operators of the Beckwith Manufacturing Company, producing cosmetics from 1911 to 1940. Theirs was a big business in Cleveland and elsewhere.

Mrs. Daisy Marshall, Undertaker for Marshall Funeral Home, served several years as the Vice President of the Cleveland Funeral Directors Association

In December 1953, I represented the Rogers-Daisy Marshall Funeral Home with about 400 other Clevelanders. We braved the weather to attend the testimonial Elks banquet, held at the famous Hollendon Hotel, where my brother-in-law, Israel Marshall, was the famous crème de la crème headwaiter.

My mentor, James A. Rogers died in October 1957. Besides losing a business associate and dear friend, I was out of a job. It would soon be time for me to move on.

LIVING IN A FUNERAL HOME

As you might assume, my immediate family didn't have a typical home life in Cleveland. A dozen people (including me, my husband Austin and our five children, brothers Thomas and Clifford and their wives) had, at one point or another, lived in our first house on East 81st Street. Or, some lived upstairs in the Marshall Funeral Home a few blocks away, where bodies were embalmed and prepared in the basement. There was a door on the back of the funeral home, where the bodies were taken from our hearse and delivered into that lower "working" level.

Austin named our middle son after his brother. Our son, Thomas Richard, was a Boy Scout, lifeguard at the Cedar YMCA, and long-distance runner. Besides being brilliant in math and chemistry, he was also a drama king who, following our long line of storytellers, learned how to craft a good tale. He often told many frightening and funny stories about growing up in our family funeral home.

I remember one time in particular when I asked my eleven-year-old son Thomas to finish dressing Mr. Brown's corpse for a viewing that afternoon. Instead of doing what he was supposed to do, that boy decided to play around with Mr. Brown's not fully stiff arms. He inadvertently messed up the makeup I had applied to remove the gray hue of the deteriorating facial skin.

"Thomas, what do you think you're doing?" I barked, when I came down the stairs and saw him playing around. The boy had the gumption to say something smart-alecky to me which, of course, rubbed me the wrong way. Everybody knows I have a quick temper. Well, I reached for something, anything, to throw at that boy to make him mind me. The closest thing was a cleaver—used to help shorten parts to fit in a casket…Sorry, you probably didn't want to know about that.

When I reached for that big knife, the little rascal understood I meant business. Thomas lunged for the stairs some ten feet away, afraid I would cut *him* down to size too. As he bounded up the steps yelling, "Mother's trying to kill me!" I aimed, and threw the knife. *Zing!* It's a good thing he's a fast runner because the knife just missed his skimpy buttocks, and became firmly embedded into the stairwell wall. I ran after him, trying to remove the knife and finish what I started, but it was stuck too deeply. Well, I chuckled, at least I gave the boy a scare!

Truthfully, that experience didn't stop Thomas' smart mouth from irritating my last nerve on many occasions. I must admit, though, I loved his moxie. Very few people, except him and his younger sister, Shirley Jean, have ever felt comfortable enough standing up to me like they did on a regular basis.

[Author note: My father, Thomas Richard Marshall, adored his mother. In her old age, he visited her many times in Cleveland, or had her fly out to visit him at his home in Loomis, California. We have many photographs of them together, with Dad sometimes holding his laughing mother like a baby in his chiseled arms. They had a strong bond, forged in love and mutual respect.]

Artist: Mary Ellen Marshall

CHAPTER 23 - THE BREAK AWAY

(Cleveland, Ohio, 1952, Daisy)

My husband Austin and I had been growing farther and farther apart for years. Admittedly, I am just as much to blame for the dissolution of our marriage as Austin. I'm a strong God-fearing woman and I like—no—I demand to have things done *my* way.

Austin worked as a Pullman porter for nearly all of our marriage, usually away from the family for weeks at a time. I had to be the woman *and* the man of the house, ensuring our children learned what they needed to know to become good citizens. I wanted them to be successful in this world, like my parents taught me and my siblings.

Talking on the phone with my girlfriend, I bragged, "When Austin returns home for a few days between work assignments, I treat him like any of the other children. He has to fit into the system I developed for running a household. He has to put his clothes in the laundry area, brush his teeth properly, keep his elbows off the dinner table, and speak softly while eating, like everybody else in the house," I cackled.

Unexpectedly, coming from around the corner, Austin bellowed, "**I AM A MAN!** The man of this house! I don't take kindly to being treated like one of the children." He had been listening to my telephone conversation from the next room.

I told my friend I'd call her later.

"When I am working on the train, I have to kowtow to every white person who wants to lord over me that they are in control of everything I do," he continued to rave, grimacing, as his hands grasped the lapels of his signature white suit jacket.

Austin was not particularly handsome, in the traditional sense, but he was a snappy dresser. Everybody said so. He had a hat for every occasion, not just to cover his shiny bald pate, but also to match his latest ensemble. He loved alligator shoes, and white and black spats. He used a mahogany-colored leather briefcase as his suitcase. That made him look more like a traveling businessman than a Pullman porter who worked long hours on a train. Inside his briefcase was a starched white uniform shirt, buttoned-up black jacket, and pants. In addition, were two changes of clothing for his rare off-hours. His shaving kit, socks, bow-tie, black shoes, underwear, and a deck of cards, flask for a nip or two, also fit into the trim suitcase.

Austin bellowed, "Daisy, you can't possibly understand how hard my job is. I have to cater to every whim of those passengers, no matter what the time of day or night. I have a whole carload of twenty-four or more passengers to service, twenty-four hours a day. I am theoretically allowed three hours of sleep a night, but I must do my job perfectly, or get written up or have my meager pay docked, or risk not getting a tip at the end of the ride. And you know, you don't want me to miss getting paid.

"I must endure indignities every hour of every day. If a passenger wants to spit in my face for whatever reason, I have to smile and clean it off, then do as they wish. I can't complain to management, because the customer is always right. I am, in essence, a glorified slave who has no recourse, no way to stand up for myself.

"To keep you in those fancy formal dresses, my dear, our kids going to the best schools, and a roof over your head, I have to depend upon the tips my passengers give me. We are low man on the totem pole, with the Pullman Company paying us porters a scant $80 per month, for our twenty-four-hours-per-day efforts. If I'm lucky, every passenger will give me a dollar or two when they leave the train. I always give exemplary service, but sometimes I get no tip at all. Even so, I must still have a big grin on my face and say "Thankee" or "Yessuh" in traditional, lowly slave dialect. I'm not treated like a man at work," Austin fumed, "nor here at home." His gaze rested on my eyes, his lips tightened together, in an effort to force himself to stop ranting.

I shifted my position, feeling a bit uncomfortable on the olive green sofa in the living room, where Austin had been talking *at* me. He was getting more and more animated as he unloaded his anger toward no one in particular. It's like he *had* to speak. He *had* to unburden himself. He *had* to make me understand, and I didn't dare interrupt him.

My husband continued his heartfelt speech. "The only time I've been treated like a man was in France, during World War I, before I met you." He paused a moment, glaring at me. "As you know, I joined the Army when I was twenty-five. I was assigned to Company C, the 325th Field Signal Battalion of the 92nd Division. We were the first all-black signal battalion in the world. About 400,000 Negroes served in World War I. The 325th was considered to be the most elite group of Negro soldiers. We were one of the best educated battalions in the Army, as many of our soldiers were graduates of the nation's best colleges and universities.

"I was a Private First Class. We left Cleveland on April 28, 1918, for Camp Sherman in Chillicothe, Ohio. We didn't know what to expect. After initial signal and combat training, we were sent to fight in the Meuse-Argonne Offensive, located in the region of Alsace-Lorraine in northeastern France, bordering the countries of Germany, Belgium, and Luxembourg.

"The 325th was part of the defensive sector of the American Expeditionary Force, serving from June 1, 1918, to February 27, 1919. It was a major part of the final Allied Offensive Coalition that opposed the Central Powers of Germany, Austria-Hungary, the Ottoman Empire, and Bulgaria.

"Arriving in France in June, the 325th had to undergo signal training. Then we served in the trenches of the St. Die sector for four weeks before heading to the Argonne. We *men* saw lots of action during battle.

"Negroes were responsible for splicing telex phone wires in trenches captured from the Germans. Wire communications, in particular the field telephone, proved to be the chief means of signaling that was used by the United States Army. A field telephone could operate over a range of fifteen to twenty-five miles. A field telegraph could relay messages up to hundreds of miles. We ensured there were continued, unobstructed communications between the front and Army headquarters. We performed our duty amidst constant fire. It was not for the faint at heart, I can assure you.

"In addition to our signal duties, several platoon members volunteered to capture a German machine gun nest that was encountered while scouting a location for a new command post. Their bravery succeeded in capturing the enemy position.

"The 325th served from September 26th, until the Armistice on November 11, 1918, which ended the fighting on land, sea, and air. The Meuse-Argonne Offensive was the largest in United States military history, involving over one million American soldiers. I'm proud to say it was one of a series of Allied attacks which brought the war to an end. While we were afraid for our lives the whole time, we looked forward to our free time off after the Armistice."

In a gentle voice, I interrupted his reverie, "Austin, what did you do on your time off?" I knew his time in France was a bright spot in his life. I wanted to quench his anger toward me before our fight deteriorated, as it often did, to physical violence.

"Oh, the French were *fascinated* by us Negro men!" Austin started, with a big smile. "They wanted to touch our warm brown skin...and we let them. They wanted to see how we fit our monkey tails into our pants. Yes, they were told by Caucasian American soldiers that we had tails. Some of us invited the women to see our tails...as a result, I am sure many of us left *lasting* remembrances behind in France!

"What did we do there? What *didn't* we do! Bars, restaurants, babes. That's all an unmarried soldier needed. A little love and care. We had seen enough of the countryside during the fighting. Romancing, playing cards, drinking booze, and socializing with the lovely ladies filled our time off.

"We soon learned basic French expressions to get by:
* Bonjour (pronounced "bone joor" meaning "Hello")
* Au revoir ("Oh ravwar" for "Goodbye")
* Mademoiselle ("Mah-dem-wha-zell" for "Miss")
* Madame ("Mah-dahm" for "Mrs.")
* Oui Monsieur ("Wee mohn-sure" for "Yes, sir")
* Ou est la salle de bain? ("Ooh ay la sall da bahn" for "Where is the bathroom?")
* Combien pour cette biere? ("Com-bee-yahn pour set bee-air" for "How much for this beer?")
* And last, but not least...the most important phrase of all:

- Voulez-vous coucher avec moi? ("Voo-lay-voo koo-shay aveck mwah?" for "Would you like to sleep with me?")

"If I could have stayed in France, believe me, I would have! After representing our country overseas in a war, I was honorably discharged.

"We had saved the world from the Germans, and assumed we would be treated with a newfound respect when we returned home to America. But no, it was the same racist treatment all over again. It was almost worse, because we had tasted what it felt like to be treated as a man. Jim Crow back home. It didn't matter if we wore our military uniform. Once our feet touched American soil, it was back to normal. Negroes were still treated like slaves. I resumed my job as a Pullman porter, making less than any other worker on the railroad, just like before.

"Daisy, you can't imagine how stressful and demeaning it is to have to act like a good Pullman porter *boy*: bowing my head, not looking white passengers in the eye, smiling until my jaws ache, waking at the sound of a passenger's bell to service their latest need, and having few moments to rest my sore feet in a bowl of Epsom salts at night. If I want that two-dollar tip at the end of the ride, I have to potentially demean myself every second of every day." A heavy sigh ended his soliloquy. He looked downtrodden.

Austin was right. I would *never* be able to keep my mouth shut and abase myself like that. Lord knows, I must acknowledge that Austin has always been a responsible provider, bringing home most of the money he made, to pay for our needs. It can't have been easy for him to afford my Mortuary School, Patricia's Oberlin College fees, then Thomas' medical school tuition at Ohio State University. That's in addition to paying for our mortgage and the other financial needs here at home. Admittedly, he had done his fatherly duty, without much complaint.

Because he is so amiable, the big shots sometimes gave him more than just a good tip. Austin said one Senator wrote a letter of recommendation for our son, Thomas, to get him into medical school. Maybe I should try harder to be nicer to my husband of thirty years.

Pacing back and forth to walk off some of his ire, Austin revved up again, "No, I am not treated like a man at work, nor at home. The only fun in my life is the few hours I have off once a week when the train stops at the bigger cities, where I can listen to some good music, smoke a cigar, and have a beer or two."

A lightning bolt hits my left temple, sizzling. *There he goes again, hitting on my last nerve, baiting me to say something back.* Without thinking, my voice rises to the occasion. "And who is it you spend your time with on your days off in the big city? I've heard rumors you have a girl in every major stop. I smelled some woman's perfume on your clothes when you came home the other day. Don't think I don't know that you 'get around' when you're away from me." My head was bobbing and weaving side to side on my neck, as I snapped. *Game on.*

Our arguments were often loud and sometimes physical— at least I can't help taking out my anger on him in violent ways. My anger has always been intense and surges forward uncontrollably, like a wild beast. My children can vouch for that! That's just how I was, and am. My daddy was the same way. It's how I was raised. But Austin, too, can get into the swing of things when the devil liquor gets into him. We each get as good as we give.

Yes, when Austin comes home a few days each month, I make him conform to my way of doing things. Consistency is important when raising children. As usual, it doesn't take long before Austin grabs his hat and wallet, and slams the door behind him, leaving the house, to cool off from our latest fight.

Austin:

Oh, that woman! If Daisy weren't so beautiful and accomplished, I would have left her years ago! I must admit, though, she is a good mother, if not a bit too strict on the kids…and me. I can't imagine living everyday with her never-ending rules. Her upbringing in Mississippi must have been difficult for her to be so mean and violent at times.

I do my part as a father and husband, to the best of my ability. I may not be there to raise my kids, but I sure provide for them financially, and I enjoy them immensely when I'm in town.

Enough! I think I'll go visit my son, Austin Jr., at his home on Throckley Avenue. I can get a drink or three there, and loosen my tie. Maybe I'll take the grandkids out to the corner store for some fun. It delights me so when their eyes get big, looking at my wallet stuffed with dollar bills, or at my purse full of silver dollars given to me as tips. I enjoy letting them buy whatever they like—which is always candy. Our dentist sure likes seeing us coming, with all the work we give him to fix our teeth!

Sigh. I feel better already, getting away from that shrew of a wife!

THE SEPARATION

Daisy:

Now that all of our children are grown, except for eleven-year-old Bruce, it was time to cut the ties that bound our bickering selves. Austin had moved out of our home by 1952 and was staying a few miles away at 768 Parkwood Drive, with a friend named Mr. Upshaw. Austin's diabetes had progressed so he could no longer work on the train. He got a job at the Majestic Hotel where his friend, Mr. Upshaw, worked. I hear he took up with a lady friend who grew up with him in Columbus, GA. The kids say their dad and Vernelle are planning to move back to GA soon. Well, that's the last of him. It will be easier here at home, now that Austin has moved out…as long as he continues to pay child support for Bruce.

[Author's note: Austin did marry Vernelle, a former teacher, and they moved back to Columbus, GA, to live out their days. Austin's never-ending faith in his son, Thomas's abilities—over naysayer warnings that his son was squandering money instead of studying medicine—was well rewarded. My Grandpa Austin and Vernelle visited us in Sacramento, California, during the summer of 1966. Austin was able to view my dad's first private practice office on Florin Road, in south Sacramento. My grandfather, Austin Henry Marshall Sr., died the following year, on November 30, 1967, in Columbus, GA. He was

buried in Porterdale Cemetery, which is also called the Colored Cemetery. Austin Marshall rests there with his:

Mother, Mary Marshall (1866-1928);
Grandmother, Laura Ligon Smith (1848-1926);
Grandfather, Israel Smith (1830-1901);
Aunt, Laura Smith Pitts (1879-1907);
Uncle, Hampton Smith (1879-1929 who married Daisy's Aunt Eva); and
Sister, Cora Lee Marshall (1898-1919).]

Porterdale Cemetery, Columbus, GA. Photograph: Kathy Marshall, 2009.

CHAPTER 24 – PROLONGING LIFE

(Cleveland, Ohio, Mid-1950s, Daisy)

I had to find a new occupation, so I could help support myself and son, Bruce, still living with me. Although Austin moved out of our house in 1952, divorce proceedings didn't culminate until years later.

Truthfully, I had become tired of tending to dead bodies. I yearned instead to become a healer like my middle son, Thomas Richard. I wanted to fix broken people and keep them alive for as long as possible.

My tender side always came out when I encountered people or organizations that needed my help. When my children were sick—not the "I don't want to go to school" fake sick—my nurturing side bubbled up from my depths and I would wait on them hand and foot. At those times, I felt remorseful for the times I was so prickly, so tough, so demanding, so unbending, with my children and my husband.

When someone was truly at their lowest point, I could show tenderness. I guess in my middle years, I wanted to turn over a new leaf. Maybe I could fix what I had broken in others and in myself. I wanted to become a nurse.

I enrolled in the Frances Payne Bolton School of Practical Nursing on Cornell Road, in Cleveland. The School of Nursing, at Case Western Reserve University, had earned a reputation as an innovator in nursing education, research, and leadership.

Taking an experimental approach to education was one of the key conditions of Congresswoman Frances Payne Bolton's 1923 gift of a $500,000 endowment to the school. That was the largest ever for a university school of nursing.

In 1954, Betty Smith Williams earned the school's first Master's degree granted to a Negro nurse. She later founded the National Association of Black Nurses. I attempted to follow in her footsteps, graduating from the Bolton School of Nursing in 1957, as a Licensed Practical Nurse.

To help me learn the nursing concepts and procedures from class, I sometimes experimented on my family. I took their temperature, applied bandages, practiced turning them in the bed to discourage bed sores, washed them in the bed, and administered medical treatments to my grandchildren, when needed.

One day, my granddaughter had a tough bout with bronchitis and strep throat, which was a painful combination. I administered a home remedy consisting of castor oil, followed by a chaser of whiskey, turpentine, and sugar. That's what my Mama used on me when I was young. But it didn't work and my granddaughter ended up at the doctor's office, sicker than ever. After that experience, I learned to admit when a malady was beyond my capabilities.

Get well wishes were announced in the *Call and Post* newspaper in 1957, listing me as "a mortician who was confined in the Cleveland Clinic for a short illness." It was exhaustion, to tell you the truth. I was running on all cylinders, night and day, as usual. I wasn't sleeping, eating, or drinking enough water, while I attempted to pass the nursing test, caring for Bruce, while going through a divorce.

All those things took their toll on me, but I had to get well. In a few months, my daughter-in-law, Mary, was coming to live with me. She was in the last couple of months of her pregnancy with her and Thomas' first child. There's no better impetus to get well when a new baby is on the horizon.

I worked for University Hospitals, in Hanna Pavilion, for ten years, until I retired in 1967.

CHAPTER 25 - THE NEW GUY

(Cleveland, Ohio, 1958, Daisy)

Austin had already moved out of our home and divorce proceedings were being finalized by the mid-1950s. I had come a long way since arriving in Cleveland thirty years prior, but I wanted more: more prestige, more acumen, more respect, more money, and an honorable man with whom I could share my full life.

My eyes set their sights on Dr. Lawrence Powell Schumake Sr. early in my nurse's training at Lakeside Hospital. He had been a successful chiropodist—a foot doctor—since the 1920s, and his namesake son was also a well-known doctor in Cleveland.

[Author Note: for some reason, Dr. Lawrence P. Schumake Sr.'s obituary incorrectly indicated he had worked for the Post Office for fifty years. Contradictory newspaper accounts of Dr. Lawrence Schumake, Sr. through 1959, memories of his living grandchildren, and his medical bag kept in the closet of his East Blvd. home, refute the veracity of the obituary.]

In 1958, I had asked Larry Sr. to examine the arch on one of my granddaughter's feet. After that medical interchange and successful surgery, I invited him to my house on East 81st Street for a thank-you dinner. My life changed for the better after that sumptuous dinner. Larry and I began dating seriously.

If one didn't know better, they might think Larry was Caucasian, his skin having only a slight olive shade. In fact, he was listed as white on the 1930 US Census. He had large, wide-set eyes behind glasses, a Cupid's bow mouth, and a five-feet seven-inch frame that became more portly with age. He wasn't a bad-looking guy, but looks were not what attracted me to him.

Larry was an activist: a member of the Boydston Post of the American Legion, the Royal Vagabonds, the Veterans of Foreign Wars, and Excelsior Lodge No. 11, along with other houses of Prince Hall Masonry. He was also a member of Toastmasters International. He was erudite, dressed and carried himself like a gentleman, and was a 33rd degree Freemason.

Everyone knew he was an honorable man who cared about bettering veterans and our Negro community.

Larry served in World War I as a Private First Class. Like my first husband, he was part of the American Expeditionary

Private Lawrence Schumake, World War I, 1919.

Forces at Meuse-Argonne, in France. He was wounded in action and walked with a slight limp forevermore. He advanced to Corporal, before being honorably discharged from the National Guard in April 1919 with a fifteen-percent disability.

My *intended* was born in 1891 in Portsmouth, Ohio. His family moved to Cincinnati ten years later. Larry married his first wife, Francis Epps, in 1911, and they had a son—his doctor namesake—a year later. After a divorce, he married Mary Lucretia Grant, in Cleveland, in 1928. Austin and I knew them as members of St. James AME Church, but we weren't particularly close. Hi wife passed away in 1958. Not to be unfeeling, but now being a widower made him fair game.

Because Larry was so interested in the treatment of Negro veterans, he fought for their cause all his life. Through the special interest of various Cleveland judges, he was appointed as a Commissioner to the Soldiers Relief Commission, where he served for fifteen years. Yes, he was a cultured, educated, caring man who could speak on many subjects.

I was fifty-four years old when we started dating. I still looked pretty good and had plenty of verve to share. I desired to be seen with a successful, educated man on my arm for the many social functions I regularly attended.

During most of my adult life in Cleveland, I was forced to attend those events alone because Austin was usually working on the train. The past stigma of being an unescorted woman would now be remedied.

Daisy Dooley Schumake, circa 1958.

Larry and my courtship was at its apex during the time my daughter-in-law, Mary, and grandbaby, Kathy, were living with me. Larry and I married in 1958, after the newly appointed Dr. Thomas Richard Marshall whisked his family off to Washington for his military and medical residency requirements.

225

Daisy moved into Dr. Lawrence Schumake Sr.'s upscale tri-level apartment at 1431 East Blvd., Cleveland, OH, when they married in 1958.

CHAPTER 26 - THE ELITE

(Cleveland, Ohio, 1930s-1970s, Daisy)

It was at the suggestion of my father that *I* decide the course of my life by saying I was born in St. Louis, instead of my original Deep South homeland. I must admit that I've done a darn good job of it.

The infrastructure in segregated America made for a strong Negro community of businesses which accommodated every need of an upwardly mobile society. Daddy showed us plenty of successful Negro businesses in St. Louis, with their impressive shops lining the streets in colored neighborhoods. Negroes were doctors, lawyers, accountants, beauticians—every possible profession you could imagine. Their houses were on a par with the white-owned plantation houses in the south.

For the first time, well-dressed women invited me to tea parties. The teas accompanied fundraisers for organizations, bridge games, or musical programs. Rich silver tea services adorned tables, alongside beautiful flowers on lace-covered tables, sumptuous appetizers, and sparkling drinks. Social events for whatever reason abounded in St. Louis and Cleveland. We looked for any reason to get together and rejoice in how fortunate our lives were, away from the Deep South.

Oh, the dresses and hats and gloves. Women had their hair done weekly at the best hair salons: pomades, hot combs, chemical "permanents" to straighten our nappy or frizzy natural hair, in addition to hair coloring. Nails must be manicured. Skin lighteners were all the rage. Shoes were stylish. One didn't leave the house without being 100 percent "made up."

Negro newspapers captured our transformation from a rural agrarian, former-slave society, to the bright new day we experienced in St. Louis and now in Cleveland. I was an activist, involved in various and sundry organizations to better our community. My name and photograph were often found in the Cleveland *Call and Post* newspaper, in the "Social Whirl" section. Since my first husband, Austin, was often away, working on the train, I often attended these events by myself.

I was referred to as "Mrs. Daisy Marshall" in the papers, whereas most women are mentioned as "Mrs." followed by their husband's first and last name. People who knew me understood that my husband had a good job on the train, providing for our upscale lifestyle. I felt no shame in attending those events alone, even though other women came with their spouses. If people considered me a wanton, unaccompanied, woman behind my back, I didn't care. I had crafted my life to be full, like that of Auntie Mame. "Live, Live, LIVE!" was my motto, and I did it to perfection.

I love music. It soothes my inner beast and puts a smile on my face. I ensured all my children were exposed to music at an early age and learned to play at least one instrument: Patricia, the piano, Thomas the trumpet and flute, Austin the violin, and Shirley Jean and Bruce the piano. Being an accomplished musician was seen as being an important part of one's grooming. It signaled you were an upper class sort of individual.

Our slave ancestors employed music in the plantation house, as well as in the fields, probably being an important remnant of our African past. But theirs were drums and banjos, syncopation, call and response. We wanted to put as much distance as possible between the new Negro and the perceived degradations from slavery. Right or wrong, many of us Negroes in the big cities gravitated toward traditionally European musical instruments and songs, instead of those from our African roots.

To be perfectly honest, I was happiest donning formal gowns and attractive outfits at social events. It signaled that I had *arrived*. I felt like a princess among the crowd of notables— the best of Negro society, discussing important events of the day, dancing with multiple partners when my husband was away, eating fine food, drinking fine wines, raising money for the many activist organizations I held dear. Like my older sister, Wilda Lee, sometimes we just wanted to have a nice time with like-minded people. Looking back on those days, I wish I would have bought stock in tea!

Yes, some might consider me to be bourgeois, or "bougie" but that's just how we felt, finally being able to live the American Dream like whites had lived all of their lives. Let me share a smattering of examples of my time in Cleveland, many of which were reported in the *Call and Post* newspaper so you can get an idea of how I spent my time, in addition to being a mother, wife, and a business professional.

In June 1934, my husband, Austin, and I had a musical afternoon at our East 81st home for the benefit of St. James A.M.E. Church. The program consisted of music, group songs, readings, and dances. Among the performers were my daughter, Patricia Rae, and my nephew Prince Marshall.

In July 1936, I attended a tea near my house in honor of Miss Ethel Brown who was a delegate to the Youth Congress, visiting her sister in Cleveland.

In November 1941, I was one of many houseguests who came to enjoy brunch and bridge at the home of Amanda Wilkerson, who was honoring a houseguest from St. Louis, Missouri. Two months prior, they staged a 'tonk and pokeno' party before which there were invigorating cocktails and a swell turkey dinner, served on floral-laden tables. The guests with their smart frocks and enchanting hats with wide brims, made a pretty picture.

In February 1944, my talented daughter, Patricia Rae Marshall, was presented in a piano recital at the St. James AME Church. I was the Chairman of the affair. Patricia made a charming picture in a youthful evening gown of ice blue satin and net, satin fitted bodice and three-quarter length shirred sleeves, and bouffant net skirt with a band of satin. The newspaper wrote, "Miss Marshall has the poise and presence of a much more mature artist and plays with confidence, keen understanding, a good sense of rhythm, and flawless technique. One recognizes at once her complete mastery of the instrument, and it is easy to predict a bright future for her as a concert pianist." I was proud of her accomplishments and the time I invested in her future because she indeed did become a concert pianist who traveled to several different countries.

In July 1944, I entered my fourteen-month-old son, Bruce, into a baby contest to help raise funds for the 22nd Annual Cleveland Convention Committee of the National Association of Negro Musicians, Inc.

In November 1944, at the spacious home of Mr. and Mrs. Clarence Wilson, the St. James' Flower Guild presented a most successful musical tea program to one hundred and twenty guests. My daughter, Patricia, was one of the pianists, among sopranos, tenors, baritones, readers, and full choirs.

In October 1945, I was a guest at the informal wedding reception of Miss Georgia Harper, whose aunt was Mary Clayton. I attempted to learn whether she was related to my Claytons from Mississippi, without her suspecting my roots were actually from the Deep South.

In September 1946, a host of friends gathered at the home of Dr. and Mrs. Evans to celebrate their wedding twenty-five years earlier. My daughter, Patricia, called 'the brilliant pianist and student from Oberlin," played various musical selections at frequent intervals during the celebration.

In February 1952, I participated on the Folk Festival Ticket Committee to help bring the Kent State University A Cappella Choir to Cleveland, as well as inviting Dr. Ralph Hartzell, head of their Music Department, who would give a talk on Folk Music and its contribution to America.

In December 1958, holiday meetings often became gay yuletide parties. Our "Present Day" club meeting was turned into a real Christmas party at our home on East Boulevard. Gifts were exchanged, and a delicious dinner served. After dinner, the ladies played cards. On hand for the fun of the evening were my friends Lucille Mitchell, Sue Johnson, Sophia Bailey, Bertha Bolt, and Harvey Adkins.

VAGETTES ...Officers of the Vagettes, auxiliary of the Vagabond Club, installed the dinner fete are Elizabeth Smith, Julia A. Donato, Maryette Fuster, Daisy Scumoke and Fannie Cockfield. (Crawford Phot)

230

In May 1962: wearing white carnation corsages and gowned in colorful cocktail dresses, we members of the Vaguettes Club greeted over 300 guests at our Third Annual Cocktail Party at the Kappa House on East 100 Street. The canapes were plentiful and soft background piano music was furnished by Virgil Vincent. The Vaguettes Club, whose membership is made up of wives of the Royal Vagabonds, including me, of course, was headed by Emma Short. Among the many prominent guests were Mrs. Amable, from Port Elizabeth, Union of South Africa. These ladies are in Cleveland as part of the Cleveland International Youth Program.

[Author's Note: The reader is encouraged to go beyond the social atmosphere of the aforementioned events. It is important to understand that teas and soirées were often opportunities for fundraising for humanitarian and other causes, as well as networking with like-minded people. It was not only an avenue to see and be seen, but also to "do" for the community at large.]

CHAPTER 27 - MY CIVIC DUTY

(Cleveland, Ohio, 1921-1976, Daisy)

I am proud to be an American, even with all of this country's faults and foibles. I was raised to participate in all aspects of the American Dream, which includes giving service to my community, as well as to my family. Looking back on my life, it is hard to imagine I was involved in so many organizations, in addition to being a wife and mother, and often working full-time jobs. Having an abundance of energy and a fervent desire to build the Negro community, are the keys to my success.

With my smile and one look from my almond eyes, I can win over anyone's heart, but I can be prickly at times. I want things done the way they *should* be done, and I'm not always patient when others do things too slowly, or inefficiently. My looks may fool people, but they soon find that I am not a weak, simpering female.

I'm a doer, not one who blathers on about doing things. And I love competition, holding my own with the best and the brightest of my male and female peers in the mortuary business, church, and schools. Fundraising is one of my strengths. One of the best ways to raise money for a needy cause is to have two groups of people competing against each other to see who can raise the most money for the cause. As an example, our St. James AME Church has a healthy competition to see whether men or women can raise the most money for the church. Trust me, as a fundraising team leader, my team often wins.

At the YMCA, the Red, White, and Blue "Armies" compete to see who can raise the most money for the youth. As an Army Captain, I led my team to fundraising victory. That not only benefits the organization, but also gives me bragging rights…not that I would ever brag…

I am an activist who is always trying to make my community better. That often entails being seen at parties and other social events that revolve around improving the lives of Negroes in Cleveland, and the United States at large. I am interested in higher education for our Negro children, fair housing and employment, and making the Democratic Party more responsive to our race, etc. That's why I am an active, participating member of numerous organizations which further those purposes, as illustrated by the following examples.

POLITICS

When I was a little girl, I remember adults conversing about the despicable Poll Tax that adversely impacted most Negroes. As a young child, I vowed to change things for our people when I grew up, if I could. Becoming a part of the political process in some way could help change the laws that governed all people. That became a focus of mine. In Cleveland, the time was right.

I was a Precinct Committee Woman for the Democratic Party for 15 years, and a proud member of the American Legion. I prided myself on being a formidable woman who commanded respect, and exhibited excellence in whatever I did. My children were expected to perform in the same exemplary manner at all times.

Because their father was so often gone, I often had to bring my children (and later, my grandchildren) with me to formal precinct committee meetings after dinner. Most meetings were held in the University Circle area near Wade Park and Magnolia Drive, close to our home. I doubt the kids listened to the issues discussed while they were doing their homework at the meetings. They could eat whatever snacks were available, and try to nap until I nudged them when it was time to go home.

On voting day, my children (and grandchildren) and I would work in the basement of a church. When I worked the polls, they worked them too, standing outside the polling place, handing out election materials for the candidates I supported (even though it may not have been kosher for an election worker to do that). We wanted to inform voters of the best candidates who would forward the Negro agenda of equal housing and equal employment.

Cultivating strong political connections in Cleveland, I became attached to the Russo family. Basil Russo was a formidable jurist and I am not ashamed to admit that I dropped his name in conversation whenever I could. I wanted people to understand that I was well-connected to power, in the hope that they would buy whatever I was selling. Being respected helped loosen the pocketbooks of high-rolling donors to our causes. My parents raised me to strike while the iron was hot, to improve conditions for the community, and that's what I did...some might say, by hook or by crook, but I believed my motives were pure.

My family contributed to political fundraisers, the police athletic league, and political events. We ensured our faces were seen in all the right places, and our names noted in the newspapers as often as possible. I also volunteered to serve on numerous committees, and lobbied to be the President of organizations, to further lead their agendas.

In August 1942, the formation of the League of Independent Colored Women Voters of Cleveland numbered more than 1,000. We worked in the Democratic primaries to assure the nomination of Negro candidates to the Ohio Legislature. This followed a meeting of women leaders held at our Marshall Funeral Home on Cedar Avenue.

In February 1944, I attended the annual Lincoln-Douglass Banquet, sponsored by Councilman Gassaway and the 18 Ward Republican Club. The Attorney General was present and President Charles Wesley of Wilberforce University was the main speaker to an interested audience.

MISCELLANEOUS CIVIC ORGANIZATIONS

In February 1936, as part of the Cleveland Committee, I contributed to a fundraiser that sent $100 to New York for the Joint Scottsboro Defense Committee.

In January 1942, I was asked to join a new Committee on Juvenile Welfare which would be comprised of all persons interested in the welfare of the youth in the area bounded by East 14th Street, East 105th Street, Carnegie Avenue, and Woodland-Kinsman Avenues. We were concerned that the behavior problems of our youth reached a point where concerted public action was necessary.

In September 1944, I attended the "Delegates to the Fourth Biennial Convention of the International Sleeping Car Porters" dance, even though my husband had to work on the train that evening. I enjoyed chatting for a few minutes with dedicated International Sleeping Car Porters Union President, Philip A. Randolph.

In May 1947, Louis B. Seltzer, Editor of the Cleveland Press, spoke to an overflow audience at our Second Annual NAACP meeting. He highlighted the necessity of education as a remedy to racial differences and conflicts. He responded to questions about anti-lynching legislation, fair employment practices, and application of the Bill of Rights for all citizens— all topics near and dear to my heart.

As part of the NAACP's Junior Women's Auxiliary, I helped organize the accompanying tea, which included decorating several tables with colorful flowers, pouring tea, and doling out refreshments for the erudite crowd of 500 attendees.

PARENT-TEACHERS ASSOCIATION (PTA)

In October 1941, as President of the Bolton School PTA, I ensured that parents and teachers had many pleasant teas at which we discussed plans for enlarging the membership. In February 1942, while I was President, eleven members of the Bolton School PTA were sponsors and actors wearing period costumes in a fast-moving play called *Turning Back Time.*

Parent Teacher's Association leadership, Daisy
Marshall was President. *Call and Post* Newspaper,

236

In May 1942, I placed an advertisement in the Cleveland *Call and Post* newspaper, reaching out to give important information to parents of children who would be entering kindergarten.

In February 1953, I, and six other past presidents of the Bolton School PTA, were honored at the Silver Anniversary Founder's Day celebration. Our photograph was included in the *Call and Post* newspaper. As usual, I stood out in a fashionable white dress, but all the ladies were dressed to the nines.

YOUNG MEN'S CHRISTIAN ASSOCIATION (YMCA)

In April 1944, I attended an enlightening meeting of the Cedar Avenue YMCA which indicated the membership was up at the end of 1943, the budget had been balanced, and that the YMCA had become the hub of community activities in the east end of Cleveland.

The same year, Ralph Findlay, member of the Board of Managers of the Cedar Avenue YMCA, was named Chairman of the "Back-A-Boy" campaign to raise $20,000. Half of that money would be used to complete the Cedar Y's new physical plant, $6,500 to provide service for local boys, and the remaining $3,500 going to the World Youth Fund. I was an active participant in raising money for this important objective, in addition to being a Team Leader for various all-boy sports groups at the Y.

I was a "B" Team Captain at the Cedar YMCA in April 1947, along with eight other men and women and one aide. There were just as many "A" Team Captains.In March 1951, I was voted President of the Cedar branch YMCA Mother's Council. Our objective is to protect the welfare of boys and young men in the home and community and foster a closer working relationship between home, community and the YMCA.

THE CEDAR BRANCH YMCA MOTHERS' Council was organized last Wednesday evening at Cedar Y. Officers elected were Mrs. Daisy Marshall, president; Mrs. Rosa Williams, vice president; Mrs. Randolph Russell, treasurer; Mrs. June Brown, secretary; Mrs. Lorena Jefferson, reporter.

The objective of the Mothers' Council, according to a statement by C. W. Hawkins, executive secretary, is to promote the welfare of boys and young men in the home and community, and to bring about a closer working relationship between the home, community and the YMCA.

Regular meetings will be held at the Cedar Y on the fourth Wednesday evening in each month. Membership is open to all mothers and interested women of the community.

YMCA Mother's Council. Daisy Marshall was President. *Call and Post* Newspaper, 1951.

AMERICAN LEGION WOMEN'S AUXILIARY

The American Legion Women's Auxiliary is the oldest and largest women's patriotic service organization in the world. Organized in 1919, by 1951 they were almost one million women strong. The mission of the American Legion Women's Auxiliary was to support The American Legion and to honor the sacrifice of those who serve the country. This could be accomplished by enhancing the lives of our veterans, military, and their families, both at home and abroad. For God and Country, we advocate for veterans, educate our citizens, mentor youth, and promote patriotism, good citizenship, peace and security. We empower our membership to achieve personal fulfillment through Service, Not Self. My second husband, Larry, made these goals to improve the lives of Negro veterans his life's work.

In June 1951, I was chosen as President of the Lemuel T. Boysden Post, No. 94, Women's Auxiliary of the American Legion, located at 8508 Cedar Avenue. At the June meeting we discussed the Legion Day celebration planned for June 24 at Geauga Lake Park which, at the time, was described as the World's Largest Theme Park. We also talked about setting up a fund to upgrade the machinery at the Salvation Army and the ways our Women's Auxiliary could help make both events a success.

One of my first plans was to sponsor a membership tea, inviting all members and encouraging them to bring friends. The program would be made up from the talent of our own members. *Hmm, I wonder if Patricia will play Claude DeBussy's "Claire de Lune" for us? It is my favorite song.*

In February 1952, Doris M. Haynes, spoke about "Courage and Americanism" and this month, Martin Kelly of the Hudson Boys Farm, spoke about "Community Service."

> POST No. 94 of the American Legion had as its speaker last month Doris M. Haynes who spoke on "Courage and Americanism". This month's speaker was Martin Kelly of the Hudson Boys Farm who spoke on "Community Service." Mrs. Daisy Marshall is president; Mrs. Ethel Mayo, first vice president; Mrs. Florence Wray, secretary; and Mrs. Ruth Hayes is treasurer.

Article about a speaker at the monthly American Legion meeting. Daisy Marshall was President. *Call and Post* Newspaper, 1952.

We held our Annual Memorial Day Service in May 1952, in the sanctuary of the Cory Methodist Church. Guest minister, Reverend John H. Riggins, preached an informative message on "Our Victor." An officer of each American Legion group called the roll of members who had died during the previous year.

ORDER OF THE EASTERN STAR

The Order of the Eastern Star is the largest fraternal organization in the world to which both men and women may belong. Worldwide, there are over 500,000 members. The organization was created in the United States in the early nineteenth century to allow women to join with their Masonic relatives in promoting the values and charitable purposes that are such an important part of the Masonic fraternity. While the Order of the Eastern Star has evolved over the centuries, it still remains rooted in its charitable endeavors and fraternal fellowship.

In 1850, Dr. Morris, the Poet Laureate of Masonry, is acknowledged as the "Master Builder" of the Order of the Eastern Star. He developed the Eastern Star Degrees in their present initiatory form using selected women of the Bible who personified heroic conduct and moral values. My second husband, Larry, was a 33rd Degree, Prince Hall Mason. Today, the Order has more than 650,000 members in over 5,000 chapters.

There are five "degrees," or lessons, in the Order of the Eastern Star, to teach the Masonic principles of charity, truth, and loving kindness. Each is based on a Biblical heroine—three from the Old Testament and two from the New Testament. Each of the five degrees also represents a woman's relationship to her family—daughter, sister, wife, widow, and mother. Each of the degrees teaches a moral lesson that is designed to improve and build character.

Some of the Eastern Star heroines are well-known Biblical characters—Ruth, Esther and Martha. Among those who are best known Eastern Star heroines are American Red Cross Founder Clara Barton and author Laura Ingalls Wilder.

I was proud to be a part of this organization, sharing the moral lessons learned there to my children and grandchildren.

OTHER ORGANIZATIONS AND CAUSES

I fought for many causes during my lifetime. When I could better my community, I would, whole-heartedly. For example, in 1966, during the Civil Rights era, my Glenville housing community pleaded with Police Chief Wagner and the City Council's Safety Committee to protect our neighborhood from riots from black nationalist groups. The *Call and Post* newspaper covered our impassioned efforts.

TOTAL CONCERN ABOUT THE PROBLEMS -- Sister Patrick Marie, St. Aloysius Catholic Church, and Mrs. Daisy Schumake, president of the East Blvd. Triangle Club, gave their strength to others by their presence at the hearing.

CHAPTER 28 - GRANDMA TO THE RESCUE

(Cleveland, Ohio, 1957-1980, Daisy)

A daughter is not supposed to die before her mother, but that's what happened in 1971 to my spirited second daughter, Shirley Jean Marshall Chick. Her unexpected death left her three children—Michal, Carolyn, and Lori—for me to raise full-time, as their father was not in a position to raise them himself.

Carolyn Chick, Daisy Schumake, Lori and Michal Chick,
1543 East Blvd., Cleveland, OH, circa 1966.

WHAT IS LOVE?

Truth be told, Michal, Carolyn and Lori had been living with me off and on for most of their lives, starting in 1957 when Michal was born. Their parents cared about them deeply, but folks who love the nightlife may not be as attentive as they need to be. I was *not* going to let my grandchildren slip through the cracks because of their parents' lifestyle. They spent most of their time with me, periodically visiting with their parents at the 2182 East 81st Street house.

By 1958, I was married to Larry, who was an excellent influence on my grandchildren. He was as preoccupied with education as I was, perhaps even more so. Larry was brilliant, patient, and knowledgeable about an infinite number of subjects, in addition to being a successful chiropodist.

In fact, he spoke French fluently, having lived there for a few years after World War I. He was quite disappointed that he could not convince me or my grandchildren to speak French conversationally at home. He even put the youngest, Lori, into "French School" before she was old enough to even learn the English language. She looked so cute in the Baby Bear costume I sewed for her performance in the play, "The Three Bears," which was "toute en français" (all in French). But the immersion Larry so desired did not take hold in our "maison" (house).

What was perhaps more important than being intelligent was Larry's loving nature. "Come on over here and give Grandpa a hug!" he would welcome when the children returned home from school. They ran to him and enjoyed his embraces, as they told him all about their day. I watched, with a modicum of jealousy that morphed into a deep, simmering anger.

As you may have already gathered, I have never been a Particularly affectionate person physically, at least not to my kids, grandchildren, or husbands. I can be friendly, but am generally more of a purposeful person. Smiles and hearty guffaws don't come to me often, except at social events when I enjoy being the life of the party.

I can't remember the last time I said, "I love you" to the kids, or even to Larry, or to my first husband. I may never have uttered those three little words that are so important to many people. It's just not part of my nature. I observed the lessons from my detached parents and grandparents, and followed suit. What's wrong with that? They should know I love them by all the things I do for them, right?

According to author Gary Chapman's *Five Love Languages*, there are five ways through which one can show love for others: using words of affirmation (compliments, loving statements), spending quality time, delivering acts of service, receiving gifts, and providing physical touch.

Mine love language is the middle choice. I show my love and caring by providing acts of service to people. I've already described the civic, church and other organizations I belong to, as well as the never-ending fundraising and other activities I gladly perform to make other's lives better.

Being "loving" in my mind has always been ensuring my kids and grandkids had what they *needed*, such as: nice clothes, school supplies, cooking healthy food, doing their laundry, and taking them to their many extracurricular enrichment activities on Saturdays. I cleaned up after them, taught them etiquette lessons, and administered healing treatments when they were sick. "I'm sending you to this school," "I'm paying for classes here." That's how I displayed my affection for them, not by hugging, kissing, or idol compliments.

I led by example on how to be a responsible citizen. I taught them to practice the Golden Rule and treat others as they would like to be treated.

I didn't need to assuage my family's egos by empty compliments or needless hugs or expensive gifts. *(Although, I did buy that piano for Lori, thinking she would love what I got for her, but I didn't receive the level of appreciation I had expected.)*

No, I needed to teach my kids and grandkids to be tough. The world would not coddle them, and neither would I. Now that's what I call love. It's how my parents taught me, and I turned out just fine.

Oddly enough, I never taught my grandkids how to cook, nor talked with Carolyn and Lori about female-related issues, ironing, nor washing clothes, like I had taught my daughter-in-law, Mary, in 1957. I kept those household responsibilities for myself.

WORK BEFORE YOU PLAY

My internal "church" was on Saturdays. It was to enrich my grandchildren with not only chores, but also exposing them to cultural experiences like dancing and music.

I gave my grandchildren assigned chores on Saturday mornings. Lori was responsible for dusting all the living room and dining room furniture. That included cleaning the table tops, bottoms and legs, and dusting around the baseboards. "Lori, make sure you dust everything sitting on top of the furnishings too," I would remind her.

"OK, Grandma," which was always the preferred response. No questioning what I said, just do it and say, "OK, Grandma" and we would get along just fine.

Carolyn's chores were to wipe down the walls and countertops in the kitchen, clean the refrigerator shelves, and put everything back neatly.

Michal was responsible for taking out the garbage, and sweeping and vacuuming all floors.

Each child was responsible for putting their dirty clothes in the hamper so I could wash, dry, and iron them while they were at school. I would hang them on hangers for the children to put away when they returned home.

After they completed their chores, they got dressed and I drove them to "The Music School Settlement" on Magnolia Drive, close to the Cleveland Art Museum, for cultural enrichment activities. It was a beautiful old mansion they converted into a recital hall with practice rooms for music lessons. There was a small dance studio in back which might have originally been an in-law suite. Lori had dance and piano lessons. Carolyn had piano lessons, and Michal played the saxophone. That was the kind of church program I imbued the children in my care with: chores and culture.

After their work had been completed, they could turn on the TV. They loved watching a program called *Super Host* in the afternoon, where a quirky fellow aired *Godzilla, Dracula,* and other monster movies.

The children knew full well that whatever they wanted to do on the weekend, whether that was visiting friends, going to a movie, or watching TV, had to be preceded by the completion of their homework and chores. Some did this willingly, some didn't.

DAILY ROUTINE

Every morning, seven days a week, I got up at five a.m. sharp. I did my calisthenics and stretching exercises, like sit-ups, push-ups, and touching my toes. Then I made coffee, got dressed for the day, and started making a full breakfast for Larry and the kids.

On school days, I woke the children up at about six a.m. Even though they took a bath every night, in the morning I made them take a "whore's bath," which consisted of washing their faces, armpits and private areas, at the sink. They got dressed in the clothes I had already pressed and laid out for them the night before. Lori wore a uniform to the Catholic school she attended, but Michal and Lori selected their own clothes.

Carolyn and Michal had declared their independence once they reached a certain age, ten, I think, and did their own grooming. But there was a stool in the bathroom at which I enjoyed combing, brushing and plaiting Lori's fine, long, light brown hair.

"Lori, who's been playing in your hair?" I would question her after school. I could tell at a glance when someone had loosed, then attempted to re-braid my masterwork.

"Um, well," Lori would respond in a mousy little girl voice, "The girls at school are always, um, saying how pretty my hair is, and, um, they like to touch it, and, um, sometimes they accidentally unbraid it. They say I should let it stay loose and wear it like that, because it's so nice and soft."

"Don't let them touch your hair again!" I would command. Lori knew she had to stop that practice, no matter how nice it felt to have someone play with her hair, or how good the compliments made her feel.

We had a similar breakfast ritual of orange juice, eggs, bacon, sausage, pancakes, and toast that I described earlier in this story. However, the castor oil was only administered a few times a year, like when we did spring cleaning. My grandkids would not be like the typical American child who received sugary cereal or a candy bar to fuel their brain for the day. No. I made sure they had proper nourishment to excel in school.

As the kids got older, it became more difficult for all of us to eat breakfast together. I gave them money to eat lunch at school, since it was getting harder and harder for me to make their lunches the older they got. Peer pressure—not that I cared about that—weighed on their minds. They wanted to be accepted by other students. They wanted to eat what the other kids ate.

I drove the kids to school most mornings while they were going to Margaret Spellacy Junior High School, on 162nd Street. It was a medium-sized school which served about 300 students in the seventh through ninth grades. Minority enrollment was 97% of the student body, with a majority Negro. It's 72% graduation rate was lower than the Ohio state average of 82%. My grandkids needed a better education than what was offered in public school so they would be prepared to get into, and graduate from, an excellent college.

I sent Michal and Carolyn to Collinwood High School, which is in an Italian neighborhood on the east side of Cleveland. Collinwood High School was considered one of the best in the county for preparing students to enter the professions. I personally knew the political powers that be and was able to get them enrolled in this previously segregated school. While there was considerable animosity and negative social interactions toward Negro children during the turbulent desegregation efforts of the 1960s and 1970s, my grandchildren received an excellent education there.

In fact, all of Michal's friends were straight-A students. You better believe that Larry and I made sure of that. Michal had been in Honors classes since the second grade and, as I once heard him say, he was "on the Geek Squad" from then on. He was in the band and a member of other organizations at the high school, so he often left the house earlier than the other kids. He took the city bus, or got a ride from other students, to get to school early.

Carolyn was a spicy child, like her mother, always asking, "Why this, and why that?" to my rules. But she understood there was no choice. There would be no debating where they went to school. All of her friends were on the same track anyway, getting good grades, and that studious behavior rubbed off on her, thankfully.

Even if their friends weren't good students, it wouldn't have mattered. My grandchildren knew better than to come home with anything other than A's with maybe one B. They all knew full well that getting a "C" on their report card would result in some kind of *disagreeable* and immediate consequence.

Larry and I were on the same page, as far as education was concerned. He was the one who corrected the kids' spelling and language at the table. If a child asked us about any topic, Larry would respond succinctly, "Get the book." "The Book" was a huge Random House dictionary, which presided on an ornately carved pedestal in the front room. The children would sit with Larry, look up the topic, and read the entry aloud. Larry would ask all sorts of questions about what she or he had just read and they would discuss the item until it was well understood. He would explain whether the word came from the Greeks or Latin. Often, all the children—even five years younger Lori—would be summoned, so they could hear the same information. That resulted in young Lori's knowledge base being aggrandized well before her time, her brilliance helping her to graduate from high school at the age of sixteen.

Yes, we provided a text-rich household for all of our grandchildren. You couldn't go two feet without finding all types of books. *Esquire* and *Time* magazines, McGuffey Readers, and other types of books were everywhere in our house.

Larry and I helped our grandchildren understand that their way *out* was to get a great education in Cleveland, so they could get into whatever college they wanted, so they could become whatever they wanted in life. The key to get *out* of the doldrums of the confining life white America placed upon Negroes, was to become educated. On that score, Larry and I were on the same page.

Hmm, I had never thought about teaching the children under my roof how to sew. Come to think of it, I didn't teach them to cook either, like I did for my daughter-in-law, Mary, when she lived with me in 1957 to 1958. I did all the cooking and ironing for the members of my household, as proof of my love for them. They had some basic cleaning chores on Saturday mornings, sure, but I did quite a bit of house cleaning too.

For someone who wanted to prepare my kids to be successful in the world, it is unfathomable that I didn't teach them the basics of self-preservation, such as cooking, nutrition, washing clothes, etc. But I'm sure they will do just fine, having become well-educated, critical thinkers. After all, they can always hire a maid!

THE ALMIGHTY

Some people may think it odd that I didn't preach to my grandchildren, after having been a Trustee and devoted member of St. James AME Church for fifty years. But I didn't speak to them about God or Satan. I didn't quote Bible verses. They didn't hear me saying, "Praise the Lord" or "Amen" or "God Bless" like most church people profess every other sentence. I faced the fact long ago that to get ahead in the Black community, one must regularly attend a Christian church, or be shunned as a blasphemer.

It bothered me that many who profess to be children of God, show their faces in church every Sunday, but break every one of the Commandments when they're not there: coveting thy neighbor's wife, lying, stealing, killing. Then they seek absolution for their ill deeds in confessional during the next week in church. "After all," they say, "Jesus died for our sins." For some hypocritical people, they feel *that* powerful phrase gives them license to do whatever they want, to whomever they wish. I don't buy it.

I don't follow the adage that all you have to do is "Pray on it" either, to get good things in your life. No. I believe one must take personal responsibility for one's actions, suffer the negative consequences of poor choices, or relish the good consequences of smart choices. That's what my parents taught me. It made sense, so I taught the same to my kids and grandkids. Truthfully, I was always there for my kids, even when they made stupid choices, but the concept of personal responsibility was, and is, sound.

With that said, I did, of course, take the children to church every Sunday when they were young. We ate breakfast, dressed in our finest clothes, grabbed our Bibles and drove to St. James AME. But as the children got older, they sometimes had other plans, so it was just Lori and me going to the Catholic church by the mid-1970s. It was really pretty routine.

Some may think this heresy, but I drilled into their heads that, "Self-preservation is the first law of life." You can't help other people unless you've taken care of yourself first. I learned that from the reverends.

My Other Grands

Larry and I had ten grandchildren living in the Cleveland area, not just Shirley Jean's three. Patricia had five kids: Jocelyn, Scott, Francina, Marsha, and Kevin. Austin Jr. had Pershell and Austin David. Our local descendants often spent every major holiday at our house, all of us looking forward to the three FFFs: fellowship, food, and family, at those get togethers. I don't know who had more fun, the grownups watching the children, or the young cousins playing together.

My daughter, Patricia, and her five children, lived in an apartment complex next to my much bigger, nicer, and more immaculate East Blvd. apartment. Even though I was stern with her and her children, every morning at about seven a.m. I looked through my kitchen window, watching Patricia's children walk from their apartment to the bus stop. I continued keeping an eye on them until they got safely into the bus. We lived at the edge of a difficult neighborhood, so I always made sure my grandkids were safely on their way to school, before I could continue my day.

When the grandchildren were young, I was more hands-on with regard to attempting to impart solid ethics and values on their psyches. For example, I knew Pershell was interested in sewing, so I purchased a Singer sewing machine for her, so she could make extra money sewing garments for herself and others. *Hmm, I probably should have taught Carolyn, Michal, and Lori a thing or two about sewing too.*

Pershell ended up being a teacher. Always an energetic and positive person, she spends time with her Jazzercise exercise group, along with fundraising for breast cancer research and other worthy causes. She maintains a big beautiful smile and makes people feel at ease around her.

251

Austin David worked for the Greater Cleveland Regional Transit Authority, in the Engineering and Construction and Track Department. When he retired, he worked for RIG Engineering Consulting as a Transportation Construction Inspector. He married Marie James and they had two talented and successful daughters. Shamira became a lawyer from Stanford University, after playing golf competitively for Kent State University, Ohio. Younger daughter, Nia, was a three-time All-Ivy honoree basketball star at Cornell University, ranking in the top four, nationwide, in scoring and steals.

Patricia's eldest daughter, Jocelyn, a retired teacher, moved to Atlanta, GA, where she had two children. Brittanie, a teacher at a charter school, known as Brookhaven Innovation Academy, has a son named Braylon. Jocelyn's son, Sterling, works for The City of Atlanta as a Watershed Manager in the Office of Performance and Accountability. He and his wife, Laura, are the proud parents to daughter Keora.

Patricia's son, Scott, recently retired from his job with the City of Cleveland. He is father to son Jason, and daughter, Sydney.

After caring for their mother, Patricia, until her death in 2010, daughter Marsha gradually resumed her work as a talented artist, and continues to reside in the Cleveland area. She is mother to Owen, and grandmother to Jaelun.

Daughter Francina took off early in her adult life for New York to become a jazz singer. For more than thirty years, she has remained active in the Harlem community and continues to sing professionally at various events.

Son Kevin, an entrepreneur, happily resides outside the Cleveland area with his wife, Becky, and their combined brood of five sons (Christian, Joshua, Gabriel, Gregory, and Douglas).

My middle son, Dr. Thomas Richard Marshall's, eldest daughter Kathy—the author of this book—lived with me from 1957 to 1958 for a year after her birth. She worked for the California Highway Patrol as a researcher, analyst, and technical writer for thirty-six years. She also ran her successful Kanika

African Sculptures art business for twenty-six years. Her oldest son, Isaac, served our country in the U. S. Marines as a career after high school, serving in Iraq, Okinawa, North Carolina and California. He and his wife, Jameillah, had three children: Jazmine, Isaiah, and Jeremiah. Kathy's youngest son, Matthew, was a computer programming expert with the State of California, as well as an impressive black belt who was the National Free-Style Taekwondo Champion in 2015-16.

Thomas's daughter, Carrie, ran her own designer clothing, jewelry, and Mary Kay consulting businesses before becoming a teacher in two Sacramento area K-12 school districts. She ended her thirty-year career as a High School Vice-Principal. In retirement, she devoted many volunteer hours as a member of Eta Gamma Omega Chapter of Alpha Kappa Alpha Sorority, Incorporated®. Her organized daughter, Lauren, worked for the State of California, and has a handsome son E'Drece. Carrie's husband Romeo retired from the Sacramento Metropolitan Utility District.

Thomas' son, Gregory, joined the Sacramento Fire Department serving as an engineer on the Light Plant truck and Hazardous Materials Team. At the age of thirty-six, he and his wife bought a rural hilltop property, then purchased a Hypnotherapy School for a few years. After their divorce, Greg became a building contractor and licensed life insurance salesman, along with maintaining his physical fitness riding bicycles competitively, like his father.

My youngest son, Bruce Sr., and his wife, Rae, had four sons—Bruce Jr., Terrell, and twins Jason and Christopher. I saw my California grandchildren a few times during my senior years when I visited them in the 1960s and 1970s. I remember them being the most beautiful children. Coming from my handsome son, Bruce, and his stunning wife, Rae Evelyn, they couldn't help but be gorgeous. Bruce Jr. moved to Las Vegas, married, and had three daughters. Terrell retired from the Sacramento Police Department and has two sons by his first wife and one daughter by his second. The twins are making their way the best they can.

The entrepreneurial bug from some of my ancestors trickled down to some of my descendants: Pershell, Bruce Sr., Kevin, Michal, and all of Thomas' kids. They all got *it*: the desire to be in business for themselves, at least part-time.

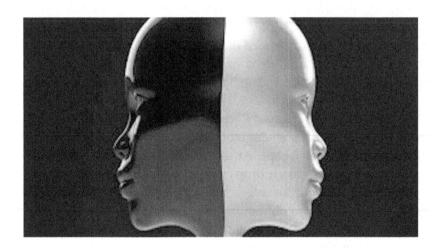

CHAPTER 29 - THE BEAST

(Lifelong, Daisy)

My temper was not that of a cute little lamb, gently bounding up a bucolic hill, nuzzling a lovely clump of yellow daisies. No, my anger was that of a behemoth lioness, galloping toward her prey with uncontrolled ferocity.

If I heard my grandson calling his sister a foul name, he felt my full wrath exiting my hand, stinging the side of his cheek.

If children were playing around instead of doing their homework, they received a hard smack on their bare buttocks with whatever object I had handy.

If someone had their elbows on the dinner table, I smacked them off and into their lap, where their hands belonged.

If children wouldn't stay away from the hot stove, I put their hand over a hot burner so they felt the sting of heat, reminding them to keep their distance in the future.

If young children were talking too loudly while I was watching my stories on TV, I might lift them off the ground by their ears cluing them they made it impossible for me to hear TV.

If children were acting wild and not following my regime, I might lock them in the hall closet for a while and let them think about my rules, so they would do better the next time. The more banging on the door, calling out, crying or pleading, the longer they would stay in that dark, lonely closet.

The rules were clear and didn't change. So when they were broken, there was no preamble, no verbal warning, no anger, no "please stop doing that." I didn't scream at the offender, except in the case of one particular child, and one grandchild, who gave as good as they got.

I posed no useless questions like, "Why did you do that?" or "I told you not to do that again," like the lenient parents of today say over and over to their spoiled kids.

There was no "time-out" before I pounced on the offender with a violent act which they would certainly remember. The contact was generally quick—a smack, a punch, or a fork lodged in the arm. Whatever was in my hand at the time could become an implement of discipline. Rarely did I deliver an actual beating that lasted any length of time.

I believed my response was always warranted. It was justified. It wasn't arbitrary or capricious. It was fairly distributed amongst the kids, because I had no favorites. My response to anyone ignoring my rules was immediate and generally physically violent. Cause and effect. Just as it should be. And then it was done. No lingering words of wisdom, or shouting, or pouting on my part, at least. The remedy was quick and effective.

If a child dared ask, "Why did you do that?" as they covered their slapped cheek or bottom, then I might give them an explanation, but usually they already knew what they did wrong. They broke the rules, plain and simple.

The children in my care didn't have to tremble, worrying to themselves, "Oh, I wonder what she's going to do to us today." If they weren't guilty of anything, there was no punishment. They didn't have to live in fear that I would be a Dr. Jekyll or Mrs. Hyde. If they did what they were supposed to do, when they were supposed to do it, I honored the rules and nothing undesirable would happen to them.

I had hoped they would take note of what happened if a sibling did something wrong, learn from their sibling's painful experience, and avoid doing the same thing. But hard heads are in every family, I guess, and some people just have to push the boundaries and find out for themselves. Some people are just deviant and want to provoke or needle others, talking back, and rolling their eyes, etc. I am choosing not to mention names here, but they know who they are!

After each outburst of discipline, I convinced myself the violence was warranted because of *that* person's actions. No, I was not abusive. Absolutely not. I simply meted out discipline that was *earned*, just like my parents did to us kids and, I imagine, like their parents did to them. In fact, every adult I grew up with handled discipline in the same manner. That was how we showed our love: trying to teach our children how to survive the cold, white world.

"Abuse," in my mind, would entail someone playing by the rules but still getting punished for no good reason. *I* didn't do that, although my daddy and other male elders did seem to take out their frustrations on their wives and children, whether it was merited or not. I could personally vouch for that type of misguided behavior.

Now to be honest, what I just said about fairness and deserved punishment didn't always apply to my husbands. If a husband came home drunk and dared to cross me, or tried to pick a fight with me, he felt my wrath just as surely as Jesus was on the cross. If a husband disagreed with my point of view, harsh words might fly out of my mouth in frenetic response, possibly accompanied by physical contact—like pummeling him with my fists, or busting a lamp on his head. Sometimes I was irrational and arbitrary, and lashed out with the ferocity of a lioness. And more often than I care to admit, I could not stop myself.

Perhaps because of ill treatment I received as a child in Mississippi, and the nasty paternalistic behaviors that were heaped upon female relatives, I vowed to never allow myself to be in a submissive position. Admittedly, I was sometimes the perpetrator of verbal or physical skirmishes, getting first dibs on adult males. It made me feel powerful, when often our history dictated that women must just *take* the abuse.

Larry and I believed children needed to be taught strong survival lessons. We didn't spoil them by letting them have everything they wanted, or letting them disrespect their elders or each other for that matter. America would not willingly let Negro children do whatever they pleased. Children had to know their place, but they also needed to use their brains and, along with our instruction, learn to excel at whatever they decided to do with their lives.

It was Larry's and my job to teach the value of education and living a life of service to the community at large. They needed to be leaders. But before one can be a leader, one must learn how to follow. I taught them well to follow my rules, but if they chose otherwise, I would let my beast remind them, each and every time I must admit that Larry and I had some nasty, knock down—literally—drag out fights.

My beast calmed considerably after Larry had a stroke. I cared for him to the best of my ability when he needed me: changing bedpans, helping him eat, keeping him clean, the whole nine yards. Some may have felt that I was a little heavy-handed and didn't have as light a touch as perhaps a nurse needed, but I did my best to make Larry comfortable during his last year. I felt remorseful after he died in 1976.

PART IV - THE FALL

Daisy Rae Dooley Marshall Schumake, Cleveland, OH, circa 1980.

CHAPTER 30 - DESTITUTE

(Cleveland, Ohio, 1979, Daisy)

"Where did all the money go?" I asked myself, glancing at the ever-increasing stack of unpaid bills on the desk. A heavy sigh escaped my lips. With Larry gone, I was like the proverbial ship without a rudder. Though we (I mainly) fought constantly, I so loved and respected that educated man. No one had a more complete intellect than Lawrence Powell Schumake Sr. But why oh why did he not leave a Will, or any kind of financial provision for me?

I had been the primary caretaker of the household and everyone living in it when Austin was a Pullman porter, gone most days of the month. I handled everything with precision: raising five children, ensuring they were fed, healthy, used proper manners, got to and from school, and earned good marks in class.

By 1975, grandson Michal had graduated from high school and had secured a scholarship to attend the prestigious Stanford University in California. Larry was as proud of him as I was! Those days of researching from the *Random House Dictionary*, having access to reading material here at the house, and his being in Honors classes throughout most of his educable years, paid off. Only five percent of applicants are accepted at Stanford. Mostly due to his exemplary grades and achievements, Michal was one of the lucky ones who had been accepted. Unfortunately, after tuition and housing, there was no scholarship money left for food or transportation, so Michal needed to find a part-time job once he arrived at the campus.

During our seventeen-year marriage, Larry took over the finances for our family. I let him handle that burden to give me a much needed break. But after he died so suddenly, I had rather forgotten the importance of paying our bills in a timely fashion. I suppose it was grief, or maybe age was starting to creep up on me. I was seventy-four years old when Larry died in June 1976. At that time, I was still taking care Carolyn and Lori, while Michal was a student at Stanford University in California.

Carolyn graduated from Collinwood High School in 1977. Larry and I had already decided she should go to Cleveland State University. After earning her Bachelor's Degree, Carolyn studied Executive Management at Baldwin Wallace University, an independent liberal arts college in Berea, Ohio. She would parlay her education and drive into the banking industry, holding leadership positions throughout her career.

I had retired from my nursing job in 1967 to devote more time to raising my grandchildren, but after Larry died, I gave up many of the glamourous society liaisons Larry and I had together. I lost something of myself in the process, and I guess my mind began to slip. So the bills mounted, late fees were applied to the balances, and creditors began sending letters and knocking on my door.

I couldn't concentrate. I was dumbfounded with the letter from the bank indicating we would be evicted. My brain could not focus on the import of our depleted status. Embarrassed, I consulted with our reverend and asked his opinion on what I should do. Through his many contacts, he suggested I rent a small place on Tungsten Avenue in 1979, which would be more in keeping with our meager means.

We had to downsize our lifestyle. Carolyn, Lori and I painfully sorted through the precious possessions I had collected over the past five decades in the Promised Land.

Our extensive library of books had to go. Hundreds of tomes we had perused over the years were given to the church and local libraries. But we saved the huge *Random House Dictionary* and a dozen "must keep" books to take to our new abode.

I no longer needed, nor fit into, the fine clothes that had contributed to my triumphant presence at banquets and balls over the years. We were able to sell some outfits to consignment stores, and delivered armloads of others to the St. James clothes closet.

Many of our friends during the good days were kind and assisted our flight to a smaller footprint. But I felt some smirked with glee that I had fallen so low. Thankfully, there wasn't much time to dwell on those thoughts. We had to move.

CHAPTER 31 - SOMETHING IS WRONG

(California, 1979, Daisy)

When was the first time I realized something wasn't quite right? Perhaps it was yesterday when I couldn't find my car keys on their assigned hook. I finally found them two hours later in the laundry basket. How did they get there?

Perhaps it was last week when I left the grits boiling on the stove until the alarming smell of burning grains reached my nostrils, after the water had evaporated from the pot, leaving a crusty black carbon residue.

Perhaps it was when Lori and I had to move from our luxurious home on East Blvd., to the tiny hovel in the Euclid area of Cleveland after Larry died. Is that when my brain started to misfire?

Perhaps it was the 1979 trip to Sacramento, California, for my granddaughter Kathy's June wedding.

Chuck , Lovey, and Ken Anderson, Kathy, Thomas, Mary and Daisy Marshall, Ken and Kathy's wedding, June 1979, Sacramento, CA.

Yes, I think that was the beginning. Thomas had paid for my plane ticket and Patricia drove me to the Cleveland Hopkins Airport the day before the wedding. I felt fine in the large Boeing 747 plane, with my black leather purse in my lap. I was nestled in the middle seat between a young woman and an overweight, middle-aged man. I didn't make much small talk with the other passengers. I wasn't wholly comfortable with airplane travel so thankfully, I was able to sleep during much of the flight.

Thomas' auburn-haired girlfriend, Susan, was waiting for me as I got off the plane at the Sacramento Airport. My brilliant son was at the hospital delivering a baby and had asked his girlfriend to bring me home. Susan was pleasant enough, chatting in a soft voice on the hour long ride to Thomas' modern, tri-level home in the small rural town of Loomis.

Wooded and pastural properties bordered Wells Avenue to the edge of his long, black, asphalt driveway. I couldn't believe this setting! We meandered past a huge rectangular pond on the right side of the road. Thomas had mentioned in casual conversation on the telephone that he had filled the lake with small-mouth bass. The driveway continued up a steep winding blacktop road to a majestic house on a hill.

I had never seen a house like his before! I almost wouldn't even call it a house. It was built into the side of the grassy hill, overlooking the pond down below. The top floor of the house had two large rectangular rooms, each probably sixteen feet deep and thirty feet long. The living room took up one side of the top level. In the sparsely decorated living room was one TV, one wood-trimmed white leather couch and chair, and a black leather bean bag chair for people more limber than me to nestle into.

Thomas' bedroom was on the other side of the expansive top floor. It had built-in closets and drawer cabinets whose door fronts blended seamlessly into the wood-paneled walls. His large bathroom had a rectangular sunken black slate tub with jacuzzi spa jets in the sides; lots of mirrors; a commode set inside its own tiny, wood-paneled room; and built-in teak-wood drawer cabinets under each of two sinks.

The top floor was covered with two-inch-high, thick black shag carpet. I had never seen anything like it! I thought it was hideous, like a nappy head in need of a good comb out.

The second floor had a tiny kitchen, maybe ten-feet wide and twenty-feet long. It included a cramped, tiled table big enough to seat four people. On the other side of the kitchen wall was an oval, glass dining room table that could barely seat eight people. Who designed that inhospitable kitchen and tiny dining room?

Next to the dining room was an eight-by-eight-foot wooden atrium, five feet off the floor, with plants and trees that extended up to the third floor ceiling. Wow!

Walking down satiny black slate stairs led to the lowest level, looking onto a large open room. One side of that room was a sunken ten-foot-by-ten-foot seating area. The floor was covered with long, purple shag carpet—imagine that! But there's more: a red, orange, and purple striped velvety sofa bordered three sides of the sunken space. Thomas' second wife, Pam, had quite the imaginative design sense!

Two small bedrooms and one bathroom led down the hall to the garage. At the base of the stairs was a pool of water with koi fish swimming slowly around and around the confined four-by-four-foot space.

The most striking aspect of Thomas' home was that one side of the house, from the bottom floor to the top was entirely made from glass! The view was incredible, looking out past the fifty-foot-long oval swimming pool, just outside the lower-level bedrooms. To the right of his property was a lush peach orchard, and to the left, was his neighbor's horse ranch way down the hill.

This was a most unusual house, certainly, but it seemed familiar to me somehow…Oh, yes, now I remember it vividly. In 1971, eight years earlier, I brought Michal, Carolyn, and Lori here after their mother, Shirley Jean, had died. How could I forget that earlier trip? What's wrong with me?

I now remember that 1971 visit to California from Cleveland. I would admonish the kids to "stay out of the sun so you don't get too dark," when the kids swam in Thomas' pool. And can you believe those children thought they could swim in that pool at night? "Get out of that pool," I demanded. "You're all going to drown!" But they paid me no mind at all, just laughed and kept on playing "Marco Polo" in the pool. These kids nowadays have no respect for their elders.

I was glad the first cousins were enjoying themselves, even though they were louder than my ears would like. While they were playing all day long, I decided to wash Thomas' many floor-to-ceiling windows. You see, I can't sit still. My joints get stiff with arthritis. Being busy eases the pain in my fingers and toes. *Why didn't I remember that earlier trip to California?*

Not in Kansas Anymore

Tomorrow, June 6, 1979, is Kathy's wedding day and she asked me to wear something colorful and comfortable. The wedding ceremony and reception would be held outdoors in her in-law's home garden, and the weather was predicted to be well over one hundred degrees. I brought just the right dress for the event with me. It was a long, cotton dress, tight at its high-waisted white bodice, over a long skirt of bright Caribbean colors. It should be perfect.

Unfortunately, Thomas was running late, as usual, and by the time we finally got to Kathy's in-laws' home, the wedding ceremony was over. I was *so* disappointed! To have come all that way but to miss the main event! Thankfully, the reception was held there, and I got to see my three California grandchildren—Carrie, Greg, and Kathy, of course. I got to meet the bride's handsome new husband, Kenneth Wayne Anderson, his welcoming parents, Lovetta and Charles Anderson, their large family, and dozens of friends. But most treasured of all was being able to mingle with my dearest daughter-in-law, Mary, once again. She and I made plans for me to visit her home the following day.

I was so excited to be able to spend the whole day with Mary! Thomas dropped me off in the morning on his way to work and said he would be back to pick me up at four-thirty p.m. Mary and I talked and talked, just like the old days when she was living with me in 1957, in Cleveland, just before and after Kathy was born.

Mary fixed me a lovely lunch with turkey and avocado sandwiches and a fresh fruit salad, with an unusual marshmallow and mayonnaise dressing. She also served the potato salad I taught her to make two decades earlier. She had made delicious

266

homemade ice cream made from the fruit off her forty-foot-tall peach-laden tree in the backyard.

"Mary, this has been a lovely day, and I've enjoyed myself immensely catching up with you. The meal was delicious. I hope we can do this again soon, but now, I've got to get back home." I got my purse and walked toward the front door.

"Wait, Daisy, Thomas is going to pick you up in a couple of hours," Mary said, as she kept her hand firmly on the door handle, not letting me leave.

"That's all right, Mary, I know my way home. I've got to water my flowers soon or they will die from the heat," I responded, trying to remove her hand from the door knob.

"But Daisy, you are not in Ohio. You are in Sacramento, California, remember?" Mary countered, her voice sounding oddly concerned.

"Now, Mary, don't try to pull the wool over my eyes. I'm right down the street from my house. I thank you so much for your hospitality, but I must go now," I insisted, starting to use my stern "Mother" voice, and fumbling to remove her hand from the door knob.

Mary looks so agitated, but I don't know why. I told her I liked her food and her house, and that I had enjoyed a wonderful visit with her. Why won't she let me go home now? Why is she rushing to the telephone on the wall? Why is she trying to get a hold of Thomas? Doesn't she know he is busy working? She can't disturb the doctor while he's working. Well, I'll just take this opportunity to make my exit and walk home. It's not far. I know the way. I'll take my purse and start walking down the sidewalk, then around the corner...

"Oh mother, there you are," said Thomas, speaking from the rolled down window in his car.

"Mother, Mary called and said you decided to walk home instead of waiting for me to pick you up. She was worried about you because it's so hot today and you didn't take any water with you before you left."

"That Mary is such a sweetheart," I responded. "I had a wonderful time with her, but I needed to water my plants."

"Well, Mother, it is hot outside. I'll drive you home, OK?"

After a while in the car, I realized I didn't know where I was. This didn't look like Cleveland at all. Where were the tall buildings? I didn't recognize any of the street names. Oh...I remember now. I'm not in Cleveland. That's right, I flew to Sacramento a couple of days ago for Kathy's wedding. What's wrong with me?

CHAPTER 32 - SLIPPING INTO DARKNESS

(Cleveland, Ohio, 1979-1980, Daisy)

Maybe the first time I noticed something was wrong was on a day in April 1979, when I got into my Ford Maverick to take Lori to Collinwood High School. It was a magnet school fifteen-minutes away, located in a predominantly Italian neighborhood. It was during the forefront of the difficult integration movement of the 1970s. Imagine that thirty years after my husband, Lawrence, had been working night and day to attempt to integrate the U.S. military, we were still experiencing de facto segregation, even Up North in the Promised Land of Cleveland.

On that crisp spring morning in April, I slid my body into the too-big-for-a-petite-woman driver seat, laid my purse down next to Lori in the passenger seat, then firmly closed the heavy car door. We adjusted our seatbelts, I craned my neck to check the mirrors, then turned on the engine, stretching out my right foot onto the accelerator to give the engine some extra gas to warm it up. All I was going to do was take Lori to school. Like always.

The car ride was about fifteen minutes away from our home. I had made this short trip countless times with Lori's brother and sister years before. Nothing would be different this time. I put the car into reverse, backed out of the carport, stopped, shifted into drive, then proceeded to travel along East Boulevard toward Superior Avenue, to East 123rd Street, toward the school on St. Clair Avenue.

All of a sudden, in the distance, I saw fingers of wispy mist seeping toward my car. To see such a thing on a summer day in Cleveland is strange indeed, but the fog came closer, soon surrounding me. I could see nothing past the windshield but a dense whiteness.

In the distance, I started to hear something like the trumpets of angels coming into earshot. The swirling air was thick inside the car now and I didn't know where I was. I lost track of time. More sounds from the angels, and what sounded like someone screaming my name, and then a jarring *bump*. All of a sudden, I stopped moving, and the murk slowly began to clear. What just happened? I blinked and opened my eyes wide. My large car was perched on the median strip in the middle of a busy street during morning commute. Oh my!

"Grandmother, what's wrong? Are you feeling sick?" said a high-pitched young voice. It was Lori on the passenger seat, looking worried. "Grandmother, you drove the car onto the median strip. We've gotta get out of this traffic right now."

Oh, I guess I blacked out or something and must have driven across both lanes of traffic, with my car running over the curb, and stopping on top of the median strip. Thankfully, my car didn't hit anyone before it stalled in the middle of this busy road. I didn't know what to do. Cars were honking all around us and that made me more anxious. I didn't know where I was headed, or how I got in to that predicament. I felt confused and anxious. "I'm done," I replied, not knowing what else to say or do.

Lori, thank goodness, assumed control of the situation. Although she had never driven a car (as far as I knew), she opened her side door, got out, and told me to scoot over. She ran around the back of the vehicle and got into the driver seat, while I sat on the passenger side. She had watched me drive and I guess figured out how to start the car. With some trepidation, she put her foot on the brake, then eased the car into "drive" as she cranked the steering wheel to the right. She looked over her shoulder to see when there was a break in traffic, then slowly lifted her foot off the brake. The car started to move slowly and thudded off the median strip, moving into the traffic lane. Cars were coming up behind us fast now, honking, as Lori tentatively put her foot down onto the accelerator pedal to speed up the car. Mercy, she was able to move the car over to the slow lane, turning onto a residential street. Recovering her nerve after a few moments, she decided to drive me home. She made sure I was safe inside the house, then drove herself to school.

Hmm. I'm hungry. I think I'll fix myself some breakfast. In the midst of biting into my buttered toast, I remembered being stuck on top of a median strip. What is happening to me? I pray nothing like that will ever happen again, but deep in the recesses of my brain, I feel I am slipping into darkness...

THE BAD MAN

A few nights later, I was watching television after Lori went to bed. I began to notice wispy tendrils appearing around the edges of the television screen. The fingers of fog were coming toward me again.

I knew it! That horrible Mr. Brown, the maintenance man who lived in the basement of my apartment, was up to no good, again. I could hear him walking around downstairs plotting his next move. I knew he was waiting for me to doze off so he could use his house key to come into my bedroom and steal my jewelry. Well, that wasn't going to happen tonight.

"Lori! Lori!" I shouted, "Call the police now! Mr. Brown is coming up the steps to grab my jewelry. Lori! Lori! Where *are* you?"

My granddaughter ran out of her dark bedroom, her eyes squinting from the bright light coming from the television. "What's wrong, Grandmother?" she asked, fear detected in her worried voice.

"Mr. Brown has a knife and he is going to hurt us and take our money and jewelry. Can't you see him right over there? Call the police! Quick!"

"Grandmother, what are you talking about? There's nobody here but you and me. Are you OK?"

"Get out of here!" I screamed toward Mr. Brown who was obviously standing in the room with us.

"Who are you yelling at?" Lori questioned. "You and I are the only ones in this house, besides the hamster."

Lori could not see the criminal right in front of her eyes! Was the girl blind? I tried to put on a brave face and order him out of my house, but he just stood there with his knife pointing at me, laughing at me, with his tall big blue hat on his huge head. His mouth grew wider and wider, as though he might be able to swallow me whole.

After what seemed like hours of terror, that bad man started to get smaller and smaller, receding back down the stairs, where he belonged. My pulse was still racing, though. I was so unnerved by that man entering my house.

"Grandmother, what is wrong with you? How may I help you? There is nobody else in our apartment. It's just you and me." Lori insisted, her voice calming down with each sentence.

As the haze left my head, I realized I was in my living room. My granddaughter was standing there in her night clothes, looking panicked.

"What's wrong, Lori? Why are you up, and why do you look so scared? Did you have a nightmare?" I asked. Lori had tears streaming down her face. "Lori, are you feeling ill? Why do you look so worried?"

"Grandmother, you kept shouting for me to call the police because you said Mr. Brown was in our house holding a knife on you. You said it over and over again." Lori cried.

"Nonsense. Now you stop trying to play tricks on me, Lori. Go back to bed. I won't stand for this behavior. You're just trying to stay up late to watch television. To bed, young lady! You need to get up early for school" I ordered, in my usual stern voice. Lori shook her head, but did as she was told, and I resumed watching television.

LARRY IS THAT YOU?

My second husband, Lawrence Schumake died in 1976. I called him Larry, but some people called him "Schu" for Schumake.

We shared many of the same dreams and both felt strongly in our leadership role as grandparents. Education was key in our household and we constantly encouraged all of our grandchildren, not just the three who were our wards in the East Blvd. house, to love learning in all of its forms.

Even though Larry and I *often* fought over *many* things, I still loved him and missed him terribly now that he was gone. Sometimes I felt the ache so intensely I believed he began to…well…reincarnate into…you'll think this is crazy, I know, into…my grandkids' hamster.

"Good morning, Larry. Did you have a good sleep? Were you warm enough last night? Do you want breakfast?" I would ask, as I prepared his usual breakfast of eggs, bacon, dry toast and prune juice. "Stop wolfing down your food. You'll get sick eating so fast!" I reminded him. Later in the day, "You'd better eat some dinner before we go to the church meeting tonight. I gave you an extra helping. Do you like it?" One day my Larry did not move, when I gave him his food. Oh my, he must have died in the night. I'll miss him.

[Author's Note: The real life hamster was named Freddie. He died from being overfed, but that didn't stop Daisy from sometimes speaking to an invisible Larry. Granted, most people never saw those behaviors, but some family members did witness inexplicable abnormalities in Daisy's behavior. She was observed talking to someone who was invisible to others.]

Now it's time for my stories. *General Hospital* is my favorite. It reminds me of my last job working as a nurse at Hanna Pavilion. "Now Ruby, you know you are too old to be a prostitute anymore," I shouted at the TV screen. "No, Jessie, don't give her a job at General Hospital! You don't know what kind of germs she would be bringing there!" I continued, acting like the actors on the screen could hear my every word. "See Jessie, I told you. Now that heffa, Ruby, is dating your old boyfriend, Dan Rooney, who wanted to marry you. Um-hmm, now you're jealous of their relationship."

I felt like I was part of their lives, trying to guide doctors and nurses on General Hospital to make good decisions, like I did all of my life with my children, grandchildren, friends, and acquaintances. There's nothing wrong with that, is there? Lots of people talk to the characters on their TV set, don't they? Anyway, it calms me and makes me feel good.

Don't Fail Me Now

I have always been unambiguous about my intentions, my actions, and my reactions…until recently. I think I started to have difficulty remembering simple things when I was about seventy-five. Sometimes I couldn't remember the correct word to say. Many times I forgot peoples' names, sometimes forgetting what I had just said. Yes, sometimes I would forget what I just said.

How can this be happening to me? My brain has always been sharp as a tack. I went to night school at the age of thirty-four to complete my high school diploma, then was one of few Negro women to graduate from the Western Reserve School of Mortuary Science. In the 1940s, I was a Co-Director and Embalmer for the Marshall Funeral Home, my first husband's family business. In the mid-1950s, while being the primary caregiver for my five children, I studied hard and became a practical nurse at Lakeside Hospital, until retiring in 1967. I was an active member of the St. James AME Church for fifty years. I served my country in the Women's Auxiliary of the American Legion, and the Order of the Eastern Star Jurisdiction of Prince Hall Masonry.

I enjoyed dressing up and being part of the exclusive private social club called the Royal Vaguettes and Vagabonds, made up of the most prominent Negroes in the greater Cleveland area.

I was a precinct leader for the Democratic National Committee. I served as President of the Bolton PTA. I was involved with the YMCA for numerous terms and was a youth sports team leader for years.

I held all of these overlapping positions with authority and accuracy, deserving the respect I received from the Negro community in Cleveland.

How could this be happening to *my* brain?

Daisy, youngest con Bruce, Lawrence Schumake, 1543 East Blvd., Cleveland, OH, circa 1966.

CHAPTER 33 - MY DIRTY LITTLE SECRET

(Cleveland, Ohio, 1980-1983, Daisy)

Who's left to help me now?

My first love, Austin Henry Marshall, died in 1967.

My fiery daughter, Shirley Jean Chick, died in 1971.

My second husband, Larry Schumake, died in 1976.

My son, Austin Marshall Jr., died of an aneurism in 1979.

My grandchildren, Michal and Carolyn, were in college.

My sons, Thomas and Bruce Sr., lived in California.

Patricia still lived in Cleveland but she was handling her own physical maladies and marital issues with her husband.

Lori was the only grandchild left living with me, but she was too young to drive, or do errands for me when I was feeling too poorly to do them myself.

I knew by now that my once magnificent brain was faltering, but I didn't know what to do about it. The apparitions came back to worry me night after night. I couldn't sleep for fear they would get me while slumbering. I didn't want to go to the hospital and have them lock me up in Sunny Acres, like we did to my poor brother-in-law, Israel Marshall, in 1955. What would happen to my granddaughter then?

My once-orderly synapses were now firing at will—their will. I would get lost while driving. I would forget what I was supposed to do at any given moment. I would forget the stove was on, which could have resulted in carbon monoxide poisoning if the flame went out. I couldn't find the words to describe my distress.

I didn't know who to tell about my problems and fears. I was Daisy Dooley Marshall Schumake, an ex-funeral home director, ex-nurse, civic activist, daughter of the church, leader and member of many organizations, widow, mother, and grandmother. I was a strong, independent woman. Who could I tell about my dirty little secret? Who could help me through these frightful days and nights?

Lori tried to get her Aunt Patricia and Uncle Thomas to get medical assistance for me, but they didn't believe her stories about my behavior. They couldn't fathom their mother sometimes speaking to a stuffed doll or to my invisible dead husband. They wouldn't accept that my mind was slipping away. I was the strongest person my children knew. They believed Lori just wanted attention since she was the last child living here with me…but her stories were all true. I needed help.

Late one night, I heard Lori calling her cousin, Kathy. She was worried to death that I would do something terrible to rid myself of the ghosts that haunted me. Sometime later, though, I heard Lori tell her cousin to stop ringing the alarm. Lori worried she could be sent away to foster care if our secret was discovered.

Yes, Lori saw the writing on the wall, my crumbling wall. My intrepid youngest grandchild taught herself how to drive, transporting herself to and from Collinwood High School every day. She did the grocery shopping and ran errands for me. Lori also began studying like a mad woman. Lo and behold, she was able to graduate early from high school. I so admired her chutzpah! She became a totally independent girl-woman by the age of sixteen, taking care of both of us.

One day, Patricia came over while I was having one of my "spells," chastising (dead) Larry about something or other. She saw with her own eyes what Lori had been trying to tell her the prior years. It was clear I desperately needed help. Patricia must have called Thomas because, finally, oh blessed be, they took over and I was no longer in torment. They had me evaluated by a doctor, and had to accept his diagnosis that I had full-blown Alzheimer's disease.

By then, Lori was eligible to enter college on a full ride scholarship, since she classified herself as an emancipated minor, living on her own.

Patricia and Thomas made arrangements in 1980 for me to live in a care facility—I never knew the name of it. During the few times my brain-fog disappeared, I realized how awful that place was. Thankfully, Carolyn and Lori visited me one day and saw how woefully inadequate the place was, especially for someone like me, who had always been so fastidious about cleanliness and orderliness.

There were obvious indicators of vermin and roaches at that place. Some elderly patrons were tied to chairs so they couldn't walk away. People were moaning and screaming to be let loose.

We called out for our families—families who didn't care to visit. Our faces were unclean, our hair uncombed, our bodies unwashed. The staff kept us overmedicated, so we didn't often realize how terrible the place was.

SALVATION

My granddaughters, whom I had raised well, could not believe that I—who had been so remarkable in my lifetime—was deteriorating in this rat-infested hell-hole. They must have forced Patricia to come and witness the deplorable conditions for herself. Only then did my grown children admit that their Amazon mother—me—was being treated so poorly. They rescued me and transported me to a beautiful memory-care facility near Lakeside Hospital, where I was treated well.

Every morning, the nice staff bathed me, then brushed my still-long, silvery-white, frizzy-wavy hair. Sometimes they braided it, or let it flow from a ponytail at the side of my head. I *loved* having my hair brushed. It soothed my beast. Sometimes when I flew into a rage, the only thing that could calm me was to have my hair brushed. And people had to use soothing voices to bring me out of the bewildering haze.

The nice ladies would rub lotion onto my hands and skin every day. People who visited from the church and American Legion would hold my hands and say how soft and beautiful they were.

The staff gave me baby dolls, and stuffed animals, to hold and love. But sometimes I became frightened when the dolls and animals turned evil. Then I had to punish them. Sometimes I wrenched their heads off, or their arms, or legs. I thought I was protecting myself from those bad men, those bad doll men who came in the night…

Some mornings, I would wake up and be fine, well, except that I could no longer speak in words that others could understand. Every day the nice nurses spoke to me in such gentle voices, and I would smile at them, and they would smile back at me. I couldn't find words to express what I was feeling, though.

Sometimes I felt so good…then my stomach would ache so much after eating, and the nurses would bring medicine that made me feel better. Sometimes the brain muddle would come back, and the bad dolls would need to be punished again and again.

People would visit me, smiling so kindly. "Are you Patricia?" I tried to ask, but it was actually Patricia's daughter, Jocelyn. I would smile at my son Austin Henry Jr., but he would correct me and say he was Austin David, my grandson. I couldn't usually remember the people who came to visit me. Then I would get mad at myself and take it out on them, by trying to slap them away.

The nurses would feed me and treat me well. But I felt so betrayed by my brain and body that I was quite cantankerous. I would get angry and lash out at them, hitting, biting, and kicking them when I felt like it. Kick? Wait…where's the bottom of my left leg? Oh, yes. Somebody told me they had to amputate part of my leg because I had diabetes, which caused a circulation problem. But why can I still feel the leg itching me sometimes?

THE LAST VISIT

Who's visiting me today? So many people are here with me, smiling at me, hugging me, giving me kisses on my cheek, and holding my lotion-soft hands. I like that. I smile back at them. Who are they? They take pictures, so many pictures. They speak to me in such nice, calming voices. I like that. I smile.

Oh, look at the precious little baby girl over there in her mother's arms. She's so cute, and…she has a baby doll in her arms. I want it. *Give me that doll!* But the baby won't let me play with it. I want it! It's a bad doll and must be punished! The baby cries when I grab at her doll.

The people stop taking pictures. They stop smiling at me. Instead, they look afraid. I fight to get that bad doll.

One by one, they leave. They all leave. I'm alone, once again.

278

Austin Jr., Mary, Lori, Daisy, Lauren, Carrie, Cleveland, OH.
Photograph: Kathy Marshall, 1983.

CHAPTER 34 - EVER AFTER

(Cleveland, Ohio, November 30, 1986+, Daisy)

Well, that was interesting.

A few days after our Thanksgiving dinner in 1986, I felt a strange sensation during my dream. I believed I had been tied up on my bed with a rope just below my ribs. It was squeezing tighter and tighter. I thought my stomach would burst out of my torso. I couldn't speak or yell. Then when I didn't think I could take the pain anymore, the ropes disappeared altogether, and I felt light as a feather.

Instead of the usual confusion in my brain, I could think lucidly again. My rusty synapses were firing on all cylinders, just like when I was young. I felt *no* pain and became limber of body, easily stretching my arms and legs and spine to their full extent. Did I perhaps just add a couple of inches onto my once-stooped frame?

Oh my, I had both of my shapely legs again, with no varicose veins anymore. My skin felt smooth to the touch. My silver hair loosed itself from the nighttime braid, flowing over my now straightened shoulders.

The morning nurse rushed in, glanced at me, then looked at the blinking whirring machines that were connected to my body via transparent rubber tubes. A low, audible hum came from the machine whose graph showed a solid horizontal line, going from one side of the monitor to the other. Every nurse knows that's not a good thing.

"Daisy, time to wake up now," the nurse ordered, but I didn't open my eyes. She shook me to wake me up, but the low flat-line hum persisted. The nurse used the pager at her waist to call for the crash cart, Code Blue, then she began administering CPR, trying to get my heart started again. Hum.

I watched with interest as she took my pulse and pried open my left eye. My iris did not enlarge or contract; no response means no brain activity. More CPR. She looked at my vitals on the blinking machines. Nothing. A flat line. My body lay inert, as I watched in fascination.

How did I know this? Well, believe it or not, I was floating above the bed, my back against the ceiling, as I gazed down at my Alzheimer's-riddled corpse. It was surreal. It was serene. It was marvelous.

My head was uncluttered. I felt like a young woman again. I saw no silver cord, though, as Shirley MacLaine described in her book, *Out on a Limb*. I saw no white light as many who claim to have died and gone to heaven, then came back again. Yet I was here, watching, like a surgical student watches an operation from the glassed room above the operating table. Interesting.

"Yes, the old girl's gone," the nurse said when the doctor arrived.

"Based on her basal temperature, I estimate the death took place at 7:00 AM on November 30, 1986," the doctor proclaimed. He wrote the information on my chart. This would become my official record of death. The death must be officially pronounced by someone in authority, like a doctor or the coroner. This person also fills out the forms certifying the cause, time, and place of death. Since hospice was already helping me at Lakeside Hospital, a written plan for what was to happen after my death was already in place.

"Doctor, I'm surprised we didn't get an alert in the nurse's station. I'll have the technicians check out this monitor right away. She must have died during shift change," the nurse said.

The doctor nodded and said, "Better call the family."

Checking my chart for contact information, the nurse phoned my daughter, Patricia. I listened to her suggest that Patricia come right away.

Who cares? *I am loosed* from my earthly bonds. I feel free as a bird. Can I actually fly like one? Even through these walls? Can I go anywhere I want? To Paris or Rome or even back to Noxubee?

"Technically yes," said a low, disembodied voice. Coming into view from the ceiling was my second husband, Larry. "Welcome, my dear," he said, as calmly as ever. For some reason, I wasn't surprised. I was glad to see him. There was no animosity or anger anywhere in my being. My beast was finally at peace.

The nurse telephoned the administration office to let them know about my death. Then the all-too-familiar process of calling the undertaker, and the "after" life activities began.

Time passed...or it didn't. I couldn't tell how many minutes or hours had passed since my death, nor did I care. I felt free. Buoyant.

My life does pass before my eyes, just like they say. What a joy! I can review all that happened to me from birth to death, like watching a technicolor movie about all I had accomplished in my eighty-four years on Earth. The accounting only takes the blink of an eye.

"Do you know what, Larry? I would not have changed one single thing about my life. I bet there aren't a lot of people who can say that."

"Well, Daisy, I would have liked you to have been nicer to *me*...but I understand what you mean. Everything happened for a reason. Whether it was the Good Lord or something else, we are both now at peace," Larry said.

Patricia came in with her tall, ebony, third husband, Bennie, holding her hand. Wails. Drapes herself over me in an embrace for a long moment, whispering her love. She uses the telephone in my room to call other family members to come right away.

"There's no hurry, Patricia. I'm free as a bird now," I shout, but of course, she can't hear me.

Bennie, an ordained minister, says some words to comfort his wife.

"Oh, so now he's acting all concerned about me. He always made such a fuss when Patricia wanted to visit me in the rest home," I commented to Larry who, of course, had seen everything for the last ten years from his lofty perch.

"It's just like watching TV, Daisy. You can dial into whichever channel you like, watching the lives of whichever person you wish. You find yourself shouting at them to make the right choices and then chastising them when they don't, or cheering them when they do."

My granddaughters, Carolyn and Lori, arrive, then Pershell and Austin David. Some time passes, then Scott, Kevin, and Marsha come in together. Cino must still be in New York, Jocelyn in Atlanta, and Michal, Thomas and Bruce in California.

283

Then the Reverend—what's his name—from St. James Church comes, blesses me, talks with the family for a few minutes, and then leaves.

My kids and grandkids speak in hushed, somber voices, which get louder as they talk about me and my remarkable life. They seem glad that my torment is over. Then Patricia cracks a joke, remembering something funny from the past, and they all laugh. Scott brings up another funny memory. Soon the whole lot of them are telling tales about me, while sitting around my inert body. They smile. They acknowledge that my tutelage prepared them to get into good schools, got them jobs they liked and which paid their bills. What more can you ask—learning that your children appreciated what you did for them? I feel proud.

A big man comes and carefully places my body on a stretcher. I watch it all from above. Larry and I float along as the gurney is rolled out of my room, into the hall, into the elevator, through the back door, then placed into the black hearse. Oh good! The big man drives me to E. F. Boyd's Funeral Home, which was our strongest competitor in the business. Nothing but the best for me.

Hours, or days, later, Thomas comes to Boyd's with Patricia. My eldest living children hold each other as they speak with the Funeral Director. They leave my favorite light gray suit for Boyd's staff to dress me in for my big day.

The embalmer prepares my body for the memorial service. My silver hair is stylishly coiffed above my head and my makeup is applied as I would have done. Family, friends, parishioners from St. James, and acquaintances from my other organizations will remember me at my best, at the open-casket service a few days after I died.

I was interred at Highland Park Cemetery, in Highland Hills, Ohio, alongside my daughter, Shirley Jean Chick, and son, Austin Henry Marshall. An American flag flies over my grave.

My body is gone, but my spirit soars. I find my mother, father, sisters, brothers, son, daughter, and even my first husband and his wife, Vernelle. They welcome me, and we laugh and rejoice in our reunion. All is good, just like the Good Book said it would be.

I see GramFannie! All of a sudden it dawns on me that she may have also had Alzheimer's or dementia, and maybe even diabetes. Is that why the 1910 Census said she was blind? Was that from diabetes? Is that why her husband signed her into the "Home for the Incurables" in Memphis, Tennessee, in 1915? Maybe this disease is hereditary…

Kathy Marshall at Daisy's grave at Highland Park Cemetery, Highlands, OH. Photograph: Pershell Marshall, 2018.

More time passes. We free spirits watch the youngsters as they age and navigate through their lives. Sometimes they seem to hear our whispered suggestions, sometimes not.

Granted, living with me was no walk in the park, but I overhead Lori telling her cousin Kathy that if she had to do it all over again, and could handpick her childhood experiences, she wouldn't have changed a single thing. Having to navigate the adult world and take care of me those last few years by her teenage self, made her strong and confident, she said. Being the youngest of the grandchildren in Cleveland, she was often excluded from older kid activities. She felt being my caretaker helped her to become comfortable in her own skin. She taught herself how to drive, pay bills, and shop for household necessities, while keeping my secret. Lori went off to college as a confident seventeen-year old, and carried those skills and abilities to numerous high-profile jobs and successes during her lifetime.

What's this? My granddaughter, Kathy, is writing a book about my life, in 2019? Well, believe you me, I shall guide her to find the truth about my adventure on this third rock from the Sun, just like I guided all my kids and grandkids. Just you wait and see!

The ancestors are smiling!

2018 Marshall family reunion in Cleveland, OH.
(Back) Austin, Michal, Kevin, Scott, Carolyn, Carrie.
(Front) Pershell, Jocelyn and Kathy.

CHAPTER 35 - EPILOGUE

(Cleveland, Ohio, October 2018)

The last Saturday in October 2018, a cold, sleety rain storm left a lifeless gray pall on our visit to the Cleveland Clinic Hospital in Akron, Ohio. Trepidation about what my sister, Carrie, and I might encounter there caused us to linger in the cheery bakery downstairs, eating a late lunch of hot vegetable soup and bread, instead of rushing up to the fifth floor right away. Yet…I had craved this meeting for months.

Our benefactrice, my first cousin, Lori, had invited all living Marshall relatives to come to Cleveland for a surprise sixtieth birthday party for her older sister, Carolyn. But three days before the October 27th event, Lori had been involved in a tragic car accident. None of us knew about the crash until the party began, because Lori didn't want to taint what she intended to be a joyful celebration for her sister. Due to her incredible planning and organizational skills—no doubt learned from our Grandmother Daisy—the party went off smoothly, without a hitch, even in her unfortunate absence.

The day after the party, several of us visited Lori in the hospital. Thankfully, her pretty face had not been marred, and the wounds to her core, hips, and leg were healing under a light blanket. The days of sharing memories of Grandma Daisy—which I had dreamed about for months—had been reduced to a couple of hours with a few key players: me, my sister Carrie, Lori, Michal and his wife, Ronda, and Carolyn and her husband, Dwayne. But what a raucous, informative two hours it was! With my smartphone videotaping the conversations, we talked about what it was like growing up in the home of Grandma Daisy from 1957 to 1980 when Lori, the youngest, was the last to leave for college.

Prior to that momentous day, even though I was born in Cleveland in 1957, I had only visited my hometown a couple of times. I knew almost nothing about that northern city in the Promised Land, where Grandma Daisy made her indelible mark on this world.

A few months prior to the 2018 birthday party, I had quickly pieced together a shell of a book about Grandma Daisy, using her chock-full obituary to determine the chapter headings of her life. I filled in what I had gathered about her since 1976, when I wrote that first letter inquiring about our heritage. I got tired of hearing "Are you mixed?" and wanted to find out the truth.

I spent days before the party, videotaping the Cedar Avenue and East 81st Street area, where my grandparents bought their first house in 1923 and established their Marshall Funeral Home in 1940. I spent a day at the Cleveland Museum of History, looking through the historical archives for any mention of my grandmother's footprint. Days earlier, I had visited the State Archives and Ohio History Museum, in Columbus, Ohio, looking for more clues about Grandma Daisy's incredible life.

At every opportunity, I interviewed and videotaped my cousins in the car, at the party, and in the hospital. I soaked up as much juicy information as possible from their memories growing up with Grandma Daisy and her two husbands, Austin Marshall and Lawrence Schumake.

In December 2018, I relished the opportunity to speak with Lori for five hours on the phone, as well as to my siblings and cousins Pershell, Jocelyn and David several times via phone and email. I gleaned snippets of fascinating stories from my living relatives. One told the disturbing tale of Daisy's brother, William, being tied to a tree and beaten by his sons, because William had been abusing their mother. That, in addition to what I knew about my father and Grandma Daisy, caused me to wonder whether that type of behavior was passed down from generation to generation. I tried to be as truthful as documents and stories presented.

The Cleveland *Call and Post* newspaper was a treasure trove of articles about my Dooley and Marshall family lines, yielding over seventy separate articles that referenced Grandma Daisy in some manner or another. Many of those references included photographs of her as the Marshall Funeral Home co-Director, PTA leader, YMCA leader, church trustee, and socialite. I also found numerous news articles about her husbands, sisters and brother too, but few photographs (except for Larry, who had articles and photographs regarding his work with veterans).

Online city directories and land deeds were useful sources of information to help me determine exactly where Daisy and other family members lived during the 1920s until her death in 1986.

This book was largely written from Grandma Daisy's point of view, as imagined by me, the author, using as many actual documents as possible. Daisy gives us a colorful glimpse into her complex life. Her ancestral background from the Deep South is presented as conversations, imaginatively presented by Daisy's grandmother, GramFannie, as "The Storyteller" in Part II. I began to appreciate through this project that I am an overachiever, just like my grandmother, and that brought me even closer to her.

Nearly every morning at five a.m., I felt a nudge (from Grandma Daisy?) and my eyes would pop open, my mind full of phrases to write in the book. Maybe it was an idea for a new resource to check, or another insight into my ancestors' lives that needed to be explored. Part IV came to me in a long dream sequence which I typed upon waking. I pleaded with my relatives to edit the manuscript for accuracy. I did the best I could.

Daisy Marshall Schumake

a pioneer for Black women

Daisy Marshall Schumake, a 50-year member of St. James A.M.E. Church; a graduate of the Western Reserve School Of Mortuary Science, and the Francis P. Bolton School of Practical Nursing, was eulogized in the East 89th street Chapel of the E.F. Boyd and Son Funeral Home on December 4. The Reverend Elmo BEan officicuated.

Mrs. Schumake was born in St. Louis, Missouri, on January 16, 1902. She died on November 30 following a lengthy illness.

After her move to Cleveland, she married Austin Marshall in 1925. He preceded her in death.

They were parents of five children: Patricia Connors Mosley; Dr. Thomas Marshall; Bruce Marshall, Austin H. Marshall (deceased) and Shirley Jean Clark, also deceased. Mrs. Schumake later married the late Dr. Lawrence Schumake, Sr. She and her first husband (Marshall) were associated with the Marshall Funeral Home which he operated with his brothers from 1939 - 1950.

Mrs. Schumake retired from University Hospitals in 1964, where she had been employed as a practical nurse.

She was a pioneer for Black women in the funeral business, she acted as associate director and embalmer for the Marshall Funeral Homes. Mrs. Schumake also served as a precinct committeewoman for more than 15 years, was active in the women's auxiliary of the Boyston Post of American Legion; the Order of Eastern Star, and was a member of the Vagettes.

Daisy Marshall Schumake leaves to mourn and remember her, three children, 17 grandchildren, seven great-grandchildren, and a host of relatives and friends.

DAISY MARSHALL SCHUMAKE

Daisy's 1986 Obituary in the "Call and Post" Newspaper. 1986.

Using various genealogy websites, social media, and old-fashioned boots-on-the-ground, deep genealogical research in Ohio, Mississippi, and Alabama, I validated who Daisy's ancestors were, took thousands of pictures and dozens of videos. All of those careful measures added to my contextual understanding of the lives of my paternal ancestors and their descendants. I wanted to viscerally grasp why Grandma Daisy chose to exorcise her Southern roots from her life story.

I hit the jackpot, finding so many paternal relatives through DNA testing with Ancestry.com, 23andme.com, gedmatch.com, and FamilyTreeDNA.com. Those were the major DNA testing/analysis companies that I used, as the manager of DNA results from six descendants of Grandma Daisy. I made the biggest breakthroughs using Ancestry's "Member Connect" and "DNA ThruLines" features, to see who else was searching for the same people so I could uncover our relatives in common.

DNA analysis is an art which is not for the faint of heart. Many uncontrollable events occurred during slavery, without our consent, so skeletons can jump out of the closet, and exciting revelations can result from DNA testing. With tutoring and membership in several social media websites, and through genealogy classes and conventions, I learned how to decipher some of those fascinating secrets.

Trust me, if you are African American or an adoptee, or an immigrant, DNA analysis may help you find your African, European, Asian, and Native American ancestors too. You can achieve heights of knowledge with DNA that would *never* occur without that genetic information.

A major desire of mine is to encourage you, the reader, to purchase a DNA test for yourself and your relatives NOW, while your elders are still living. But which DNA test should you take? Chapters 17 and 18 in Part IV of my *Finding Otho: The Search for Our Enslaved Williams Ancestors* book are dedicated to helping people understand what DNA is and what the major DNA testing companies offered, as of November 2018.

Chapter 19 in *Finding Otho* describes how to use DNA to find European ancestors. In it, I detailed how I was able to find the white slave owners in Grandmother Daisy's family line, using DNA testing. Without DNA, I would *never* have found my Borders and Cunningham connections.

I saved the best for last. Chapter 20 in *Finding Otho* details how to use DNA analysis to have a "Kunta Kinte" moment, like author Alex Haley did in his masterwork, *Roots: The Saga of an American Family*. I detail how I found specific African ancestors and present day relatives who share those common ancestors. Further exploration of my African roots will be for a future book.

I believe that adding our African American stories to the stilted American historical record is one of the most loving things we can do for our generations to come, *and* for our country at large. America is made up of many diverse populations and all of our histories should be included in the books taught to our children.

To that end, Appendix D, Solving *Your* Mystery, contains a list of hints and tips that I used to write and self-publish this book. I have vowed to become a missionary for encouraging people to publish their family history stories, to help them leave a lasting, written legacy. I hope you have enjoyed this glimpse into the incredible life of my Grandma Daisy Dooley Marshall Schumake.

The Ancestors Are Smiling!

ACKNOWLEDGMENTS

Finding Daisy: From the Deep South to the Promised Land has been a work-in-progress since 1976 when I first wrote to my paternal Grandma Daisy asking about our family lineage. It is indeed a feeling of accomplishment to bring her remarkable story to light, but I could not have completed it without the assistance of numerous helpful people.

My father, Dr. Thomas Richard Marshall, passed away in 2014. I am the lucky steward of two cigar boxes of memorabilia that he collected, which included letters to and from his parents. He also commented fondly on the stern parenting style of his beloved mother, Daisy Dooley Marshall Schumake. Those personal items became part of a biography I wrote about his full "can do" life in 2014.

My siblings, Carrie and Greg, supplied me with their personal, sometimes shocking and funny memories of our visits with Grandma Daisy in Cleveland, as well as her trips to Sacramento, California.

Our first cousins, Michal, Carolyn, and Lori, were raised by Grandma Daisy. In October 2018, Lori's impromptu reunion/birthday party with my first cousins Jocelyn, Pershell, Austin David, Kevin, and Scott, supplied me with a plethora of additional quirky, disturbing, heart-warming, and wonderful stories that revolved around our incredible grandmother. Sally and Jamie were other long-lost Marshall cousins who provided stories.

I also came into contact with several heretofore unknown black and white relatives through DNA testing and analysis. Many of them agreed to communicate with me to find our familial connections. Of particular assistance were Monica W., William Walker, Cheston and Audrey Dooley, and Anna Cunningham.

Some specific DNA experts were particularly helpful to me, including a fellow who wishes to be known as HDG, Anthony Mays, Melvin Collier, Bernice Bennett, Clevlyn Anderson, Shannon Christmas, and the excellent published books and blogs by Blaine Bettinger.

One of the most memorable experiences was being able to spend the day at the plantation house where my fourth great-grandparents lived in Calhoun County, Alabama. Many thanks to owners Dr. George and Susan Gibbins who welcomed me with open arms to visit that important place in my family history. Thanks also go to architectural historian, Christopher Lang, who supplied me with excerpts from the *Made in Alabama* catalog created by the Birmingham Art Museum which profiled four of my enslaved Borders ancestors.

Sharon Morgan, professional genealogist specializing in my Gavin and Nicholson families, opened her home and heart to me for five nights, drove me to areas in Noxubee County, Mississippi, where my ancestors toiled during slavery. She taught me how to access birth, marriage, death, and other records in the Noxubee Courthouse and Public Library. She, and genealogist Darlene Webb Nowels, Anthony May, and DNA cousin Clevlyn Bankhead Anderson, also helped break down several brick walls in my search and/or edit the manuscript.

I thank the content editors from the Elk Grove Senior Center writing group who provided helpful weekly suggestions for improving my writing efforts, with special thanks to author P. L. Clark, author Cynthia Hobson, author George Hahn, and author Jacqueline Canoose. The Sacramento Black Women Tell Tales group provided cherished support.

Sincere thanks go to my talented editor, Jean Cooper, Metadata Librarian and Genealogical Resources Specialist at the University of Virginia Library, for ensuring the manuscript was grammatically correct.

And I cannot forget the daily patience and support my boyfriend, Michael Fitzwater, showed towards my unwavering commitment to writing stories about my family's obscured past.

It was through DNA testing, combined with traditional history research, that I was able to validate truths and unmask the many mysteries about Grandma Daisy's ancestral past. She was a remarkable woman and I am extraordinarily proud to be her granddaughter.

KATHY MARSHALL'S BIOGRAPHY

For twenty-five years, my goal has been to share the strength and majesty of ancient cultures via beautiful, spiritual sculptures and clay pottery I hand-sculpted for my Kanika African Sculptures business, in my private art studio near Sacramento, California. Clay was the foundation of my artwork, but other earthly materials such as stone and glass, as well as vivid textiles, leather, shells, beads, and recycled metal enhanced the art. I believe my African ancestors work through my fingers to create each collectible ceramic figurine draped in African fabric, mask, tribal jewelry, mixed media bust, and seven-foot-tall welded steel garden sculpture.

But in 2016, living the sixtieth year of my life, I realized the forty years I had spent collecting family history research data would be lost if I suddenly passed away. I needed to compile that collection of interviews, vital records and other documents, into stories my relatives would not only understand, but enjoy. I felt the urge to ensure our contributions would enhance the American historical record, by donating my books to the Library of Congress, local libraries and historical societies in the lands where my ancestors toiled as slaves.

After publishing my first book, *The Ancestors Are Smiling!* in 2017, I began to receive requests to speak about my genealogical journey to various genealogy, African American, art, and school groups. My mission is to encourage you, the reader, to do the same thing for your family, by leaving a printed legacy of your family's footprint on the world. To that end, my published efforts may be used as guidebooks for your journey.

KANIKA MARSHALL ART

PUBLISHING HISTORY

2019 Won the 2019 International AAHGS Book Awards Best Book in the Non-Fiction—Regional History/Genealogy category for *Finding Otho: The Search for Our Enslaved Williams.*

2019 Published "Wolf Song" in the *Birds of a Feather Anthology*, sponsored by the Northern California Publishers and Authors.

2019 Published "A Nickel for Your Thoughts Dad" in *Daddy Issues: Black Women Speaking Truth and Healing Wounds.*

2019 Interviewed on the Wanda Sabir Blog Talk Radio Show.

2019 Won an award at 26th Annual Northern CA Publishers and Authors Book Awards Competition for *Finding Otho*, Sacramento.

2019 Spoke at ten events, including the "Annual Family History Seminar," "CA Writers Club" and "Black Book Fair," in Sacramento, CA.

2019 Had a book signing at Underground Books, Sacramento, CA.

2019 Conducted a book release party on Facebook for *Finding Otho: The Search for Our Enslaved Williams Ancestors.*

2018 Published *Finding Otho: The Search for Our Enslaved Williams Ancestors* on Amazon and www.KanikaMarshall.com.

2018 Had book signing for *Finding Otho* at Underground Books, Sacramento, CA.

2018 Was a speaker on "Research at the National Archives And Beyond" Blog Talk Radio, Maryland.

2017 Had book signing at Elk Grove Fine Arts Center, Elk Grove, CA.

2017 My *The Ancestor's Are Smiling!* book was profiled in the "Elk Grove Citizen" newspaper, Elk Grove, CA.

2017 Published *The Ancestor's Are Smiling!* for sale on Amazon.com, www.KanikaMarshall.com, and Underground Books, Sacramento, CA.

2017 Created Kanika Marshall Art and Books Publishing business.

2017 Published "Answering the Ancestor's Call" in the Baobab Tree, Journal of the African American Genealogical Society of Northern California, Inc., Vol. 22 No. 3, Summer 2017.

2010-2019 Published assorted travel and family history photo books.

BOOK RESEARCH BIBLIOGRAPHY

Abbott, Dorothy (Editor). *Mississippi Writers: Reflections of Childhood and Youth,* **Volume II: Nonfiction.** *University Press of Mississippi, Jackson and London, 1986.*

Adams, E. Bryding and Leah Rawls Atkins. *Made in Alabama: A State Legacy.* **Birmingham Museum of Art, 1995, pages 112, 113, and 224.**

Bettinger, Blaine T. *The Family Tree Guide to DNA Testing and Genetic Genealogy.* **Family Tree Books: Cincinnati, Ohio, 2016.**

Cleveland *Call and Post* **(1934-1962), Cuyahoga County Public Library. Proquest LLC, 2019**

Collier, Melvin J. *150 Years Later: Broken Ties Mended.* **Charleston, SC: Write Here Publishing, 2015.**

Collier, Melvin J. *Mississippi to Africa: A Journey of Discovery, Second Edition.* **Charleston, SC: Write Here Publishing, 2nd edition, August 2015.**

Cooley Farms **(Sunny Acres), Asylum Projects Reserve Preteritus.** http://www.asylumprojects.org/index.php/Cooley_Farms

DuBois, W.E.B. *The Souls of Black Folk.* **New York, NY: Dover Publications, Inc. 1994. First published in 1903 by A.C. McClurg and Co. in Chicago, IL.**

Ervin, E.K. *Riot: From Their Reconstruction to Our Revolution; A Chronological Reflection of Race Riots since 1865.*

Ewing, Linda Cunningham, *My forebears : history and genealogy of the Cunningham, Knox, Gibson, Borders, Ewing families.* **Atlanta, Ga.: J.T. Hancock, 1946.**

Hensley, Walter P., *History of The Cleveland Cincinnati Chicago and St Louis Railway Company.* **http://madisonrails.railfan.net/bigfour.ht ml. 1998.**

History of the Land, Choccolocco Park. **http://www.choccoloccopark.com/i nfo/history/**

Hurston, Zora Neale, *Barracoon: The Story of the Last "Black Cargo."* **Amistad, an imprint of HarperCollins Publishers, NY, 2018.**

Know Our Heritage: The African-American Experience in Cleveland, **Cleveland Restoration Society, Sarah Benedict House, October 2014.**

Kusmer, Kenneth. "The Black Experience in Cleveland, 1865-1982," in Cleveland Heritage Program. Cleveland: The Industrial City (program), 1982.

Lang, Christopher. Borders Brothers – Alabama Joiners: From Slavery to Freedom. **Alabama Humanities Foundation. https://www.alabam**

ahumanities.org/programs/road/christopher-lang/borders-brothers-alabama-joiners-from-slavery-to-freedom/

LaRue, Paul, *The 325th Field Signal Battalion: Elite African American World War I Soldiers.* **Ohio WWI Centennial Commemoration, 2018.** *https://www.worldwar1centennial.org/index.php/ohio-in-ww1-articles/5479-the-325th-field-signal-battalion-elite-african-american-world-war-i-soldiers.html*

Lumpkins, Charles L. *Black East St. Louis: Politics and Economy in a Border City, 1860-1945.* **Dissertation: 2006, Ph.D., Pennsylvania State University.** *https://etda.libraries.psu.edu/files/final_submissions/1032, May 2006.*

Macon Georgia Photographs on Pinterest, *https://www.pinterest.com/visitmaconga/*

Marshall, Kathy Lynne. *Finding Otho: The Search for Our Enslaved Williams Ancestors.* **Elk Grove, CA, 2018.**

Marshall, Kathy Lynne. *How to Write and Self-Publish a Book of Family Stories.* **Elk Grove, CA, 2019.**

Marshall, Kathy Lynne. *Mary Ellen Carter Marshall: The Life of a Hero, Educator, Mother, Artist, Citizen, Mentor and Friend.* **Elk Grove, CA: Kanika African Sculptures and Books, 2015.**

Marshall, Kathy Lynne. *The Ancestors Are Smiling!* **Elk Grove, CA: Kanika African Sculptures and Books, 2017.**

Marshall, Kathy Lynne. *Thomas Richard Marshall: A Life Well-Lived, 1931-2014.* **Elk Grove, CA: Kanika African Sculptures and Books, 2014.**

Marshall, Mary E. *Reflections from a Mother's Heart: Your Life Story in Your Own Words.* **Dallas, Tx: Word Publishing, 1995, pages 24, 35, 38, 39, 45, 70, 72, 95, 150.**

Mississippi Encyclopedia, **a variety of subjects for Noxubee County,** *https://mississippiencyclopedia.org/staff/mississippi-encyclopedia-staff/*

Noxubee County Churches, in Mississippi Encyclopedia. *https://mississippiencyclopedia.org/entries/noxubee-county/Churches*

An Overview of the Historical/Genealogical Records Concerning the Muskoke (Creek) Indians. **State of Alabama Indian Affairs Commission,** *http://aiac.state.al.us/Gen_Creek.aspx.*

Porterdale Cemetery, Columbus, Muscogee County, GA. *http://www.interment.net/data/us/ga/muscogee/porterdale-cemetery.htm*

Roland, Dunbar. "Macon Mississippi Ice Factory," Encyclopedia of Mississippi History, **page 158.**

Rose, Lisa. *"Black History Month: African-American funeral directors as community leaders."* NJ Advance Media for NJ.com, Feb. 18, 2011, https://www.nj.com/news/index.ssf/2011/02/black_history_month_african-am.html

Rubin, Gail. *"A History of Women as Funeral Directors,"* March 2011. http://agoodgoodbye.com/funeral-news-bits/a-history-of-women-as-funeral-directors/

Sellers, Janice. *Freedmen's Bureau 2.0: A Better Way to Do Slave Research (but still not perfect). Ancestral Discoveries, 2017.* http://www.ancestraldiscoveries.com/

Slave Narratives: A Folk History of Slavery in the United States from Interviews with Former Slaves, Mississippi, **Washington DC: Work Projects Administration, 1941.**

Slave Narratives: A Folk History of Slavery in the United States from Interviews with Former Slaves, Alabama, **Washington DC: Work Projects Administration, 1941.**

Smith, Jeffrey E. *A Preservation Plan for St. Louis, Part I: Historic Contexts, 2- Transportation.* **St. Louis, Missouri, Cultural Resources Office, 1995.** https://www.stlouis-mo.gov/government/departments/planning/cultural-resources/preservation-plan/Part-I-Transportation.cfm

Spreen, J. Orville. *St. Louis Railway Enthusiasts Club Tour of Structures or Sites of Railroad Passenger Stations of St. Louis, Mo., September 23, 1951.* https://archive.org/stream/STLRRTour/img268#page/n1/mode/2up

Tadema, Lalita. *Cane River,* **Grand Central Publishing, 2002.**

Taylor, Frazine K. *Researching African American Genealogy in Alabama: A Resource Guide.* **Montgomery, AL, New South Books, 2008.**

"The Price of Cotton, 1800–2000: A Table." **Cornell University, 2002.** http://usda.mannlib.cornell.edu/data-sets/crops/96120/

"What is Order of Eastern Star?" **Ohio Grand Chapter, Order of the Eastern Star, https://www.ohiooes.org/about-us**

"World War I," **Chapter 5 in Raines, Rebecca Robbins,** *Getting the Message Through; a Branch History of the U.S. Army Signal Corps.* **Washington, D.C., Center of Military History, United States Army, 1996.** https://history.army.mil/books/30-17/S_5.htm

Appendix A – Dooley Land Deeds

Compiled by Sharon Morgan, Macon, Mississippi, 2019.

SURNAME	1st NAME	DATE	ACRES	LOCATION	SOURCE	NOTES
DOOLEY	W.W.	1853	292 acres	Sec 22 Twp 14 Range 17	Land Roll Book	
DOOLEY	W.W.	1853	160 acres	Sec 21 Twp 15 Range 17	Land Roll Book	
DOOLEY	W.W.	1853	40 acres	Sec 28 Twp 15 Range 17	Land Roll Book	
DOOLEY	W.W.	1853	80 acres	Sec 23 Twp 15 Range 16	Land Roll Book	
DOOLEY	W.W.	1853	160 acres	Sec 24 Twp 15 Range 16	Land Roll Book	
DOOLEY	William (Estate)	1853		Lot 3 Block 19	Land Roll Book	Lot 3 + Residence
DOOLEY	Lavenia	1853			Land Roll Book	House & Lot
DOOLEY	Louisa	1853	40 acres	Sec 8 Twp 14 Range 17	Land Roll Book	NW 1/4 SW 1/4
DOOLEY	Billy	1870		Macon Town	Land Roll Book	North of lot 1; North of Block 12 -$100 value
DOOLEY	Billy	1870		Macon Town	Land Roll Book	NW part; North of Block 19; 80X132 Lot - $200 value
DOOLEY	Billy	1876	15 acres	Sec 32 Twp 15 Range 17	Land Roll Book	
DOOLEY	Billy (Estate)	1879	46 acres	Sec 5 Twp 14 Range 17	Land Roll Book	
DOOLEY	Louisa	1879	41 acres	Sec 7 Twp 14 Range 17	Land Roll Book	
DOOLEY	Elias	1881		Sec 32 Twp 15 Range 17	Land Roll Book	Elias DOOLY & Ann HARRIS > Amanda DOOLY & Savannah
DOOLEY	Elias	1882		Sec 5 Twp 14 Range 17	Deed Book	Conveyed by A. KLAUS > Elias DOOLY
DOOLEY	Lavinia	1883		Macon Town?	Land Roll Book	House & Lot - $150 value
DOOLEY	William (Estate)	1883	22 acres	Sec 5 Twp 14 Range 17	Land Roll Book	
DOOLEY	Elias	1922		Sec 7 Twp 14 Range 17	Land Roll Book	
DOOLEY	Ann	1913-1914	10 acres	Sec 7 Twp 14 Range 17	Land Roll Book	
DOOLEY	Ann	1913-1914	5 acres	Sec 7 Twp 14 Range 17	Land Roll Book	
DOOLEY	Ann	1913-1914	15 acres	Sec 7 Twp 14 Range 17	Land Roll Book	
DOOLEY	Elias Sr.	1913-1914	40 acres	Sec 8 Twp 14 Range 17	Land Roll Book	NW 1/4 SW 1/4 - $240 value
DOOLEY	Lewis	1913-1914		Sec 9 Twp 15 Range 16	Land Roll Book	E 1/2 SE 1/4 + E 1/2 W 1/2 SE 1/4 @ District 5
DOOLEY	Elias Sr.	1913-1914	20 acres		Land Roll Book	School district - 20 acres off South End, Lots 3&4 - $50 va
DOOLEY	Elias Sr.	1913-1914	15 acres		Land Roll Book	Separate school district - 15 acres off East Side, Lot 10
DOOLEY	William	1919-1920		Sec 5 Twp 14 Range 17	Land Roll Book	
DOOLEY	Elias Sr.	1919-1920		Sec 5 Twp 14 Range 17	Land Roll Book	
DOOLEY	William	1919-1920		Sec 8 Twp 14 Range 17	Land Roll Book	
DOOLEY	Elias Sr.	1919-1920		Sec 7 Twp 14 Range 17	Land Roll Book	
DOOLEY	Annie	1921-1922		Sec 7 Twp 14 Range 17	Land Roll Book	
DOOLEY	Elias	1921-1922	6.5 acres	Sec 8 Twp 14 Range 17	Land Roll Book	

Appendix B - Family Timeline

YEAR	EVENT
1707	Matthius **Bader**—author's 7x great-grandfather—born in Jettenburg, Wuerttemberg, Germany
1751	Michael Bader **Borders**—author's 6x great-grandfather—born in Baden-Wurttemberg, Germany
1779	John **Borders**—author's 5x great-grandfather—born in TN
1813	Narcissus **Borders**—author's 4x great-grandmother—born in Jackson GA
1820	Billy **Dooley**—author's 3x great-grandfather—born in GA
1833	John Borders **Cunningham**—author's 3x great-grandfather—born in Jackson, GA, to Narcissus Borders and Ansel Griffin Cunningham.
1835	Elias **Dooley** Sr.—author's 2x great-grandfather—born in GA
1835	Lavinia Olmstead/Armstead?—author's 2x great-grandmother—born in AL?
1835	Julia **Borders**—author's 3x great-grandmother— born in GA.
1853	Charles **Nicholson** born in Noxubee, MS
1857	Fannie **Cunningham** born in AL
1873	John **Borders** died in Choccolocco, Calhoun County, AL
1878	William James **Dooley** born in Noxubee County, MS
1878	Julia **Nicholson** born in Noxubee, MS
1880	Griffin **Borders** living in Richland, AR.
1889	Narcissus **Borders** died in Choccolocco, Calhoun County, AL
1892	Austin Henry **Marshall**, Sr.—author's grandfather—was born in Columbus, GA
1900	Julia **Borders** Cunningham died after 1900 in ?
1902	Daisy Dooley—author's grandmother—was born in Noxubee County, MS

1912	John Borders **Cunningham** died in LA
1912	Fannie **Cunningham** Nicholson Clayton—author's 2x great-grandmother— died in Memphis, TN
1919	Elias **Dooley** died in Noxubee, MS
1921	Julia **Nicholson** Dooley died in Cleveland, OH
1923	William James **Dooley** died in Cleveland, OH
1927	Patricia Rae **Marshall** was born in Cleveland, OH
1929	Austin Henry **Marshall**, Jr. was born in Cleveland, OH
1931	Thomas Richard **Marshall**—Author's father—was born in Cleveland, OH
1933	Shirley Jean **Marshall** was born in Cleveland, OH
1940	Bruce Cyril **Marshall** was born in Cleveland, OH
1957	Kathy Marshall—author—was born in Cleveland, OH
1967	Austin Henry **Marshall**, Sr., died in Columbus, GA
1986	Daisy Dooley Marshall Schumake died in Cleveland, OH
2014	Thomas Richard **Marshall** died in Carmichael, CA
2019	Kathy Marshall writes *Finding Daisy: From the Deep South to the Promised Land* about her beloved Grandmolther Daisy.

Appendix C - Family Trees

Dooley Family:

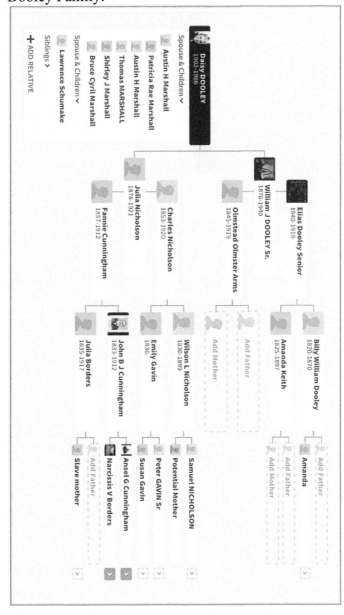

Nicholson Family:

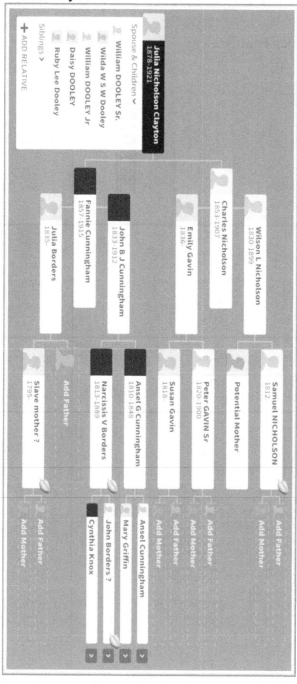

Cunningham Family:

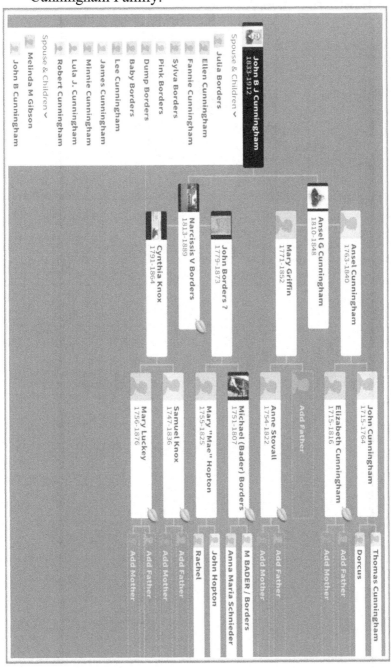

Borders Family:

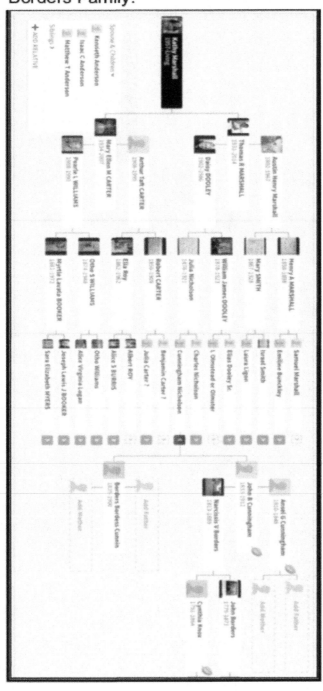

Appendix D – Solving *Your* Mystery

I have been researching the lives of my African American family for four decades, creating the requisite genealogy binders full of vital records, census and other documents for six of my family lines, including the Williams, Bookers, Marshalls, Dooley, Carters, and Myers family lines.

An alarming thought entered my head in May 2016 when I began my sixtieth year of life. There are only three people older than me in my mother's family and three older in my father's. Soon I may be the matriarch of the family. If I don't write a book about my ancestors, who will? Now is the time to commemorate the lives of those enslaved and free people who have gone before me, and of those of us still living who are their proud descendants. I have a burning desire to ensure that my family is remembered in a tangible, written way.

After a gentle push from my spirited ancestors, I began writing *The Ancestors Are Smiling!* on October 1, 2016, and published it in July 2017. The next fifteen months were spent solving the mystery of my enslaved relatives in *Finding Otho: The Search for Our Williams Ancestors*. Then came *Finding Daisy: From the Deep South to the Promised Land* in 2019.

There are a number of reasons why I was finally able to accomplish this momentous goal successfully. I had heard most of the following how-to tips numerous times over the years, but this time I ACTUALLY DID WHAT WAS SUGGESTED.

Please note that the following ideas are only one way to write a book about your family, but they are steps that worked well for me. Will any or all of them work for you? Give them a try. See if they will help you to get started (and finished) with your book.

* Planning to Write Your Book *

1. Adopt an **ATTITUDE THAT YOU MUST PUBLISH THE BOOK,** before all else. Your mantra must be: "I live and breathe to publish a book about my family." Otherwise, any mundane activity will divert you from your goal to leave a written legacy for your family.

2. **FOCUS ON ONE** specific family line, or one person, or one specific aspect of the family, for example, a specific enslaved ancestor from one of your family lines.

3. Determine the **SCOPE** (extent) of the book. I wanted to find my third great-grandparents, write about their lives, then publish this book. What, specifically, do you want your book to be about?

4. Develop a **LIST OF QUESTIONS** you want to answer (e.g., who were my third great-grandparents, what jobs did they do, where did they live, who were their slave masters?).

5. Understand that you may not be able to answer all your questions but accept that it is OK. Write about the **steps you DID take and** present what you *did* and *did not* find. Indicate that you may resume your inquiry in the Second Edition when more information becomes available.

6. Decide on the **AUDIENCE** for your book (e.g., children, family, genealogists, the public).

* Developing the Book Framework: Type Book as You Research * *(This will make you feel so successful!)*

7. Decide on a computer **WORD PROCESSING PROGRAM** for your book, such as Microsoft Word or Apple Pages.

8. Open a **NEW DOCUMENT and NAME IT** (e.g., My Family Book) and **SAVE** it to a folder on your computer.

9. Be sure to **SAVE** your word processing manuscript every hour or so and **BACK UP** your book file every day (e.g., keep a copy on the Internet cloud or on a portable backup drive).

10. Develop a **BOOK OUTLINE** in your new word document, like the following:

11. **Title of your book** on the first page.

12. **Copyright** on the second page (copyright.gov).

13. **Dedication** on the third page.

14. **Filler** on the 4th page: add a picture, or a quote, or a poem, or a **Foreword** from a professional.

15. **Table of Contents (TOC): Microsoft** Word and Apple Pages automatically generate the TOC with the "Styles" Function.

16. **Acknowledgments** page thanking people who helped you write your book.

17. **Introduction** that explains what the book is about; write it early in the process, then refine it.

18. **Timeline** of historical events, if desired.

19. **Chapters** about certain characters or topics (NOTE: Start chapters in the printed book on an odd-numbered, right-side page for chapter headings in the header).

20. **Epilogue**/Conclusion/Coda/Wrap up to summarize your efforts.

21. **Appendices**, lists of tables and maps (if appropriate).

22. **Bibliography** listing which sources you used to develop your ideas in the book.

23. **Endnotes** (optional) with complete the citations, using this basic format: Author, *Title*, (Publisher State, Publisher, Year), page number.

24. Refine the **book layout** after some of the manuscript has been written (e.g., add photographs or quotes to the first page of each chapter, if desired).

* Writing Your Book *

25. **START WRITING TODAY** with what you already know (e.g., your life story, parents, grandparents). Don't worry about perfect sentences; just type your thoughts and revise them later.

26. **COPY AND PASTE** into the correct chapter any documentation that has already been written. For example, a memory about your fifth birthday party would go into your chapter; your grandparents' wedding picture would go into their chapter, etc.

27. **TYPE THE BOOK** as you are conducting your research and getting stories. Include your emotions at that time when they are fresh.

28. Include **FOOTNOTES/CITATIONS** citing your information sources as you write.

29. **RECHECK YOUR FOCUS** and scope often, to remain on track with what your book is about.

30. Consider writing the passages as though you are telling the story directly to your audience or writing the stories from the **POINT OF VIEW** of your family members.

31. **READ OUT LOUD** what you have written to uncover awkward sentence structure or to notice missing words and to hear whether the text is too conversational or too technical, keeping in mind your audience.

* Gathering Information *

32. **INTERVIEW YOUR ELDERS** and other family members and type their stories in the book.

33. Do **DNA TESTING NOW** for yourself, your elders, and other family members. The major DNA companies are: ancestry.com, 23andMe.com, FamilyTreeDNA.com, My Heritage, and Living DNA. For more information, check https://isogg.org/wiki/List_of_DNA_testing_companies.

34. Gather **FAMILY PHOTOGRAPHS**, using your camera or smartphone to take high-resolution photos. Copy the photos to a folder on your computer. Save them as 300 dots-per-inch (dpi) resolution for printing. Label the photos with the date, place, and names of the subjects.

35. Read **PROBATE, CENSUS, and LAND RECORDS** documents pertinent to your family.

36. Visit family **HOME SITES** and **CEMETERIES** (search Findagrave.com), take photographs and type your findings, and **YOUR FEELINGS,** about visiting these places in your book.

37. **PRINT DOCUMENTS** within each family line and organize them into separately named **GENEALOGY BINDERS**.

38. Start an **ONLINE FAMILY TREE** (e.g., **ancestry.com, familysearch.org**) with names, dates, locations, etc., and **KEEP IT PUBLIC** so others may connect with you and share information about your family.

39. Also keep **FAMILY TREE DATA ON YOUR COMPUTER** (e.g., Family Tree Maker).

40. Use **ONLINE GENEALOGY SITES** (e.g., ancestry.com, familysearch.org, USGenWeb.com, WikiTree.com, newspapers.com, fold3.com, and Genetic Genealogy Tips and Techniques.

41. Become a member of **GENEALOGY FACEBOOK PAGES** and other web pages (e.g., Our Black Ancestry, Our Black Legacy, Research at the National Archives and Beyond, Black ProGen Live).

42. Watch free **GENEALOGY HOW-TO VIDEOS** from ancestry.com or youtube.com.

43. Do a simple **online Google search on your ancestors' names and states** to see if any books or other resources contain their name. Recheck these resources often.

44. Take **GENEALOGY COURSES** and join genealogy guilds to learn the best genealogy practices. Conduct an exhaustive search. Document accurate citations. Analyze information. Resolve conflicting evidence. Develop a reasoned written conclusion.

45. **DEVELOP THEORIES** and prove or disprove them, but do not be too rigid. Review and revise theories and update the book accordingly. Avoid obsessing on preconceived ideas from family lore.

46. Discuss your book ideas and theories with other authors, editors, and family, and **ASK THEM TO GIVE FEEDBACK** on your work in progress.

* Self-Publishing Your Book *

47. Have the book professionally **COPY EDITED** and PROOFREAD to ensure the manuscript is perfect before publishing.

48. Export your book manuscript to a **.pdf FILE** on your computer.

49. If you want to sell books, obtain an International Standard Book Number (**ISBN**) through **bowker.com** ($295 for 10 or $125 for one); include one ISBN on the back cover of your book file.

50. **COPYRIGHT** your book (e.g., copyright.gov).

51. Choose a **SELF-PUBLISHING WEBSITE** (e.g., **lulu.com** or **Kindle Direct Publishing,** KDP.com,) and read their online instructions on uploading a .pdf copy of your book. Create an online account for your book. Choose a book size and number of pages. Upload an initial .pdf of your manuscript.

52. Use the self-publishing website to create a **BOOK COVER** (front, back, and spine). Or, make your own cover on your computer, or pay someone to make one. Be sure to use the precise measurements supplied by the self-publishing service. Export your book cover to a .pdf file.

53. After your book manuscript is perfected, export it to a .pdf file, then **UPLOAD THE MANUSCRIPT AND COVER .pdf** to the self-publishing website. Make sure you review any corrections the book website suggests (like ensuring the photos are 400 dpi), make the changes, then upload the .pdf files again.

54. Prepare a summary of the book, for the online **DESCRIPTION** of your book (you may use the text on the back jacket of your book). Look at several amazon.com memoir book examples to see what kinds of things are written in the book description. Make it pop!

55. Decide on a retail **PRICE** for your book. The book service will tell you how much revenue you will earn depending on your retail price, the book size, and number of pages.

56. Once the manuscript is submitted for printing, order an **ADVANCED READER COPY**. Carefully **REVIEW** the printed book, make corrections, create a new .pdf, re-upload the file, recheck the uploaded file, order another Advanced Reader Copy. When you are absolutely certain there are no errors in your manuscript submit it for **FINAL PRINTING**. It takes 24-72 hours for book approval and about a week to print the book(s).

57. If using Amazon.com's <u>Kindle Direct Publishing</u>, choose **MARKETING CHANNELS** for your book (e.g., Amazon in America and/or Europe, resellers, research channels).

58. **MARKET** your published book (e.g., **amazon.com**, Facebook page, webpage, newsletter, blog, local bookstores, donate to research libraries, and/or offer to be a volunteer speaker at local networking groups and service clubs).

* An Alternative, Photo Book for Genealogy*

59. Instead of a narrative, self-published book as described in the previous steps, you could create hard-cover, photo album style books. Simply upload your high-resolution (300 dpi or more) .jpg family photos, charts, graphs, or maps to <u>shutterfly.com</u> or <u>photo.walgreens.com</u> or <u>costco.com</u> or other online photo book services. Get on their mailing lists to get periodic discounts. This is an easy way to commemorate your ancestors' lives, and/or to write story books of any kind.

* Always Remember *

Be so passionate about commemorating your ancestor's stories that you have an overwhelming need to publish your book. Be focused on writing about a specific person or family line. Create a book template and begin typing what you already know into it and type all your new findings into it. Include source citations as you enter information. These most important actions will result in the quick development of a manuscript that looks like a ready-for-printing real book. I hope these lessons I learned help you write and self-publish your own family stories. Remember, when the ancestors call, we must listen.

The Ancestors Are Smiling!